The comatosed young pilgrim lying in a northern Spanish hospital after being garrotted by his own rosary, feverishly dreams of a creaking wooden gibbet with a tragic disabled youth swaying beneath. Suddenly the present seems to reflect the past.

Elsewhere the romantic history of an incredible uncut diamond newly discovered in the vaults of a London bank rekindles a bitter ancient vendetta, together with the vengeance and avarice of ruthless and powerful antagonists each determined to possess this jewel with its provenance of such historical importance.

When past meets present innocent bystanders become the victims of an international intrigue.

FORGOTTEN DIAMOND

Published by : Charles Ranald and John Sorrell
c/o West House,
Itchen Stoke.
Hampshire.
SO24 0QZ
United Kingdom

charles.ranald@tiscali.co.uk
john.sorrell@wanadoo.fr

A catalogue record for this book is available from the British
Library from January 2007

Cover design by baudoinsorrell@hotmail.com

ISBN 978-1-84728-358-0

FORGOTTEN DIAMOND

CHARLES RANALD & JOHN SORRELL

ACKNOWLEDGEMENT

The authors would like to place on record their very grateful thanks to Margaret Crosland for her most useful practical help and advice at every stage. This, together with her continual enthusiastic encouragement and support throughout the whole process coupled with her kindness in taking time out from her own busy writing schedule to provide this, has all been most valuable and very much appreciated.

CHAPTER ONE

NAJERA NORTHERN SPAIN

He had done everything he humanly could. Now the patient's fate was out of his hands and in the lap of the gods. It had already been a very busy day before this last case had arrived and he was tired as he left the ground floor intensive care room feeling helpless to do more but looking forward to some well earned sleep. Wearily he turned to one of the two policemen who had been keeping their sentry like vigil just outside its door since the patient had arrived and, in answer to the unspoken question, said, "He is in a very deep coma indeed, heavily traumatised and probably dreaming all sorts of nightmares, poor kid. Only the next thirty-six hours – if he survives that long – will tell, and while there's life there's hope I suppose, but from everything I have seen, I'm afraid the most likely outcome is that you're going to have a case of murder to investigate."

Earlier he had been having a snatched meal with a colleague when his mobile rang and he'd had the warning that an ambulance was bringing in an emergency case – a victim of a serious assault. The doctor and his specialist nursing team had quickly assembled and were waiting with quiet professional calm for the patient's arrival. A second call from the accompanying medics in the ambulance had warned them of a delay caused by the victim suffering a cardiac arrest, which luckily they had dealt with by using their portable fibrillator – shock starting his heart by several large electric shocks, which had rocked the whole ambulance. There had been two more short stops as his pulse seemed to vanish and then fortunately return. Pacing the room the doctor looked at his watch as, at last, the waiting team heard the vehicle's siren getting louder as it forced its way through the traffic on its final approach to the clinic in the Northern Spanish town of Najera.

Immediately it arrived nurses accompanied the inert body of the young pilgrim as the ambulance staff wheeled the trolley into the prepared room, one of three emergency intensive care units which the clinic maintained. Supervised by the sisters the porters gently transferred him onto the bed. Although pleasantly cool, with the window blinds pulled down against the sun, the stark white painted walls gave the room an extra impression of brightness and space. Two nurses methodically attached the various monitors which would give a continuous record of the patient's blood pressure, breathing, heart beat and temperature. A third set up the intravenous drip feed through which the necessary liquid, drugs and sustenance could enter his body. As this was going on the grey-haired doctor, assisted by a young houseman on his staff, began his examination.

The rosary which had apparently been used to garrotte the victim had been cut from his throat, but the frayed ends were still tightly gripped in the right hand of the young man. Gently a nurse opened his fingers and removed these and put them carefully in the drawer of the bedside table. A vivid red weal, now beginning to blacken as the severe bruising developed, was clearly apparent. The doctor noted the slightly deeper indentations where the larger beads of the rosary had dug viciously into the skin at regular spaces – the whole thing, he thought, gave the impression of a badly done tattoo. He continued his inspection in silence, only occasionally mumbling the odd remark to his assistant. When he had finished he gave instructions for the neuro-surgeon to be contacted urgently so that as well as all the other data, the patient's brain function and any possible damage resulting from the short cardiac arrest could be assessed. Finally he told a nurse to arrange that his dangerously shallow breathing should be assisted by a supply of oxygen.

Leaving, he gently brushed away the young man's lock of hair which had fallen over his closed eyes – he thought of his own son about the same age safely at home and his prayers went out to this one's parents. They can only hope for a miracle he said to himself.

CHAPTER TWO

NAJERA

As François lay on the bed a nurse switched on the brain scanner. The immediate flickering oscillations showed that, despite being physically deeply unconscious, the patient's mind was certainly dreaming. Outwardly his body, apparently lifeless, apart from his shallow breathing, showed no visible sign of his inner sensation............ As if disconnected from his body he sensed the warm evening breeze that was making little whirlwinds in the rough and sandy surface beneath the gibbet. Two rough hewn, but sturdy wooden poles, some three metres high and hewn from local spruce, supported the cross bar. It creaked as it was caught by each gust of wind. More obvious and threatening were the groans that came from the laden structure. Not only were they coming from the straining timber, but from its human cargo in the form of Ebbo, a recently turned 16 year old schoolboy, whose slender frame carried not an ounce of surplus flesh.

A dirty cotton chemise and a loin cloth, made of material only a little less rough than sacking, were the only two items of clothing protecting the tragic figure. The pock marked youth looked frail and haggard having journeyed painfully on foot already for nearly a thousand miles. His appearance was changing rapidly with his eyes starting to bulge as a coarse sisal noose tightened around his neck. In only a matter of minutes he would be dead.

Summary justice was common place in the year 1090 with Ebbo's conviction a perfect example. Just a few hours earlier a self important, self satisfied and sadistic local magistrate, with unquestioned judicial power, had quite wrongfully and   without any manner of trial, condemned Ebbo to death by hanging before sunset that very day. Mercy wasn't a word in the thoughts and minds of many medieval township's law enforcers, but cruelty came as naturally to them as a cat would play with a mouse.

To get Ebbo onto the crude wooden structure, which acted as a hanging device, it had been necessary first to lift the lad's limp body to cross-bar height. A burly shaven headed hangman whose arms, wrists and waist were adorned with massive leather belts was charged with this grizzly task. For him the task of lifting was simple. Accustomed as he was to slinging the dead body of a fallen cow across his massive shoulders, the slight frame of the still living Ebbo was equivalent to a haunch of beef or a small sheep. He was employed on a casual basis by the town authorities of Santo Domingo de la Calzada. It was a job he was happy to do, not only for the monetary reward, but because it gave him a feeling of satisfaction that he was contributing to the safety and well being of his fellow townsfolk. Death meant little to him, so the rapid execution of a young foreigner was of no consequence.

The town was named after a hermit named Domingo, who was later sanctified having built a Cathedral and a bridge over the River Oja as well as a pilgrim's hostel. Poor soil coupled with either flood or drought ensured permanently dismal economic prospects for the frequently windswept town. The steadily increasing flow of pilgrims bound for Santiago de Compostela in the West provided the main source of revenue to the hard pressed township. About twenty days a year the hangman was called upon to carry out an execution. The fee he was paid plus the small commission he garnered from the grave diggers made the reward for this macabre task a welcome addition to the meagre earnings he gained from the dismembering of fallen cattle and the occasional intentional slaughtering of ill fed cows. In fact it paid him sufficient to feed his family for nearly a week, providing some welcome extras to their otherwise miserable existence. Only a few of the townspeople could afford the luxury of eating meat and even they would find it hard to pick much edible flesh from the carcasses of cattle much better suited to the provision of hide. News of an execution spread with the speed of the wind that blew most days and there would always be a crowd of watchers at the chosen site of death. The name, let alone the crime of the alleged culprit was of no interest to the audience - comprising gawpers, ghouls, imbeciles and would be torturers. The crowd would assemble up to an hour before arrival of the condemned prisoner. A trade in wine or stronger fortifying refreshment would spring up amongst them, so that by the time the hangman himself had lurched his way to the scene it was difficult to tell if the mob was witnessing the celebration of a victory or an imminent lynching. Baying for blood there were always amongst the rabble two or three ignorant shouters bellowing their desire to see infliction of a lashing before a hanging - masochism in medieval times was utterly acceptable. The favoured method of execution was a simple but painful one. No drop, no neck breaking, just an agonizing suffocation depending on weight as the rope dug in to the neck, squeezing the life out of its victims. Unlike a crucifixion where the fated victim was nailed to wood with arms outstretched and feet semi supported, the Spanish means of final penalty was cheaper and easier - usually finishing in a matter of minutes. As a warning to others and as a sop to a mainly peasant multitude the lifeless body was left swinging, twisting and usually dripping as bodily fluids discharged themselves from the fast decaying remains. Beneath the gibbet two slothful curs sniffed the dampening ground at the prospect of licking their reward.

An almost inaudible croak came from Ebbo as his distorted body twisted vertically from the gibbet's crossbar. Two distraught figures, slightly apart from the foul smelling mob, now drunk with pleasure and liquor, recognised the words that came from Ebbo's mouth. It was a plea to his stricken parents to leave him alone to die and to continue with their pilgrimage. Already Lucus, the father of Ebbo had endeavoured to get himself hanged in place of his semi crippled son, but this supplication however sacrificial was rebuffed immediately by a callous magistrate. The stricken couple's wailing was ignored by the semi drunken mob and they became the victims of verbal slanging with accusations that they too were as guilty as their executed son. Weeping aloud they left the scene of their offspring's body now twitching slightly as death approached.

Ebbo himself suffered in a totally different way. Half walking, half being dragged from the Courthouse to the gibbet spot, he was so dazed by the horror of what had gone before that he was semi anaesthetized and unaware that he was being lifted off the ground by human hands and about to be blindfolded. Rough hands pulled a stinking rag over his already bloodshot eyes and from that moment until unconsciousness a misty grey light was his only awareness.

The coarse fibres of the sisal warp bit into Ebbo's neck as he became aware that he was only minutes away from death. He recalled the events of the last two days with an unexpected vividness exaggerated by the light blindfolding of his eyes. Instead of fear, an unexpected feeling of warmth and uncontrollable sexual urge overcame him with a swelling of his manhood to a size he had never experienced in his short life and certainly could never have imagined possible. No thoughts of why or how this glorious sensation happened entered Ebbo's mind, but as grey light behind his blindfold turned to blackness he was joyfully relieved by a hot stream rushing through his stem accompanied by merciful oblivion. Ebbo's hands remained tied firmly behind his back as quickly they turned dark purple.

CHAPTER THREE

THE BALTIC SEA 1907

Prince Vladimir Varlov took a deep breath and allowed his vast body to relax now that he realised he wasn't going to die. His narrow almost Asiatic eyes no longer showed his fear as he allowed himself a smile. In fact instead of having to rough it in the sparse confines of the sick bay of a Naval vessel he was to be transferred aboard another grand, but rather older yacht the *Polar Star.* Following his family's ancient traditional role, Varlov, a man of huge ungainly proportions, had in turn served as a favoured courtier to Nicholas II, Tsar of Russia for most of his adult life. Although it was not just because of his status as a member of the Imperial Court, but more as a result of his undoubted charm and outstanding skills as a billiard player, that he was a regular guest aboard the massive Russian Imperial Yacht *Standart* in June 1907.

As a matter of rigid tradition and without exception, the Russian Imperial family always followed the same regular social programme each year, and this included a summer cruise from the Baltic through the Finnish fjords aboard this veritable floating palace. The *Standart,* built in Denmark had been launched in 1895 and at 401 ft long it was then the largest private yacht in the world and soon became the envy of the Tsar's jealous cousin, Kaiser Wilhelm II of Germany. By day the great yacht steamed slowly among the islands before anchoring each night in the shelter of a different cove where the steepness of the rocky coast permitted it to lie within 100 yards of land. Two white funnels with black tops distinguished the *Standart* from other ships, as did her three varnished masts. These were used for hoisting the Imperial Standards displaying the double headed eagle signifying the Tsar's presence on board. From her graceful clipper bow extended an enormously impressive bowsprit richly encrusted with gold leaf, and there was certainly never any doubting the Royal ownership of this huge yacht when the Tsar's Standard was worn from the forrard mast. At the end of an informal day of gentle cruising and deck games it was the Tsar's great pleasure to spend the early evening testing his skill at billiards. On many occasions the slightest motion by the yacht at anchor would raise howls of mirth from the ship's officers, courtiers and other guests on board, when the most skilled scoring break would be wrecked by a shifting table angle sending the balls rolling away in an unintended direction, often to end up in a netted pocket.

This afternoon Varlov's relief had followed a hectic twenty four hour period of chaos and potential tragedy. For some unknown reason the *Standart,* fortunately steaming at less than 10 knots at the time had hit an uncharted rock, and with a shuddering jolt came to a full stop, heeling quietly over at an alarming angle. Tea cups went flying, candelabra and furniture slid across staterooms and saloons, but worst of all water flooded into the stricken yacht, which as a result quickly began to settle. Alarmingly, Alexis, the sickly three year old Tsarevitch was missing as "All hands on deck" was piped around the vessel. With both the Tsar's and Tsarina's royal training hiding the panic they were both feeling, a dramatic search of the ship was immediately undertaken for the little boy, and it was Prince Vladimir Varlov, who eventually found him playing innocently with his sailor Guardian. The Empress Alexandra herded her children, with all alacrity, into the boats before returning to her stateroom to rescue her jewellery, icons and other valuable possessions. Some of the jewellery had been wrested years earlier with difficulty from her mother-in-law, the Dowager Empress, and included items of the Crown collection traditionally handed down from one Russian Empress to the next. So great was the quantity that the only way she could carry it was by stripping off a bed sheet and throwing everything into it. Then, like a peasant woman she swung the bundle over her shoulder and made for the lifeboats. Recent ship building techniques had introduced watertight compartments and thanks to the glassy calm conditions the ship didn't actually founder. Next day she was pulled off by tugs summoned quickly from the nearby port. Meanwhile Naval Escort vessels had carried out a text book rescue operation leaving a skeleton crew, including Tsar Nicholas himself, to man the wounded *Standart*. No charges were laid against the yacht's Captain as it was instantly proven that the submerged rock had never been charted.

The following afternoon, shrouded in discrete secrecy, the older Imperial yacht *Polar Star* once belonging to the Dowager Empress was called up and took on all the passengers including the much relieved Prince Vladimir Varlov.

Alexandra Fedorovna, Empress of Russia, granddaughter of Queen Victoria was a devotedly protective mother who loved her children. So much so that it was only on the rarest occasions that she would allow Alexis, her only son aged three, and the youngest of her five children, out of her sight. Only weeks after Alexis's christening Alexandra had first noticed the bruising that left its mark on his frail body if he had had the misfortune to suffer even the smallest of childhood tumbles. In 1904 the causes were not really understood and certainly there was no cure for his inherited haemophilia - the condition that was soon diagnosed by the Royal doctors.

Despite his huge girth, the otherwise ungainly Varlov, like so many big people, was remarkably nimble and light upon his feet, which were small for a man of his size - almost describable as dainty. He had astonished other dancers, and increased his popularity with his Royal hostess, by his dexterity in highland reels when staying at Balmoral some years before, a guest of Queen Victoria as a member of the household of Tsar Nicholas and the Tsarina. It was no surprise therefore that it was he who carried the little three year old Alexis to the comparative safety of a rocking lifeboat from the badly damaged *Standart*. Once aboard the rescue ship, a naval escort vessel, and having handed over his priceless human charge, Varlov was allocated what he thought a less than adequate cabin alongside the surgeon's operating theatre. Apparently meant for two it was all the poor man could do to get through the cabin door and then he found himself unable to close it behind him. Relief wasn't too long in coming however and by next afternoon he was comfortably installed aboard the *Polar Star*. A tap on his cabin door interrupted him attempting to clean up his appearance, and a steward presented his compliments and brought a command to attend The Tsar and Empress forthwith. The *Polar Star* may have been older and smaller then *Standart*, but she was nevertheless, in her own right, a floating palace on the grandest scale. Varlov was escorted in silence through the corridors to the Royal afternoon stateroom, a light oak panelled drawing room hung with English chintz. English furniture by Hepplewhite and Sheraton was carefully placed before a mock fireplace with overmantel. Above the mantelpiece hung a landscape painting in oil by Thomas Gainsborough depicting woods and cattle. With no announcement a withdrawing room door opened and the Empress Alexandra floated silently into the room stepping softly across the Aubusson carpet. While simply dressed in a floral skirt, with a white cotton blouse and covering shawl her Royal status was plain to any on-looker. Although she looked more than her 35 years, this could well be attributed to her pale Germanic complexion. Holding out her hands in greeting she welcomed Prince Varlov in English "Dear Vova, I find it hard to express my gratitude for what you have done for my family. The Tsar, will be joining us in just a minute and he will tell you that he feels exactly the same way." Happy to be addressed by his nickname, Prince Varlov proudly beamed his rather flowery reply "Madame, to lift your son and carry him to safety has brought me great pleasure and if it pleases you and His Majesty I am deeply touched and proud to be of service." The Empress beckoned him to sit, and carefully choosing a tapestry upholstered armchair of adequate size, the portly courtier lowered himself gently into it.

At that moment Tsar Nicholas II entered the stateroom mumbling his apologies for the delay and causing Varlov to struggle to his feet with respectful deference. The Tsar, as usual, was curiously dressed for yachting, but his military nature never totally deserted him. A high collared army uniform jacket of lightweight fawn barathea was weighed down on his right shoulder by plain gold aiguillettes tipped with gold gun spikes. A single medal affixed to his left breast displayed a tiny cameo of his father Alexander III. At 39, Nicholas was a fine and impressive figure of a man with a full black beard neatly trimmed, which seemed to add to his general air of authority. Formalities over, the three settled back into their chairs, whilst the Tsar, to the clear annoyance of his wife, lit another of his Black Sobranie cigarettes and waited for the tea to be brought. Lifting her head from the ever present needlework, which she picked up automatically on sitting down, Alexandra said "I'd like you to know Vova that when I left the *Standart* so hastily yesterday, I was able to retrieve my jewellery and although personally I value it so little, I realise that I have a duty to safeguard it as a sort of custodian for so long as I remain, which I hope will be a very long time, Empress to my darling husband." Varlov quietly murmured his understanding of this rather strange statement and waited whilst the Empress herself poured the Earl Grey tea into cups of the finest Sèvres porcelain.

"These summer cruises we always take are very pleasant, but I am starting to question their justification" Alexandra continued. "Yesterday, it is just possible we might have died by drowning and all the while the Tsar is terrified of any vessel getting within range of *Standart*" Tsar Nicholas interrupted, "I have given instructions that if any unauthorised ship whether a warship, merchantman or yacht approaches within 500 yards we are to open fire."

"That is only a normal precautionary step" placated Varlov anxiously, - not wishing to take sides between the Tsar and Tsarina, but feeling at the same time he should say something, "and I would be concerned if you didn't demand such security for your well being and that of your family."

"What worries me more Vova" Alexandra explained, "is that the very spectacle of our conspicuous wealth is a danger in itself." Twisting and untwisting her slender hands it was becoming clear that she was perhaps more perceptive than the Tsar and thus more conscious that the future of the Romanov dynasty was starting to be questioned and could well be threatened during her husband's reign. What happened in France just over a hundred years before could easily happen here she couldn't help thinking to herself. The Tsar shook his head and carefully stubbed out his cigarette in a gold ashtray engraved like other items with the double headed eagle and casually blew a puff of Turkish scented smoke towards the empty fireplace before looking at his wife, who nodded and then addressing Varlov said, "In that bundle of jewellery Alexandra was just telling you about, there is one single piece that we would like you, Vova, to accept in gratitude for what you have done for us over all these years."

Varlov protested immediately by saying that service in the Imperial Household was sufficient reward in itself and that he could never possibly countenance any gift of that nature. The Tsar held up his hand to stop his protest, "Please understand, Vova, that this is a single diamond, I am told weighing some 150 carats, and until now it has been left untouched and uncut. It had been my intention to have it sent to Peter Fabergé, our Court jeweller, for incorporation into a magnificent setting for display at the Tsarkoe Selo Winter Palace." Varlov visibly gasped when he heard these words depicting the size and the intended destination of such an amazing diamond. "Sir," he slightly stammered, "Am I to understand that you want me to take this priceless jewel as a gift or for safekeeping for your Majesties?"

"Vova," the Tsar expounded. "We would trust you with our lives and your loyalty is beyond any doubt. There may come a time when this trinket of indeterminate value may perhaps be necessary to secure the survival of ourselves and our children - we live in troubled times. Therefore, the Empress and I want you to take it now and look after it and treat it as if it were your own. If, in years to come our need or situation requires the return of the jewel I am sure we'll have only to make that known to you, but in the meanwhile God Bless you my dearest friend and say no more."

Without any further words between them, the Empress withdrew from her small purse what looked like a semi rough brown coloured bantam's egg and pressed it into the clammy hand of a speechless but emotional Vova.

The Prince had always enjoyed a privileged status within the inner Court of the Imperial family and it was generally accepted that this was thanks to his ancestry appearing to trace all the way back to Catherine the Great, who had indeed given birth to more than one illegitimate child. Although married, as he was, to the daughter of a General in the Russian army, his regular separations from his wife and children allowed him, unfortunately all too frequently, to indulge in his lifelong secret sexual leanings. His weakness for male companionship was quite easily and discretely satisfied from crew members of the *Standart*, not necessarily just restricted to those serving on the lower deck. The visit to the Imperial Yacht by the Emir of Bokhara, a well educated Russian speaking foreign ruler, accompanied by two of his ministers, sporting stunningly red dyed beards, was of particular appeal to 'Vova' as well as to the children with whom he was always a favourite. Bokhara, being an autonomous Muslim state within the Russian Empire near Afghanistan had always had a population very much at ease with homosexuality. So the exciting prospect of some genteel depravity with some of the Emir's entourage was too

13

tempting to the highly charged sexual instincts of Prince Vladimir. At the traditional exchange of gifts between the Tsar and his honoured guest, the Imperial family, including the five children, were astonished to see the tall black bearded Emir present a truly enormous uncut diamond to the Tsarina, perhaps even bigger than the one she had recently handed to Varlov, who with an almost casual manner handed the huge rock to her chief lady in waiting, whilst thanking the Emir in her far from fluent Russian.

Alcoholic drink was freely available aboard the Royal Yacht and as soon as the formal reception was over Prince Vladimir was moving rapidly to gain the eye of either of the two senior courtiers to the Emir. The best French Champagne flowed generously as the rotund and naturally amiable Prince worked his diplomatic charm. It took only an hour before the senior duty officer, whilst carrying out his routine 'rounds', was surprised and shocked to find, in a carelessly unlocked cabin, a trouserless Vova kneeling by his bunk, whilst being actively pleasured from the rear by a red bearded monk-like figure.

Admiral Kortaski was the nominal commander of the *Standart* and indeed he always hoisted his two red balled pennant from her middle mast to signify his presence aboard. The ship, in actual fact, was effectively under the command of a Russian navy Captain, and to whom the disgusted 'duty officer', wasting no time immediately reported this scandalous breach of both Imperial and Naval regulations. Following the rigid chain of command it was only a short while before the matter was brought to the attention of Admiral Kortaski, who as might be expected revealed no emotion or outward expression of shock as he reflected on the fact that until recently this was a crime punishable by death - and what a pity, he thought to himself, that it no longer applied.. Internally, his heart was thumping at the incredible opportunity for revenge that had just been presented to him. Despite giving every impression of utmost loyalty and devotion to the Romanov dynasty, Kortaski had been increasingly disturbed over the past two years or so by feelings developing within him of sympathy for the ever growing signs of future reformation and revolution in Russian society. As the grandeur of the Imperial way of life grew more extravagant, so did Kortaski's resentment increase and he jealously envied and hated the relaxed louche manner in which the non contributing Prince Vladimir slipped effortlessly along the corridors of power without having endured any of the former years of hardship and training which he had suffered in order to reach his own present prestigious position of responsibility. What is more Kortaski also loathed Varlov for the more personal reason that about fifteen years earlier they had both fallen for the beauty and wit of Anya Dieterisk the 18 year old daughter of General Dieterisk, a Chief of Staff in the Imperial bodyguard. It was Kortaski, who first had been swept off his feet by Anya's classic looks and her unexplained ability to find an affinity with almost any horse she was permitted to ride. Side saddle may be safe in terms of remaining mounted, but if the horse itself should fall it left little chance for its unfortunate rider. With her straight back, and the fashionable wide brimmed netted hat she wore, Anya was a desirable temptress for many a young officer participating in St. Petersburg equestrian events. Kortaski, then a mere naval Lieutenant, but shortly to receive his first command, had to tolerate being teased by other uniformed horsemen with such calls of "Where's your anchor Korti ?" as, at best only a novice rider, he vainly tried to pull up an over eager thoroughbred. Just one year younger than Kortaski, Prince Vladimir Varlov had no such trouble. Trained as a trooper from an early age by the Cossack Household Escort riding school he had no difficulty in showing off his flashy mounted skills and being much lighter in those days, he was an outstandingly competent horseman. On one occasion, in front of a bevy of young ladies including the General's beautiful daughter, he had demonstrated his favourite trick by riding at full gallop and managing to hit a target behind him with his carbine. This formidable feat of horsemanship and shooting flair was more than enough to turn the head of pretty 18 year old Anya Dieterisk. To the inward distress and frustration of Kortaski, wedding bells were not far distant and within a year Vladimir and Anya were to be man and wife. What puzzled Kortaski further was how Varlov would satisfy the natural sexual desires of Anya, knowing as he did that the bridegroom's tastes were mainly deviant.

Summoning the *Standart's* Captain to his day cabin after reading his report, Admiral Kortaski gave him clear and unequivocal instructions. "I want no mention made of this appalling incident, but I want two men carefully selected by you from the crew under your command to keep watch on Prince Vladimir secretly for twenty fours a day. At no time is he to be permitted in the company of any member of the household without one of your spies watching his every move and recording his every word." The *Standart's* Captain stumbled in his reply, but with dominant severity Admiral Kortaski repeated his orders by adding "If you wish to retain your command of this most important ship of the Imperial Russian navy you will see my orders are executed to the letter. You will also report your findings to me alone."

The Empress Alexandra suffered from sciatica and seasickness, so when Tsar Nicholas said that they were to sail in the Imperial Yacht *Standart* to England after the closing celebrations of the Kiel Regatta in August 1909, she could only moan and express her dismay. The Tsar was keen to make an appearance at the fashionable seaside town of Cowes on the Isle of Wight where the English summer season would be rounded off by the Cowes Regatta. Already that summer they had been living, albeit in considerable comfort, for two months aboard the huge stately vessel, and now the thought of the 500 mile passage across the North Sea was a most unpleasant additional prospect for her, just when she had thought that the year's sailing days were nearly finished. The Tsar, on the other hand had a competitive instinct having been encouraged by his two yachting mad cousins, Kaiser William II of Germany and The Prince of Wales. Admiral Kortaski, was still officially in command of *Standart* but was due to retire from Imperial duties at the end of the year. For him, this would come as a great relief, as amongst other reasons, it would put an end to the continually unpleasant ongoing relationship he had been forced to endure with Prince Vladimir Varlov. The 'fat man' as he came to call him behind his back, and sometimes even to his face, had become yet more entrenched as favourite of the Tsar and his family. Not so much by his natural obsequiousness or toadying, although that was a trait shared to some extent by all the Royal courtiers, but by the much more intangible quality of his personal charm with which he was abundantly blessed. The aggressive down to earth Kortaski, as much as he tried, could never, in any way, be described as a charmer and his blunt gruff authoritarian manner may have served him well as a senior naval figure, but was no asset as a member of the Imperial court.

Bidden by the Empress to the day Stateroom, Admiral Kortaski explained to her "The first 75 miles, Your Majesty, will be through the Kiel Canal, which you will remember was opened by the Tsar's cousin Kaiser William just 14 years ago, and we will steam slowly along it in daylight until Cuxhaven. The weather appears to be set fine for the coming two days and you should be able to sleep peacefully for most of the short onward voyage to Cowes."

"Then I'll take your advice and keep to my sleeping quarters and I should be all right" she told Kortaski, "but give me now your firm promise that the children, once we leave the shelter of the canal, will be kept strictly below deck. Don't forget that the Tsarevitch is frail and still only five years old. As for our daughters I want a firm eye kept on them even though Grand Duchess Olga is now fourteen. Dear Prince Varlov is wonderful with them all, but I would like your assurance that you will help him all you can if there are any signs of them behaving badly." Kortaski inwardly groaned at this repetitive semi admonishment, which seemed to be spelled out to him on an almost daily basis, coupled with the usual adulation of the 'fat man'.

The passage across the North Sea and into the Solent passed off uneventfully with *Standart* cruising at a respectable 20 knots. Arrival at Cowes Roads, the stretch of water so named just to the North of the little island sea side town of Cowes, was as dramatic as it was spectacular. A forest of masts appeared to fill the sheltered mouth of the Medina River and to a quick glance it seemed possible to envisage walking from East to West Cowes across the decks of the hundreds of yachts anchored there for Regatta Week. The Prince of Wales had already arrived aboard his late Grandmother's old yacht '*Victoria and Albert*', and Kaiser William was making a double showing by arriving earlier the same day aboard his new yacht *Hohenzollern,* which was only a few feet shorter than his cousin's *Standart.* He also had with him his latest German built racing yacht *Meteor IV,* manned by an all German crew under the command of the relatively elderly white bearded Admiral von

Eisendecker. In a spirit of Edwardian bravado, daily racing of the big yachts included the Prince of Wales's *Britannia* - the great gaff rigged yacht built by his father in 1893 the then Prince of Wales and the future King Edward VII, The Kaiser, took enormous pride in what he thought was regarded as his Englishness and was thrilled to entertain his guests at what he referred to as 'The Castle', the home of the Royal Yacht Squadron of which he had already been a proud member now for over twenty years. This year at a fateful reception he held at 'The Squadron', his 150 guests included Admiral Kortaski and Prince Varlov. In a genuine gesture of friendship he invited Kortaski to join him as honorary tactician aboard the impressive *Meteor IV* for the following day's racing - an invitation heartily endorsed by Tsar Nicholas, who himself would be aboard *Britannia*. Prince Varlov, never short of an opportunity, in turn accepted the invitation of the American millionaire Morton F. Plant for a comfortable day aboard his superb 248 ton racing yacht *Ingomar,* which was strongly tipped as the likely winner.

The fertile mind of Admiral Kortaski for many years now had continually been trying to find a way of ridding himself of the ever present 'fat man'. His orders given two years before to have him kept under 24 hour surveillance had quickly proved fruitful. Within three weeks of receiving the shocking report of Varlov's appalling sexually perverted activities, one of the Captain's spies, who worked within the personal quarters of the Imperial couple, had brought him the news overheard from the private galley adjacent to the *Standart's* day stateroom that the Empress Alexandra had given Varlov apparently for safe keeping an extremely valuable, unidentifiable single gem stone with a supposed weight exceeding 150 carats. Kortaski's bitter personal jealousy was driven to new levels as he constantly dreamed and schemed how to finish off the 'fat man' and somehow acquire the jewel for himself. In fact the whole vendetta was becoming an obsession to him.

The following day, a Saturday, promised the prospect of some good racing with a moderate Easterly breeze, calm sea and good visibility. There were fifteen yachts due to cross the Royal Yacht Squadron starting line, presenting a fine spectacle, for the hundreds if not thousands, of day trippers over from Portsmouth and Southampton. *Meteor IV* and *Ingomar* both made good starts, thanks mainly to the expert tactical manoeuvring by Kortaski aboard the German yacht *Meteor IV* and the superb technique of Charlie Barr, acknowledged to be the crack American skipper of the day, who was in command of *Ingomar.*

The first hour of the race was along the Solent towards the East, passing Osborne House, the old Queen's home and then Ryde before reaching the more open sea and making the first turning point, at the Nab Tower. With the tide under the racing fleet, progress was quite rapid despite the boats having to tack continually into a difficult force four headwind. Quite quickly after the start *Ingomar* established a useful lead of about two minutes over *Meteor IV* and for most of the time the two yachts were on the same tack in what was fast becoming a semi procession. As they neared St Helen's Fort, Admiral Kortaski advised the German Admiral von Eisendecker to put in an 'extra tack' and thus continue the race with the two leaders on opposite tacks. Charlie Barr, skippering *Ingomar*, noticed this immediately and commented to his guest Prince Varlov, lounging comfortably in a wicker chair nursing a glass of champagne and dressed in immaculate white flannels and blue boating jacket, that they would have to be exceptionally alert and to keep a 'sharp look out' as inevitably the two yachts being on opposite tacks would come onto a collision course. "Don't worry," called Varlov wanting to sound knowledgeable, "we are bound to be on Starboard tack when we cross *Meteor* and we will have the undisputed right of way." He knew little about the rules of seamanship, let alone the rules of yacht racing, but this one he had been told that very morning by one of the crew. Neither the American skipper, nor the Russian courtier or even the over confident multi millionaire owner had however, considered the supreme arrogance of the King of Germany, who believed his Royal status, took precedence and always overruled any such nautical nicety.

Within three minutes the two gaff rigged yachts, with top sails and upper jibs set, were heading towards each other with a closing speed of 22 knots. Kortaski, in sympathy with the Kaiser's preposterous notions of Royal privilege had carefully calculated that as *Meteor IV* carried a 30 ft bowsprit at a height of about three feet higher than *Ingomar's* deck, the collision, if carefully steered, should be lethal for Varlov, Charlie Barr and her owner. When the contenders were within 200 yards of each other Charlie Barr, himself at *Ingomar's* wheel, bellowed to Varlov and Morton Plant "RULE?"

"Stand firm on Starboard" came the shout in unified response, - Varlov only silently hesitant on following his colleague. The convergence became breathtakingly frightening as the crew of both big yachts prepared to protect themselves from the imminent collision. So scared were the American yacht's crew that they actually turned away from the sight of the German killer yacht bearing down on them from now just 50 yards away. At the last possible second the German helmsman slammed the tiller down allowing *Meteor IV* to fly into wind and immediately Charlie Barr reciprocated with an identical move. Danger was averted, but with the two boats within grappling distance of each other both had flapping canvas, ropes and wooden blocks threatening to smash into any innocent item in their path. Prince Vladimir Varlov, was struck violently on his shoulder by one of the huge wooden blocks attached to the mainsail as it flailed out of control and in a flash was hurled across the leeward rail. "Man overboard" came the cry from several of the crew as they saw the large splash. The realisation by Admiral Kortaski, aboard *Meteor* IV, that the 'fat man' was imperiled with little hope of rescue made it hard for him to suppress a smile.

The first thing that a panicking Prince Varlov felt as his legs thrashed weakly in the sea was a blinding pain in his shoulder and the inability to move one of his arms. Only semi conscious he also hazily noticed that he was very slowly drifting astern of a large black hulled yacht on whose transom he read in gold lettering *Meteor IV RYS*.

The German skipper of *Meteor IV* had shown exemplary seamanship the moment he realised there was a man overboard and, with the yacht still carrying sufficient way, had turned her a full 180 degrees downwind. Charlie Barr, the American skipper of *Ingomar* was too concerned with the immediate hoisting of a 'protest' flag on the signal halyard that it was a full 30 seconds before he took in the fate of his famous Russian guest. Canvas bound cork lifebelts were thrown hastily into the sea in the hope that the victim would save himself from drowning by reaching out and grabbing one. In the event it was a hefty boathook handled by two German sailors from *Meteor* that fished out the unfortunate 'fat man'. "My God" one exclaimed "this is a heavy old thing, more like a whale that we have rescued from a watery grave." Unceremoniously hauled aboard the Kaiser's yacht, Varlov was carried below and given careful attention including a few kind words from the German King himself, who had at least shown the good grace and unexpected sportsmanship to hoist a retiring flag in apologetic acknowledgment of the American's protest. To everyone's relief the unfortunate incident was closed with exception perhaps of Kortaski who would have been happy to watch the rescue take a good deal longer.

In the local clinic of the little seaside town, thanks to the solicitous attention of the senior Doctor, Prince Varlov made a rapid recovery and apart from a badly bruised shoulder, and a more badly bruised dignity, was fit enough to be physically aware that the great diamond was still safely located where it should be. Never trusting anyone but himself for the last five years, Varlov had kept the diamond either in a safe, the combination of which was only known to him, or when travelling, including time spent aboard *Standart,* he had resorted to the means adopted by slaves, convicts and traffickers i.e. a personal 'charger' worn internally. To most people the concept of such concealment would be abhorrent, but due to Varlov's occasional past sexual tastes, no such problem presented itself. The diamond was secure.

Fortunately, Varlov's near fatal mishap occurred at the beginning of Cowes Regatta week and didn't interfere with his most important plan to receive, aboard *Standart,* an English visitor from London. So it was that on the final day of the Regatta, the Imperial courtier was leaning over the rail near the landing steps of *Standart,* scanning with his binoculars the distant landing stage where the Portsmouth paddle steamer was shortly due to arrive. It wasn't long before he saw the yacht's gleaming black steam pinnace charging its way through, weaving skilfully between the vast number of boats anchored or sailing at the mouth of the Medina river. The grand little boat with its crew of four - had brilliantly polished brasswork gleaming in the sunlight distinguished by a 10 ft high inverted bell shaped funnel from which an intermittent plume of white steam puffed busily into the summer sky.

With his right arm still in a sling, the ever charming Prince

Varlov moved to the head of the *Standart's* landing steps and greeted a tall willowy young man carrying a silk top hat. To his surprise his greeting was returned in near perfect Russian, so despite his misgivings about the man's curious manner of dress, Varlov was favourably impressed.

"Welcome to this piece of Imperial Russian territory, I do hope you have survived the discomfort of the train from London and not been seasick on your short trip across the Solent."

"A very nice change for me to come down here Your Highness." the wispy fair haired Warwick Hardfells demurred, adjusting his rimless glasses and giving the impression of an easy manner and that he was perfectly at home with the protocol and formality of the Imperial Yacht surroundings. The officers aboard *Standart* knew nothing of the reason for the young man's visit now and neither would they in the future. "Please arrange for us to be served lunch in my personal day cabin," Prince Varlov instructed the senior steward. "We have private matters to discuss and I don't wish to be disturbed." Unseen by either man, the Admiral was watching their meeting from the far end of the yacht - his expression would have betrayed his curiosity. Once they were comfortably settled in his day cabin, Prince Varlov apologised for the brief notice by telegraph by which he had requested Hardfell's presence and went on to explain that there was only one opportunity to carry out the intended transaction and that would have to be today. Displaying his fluent Russian and a working knowledge of French the young banker began. "I hardly need mention to you Sir, that the Imperial family is already well known to our bank and 'The French Department', of which I have recently become the head, has had the honour of serving the interests of European Royalty since shortly before Louis XVI and Marie Antoinette were unfortunately executed in 1793. We have arranged, I would add in utter confidence, to carry valuables across Europe, to hold in safe keeping mainly in the vaults located in our London head office." It was hot in the cabin and Hardfell discretely wiped the sweat off his top lip with a silk handkerchief taken from his top pocket.

"I know all that my dear fellow." responded Prince Varlov, slightly irritated by the condescending explanatory manner of this over self confident rather pushy bank officer. "What I want to know is what form of receipt your bank is going to give me if I pass across to you for safe keeping a single diamond of enormous value?" Without hesitating for a moment the well rehearsed Warwick Hardfells explained. "I am afraid Sir, absolutely nothing at all. That is not our practice. We are the guardians of many Royal fortunes, both from reigning and deposed families. Not one of them has ever been granted physical evidence of our custodianship." He went on, "What we do is to allocate you a safe box - the size depends on your requirements - and a key. That is registered in your name, but what is kept in it is entirely a private matter for you - we retain no knowledge or record of the contents. That is entirely your personal business."

Perplexed and awed by the blandness of this announcement, Varlov asked "But surely the question of identification and payment must be of concern to your eminent bank?"

"In your case Sir, there is no problem. Our own security intelligence has a good working knowledge of your Imperial Household and already we are entrusted with redeemable bearer bonds from which we are able to draw our custodial fees. We know your position as a long standing courtier to the Family and there will be no charge to you or your rightful descendants until such time as your property is withdrawn from our safe keeping when an appropriate charge for the rent of the safe box could possibly be negotiated. As I said you will retain a key to the private safe containing your deposit and possession of that is sufficient proof of your rights and will enable access to your property at any time. In the meanwhile, we ask you to trust us without question and I understand that I am here by your request to collect the property of which you told me. Normally we would ask you to visit London and to deposit your property within the safe yourself - in this case as you agree and have requested I will take it on from here on your behalf."

By now suitably impressed and given no choice other than to accept the bank's terms, he said to his relaxed visitor "If you will wait here a few minutes Mr. Hardfells, may I leave you, whilst I go next door for a moment?" Varlov, rose and left the cabin. Within minutes he returned with the diamond, now reposing in a modest grey chamois leather pouch after an empty metal charger had been discretely disposed of through a port hole. The noise of the small splash was hidden from the Admiral looking out to sea from the deck above, by the rising wind. Varlov handed the leather pouch to

Hardfells, "Take good care of this if you will and thank you for your visit. Now I see it is time for you to return for the ferry to the mainland - so if I may I will call the bosun of the yacht's pinnace - I wish you 'bon voyage' and a safe arrival in London. Good bye."

Mr. Hardfells took the leather purse and placed it in his brief case. As he shook hands with the Prince neither man could realise that the diamond inside it would not see the light of day again for the best part of a hundred years, nor could they have foreseen the drama in which it would take the lead.

CHAPTER FOUR

HAMPSHIRE 2002

The knocking on the door was insistent and the dogs were barking with their usual ferocity. "Sleep oh blessed sleep why do you evade me?" Her trembling continued and the racket went on as well. Fear, fever and faintness were giving Ishbel a terrifying experience from which she couldn't escape and where even death would seem a relief. The knocking was getting louder in her head and a human voice was shouting from somewhere outside the house. In desperation she pulled a pillow over her head, not to suffocate, but just to block out the terrible noise created by the hysterical animals warning the unwelcome visitor or intruder that early evening in September. For months now Ishbel's doctor had told her to help her migraines by resting whenever possible and had prescribed her a series of increasingly powerful tranquillisers and sleeping pills. As the long term family doctor he was worried about her recent frailty and had done everything he could to persuade her husband, Peter, to take her away from the stressful London and country social scene, in which they had become so involved. As a Scottish girl still with a family house where her brother lived on the West Coast of Scotland, she had unwillingly, but loyally spent far too many years in the South. It was only Peter's untiring energy at work which kept them from spending at least three months of the year in the North.

It must have been three or four minutes now that this ear bashing half imagined onslaught had gone on and no way could she avoid it. The familiar ring of the bedroom phone came almost as a relief from the jangle of door bell ringing, door knocking and dogs barking. With a shudder Ishbel threw back the pillow and eiderdown under which she had been sheltering and grasped the handset of the old fashioned white telephone. It was Peter. "What is the matter darling - you sound distraught?"

"They're coming darling - I know they are - what am I to do?" sobbed the tragic figure from the protection of the bedroom.

"Don't worry my darling, I'm almost home - in fact I shall be turning into the drive within three minutes as I managed to get an early train." soothed Peter Varlov, who had grown accustomed to calming Ishbel from her repetitive bouts of imagined threats, but he was totally unprepared for the attack he was about to get himself as he parked the elderly Volkswagen 'beetle', which he insisted on still using as a station car.

The Georgian house with Victorian additions lay, in pleasant rolling countryside, and was hidden from the road with a wide curving driveway leading to an adjacent stable block, now used as a garage with another branch of the drive leading to the front entrance. It had been a long day for Peter, who had left home before 6 a.m. for The City, and he was looking forward to his usual evening drink, the best of the day he always thought, with the fire already lit in the sizeable inglenook fireplace of the listed 'brick and flint clad' house, which had been their home now for more than twenty five years and in which they had brought up two lovely daughters and a son. He hoped that he wouldn't have to spend hours settling Ishbel and getting her out of a mental state that had been developing for the past two years - for the last few months he never knew what he would find when he arrived home. He put the car away and was walking passed one of his favourite evergreen yew bushes when he saw the man appear from the shadows of the lighted portico in front of the house. In poor light it was difficult to see who the visitor was, but Peter could notice enough that he was quite out of keeping with this rather special part of Hampshire. It was a scruffy looking individual aged at least 65 and wearing a nowadays unheard of piece of clothing, a fawn coloured mackintosh. What was more he had a misshapen brown trilby on his head, which covered half his face and was carrying a rolled up carton that could be threatening as a weapon. Before Peter had a chance to greet the visitor he found himself cornered against a yew hedge. "Are you Prince Peter Varlov? abruptly demanded the unsavoury shabby man. Unsuspecting Peter replied "Yes I am, but more usually known as Mr. Varlov nowadays"

"Then take this as a legal serving of a writ" growled the stubble chinned man as he slapped the rolled up paper from the carton into Peter's hand. Perplexed, worried and unable to think of a suitable response in his surprise, he stood semi aghast and motionless as the

Macintosh man marched quickly down the drive and got into a small car that Peter had failed to notice parked in total darkness behind a solid hedge that acted as protection and a sound barrier from any passing traffic.

So shocked was Peter Varlov by this virtual assault on his person that he was unable to face up to reading the contents of the writ. In reality he knew what it was going to say, but he just couldn't face it there and then that evening. Instead, he let himself in through the massive oak front door and after throwing off his Loden overcoat he hurried up the stairs to see Ishbel. He was appalled by what he saw and all thoughts of the writ momentarily left him. The once indescribably pretty red head with the piercing pale blue eyes was now just a shadowy shrivelled creature with white hair so thin that patches of her scalp showed clearly pink and bald. Her skin, once milky white and freckled, had turned to crinkly parchment that reflected the beads of icy sweat from her forehead down to her neck. She seemed scarcely able to recognise him as she struggled to return herself to a conscious state having for the last half hour been sheltering in a semi coma partially induced by her medicine. He sat gently on the bed beside her and with a cool damp flannel dabbed her face before kissing her on the forehead. She trembled continually, but at least she was accepting the comfort of Peter's arm supporting her, as she tried bravely for his sake to pull herself together.

"You have nothing to be afraid of darling." he said softly, "absolutely nothing. You only heard the gibbering shouts of a wretched tinker. You know we have that colony of them settled just half a mile from the village and from time to time one of them gets drunk and makes a nuisance of himself by pestering one of the residents." Not really satisfied with Peter's explanation she was only content when he went on "I told him I would call the Police if he didn't get off our land immediately and if they caught him he'd be banged up for the night. Why don't you go and run yourself a bath and then put on your prettiest housecoat before coming down to enjoy a glass of champagne?" It was difficult for Peter, but at least he had the distraction of going to the office and at home he made a supreme effort to boost his wife's morale. As she disappeared into the bathroom he couldn't help sitting back on the bed with both hands holding his head in dismay.

Whilst Peter heard the noise of a running bath and smelled the familiar flowered aroma of her bath essence, he went downstairs and quickly took the dreaded writ that had been served upon him and placed it into his old fashioned leather briefcase, which he locked. He was an adequate if not an accomplished cook, so he had no difficulty in putting together a risotto dish, whilst refreshing himself with the better part of a bottle of medium expensive champagne - famous name vintage luxury champagnes were all very well, but certainly not justifiable under present circumstances. Ishbel appeared within twenty minutes looking and behaving as if twenty years younger and after two glasses of champagne even showed flashes of her gorgeous smile, which had so enchanted her husband some thirty years before. Peter had had to fight his corner to win her hand and never once in 29 years of marriage had he regretted entering the contest.

"Will you be alright tomorrow darling?" Peter queried.

"Of course I will. It's only in the dark winter evenings when I'm alone here that my mind wanders onto a subject we rarely discuss and I am terrified that one day there's going to be a catching up." Ishbel replied.

"Tomorrow will be a most eventful one for me because I am meeting George Matthews at the club for lunch. Dear old George, he's such a good friend really, but such a snob. I do wish he wouldn't keep on nagging me to put him up for the club."

"Surely Vova, he'd be a decent new member for you?" Ishbel lightly teased him, using his family nickname. "You're really more of a snob yourself. What is so special anyway about your meeting with George?" Ishbel asked.

"As you know only too well, George has been a confident of mine for more than 30 years and he is godfather to one of our children, although I have never really known why we asked him at the time, and finally he is still an executor of my will." came the lengthy reply from Peter. "Admittedly he has become unbearably pompous since he got his knighthood, but nevertheless I am going to talk to him about our problems and listen carefully to what he has to say. Sometimes his advice is good."

For some inexplicable reason Sir George Matthews was always late, so it was no surprise that it was almost one thirty when the hall porter of the austere looking club in St. James's, announced his arrival to Peter Varlov who was waiting in the smoking room. In fact the porter's announcement was hardly necessary - Peter had already heard Sir George ask for him at the front desk using his full title in a customary loud voice.

The wait however, had given Varlov time to absorb further the utter unspeakable horror of the document so brutally thrust into his hand the previous evening. Not daring to open it until this morning whilst sitting in a first class railway compartment on the train to London, the single passenger sitting opposite him must have been amazed to see the colour in the face of the elderly man change from ruddiness to ashen grey as the blood had drained away. There staring at him were the bright red words of a naked rubber stamp 'SUPREME COURT OF JUDICATURE - ADMIRALTY & COMMERCIAL REGISTRY' Beneath a Sword of Damocles it stated starkly and bluntly 'IT IS THIS DAY ADJUDGED that the Defendant do pay the Plaintiff the sum of £2,347,854.68 together with costs to be taxed if not agreed.' The Plaintiff as listed in this shattering piece of documentation was 'THE SOCIETY OF LLOYD'S'

After welcoming his guest the two old friends had a quick drink at the bar, a large gin and tonic for Varlov and a plain tomato juice for Matthews, before taking their place at a quiet corner table in the so called coffee room. It was separated enough not to be overheard in normal volume chat, yet with a hum of conversation around them as fellow members enjoyed their usual high standard of quintessentially English school cooking and fine wines. Varlov nodded a friendly good morning to two well known opposition politicians, whilst Matthews studiously surveyed the menu. Forgetting his normally courteous manners Varlov blurted out "Kidneys and bacon as usual for me" to the pretty waitress, who smiled at him as she flapped open his damask napkin. "I'll have the lamb cutlets please" countered Matthews, looking round the room enviously at the air of social acceptability and seeing who might recognise him. "And now we've got that out of the way we can have a proper chat. Starting with you bringing me up to date with Ishbel and of course my favourite godson." gushed the banker, disappointed that he had seen no one there who might acknowledge him.

"I'm afraid I've got something far more urgent to talk about than that, though God knows Ishbel is no better I'm afraid" said Varlov, who by now had re-gained at least some colour back in his cheeks. "Those bastards at Lloyd's have at last done their worst and finally yesterday I received a writ saying that I owe them coming on for two and half million quid."

"Christ, that's terrifying. However, let's have lunch first and wait until we have a coffee and perhaps a glass of your club's delicious port upstairs to discuss things. Just tell me now how you came to be involved in such a disastrous state of affairs and then we can talk later about the best way of dealing with it." came Matthew's clear headed approach - in any case he hated to talk business while he ate, such a distraction he always thought.

Gradually and painfully Varlov recalled the circumstances under which he had become a member of Lloyd's, the three hundred year old insurance market in the City of London. He reminded Matthews how it was he who had suggested that he talked to a mutual friend of theirs, actually an old school fellow of his as well, Anatole Kortaski, who was now a Lloyd's Underwriting Agent. Then, as his potential agent and a long standing friend, he had told him way back at the end of the seventies that he should consider joining as a way of comfortably meeting school fees and perhaps most appealing of all was that it was a way of using his assets twice and of helping his cash flow. All you had to do, he had explained, was to make a simple declaration of wealth and then put up a small percentage of something like 20 per cent of the amount of premium income he would like to 'write.' Then he would be an underwriting member of Lloyd's of London - an institution with an amazing history. 'Just sit back and wait for the cheques' he had said. There had been some mention of unlimited liability, but that had been passed over as briefly as possible. It's ironic but their motto is 'FIDENTIA', which crudely translated means 'Utmost Good Faith!' That rings a bit cold now thought Varlov to himself.

"I must confess" said Varlov "that I should perhaps have known better than to have picked the agent you suggested. Apparently there were at the time I joined several hundred to choose from - probably still are, but I still had this sort of loyalty to the old Imperial Court in which my Grandfather had served and there, with a seemingly good reputation, was Anatole Kortaski, the younger brother of Stanislas, -

I was at school with both of them. He was running his own quite large and seemingly profitable Lloyd's Agency business. "Like mine, their Grandfather also had served the Russian Court when he was the Admiral commanding the Imperial Yacht, but I think there was always bad blood between them. Our family histories have to a large extent run parallel in that both our grandfathers managed to escape from Russia in 1918 and spent until 1940 in Paris where both the families worked under the most menial circumstances. I suppose finally, George, it was your suggestion of going to Anatole that persuaded me." George Matthews, being a would be snob squirmed imperceptibility at being reminded of this part of Prince Varlov's background, as to the outside world he gave a good impression of being an English gentleman born and bred, which in one sense he now was. He had often wondered how Varlov's father, apparently a charming man, although he had never met him, had arrived in England, just before the German occupation of Paris, and had managed to fall so easily into a financially comfortable situation aged just 42. His connections, of course, were exceptional if ill defined, and it was generally assumed that his glancing friendship with British Royalty may well have extended beyond social acquaintance.

"I've never really gone along with this British old school tie business." Varlov protested, "but I have to admit as well that Anatole and I were in the same house at Eton, which may have been another small influence on my choice. It's funny isn't it George, that traditionally it was always the most stupid boys who left school to join the army and the next up the list went into Lloyd's? The clever ones usually went to university" Matthews avoided those remarks - he had gone straight into banking from school. Upstairs after lunch, in the library, an open smokeless fire was glowing pleasantly, and the only noise apart from the mumble of muted conversations were the snores coming from an aged member enjoying a dreamless port-induced unconscious state. With a coffee in his hand and a glass of vintage Taylors in Peter's, Matthews asked, "How do you propose to handle this Peter?" which was just the question he had anticipated.

"Quite simply George I have got to pay, but then My God I am going to try to fight for justice." Emboldened by the best part of a bottle of good claret, not to mention his pre-lunch Gin and Tonic, to which the port was now adding its   effect. "I have got no choice, but to follow this route. If I don't pay, the merciless bastards will bankrupt me - they've already said so in writing. If I go bankrupt my present consultancy business will be shut down because these modern Financial Services Authority bureaucrats, with all their red tape, don't take too kindly to their members being in Carey Street, for whatever reason. Then there is the personal hell of causing the inevitable embarrassment to my wider family and friends in Gloucestershire, who have always been so supportive and good to me. After everything they have done for our family it would be totally wrong to let them down with such a disgrace. I may have been born half Russian, but at least I've taken in some of your English sense of fair play and decency I hope."

"But Peter, how are you going to find all this money - it's a huge amount?" interrupted Matthews, looking round the room and getting slightly worried by the fury spewing forth from the now far from sober and florid Varlov and which other members were beginning to notice.   Matthews hated being involved in embarrassing situations like this looked to be developing into. "I'll tell you how I'm going to do it, my old friend" went on Peter, - his speech becoming a little slurred. "You're going to lend it to me when I come and ask." He said a little too loudly for Sir George's comfort. Matthews looked at Varlov - he saw to his alarm that he wasn't smiling.

"Steady now Peter. You certainly have a facility with my bank, but it only extends to half a million pounds, half of which you've used already and with this you're talking about one of five times that amount."

"Don't worry old boy you'll have all the cover you need and I only need a bridging loan. I'd never expect a banker to take a real risk - you'll see alright that I'm not joking. Now I'm going to tell you what I propose to do after that."

Matthews winced and realising that the drink was getting his friend steadily more excited, started to make excuses that he must be getting back to work - a bit disingenuous as he never, on principle, went back to his office unless it was absolutely necessary following drinking at lunch. Varlov ignored his attempt at leaving "Just you sit right there and listen to me - I'm going to take on these serious swindlers head first and that's another reason for not going bankrupt. I want to fight from a position of strength and I hope you'll understand as well that I don't want to be obliged to resign my membership of this dear old club. Nor suffer all the other indignities that going bust would involve" A member, apparently dozing in his leather armchair quite near them, got up quickly and left the room.

"O.K. Peter I'm listening." murmured a resigned George Matthews, who knew there was little point in not humouring a drunk. "Just you tell me slowly and quietly what you're going to do?" He looked round the room and to his relief saw that Peter wasn't attracting any more unwelcome attention.

"I've got evidence, yes proper evidence in writing, that proves how these Lloyd's buggers have cheated us. The boss of Lloyd's or Chief Executive Officer, as they like to call him, was put in by your top authority, the Governor of the Bank of England. He put him in to Lloyd's as an independent outsider in 1983 to sort the mess out, but I personally believe he found it all so distasteful and full of rotten apples that he couldn't cope and left in 1986."

"That's all very interesting Peter, but even if that were true which I think unlikely, how is that relevant and going to help you fight them?"

"A whole can full of worms have crawled out of the Lime Street woodwork and I think the whole affair stinks. Don't think I'm the only one who's going to fight - not for a long way I'm not. I intend to use any persuasion I can to get him to testify in court. If he does, the legal consequences could be catastrophic for the lot of them, hopefully, but God only knows what will happen. I'll probably be dead before it's all finished."

"I think you should be very careful what you say" warned his more restrained friend, "and even more careful what you accuse people of – you were happy enough to join at the time. Let me remind you that discretion is usually the better part of valour and the City is a real jungle." As Matthews got up to leave, it was maybe as well that he missed the look of contempt that Varlov gave him.

CHAPTER FIVE

LONDON

Sir George Matthew didn't really mean to be pompous it just came naturally to him. As the product of a minor public school and with a father who had spent a lifetime working for a building society, and had struggled financially to send him there, it was inevitable that he should adopt the symbols so cherished by the bank manager class and which he had thought so necessary for his climb up the English social scale. If someone had told him that the golden privet hedge, which surrounded his tidy garden, was the perfect give away, he would never have believed them. Similarly, he would never have understood that his mid 1930s house between Putney and Richmond, that hinterland between suburbia and town, was seen as the epitome of middle class British solidity. Only a few years younger than Peter Varlov, he had been one of the very last National Servicemen and had striven successfully to obtain a commission in the Royal Artillery, continuing afterwards for some years as a weekend territorial. As a young man he had studied for and acquired all the necessary banking qualifications needed for a career with one of the major banks. Indeed, thanks to his diligence he gained star grade diplomas in each examination.   With such a worthy c.v. to present he had not the slightest difficulty in getting offered a job as management trainee with one of the major banks. Enthusiastically, he immediately looked the part, wearing the uniform of the day including a bowler hat, stiff detachable collar clean on daily, and rolled umbrella. With considerable pride, across his double breasted waistcoat, he sported the heavy gold watch chain given to him by his father as a twenty first birthday present, but at the tender age of 22 he hadn't yet got the watch to hang on the end of it - still, no one would see this omission he had thought. On his first morning, ready for work, his proud mother had insisted on taking his photo with her 'box brownie' before he left home.

Now, in his early sixties he still wore a double breasted waistcoat covering a comfortable paunch acquired over the years, and his forty year old watch chain, now with a gold hunter firmly attached he looked just the part of the recently retired central banker, which is exactly what he was. Sitting easily behind a huge desk in the office provide for him, he was studying with not a little concern the private banking records of Prince Peter Varlov. Though now officially retired, Sir George Matthew KCB, who had been knighted just the year before by the Queen, in recognition of his services to banking,   regarded the honour as the climax of an otherwise unexciting career - for his wife it was the very apex of all her social ambitions. He had remained as a non-executive director of the exclusive bank in the Strand, to whom he had given so many years of devoted service before finishing his career as a not particularly distinguished member of the Court of the Bank of England. He was certainly not looking forward to this morning's meeting with Peter Varlov. He couldn't help recalling the lunch they had together two weeks earlier when Peter, who he regarded as a most special friend had disclosed, what he had only half expected, disastrous losses incurred through his membership of Lloyd's of London. What was worse, and what had unnerved Sir George, was that he had indicated all too firmly that he intended to meet those massive losses by borrowing from this very bank and was relying on him to arrange it.

Their friendship, such as it was, went back more than thirty years when they had both rowed together and they had even competed against one another in the coxless fours at the Henley Royal Regatta. At the time, Peter Varlov was a member of Leander after winning the Ladies plate as a member of the Eton eight and the young George had been most impressed by this.   The bank's records were fulsome in the majority of cases, but going back to the end of the nineteenth century there were some noticeable gaps. Matthews had heard of, but never known Peter Varlov's father, who had been one of their long established customers. He had apparently arrived in Britain from Spain under conditions of secrecy soon after the outbreak of World War II with evidently no worthwhile assets to his name. He read in the file that with his English wife he had previously been living in Paris, like countless other refugees from the 1917 Russian Revolution. For twenty years or more he had driven taxis, worked in restaurants and even served as a lift attendant in a smart hotel in order to keep his family. Delving back yet further in the records to 1909 he read with curiosity that a member of the bank staff had apparently visited Peter Varlov's grandfather Vladimir at Cowes in the Isle of Wight. No reason was given for the visit. No name was given for the bank officer, and no further reference as far as he could see was made to it.

Adjusting his half moon reading glasses, on the bridge of his ample nose, Matthews checked on Peter's present status with the bank and was relieved, although not surprised, to see that he kept an orderly account with attractive interest bearing balances spread over three different currencies. There had never been any irregularities or problems with his account, nor for that matter with those of his wife or children, all of whom had their accounts with the bank. Their fund management division also had a mandate for the management of a £1 million pound share portfolio and they held a floating charge over those securities, enabling them to provide Varlov with an overdraft facility of £0.5 million. This, Matthews noticed was only half used at present for the purpose of gearing his portfolio of shares. He did not appear to have any other debts, with the deeds of his house, which they kept for him, being unencumbered. All in all, before the Lloyd's problem, he appeared to be very comfortably off, thought Matthews. Although now semi retired he knew that Peter was still active in the field of mergers and acquisitions, an area which he understood well, having spent at least twenty years as a much respected managing director of one of the City's more eminent merchant banks. In all, a valued customer to the bank who, thanks to his impeccable connections had, over the years, introduced many others of greater net worth. Sir George wanted to help, his pride would not let him refuse, and indeed he was sure that he could, but certainly not by the route of providing an un-secured loan - that was too tricky as the bank might possibly hold him responsible if anything went wrong.

Unlike Matthews, who was always late, Peter Varlov made a point of being punctual so it was at precisely 1130 that there was a soft tap on his door and a frock coated young man quietly came in to the heavily carpeted office on the third floor. "Prince Peter Varlov has arrived and is waiting downstairs Sir George. Should I escort him up here?"

"No thank you Michael" Matthew replied, "I will go down personally to meet him. He is after all, one of our most special customers as well as being a personal friend." He hoped the young man would be suitably impressed. Varlov never failed to be impressed, and not a little amused by the courtesy, bordering on obsequiousness, and flattering service offered to him by the bank and now by Matthews. He couldn't count the number of times he had been invited to lunch in one of their boardrooms, been their guest with his wife at Covent Garden in winter and Glyndebourne in the summer. This time it was he who was going to impress them if not give them an electrifying surprise. After the usual courtesies and accepting the offer to bring coffee, from his secretary, Matthews gently invited Peter to explain the purpose of the visit. A glance at portraiture of the Varlov family, would show distinctly a facial similarity down three generations. More obvious, but not evident from paintings, was the physical likeness between them. Peter had the same roly-poly appearance as his forbears, but encouraged by his wife and through careful dieting and some exercise, he could be described as comfortable rather than fat like his grandfather. He had though, inherited the same easy going manner that charmed almost everybody who was lucky enough to know him and this was perhaps his most valuable asset.

With a long sigh Varlov started by apologising to Matthews for his recent verbal explosion when they had last lunched together in his club. "The only excuse I can give is that these problems I am facing, have been building for years. The evening before we had lunch was the final straw with the arrival of the £2.5 million writ from Lloyd's and Ishbel again showing dangerous warning signs of her deteriorating mental state."

Matthews stayed silent and let Varlov enlarge on his problems without any interruption. He heard once more how he had joined Lloyd's as long ago as 1978. He was quietly relieved that Varlov made no further reference to the fact that it was he who had first suggested membership and approaching Anatole Kortaski as a suitable agent. Apparently within a year he had been called upon to write a cheque for losses. This had infuriated him because despite his agent telling him that he could expect to receive neither a cheque nor demand for the first three years he either accidentally, or perhaps maybe carefully, never mentioned that this was a possibility, however remote. It had certainly happened in his case he remarked bitterly to Sir George.

"Then I began to understand the business of what appeared to be deliberate or underhand concealment of the asbestosis problem facing Lloyd's. I reckon they entered into a deliberate policy of recruiting more members - 'Names' as they call them, so as to dilute the problem of what looked likely to be future enormous claims. Of course there's no proof, but I have met two of their so called 'fishermen', who they sent to Canada on a recruiting drive. - the whole thing is my own fault I suppose - I should have looked far deeper into things before joining. At the end of the day I took the decision to join, though I believe the terms were never totally explained"

"I think I know enough about it." sympathised the wise old banker, "but let me caution you seriously about taking any legal action. It really won't help you. If you win, all well and good, but that's very unlikely. If you lose, remember you'll probably have enormous costs awarded against you and in any case you are fighting an institution with to all intents and purposes limitless resources, strong establishment backing and a ruthless determination to survive - It's virtually the State you're taking on and the odds are stacked against you I'm afraid. So unless you have recourse to unlimited funds yourself, the costs could be greater than the amount you are proposing to settle now. Don't be a masochist - any victory would only be a pyrrhic one. Remember you were told of the unlimited liability condition when you joined"

"I, understand all that George, but with me it's more personal. I would be doing it largely as a revenge for Ishbel. She has never been physically strong as you know and fear of financial ruin or insecurity has stalked her all her life. I think you know almost as well as I do that, whilst this threat has been going on she has been admitted to hospital suffering from acute depression. I am worried stiff that it will shorten her life, either through shock or even worse by her own hand - the worry has proved just too much for her, poor darling."

Without much progress being made the conversation went on around the subject for another half hour or so when suddenly Peter said "I'd like you to take me down to your vaults please. I have never been there, but I remember you telling me about the fantastic new underground facility you had created when you moved back here to the Strand. I need to show you something"

"Well that certainly changes the subject, - what an extraordinary thing to say" blurted out Matthews.

"Not really," came the easy reply, "I think I have got something there to surprise you. So let's waste no time - call an escort to take us down."

"Hold on now Peter, it's not quite as simple as that" Matthews countered. "You see, the security is such that only personal key holders in the presence of two senior bank officers, who are permitted to go there and only then can they remain in an externally locked room whilst they carry out their business relating to their property held in our vaults."

"But I am a key holder" retorted Varlov in an intense whisper, which surprised Matthews as there was no mention of such a thing in the records he had been looking at earlier in the day.

"I am most terribly sorry Peter, but I am going to have to refuse your request until you give me some time to confirm your status with the bank as an authorised person and key holder, or you come here with your key. This may take several days, but I will telephone you, of course, the moment I have got some information. If you find the key in the meanwhile or any other receipt just let me know"

Grumbling out loud, but otherwise retaining his usual jovial manner, Varlov pretended to understand the difficulty and wished Matthews luck for a speedy discovery. He couldn't afford to delay too long as the clock was ticking against him far too rapidly. Time most certainly wasn't on his side.

Later, as Peter entered the front lobby of one of Devonshire Street's small private clinics, he was met by a slightly shabby patterned carpet and the usual pervading and distinctive slightly sickening smell of disinfectant. He had never liked visiting these sorts of places, but now he blessed the day that he had started subscribing to the premium rate of a private health insurance company for him and his family. At least he hadn't had to suffer the indignity on behalf of Ishbel of producing literally at the door a minimum of £10,000 in cash or bank draft before his tragically sick wife was admitted. He had already checked with the insurance company and they had notified him that he could expect nearly 90% of the likely huge eventual costs to be met by them.

When the Doctor had explained to both of them, a short time ago, in his consulting room, his wife had been very brave. Close to tears and absolutely shattered, the sensitive Varlov had learned from the result of tests, that Ishbel had been diagnosed as having a brain tumour. Only urgent immediate treatment would give her a possible, but very slim chance of recovery and now after being welcomed by a friendly nurse he was directed up to her room. He hoped that he had managed to hide the dreadful shock that the sight of her had given him, but he feared his eyes had given him away. Ishbel, covered in head bandages concealing a totally shaven skull was lying in a semi coma not even propped up for comfort. Her once lovely youthful face was now creased with pain and the powerful drugs had induced a colour and wrinkled texture of dry moulded putty. She hardly showed him any recognition from her sunken grey eyes as he gently drew up a chair and placed it beside her bed. Despite them trying to keep her illness a secret, her room was a mass of cards and flowers - clear evidence if any was needed of the love and affection her countless friends and family felt towards her.

Neither could speak as Peter sat in silence, his mind going over the many happy memories of their long marriage during which they had shared nearly every secret, even if he had sometimes hesitated, for the best of motives to reveal some unpleasantness or other. In the present case of the horrifying £2.5 million writ received a week ago, Varlov did have serious doubts whether to tell her. Not to do so he convinced himself would be to be deny her the sharing of everything between them. To tell her might aggravate her delicate mental state already on a precipice, and put her over the edge. Possibly it was more out of an uncontrollable and selfish need to share his own misery that he finally told Ishbel that they indeed faced a serious danger of financial ruin. He needed her strength as much now as at any previous crisis they had faced together - weak as she was he found her support vital.

Within days of getting the ghastly writ and waiting for news from the medical tests, they had spent more time at home in a quiet communion with each other. The second evening after his meeting at the bank, they were sitting in the drawing room with its chintz furnishings and beautiful English watercolours - the late evening sun playing shadows on them, armed with their usual drinks, when Peter announced "I went to the bank yesterday and set out again for

George Matthews the problems I am facing and how I propose to deal with them. Then I asked him to escort me down to the vaults."

"Why on earth did you do that?" asked Ishbel.

"Because, darling, the time has come, after almost a hundred years that I am forced unwillingly to break the trust that the last Tsar and his Empress placed in my Grandfather all that time ago. Things are drastic and I have to do it whatever the rights or wrongs of the situation. The Tsar's family are all dead - mine is alive and I have to save them."

There had been just one exception to the deep trust and love between Peter and Ishbel, which he could never forget. In an extraordinary way it mirrored the intense rivalry between Peter's grandfather and Admiral Kortaski, grandfather of his Lloyd's agent Anatole, all those years ago in 1907 when they were both serving the Royal family. Within four years of Peter and Ishbel's marriage there had been an indiscretion that Peter scarcely allowed himself now to admit, even to himself. He had met at a cocktail party, been wildly attracted to, and then finally seduced Anatole Kortaski's wife. Their illicit liaison lasted for barely a year, but in that time it caused heartache and near grief for the lovely and inconsolable Ishbel. Anatole himself never knew, or at least if he did, he pretended not to. Only ten years later, as his son was growing into puberty, did he have his suspicions, confirmed by an unarguable physical and facial resemblance, that Peter Varlov was the father. Their adulterous affair had been passionate yet hopeless - bound to lead nowhere as there was an insurmountable incompatibility between them outside the bedroom - the attraction being purely physical. She, more smitten than he, in her desperation had begged Peter to give her some lasting memory when she realised that any future life for them together was impossible. During a last stolen weekend in Florence, which they both knew would be the end of their affair, they made love together free of any sort of interference. Peter, if he was honest with himself had since enjoyed mixed feelings about his misdemeanor. In one sense it thrilled him that he had succeeded in cuckolding Anatole Kortaski - giving him a sense of primeval male dominance and secondly over the years knowing that each time Kortaski looked at his son he would suffer the indignity of knowing that it was Varlov who had sired a male heir where he had so manifestly failed.

The story about the Tsar's trust in Peter's grandfather was not new to her. Ishbel had often listened to her husband repeating what she came to think of as a fanciful romantic but pleasant family legend. For, after all, the Russian Revolution was just part of history to her. She had been born after World War II and raised in a classic Scottish aristocratic manner. She enjoyed a sheltered if privileged life, being very much the afterthought of a family split for five years by war. Her father - a victim of the 1940 Dunkirk evacuation, had been captured with the 51st Highland Division at St Valerie. As a P.O.W. in the Cameron Highlanders he was marched to Stalag XXa in Poland and for him the war was finished. He was held, as it was euphemistically called 'in the bag.' This legend of the Tsar's diamond, from the distant past, seemed to her to be just exactly that. No more than a story about an enormous stone having been given to her husband's grandfather, who by all accounts had led a fairly Bohemian existence, for safe keeping and then forgotten. Peter had certainly never told her where the actual diamond was or indeed who, now, was the rightful owner. Perhaps, he did not even know completely himself.

"I know you've always regarded my story about the diamond as being just a happy family fairy tale" said Peter. "What is different now is that I think I have found the key to the safe where my father always told me it had been deposited - it was in a box of some of his old effects in the attic, which he gave me just before his death"

"What key?" replied Ishbel showing just a hint of curiosity. "If it's what I think it is, it would be the key to a safe deposit box in our bank." Peter elaborated.

"What makes you think this key is so special. It could belong to nothing other than a rusty old padlock or a spare key to a cabin trunk stored in the loft?" Ishbel queried, turning over in her hand the small, but sturdy deadlock key, noting that it carried no decipherable number engraved upon it nor a maker's name.

Peter went on "I had a phone call from George Matthews today to say that he would like me to go into the bank again sometime soon because he thinks that from their old records there is a chance that they have traced another key so far un-identified, which just might be one mixed in with some missing from about 1909. He mumbled something about the bank having received a direct hit from a German bomb in 1940 causing serious damage and fire to the subterranean vault."

At the hospital when Ishbel had been admitted a couple of days after that conversation he looked at his sleeping wife and stood up. On leaving the more or less unconscious Ishbel in the tender care of nursing staff he took a taxi to his club in St. James's where he had booked himself a bedroom for the night. He was in no mood for any pleasant talk with fellow members when he sat at the round table set aside for single diners. In fact it was obvious to any casual observer that Peter, normally a very clubbable man and a popular member, was seriously worried. He gulped his wine and pushed aside the fillet steak he'd ordered - all the while twisting and crumpling his napkin as if he was trying to wring it dry. He left the table quickly and retired to the refuge of his bedroom, not even bothering to watch the 10 o'clock television news. Peter scarcely slept that night, his many thoughts racing in his mind and it was only as dawn filtered through into the heavily curtained room that he fell into an early morning slumber.

In a similar performance to the previous week Varlov was met at the bank by a frock coated young man, but this time it was he, who took him up immediately to Sir George Matthew's third floor office. The banker waved Varlov to a seat as he noticed the nervous manner of his customer as well as the black circles beneath his eyes. Sir George leant back in his chair and began the speech he had prepared in his mind. "I'm sorry it's taken a week for us to come back to you, but as I told you on the telephone a small section of our underground strong room at the time suffered bomb damage early in the blitz and we have had identification problems ever since with about fifty safety deposit lockers dating from the period 1900 to 1910." explained Matthews self-importantly. "You know how much I want to help you and this morning I hope we'll be able to pair off your key with one of ours that we have held in a collection of hitherto un-matched duplicates and thus be able to open the safe deposit - let us hope so."

"I'm in your hands George, but at least I am relatively certain that the key I have with me now is the one that my father told me was the relevant one and that I should look after it with my life. I have to say that in one way I am very surprised that the bank has left it so long before investigating all this themselves."

"Let me ring down to our chief security officer and tell him we are on our way down." said Matthews ignoring the implied criticism "So that he can accompany us with another guard. I have warned we are coming and we can meet them from our directors' lift below ground at level minus three." He needlessly explained.

As the lift went down Matthews proudly and patronisingly explained that customers wishing to deposit or collect valuables from the vaults, could, by arrangement come by car as long as it was carefully identified, and drive down three levels with the security doors sealed behind them. Then, following the same procedure they could exit from the bank without at any stage having been seen arriving or leaving. No carpeted luxury met them as the silent lift discharged the two men into the glare of strip lighting and raw concrete. Waiting to meet them was the bank's chief security officer, a retired policeman, wearing a black frock coat accompanied by a vividly contrasting armed guard in combat gear, who was carrying what appeared to be a sub-machine gun. Varlov was shocked by the sight of this example of modern security and just for a moment he felt he was about to be incarcerated in a subterranean dungeon himself. "Do relax Peter, we are actually welcome here." laughed Matthews as he introduced him, using his full title, Prince Peter Varlov, to the chief security officer - he took pleasure ensuring that the frock coated bank servant had fully understood and appreciated his superior standing of enjoying first name familiarity with the Russian Prince.

By using a variety of codes in L.E.D. format together with laser scanning iris recognition the mighty 10 ft high door of the vault swung slowly and silently open revealing a thirty square feet chamber lined from floor to ceiling with dark green painted locker doors of various sizes. The first thing Varlov noticed was the whirring of the air conditioning plant and extractor system, which reminded him of similar strong rooms he had visited in Switzerland where every public building and in some cases private dwellings were at the time obliged to maintain an *abri atomique*. "Can you see Peter that the fifty odd lockers at the far right hand corner of the chamber are painted red?" asked Matthews, to which Peter nodded. "They are the lockers with which we have had the identification problem I explained so now we are going to try to match up your key with each of these on the two large ring holders our security officer has here. It won't take long as it only takes a second or two to insert your key, which I am glad to say looks exactly as I had expected it should. The odds will be fifty to one against as we try the first one, decreasing to even chances when we get to the last one." came the rather feeble joke from Matthews. No one laughed.

Fifteen minutes of silent checking followed as mismatch followed mismatch. Peter could feel the start of a cold sweat issuing round his armpits and dryness in his mouth that no offer of a glass of water could take away. At 1151 hrs Greenwich Mean Time, locker number V38754 clicked and the door sprung gently open. As the safe deposit opened both bank officials withdrew immediately from the room together with Sir George, leaving Peter alone to discover its contents by himself. Not quite as he had expected, inside, apart from what looked like some old legal papers mostly in Russian script, was a very small and simple grey office cash box with a chrome carrying handle. The solid little box was dwarfed by the size of the locker and it was obvious it couldn't be the repository of bearer bonds or such like. The problem was however, it was firmly locked and Peter did not possess a key. He would have to break it open.

Wile pretending not to notice, the three bank staff could not help seeing, from their position through the doorway, that Peter Varlov was now showing distinct signs of emotional nervousness and perhaps needed some assistance. The armed guard rocked steadily back and forth on his deep sole combat boots keeping the index finger of his right hand resting lightly on the trigger of a Heckler & Koch sub machine - a weapon more often associated with the S.A.S than a security guard company. It was George Matthews who moved first. Stepping forward he placed a gentle hand on Peter's shoulder. He could feel as well as see that Varlov was trembling as he struggled vainly with the clam-like closure of the little grey box. "Would you mind Peter if we broke with etiquette and offered to help you with what seems to be your problem?" Matthews asked - his pomposity never left him. And he continued "as you know it is normal banking practice always to leave any customer alone when he opens his personal safe - the contents are always regarded as purely a matter for the customer and we have absolutely no knowledge of their contents."

"Of course you can help me George." said Peter gratefully, his fingers still fumbling with the small security box, on which he had just noticed his grandfather's fading initials stenciled. "It certainly won't take a locksmith's expertise to open this. It's not much different from one of those children's money boxes you see everywhere?"

"Let me leave you here Sir." said the chief security officer, speaking for the first time that morning, and I'll just pop next door and get a set of duplicates. That box looks just like an older version of hundreds of similar petty cash boxes that we have provided for our customers. In fact, we buy the modern ones locally from a chain store in the Strand, but don't let anyone know that - we charge three times their price for them!" Sir George Matthews looked rather disapprovingly at the security man.

Peter Varlov had already been thinking how little and in what form he would need to tell the bank of the history behind the diamond. So with the armed guard standing nearby, Matthews and Varlov sat down in silence at the Spartan metal table and chairs and waited. Minutes later he was back with a large bunch of non-descript keys and true to his word had the box clicked open in a second. "Forgive me George," said Peter, "but I am going to ask you for a little privacy now, whilst I look inside. If you would be kind enough to give me just a minute or two to do just that, I'll ring the bell by the hatch and we can then carry on with our meeting if that's alright with you?"

"Take all the time you need Peter, there's no rush. I'm going back to my office and will wait for you there. As soon as you're ready my colleague here will bring you back up."

An involuntary shiver of excitement went deeply through the whole of Peter's trembling body as he sat, alone and rather frightened, locked in the dungeon-like inspection room just off the side of the main strong room. The harshness of the strip light overhead and the threatening whirr of the air conditioning made him all the more aware of the solitude and penury that he was facing unless his grandfather's legend of 1907 proved to be something other than a mere fairy tale - now was the moment of truth. Half expecting to find the box empty or perhaps containing the odd trinket or two he forced himself slowly to lift the lid. He hardly dared look inside. After he had plucked up the courage he saw, just one single item - a dried out chamois leather jeweller's pouch that looked as if it had been cut from a window cleaning leather and roughly stitched together to make an open ended purse. Peter, with a shaking hand, dipped inside the pouch and withdrew a smooth pebble-like object the size of a bantam's egg - a strangely translucent browny grey colour - it felt heavy in his hand. His sharp intake of breath nearly choked him and he couldn't suppress an involuntary shriek of joy which filtered through the metal doors of his temporary prison. "Is this really the priceless diamond my grandfather and father spoke so much about?" he thought to himself. "It has to be, please God it has to be" he said out loud.   Peter replaced the big oval pebble in its simple pouch and slipped it into his trouser pocket.

Upstairs, George Matthews was sipping his second coffee of the morning, served as usual in best Royal Doulton, as he thought only befitted his status. He looked at his watch for a third time as he was getting a little impatient at how long his old friend was taking. He had more urgent charitable matters to attend to and anyway he was due to lunch at The International Bankers Club in Threadneedle Street at 1 o'clock. Little did he know that in the next ten minutes he was going to play a part in what would turn out to be one of the most newsworthy events of the year, catapulting him and his bank to the front pages of the world's newspapers and onto its television screens. There was a soft tap on his door and the chief security officer ushered a smiling Peter Varlov into his office for the second time that day.

As soon as Peter was settled back into the carpeted luxury of Matthew's office, he gently drew out the chamois purse from his pocket and laid it on the desk in front of a puzzled George Matthews. "Don't touch it George, until I tell you what it is" said Peter quietly. "In that purse, believe it or not, is a single rough uncut diamond, which has belonged to my family from before they left Russia, and has lain untouched in your bank vaults for the best part of one hundred years. I now propose that your bank take it as collateral and provide me with a bridging facility sufficient to pay my Lloyd's debts of coming on for £2.5 million before the writ they have issued against me takes effect. I propose to sell the diamond and its value would cover any such loan many times over"

By now, Matthews was actually annoyed, and finding it hard to hide and before replying ostentatiously looked again at his watch to see how many more minutes he could spare for this fantasist. "You must be joking Peter. You know bloody well that we don't make loans against little bits of jewellery. A porn broker might be more appropriate, but of course they aren't in the business of lending the sort of sums you're talking about."

Peter made a supreme effort and somehow managed to stay calm in the face of Matthews' ignorant onslaught. He was actually starting to enjoy the possibility of pricking the pomposity of this recently be-knighted bank manager. "George" he said, "You see over there on the sideboard by the window there is a set of old fashioned letter scales?"

"Yes" he replied. "As a matter of fact they're mine - a Victorian set presented to my father on his retirement from the grateful Building Society of which he was the Chairman."

"Well, very carefully take the contents of that little bag in front of you and go and weigh it on your beautiful scales." Reluctantly, the banker tipped up the bag and allowed the object to fall with a bump onto the leather top of his desk. Clasping the stone tightly in his soft fingers with their manicured nails, he crossed to the window and placed it on the letter tray of the brass scales. Then individually he placed the little circular brass weights on and off the counter balance of the scales until the indicator needle centred. "What does it say George - why are you taking so long?" asked Peter, trying to stifle his concern. "It's just that I'm having to shuffle around the weights to get enough of them on the scale, but just a second and I'll tell you, let me see, they add up to a fraction over two ounces." came Matthew's strangulated comment.

"That stone, George, was originally dug out of the earth's crust in Bokhara, the autonomous Muslim State within the Russian boundaries, God knows when, but what I do know for sure is that it was given to my grandfather Prince Vladimir Varlov in 1907 by the last Tsar. It was originally a gift from the then Emir of Bokhara to the Tsar and Tsarina of Russia, who later, as an act of gratitude and personal affection in return for all his loyal service to both of them, gave it to my grandfather." He hoped that this explanation would be enough to more or less cover the ambiguous nature of the gift suitably for his present purposes

A now slightly chastened Matthews returned to his desk and

listened more carefully to Varlov's increasingly confident revelations, the urgency to leave for his lunch temporarily forgotten. The facts were indeed startling, and he was amazed to learn from a now positively ebullient Varlov that the last highest recorded price at auction of a cut and polished diamond had exceeded $500,000 per carat and when he had gone on to tell him that a two ounce diamond was the equivalent of about 60 grams or 300 carats he decided, for the moment to keep quiet. Fiddling with a calculator he rapidly realised that he was looking at a possible value of $75,000,000 or about £40 million pounds. Matthews's banking mind, governed by a mixture of security, fear and greed, had already formed a list of priorities. "I take it you are intending to sell this diamond?" he asked and Varlov immediately replied that diamond auctions in Switzerland were widely recognised to be the very best way of achieving the highest prices - he would indeed sell it there as soon as practical.

What was nagging at the back of Matthew's fertile mind was whether or not there could be any questions arising from its alleged provenance. He didn't want to end up with the bank, or worse still himself in some sort of trouble from a furious Russian government or oligarch accused by them of selling stolen property, but then he quickly thought it wouldn't be the bank who were selling - it was Varlov himself, he would carry all the responsibility. Anyway, he reckoned, the bank was only being asked to lend £2.5 million, so the collateral they'd be holding was enormous - the security was immense. Almost certainly any problem of that nature would happily be at worst the auctioneer's. More immediately and small mindedly he wondered how the bank was going to recoup the cost of a hundred years of safe deposit storage - that would come to a tidy sum although trivial in relation to the value of this stone. It was, as usual, his greed that overcame all the other considerations. He almost salivated as he thought of their sharing a little bit of the commission from the obviously necessary insurance that must immediately be put in place, also perhaps a little bit of the Belgian diamond cutters and polishers fees in return for an introduction, splitting a portion of the auctioneer's commission and finally all the interest and commitment fees on the initial loan that the bank might earn as well as the additional spin off from all the potential publicity. As the egg sized pebble lay quite unassumingly on the leather top desk it was all very satisfactory thought Sir George, and all down to him.

A car and driver had been waiting for some time for Sir George to take him to his City lunch and any moment now he was going to have to break off from this engrossing subject and leave. A musical jingle disturbed his train of thought and Peter rather bashfully apologised for the interruption as he reached into an inner pocket to answer his mobile phone. Matthews sat down again in shock as he saw the expression on Peter's face, on answering the call, go from one of bubbling confidence, to one of abject despair. It was the Devonshire Street clinic with the dreadful news that Ishbel had suffered a severe heart attack and requesting Peter to come immediately. There was no question, Sir George insisted - decency and kindliness prevailed over his luncheon appetite. He took his old friend gently by the arm, escorted him from the bank into the waiting car and gave instructions to his chauffeur to go at once to Devonshire Street with Prince Varlov and forget his trip to the City. He would then take a taxi.

CHAPTER SIX

NAJERA

Meanwhile back in his Spanish hospital room, as the nurse changed his drip feed, she was unaware that François was continuing to dream........During the hot summer weather the owner of a filthy run down albergo in Santo Domingo de la Calzada dreaded five o'clock in the evening. Following his afternoon meal comprising only a mouth drying frittata bocadillo using stale bread and last season's potatoes, the only thing to do was to lie in the cool indoors waiting for the searing heat of the day to drop to an acceptable level. Sleep came easily as the man had softened the fusty sandwich with a jug of Rioja Tinto, successfully dulling his already limited senses. For two months now his daily siesta time had been shattered by a hammering on the outside door, which when opened revealed sweat stained bodies sitting wheezing and grumbling as they sought accommodation and sustenance.

José Depotillo the albergo owner, had chosen to cash in on an ever increasing flow of Saint Iago disciples who, as foot pilgrims were on route to the tomb of the famous Saint some 500 kilometres to the West. They would stop overnight in his native town seeking and accepting whatever they could find in the way of food, drink and somewhere to sleep. José was a rough ill tempered man lacking any warmth for his fellow human beings. He shared his old farmhouse hostelry with his harridan of a nagging wife Manuella, their only child Portrella and no less than eight cattle all haphazardly trundled into one end of the lowly dwelling. Cows, goats and a donkey lived together on the sometime dry caked mud floor, but with the boundary between the animal and human quarters ill-defined, more often than not the whole floor was a wet, filthy and foul smelling amalgam of rain, dung, root vegetables and urine. José and the two women all wore solid wooden clogs to protect their feet from rotting or slipping in this grime. Mud built internal walls just one metre high provided something to sit on and something that vainly attempted to keep the area free from livestock. Only half successful at this it was completely unsuccessful at keeping the revolting smells away and a strong stomach was a prerequisite for a pilgrim taking José's apology for hospitality. The centre piece of the living area was a rough hewn table and two benches. Beside it was a blackened ring of earth marking the remains of an open fire, which in winter provided sufficient warmth, but in summer was only another area of un-swept extra dirt.

Only accessed by ladder was a loft beneath a crudely thatched leaky roof, furnished with what could hardly be described as a bed, but rather more a platform covered with a slightly finer variety of straw that thatched the roof. On top of that were hay bundles and rough cloth strips acting as bed clothes. It wasn't simply humans who shared this communal sleeping platform, but a permanent infestation of bugs, fleas and even rodents, all eager to take their share of nourishment from the silage or the flesh. This was the albergo owner's family sleeping room area, but at the further end of the stinking attic was a wooden partition leading to a similar, but larger sleeping facility, in which quite often as many as ten pilgrims or other foot weary travellers would collapse exhausted.

They were more often than not inebriated by an over generous intake of Rioja Tinto after their day's trek, which had brought them from the monastery town of Najera some 21 kilometres to the East, but sometimes as much as 30 or more kilometres from their previous rest at Navarette.

Daily routine in summer for the primitive family Depotillo was simple. Despite the inevitability of unbearable heat after 11 o'clock they rose late having wasted the cool of the dawn and like their mangy dogs they scratched and cleared their throats as a greeting to the coming day. Washing was something they did on only very special occasions. José swore at his wife; Manuella swore at her husband. Neither could read nor write, as was already the fate of their blossoming daughter Portrella, now fifteen years old - even at this age after continuing bullying from her father she still tamely accepted her role as farm labourer, cow herd, serving wench and bed warmer to this man she feared. Throughout the summer days some 100 metres from their basic dwelling she cut red pimentos from their bushes and set about to roast them gently over a smouldering smoky aromatic fire of bark and sticks. Dreams came naturally to the pretty maiden as the sweet smelling aroma of the roasting delicacies wafted across her clear skinned if unwashed features. Dreams of escape from daily drudgery and poverty. Maybe to accept the warm embrace from the nuns who had taught her so sternly the skills of laundering if not of words or spirituality. A life given to God and His purity seemed to her so natural in its simplicity as it sent out to her a magnetic like attraction. At the same time she was aware that there was another kind of life awaiting her as she came into contact with the hurly burly of the town's Sunday market and the mingling with the travellers visiting her family home. When the pimentos became slightly charred and wrinkled, she peeled them and laid them out in olive oil drenched trays before setting them aside to cool. They were a highly valued delicacy much sought after in that enjoyable Sunday market.

Come the evening when she helped her bad tempered shrew like mother, who never missed a chance to criticize her, to serve the simple food to both the Spanish and foreign speaking pilgrims travelers and even vagrants, she was used to getting and ignoring the rude suggestive words and signs of crude unmistakable meaning despite the lack of any language skills between them making real conversation impossible. She knew that after too much wine the supper guests would start a session of lewd ballads with ever lowering implications towards her. This night, as all the others, the guests had been herded, like the cattle before them had been sent to their part, in the direction of the lofted sleeping area. Amidst gurgles and coughing the guests collapsed soon to be followed by a cacophony of farts, belches and lastly snores.

The three Depotillos had shared a bed for the whole of Portrella's life. For a reason she didn't originally understand it was her father José who took the middle berth, but tonight after a particularly heavy intake of grog she realised that it was no coincidence.

"You're even drunker than usual you lazy sod," screamed Manuella at her revolting husband.

"You, you worn out slag are fit for nothing but animal roistering," he responded as he made his usual attempt to force himself on his always unwilling partner. She carried on her aggressive tirade "Your breath stinks, your hands are like a gorse bush and what you so regularly blow from your vast arse has the stink of a midden - what's more what you have to offer me would better suit a cat for all the meanness of its standing - you pathetic excuse for a man."

Portrella lay quiet as usual, not daring to move, in the hope that the bulky body of her father after his rebuttal would shortly do the same, As snores from the adjacent sleeping area threatened to shake the walls she was disturbed to feel the coarseness of a hand groping clumsily around her knee.

"Go to sleep Father and leave me alone" the frightened Portrella whispered. With that she turned right away and prayed with a thumping heart for peace. Sleep didn't come to the soft skinned girl and it was a moment of terror when she felt one huge hand folding across her nose and mouth preventing breath or speech whilst another hand was parting the cheeks of her backside. Powerless to stop him she lay aghast and terrified at what was happening to her until mercifully quickly his thrusting movements climaxed and she was able with super-human effort to push his whole person away. She sobbed until sleep at last temporarily hid the memory of her father's action before her revulsion returned in the morning.

Sunday in the summer meant an early start for Portrella and with sunrise at 6 o'clock it meant being up at 4 o'clock to be ready to load the handcart with the week's harvest of roasted, skinned pimentos from the family small holding just outside the walls of the town. Then herding out the animals before feeding them whilst her father lay late abed grunting and snoring.

As early morning mist cleared from La Rio Oja, the occasional stork, a more or less pre-historic bird, flew lazily from the riverbank towards the little town and landed with infinite great delicacy on the top of one of the tall spires or chimneys, where by an act of engineering skill beyond the ability of man the huge bird had constructed a rigid nest of intertwining sticks. Along with a few dozen other market sellers Portrella emptied the handcart contents carefully onto the dusty ground in front of the cathedral before converting it into a stall with a brightly coloured canvas awning to protect the valuable produce from a glaring sun Water being in short supply there was no question of washing fruit fish or vegetables and everything inevitably ended up coated with a film of grime.

A shriek loud enough to wake the dead suddenly shattered the low pitched hubbub of a community at peace with itself and in a flash everyone was cracking with laughter when they saw the cause of the screaming.

"Get off, get off you fucking animal" screamed the plump and homely peasant owner of a young donkey, who, unbeknownst to her, was happily accepting the advances of a stallion prepared to give of his best. Thanks to his carelessness and mean fistedness, José the albergo landlord had bought a young and uncut donkey instead of paying the going rate some three times higher for a female. The strength of a stallion donkey is formidable. Scenting the mare from a distance of half a kilometre, the beast had with ease kicked down the ramshackle gate of his pen and galloped full tilt towards the market place. Wasting no time the animal mounted his happy target and plunged a truly shocking length of organ into the ready orifice. "Help, oh help my little animal" wailed the donkey's owner, but her appeal was met with jocular guffaws from those round-about including suggestions that the stallion's build was a thing of awe.

"Too late", they cried with one accord, "You'll be the proud owner of a little foal in just twenty weeks from now and all you can do is give old José a good kicking for his meanness. That's if you can wake him from his drunken slumbers to tell him of his stupidity."

Portrella witnessed this small excitement in her morning's work and quite unwittingly became aware of a certain arousal in her loins whilst watching this spectacle of such power and dominance. The feeling stayed with her on and off all day as she failed to clear her mind of a subject she didn't really understand. Her wares were popular amongst the grander element of the township hierarchy. One such regular customer was the local magistrate who, because of his office, enjoyed a status in the town far above any he personally deserved or merited. The man's chief duty was trying and then sentencing those found guilty of crimes even as minor as being drunk in Church or for uttering foul oaths in a public place. Always unnecessarily dressed in his judicial attire, he was determined to impress on all who passed his way that his decisions were made in such a manner as to ensure that fellow citizens of the town would surely be the beneficiaries. He lived well with lodgings provided for him by a supposedly grateful town. Raimondo had hardly turned forty and wore a garb of green velvet trimmed at cuff and shoulder with the fur of a Russian fox. His self indulgence in terms of sartorial display was probably exaggerated to counteract a deteriorating physical affliction he had suffered for the last two years. He had a goitre swelling on his neck that outgrew any linen shirt and had become the size of a small melon threatening to burst and spew its innards On his head he wore a three cornered device of red felt stiffened by a buckram lining. Stitched to his headdress were five black stars marking the symbol of the department of Logrono, to whose authority he was theoretically subject and answerable. Boots reaching up to his lower calf made of soft unlined leather adorned his little feet, which were out of scale to the rest of his body, and like his smooth white hands, emphasised all the more that this was a self indulgent man not now, nor ever, used to physical labour in any form.

His taste for red pimentos was satisfied most weeks by a visit to Portrella's stall, but his flavour buds were possibly stimulated more by his admiration for the pretty young fifteen year old so charmingly selling the luscious delicacy and the thought of being served by her in other ways as well. Bare feet for outdoors went well with the off-white smock and bodice worn only knee length by the blossoming maiden and it was with a tremor of excitement that he made his way towards her pitch.

"Will you spread your sweet tasties out in front of me?" the Magistrate saucily requested.

"But no Sir" she replied, "If there is any spreading to be done today it'll be of your palms to show the colour of your money. No credit for you Sir, I've done enough of making favours for your courtroom and it's high time you allowed an honest girl to make an honest living." Little did Portrella know what was to follow in the hands of this lustful old goat, who grudgingly handed over some coins in return for an unnecessarily   large basket of peeled and roasted pimentos.

"Don't forget my little one" he leered at Portrella, "An evening spent with me at my court house would be one you wouldn't soon forget."

"It is one I can well do without" was her cheeky reply having been transfixed by the revolting sight of the globe like swelling of the thyroid gland on his neck.

It was not until early afternoon that Portrella was able to escape to the coolness of the cathedral's interior. Whilst there she became refreshed by the combined smell of onions, garlic and incense.   Worshippers throughout the morning had visited the glorious church, carrying baskets of foodstuffs purchased in the market and laying them beside them in the pews, had made their devotions amidst a permanent waft of incense drifting through the transept.

CHAPTER SEVEN

LISBON 2002

Stanislas Kortaski was dozing happily on the sun bed, which was placed strategically in the shade of one of the beautiful and ancient Olive trees in his garden. His book lay abandoned, with his glasses alongside, on the grass beside him. He could vaguely hear his wife talking to some friend or other on the telephone in the house. After one of his favourite lunches of Santola recheado - the deliciously stuffed spider crabs he was so fond of - helped down with perhaps slightly too much of the local vinho branco followed by a Pastéis de nata, the local custard tart of which he was also an avid fan, with which he had also enjoyed the traditional 'bica' - the local wickedly strong espresso coffee - he was feeling very content and at peace with the world. He was a man who had always enjoyed his comforts and after a successful lifetime in the financial world he could afford to indulge himself. It gave him a lot of pleasure to spoil both himself and Natasha, his considerably younger and very attractive second wife. With no children, they led what others might think a selfish, almost hedonistic life, but that worried neither of them.

As he lazed in that delicious half stage between sleep and consciousness induced by an excellent lunch he thought to himself how lucky he had been to have sold off his fund management group to one of the big foreign banks, who were then queuing up to acquire interests in the London financial markets, and how wise to have retired early to this heavenly place. The hilltop village - or rather the hilltop group of three separate villages collectively known as Sintra some 25 kilometres west of Lisbon - had, he thought, been accurately described by Lord Byron as "in every aspect the most delightful village in Europe." He could quite understand why this had originally been chosen by the old Portuguese royalty for their summer palaces where they could escape from the heat and bustle of Lisbon itself. He often, in the early evenings, made the short walk, sometimes with his wife - sometimes alone with his spaniel, up from his house to the old Moorish Castle - the Palacio Nacional - to admire its breathtaking views over the capital and he had never ceased to have been impressed by all this. His day-dreaming was broken by his wife calling him from the house - "You're wanted on the phone Stanislas," she said using his full name as she always did, "it's Anatole - he just wants a word." Stanislas got up grumpily - he had told his brother, if once it must have been a hundred times, as he always made clear to everyone else, never to ring during what he regarded as that almost sacred period after lunch when he took his regular siesta. Padding bare footed across the rough grass and then the terrace he was in no better humour when he reached the phone. "What do you want, you've certainly disturbed my rest," as the elder brother he still felt, even at their advanced ages, to be able to speak as bluntly as he liked to his younger sibling even though the age difference between them was only fifteen months. "I've told you time and time again not to call me after lunch until at least five thirty - what is it now?" At the other end of the line Anatole ignored his brother's usual rant - whatever time he called he always complained about something, "I just thought you ought to know something about Peter Varlov, that's all, but of course, if you'd rather I rang back just tell me when you will be free to talk." Even Stanislas heard the sarcasm in his brother's voice, but his words had the desired effect and now the older brother was all attention. The long standing feud between Varlov and Stanislas undoubtedly owed its origins to the long family history of jealousy and rivalry that had started generations ago between their ancestors well before the Russian revolution. One of his first memories was how his grandfather, the Admiral who he had worshipped as a hero, had always said that one day he prayed their family would get even with the Varlovs. He had been too young, or perhaps his grandfather had never told him, to know the true cause of the bitter hatred, but it was a real part of the fabric of their lives - drilled into them as children almost like their catechism had been. At the death of his grandfather, Stanislas remembered one of the last conversations his father had with the old man had been about this - whatever the reason the loathing really ran deep. On top of this however Stanislas had more recent and more personal reasons to hate Peter Varlov - their careers in the City had both been successful and in many ways very similar.

Varlov had been junior to him at school, being the same age as his brother, and as the senior boy he had been able to bully 'young' Varlov in many subtle ways, known only to cruel school children, although Stanislas always regretted that the age difference wasn't sufficiently great to allow him to pick his enemy as his fag - he would soon have had him running fast errands and get his weight down too, he thought Their paths crossed again when they were both working for different Merchant banks in the City and found themselves as advisers on opposite sides in one of the major takeover battles at the beginning of the Thatcher era. Stanislas had prepared the press statement in co-operation with the lawyers and knew that an increased bid would be announced the following Tuesday - no harm he had thought if I arrange some discreet purchase of the shares for my friends in Luxembourg through a country broker. As bad luck would have it, that weekend Peter Varlov was a shooting guest of the broker who had been angling to get his bank as a client for some time. Inevitably after an excellent dinner on the Saturday evening, when the ladies had departed and the port was making its rounds, the day's shooting was forgotten and the talk turned to business. The broker eager to impress his guests just happened to mention that he had seen what he thought was some 'canny' buying of South Dorset Breweries. "Perhaps they are worth a punt" he had said.

On the Tuesday morning after the new bid, Peter Varlov informed the Takeover Panel and shortly afterwards a small item in the Financial Times announced that a Mr. Stanislas Kortaski had unexpectedly resigned his directorship of Williams's Bank for health reasons. Perhaps by coincidence it wasn't so very long afterwards that the Conservative government introduced the anti-insider trading laws.

It hadn't helped Stanislas's temper because this happened at the same time as his divorce, when his estranged wife was being far from modest with her financial demands. However, conveniently for her, he blamed all his troubles on Peter Varlov and all his hatred went on him. After this it took a little time before Stanislas had been allowed to start his fund management business and he had always felt that having his office in the West End had been a disadvantage. Despite being able to sell out for close to twenty million pounds in the later boom when foreign banks were buying into the London market, matters between him and Peter Varlov, as far as he was concerned, were neither forgiven nor forgotten - their relationship, which had never been good, was now non-existent. So his interest was immediate, "What is it, what's that bloody grotesque man done now? Tell me," Stanislas almost jumped down the phone to get his brother's reply quicker, "What is it?"

"Just calm down, I'm sorry I called you now, but we're going out this evening and I thought you'd like to know as soon as possible that Varlov is being sued by Lloyd's for about two and a half million pounds. Perhaps you'd like to lend him the money!" Stanislas exploded, he never really shared his brother's sense of humour and certainly not when it was aimed against himself. "God!" he said, "what's he going to do - how the hell can he get out of this one? The man's ruined financially and socially at last. Bloody good thing." Stanislas was almost dancing at the news.

"That's the strange thing," Anatole replied, "he's told me that he's going to settle the debt - he's swearing blue murder against me, and Lloyd's in general, of course, but he's assured me that he'll pay and pay on time. I saw his Asset Statement he made the last time he increased his underwriting limits - that was about nine months ago, and he was quite comfortable then, but two and a half long ones - forget it!"

Stanislas thought for a moment, "Do you remember Grandfather telling us a story about the Tsarina giving away some diamond or other to their family? I've got something vaguely in the back of my mind about it - father was always talking about it, but perhaps you were too young at the time to take it in." Anatole interrupted, "No, I don't know anything about that, perhaps diamonds are a Varlov's best friend." His attempt at a joke was completely ignored as Stanislas continued. "Well he's certainly going to need some miracle or other to conjure up two and a half mill out of thin air, even today that's a hell of a lot of money. Anyway I forgive you for disturbing my siesta - keep me in touch and we'll see what happens. I suppose the loss is all down to that asbestos business? I read about that - I hope you're not involved yourself?" Stanislas asked.

"No, thank God, I saw it coming - our baby syndicates were able to steer clear of it fortunately."

"That's good - let me know as soon as you have any news."

"OK we'll be in touch, hope all goes well otherwise, give my love to Natasha." As Anatole hung up, Stanislas just stood for some time by the phone thinking. "I wonder?" he thought to himself as his wife called him back to the garden where she had taken possession of the sun bed. The sight of her stretched out in a new bikini took Stanislas's thoughts momentarily off any diamonds from Russia.

It wasn't until a while later that what his brother had told him on the phone had really sunk in, but when it did Stanislas felt very excited. "That bastard has got his pay off at last," he said to his shaving mirror the next morning, "he'll never find any bank that'll lend a member of Lloyd's anything after all the trouble there - they just wouldn't take the risk." He had been following the dreadful saga in the press of how the very existence of the entire Lloyd's community was threatened by the massive potential losses coming from Asbestosis claims largely from America. With the underwriters' incompetence being shown up all the time, hardly a day went by without some new horror or scandal coming out of the woodwork. More than once over the last couple of years he had thanked his lucky stars that he had resisted his brother's sales pitch way back in the late seventies to join himself. His fund management business was just starting to take off and he had needed every little bit of spare capital then just to keep it going - 'Thank you but not for me' he had, thank God, told his brother at the time. Now he was laughing - Peter Varlov wouldn't be telling any takeover panel about anyone else again in a hurry! He left it four days until he gave in to his longing to ring his brother. "Morning Anatole," he began when the secretary finally put him through, "You really should have a direct line for your private calls - your girl puts callers through the third degree before she'll connect anyone."

"With angry names like Varlov trying to get me all the time you'd build in some screening system yourself brother - I'm almost thinking of getting a bullet proof vest!"

"Yes I suppose you're in the front line poor chap, what a bloody mess the whole thing looks."

"Anyway, what do you want?" his brother interrupted, "I can't talk for long, I'm very late for a meeting."

"OK - I was just wondering whether you've received the cheque from my old friend Varlov yet?"

Anatole's irritation was apparent in his reply, "I told you I'd phone when I had any news - none so far and I must go - don't worry I've got your number!" He rang off.

Ten days later Stanislas had just finished a round with his usual golfing partner - Edwardo Marques, who despite his name and having been born in Lisbon, was actually half English through his Sussex born mother - at the Penha Longa Golf Club. He still hadn't got over the thrill of playing this famous championship course set in an old Monastic estate in the beautiful rolling Sintra Hills with its breath-taking views towards Lisbon on the one side and the Atlantic Ocean on the other. Although it was coming up to six years since he and Natasha had moved down here he had only been able to play here for the last two after his handicap, with a great struggle, had at last fallen below the 28 level required by the club. He still enjoyed dropping it into after dinner conversation that he had just played there or would the next day. Edwardo usually beat him, but today he was pleased to have only lost by only one hole and that after his second had landed in the water on the fifteenth. As he carried his clubs to his car he felt his mobile vibrate in his pocket - not wishing to offend the other members he always silenced the ringing tone while playing, but never felt easy if he actually turned the thing off - he hated ever being out of reach, a habit he retained from his old market days. He saw his brother's name flash up as the caller, "Hello Anatole what is it?" It was unusual for him to call on his mobile, "You've caught me just finishing my day's golf, I'll be home in twenty minutes if you want to call me there."

"Well you were so excited the other day, I thought you would like to hear the Varlov news as soon as possible, but I'll call you back if you want."

Stanislas took the bait, "No don't worry, tell me now, what - what is it? -tell me."

"Well, I've just had a rather formal call from Peter Varlov - he confirms that he has arranged everything and I'll be getting a bankers draft for the whole of his debt to Lloyd's within the time limit." It was twenty seconds before Stanislas replied, "Blast - how the hell did he do that, Anatole, he just couldn't - I don't believe it."

"Well, he said he guarantees it and he sounds pretty sure of himself, but I agree, God knows how he's pulled it off. Incidentally, his wife has just died, did she have any money?"

"Perhaps he had her insured. How did she die? - I thought her family only owned rather useless land in Scotland, you know asset rich but money poor, no cash flow, in fact, ideal fodder for you at Lloyd's!" Anatole ignored the barb - he was used to his brother's characteristic sniping at anything he did.

"Anyway there you are - that's the situation - I'll keep you in touch when the thing is actually paid, but of course, we may never know what he's done to get himself off the hook."

"Suppose not, bye Anatole," Stanislas was a disappointed man as he drove back home to pour himself in consolation a large gin and tonic. Frustrated, he just could not work out how Peter Varlov always seemed to be able to produce these Houdini type escapes whenever he seemed cornered. He remembered how once before in the City he had thought he'd set him up, only to find that finally the financial journalist had not published his story.

CHAPTER EIGHT

LONDON

A traffic jam extended from the west of Pont Street, tailing all the way back to Belgrave Square on a cold and rainy October morning in London. At the head of the jam the reason was clear. Just one large car had stopped in front of Saint Columbus, the imposing Church of Scotland building looking down Pont Street from its dominant position near the junction with Beauchamp Place. Anyone taking a closer look would have noticed a small but distinct Royal Coat of Arms emblazoned on its door and a police motor cycle escort waiting beside the church. A solitary uniformed piper from a Highland Regiment was playing a *pibroch* - a lament - as numerous mourners steadily left the church. This had been a service of thanksgiving for the life of the Princess, whose private burial had been the previous week with only her intimate family present.

Peter Varlov was tormented by the fact that Ishbel had not known of the discovery of the diamond and now she never would. She had died just hours after his final visit to the hospital, having suffered a massive heart attack from which she never recovered consciousness. It was on the very day that their recent years of financial threat seemed to be at an end. Although it could never be proved, Peter himself was utterly convinced that the ever present menace and incessant ruthless demands for money from Lloyd's had contributed in no small way to her mental state and tragically early death. If only she had been able to hold on for just a few more hours, he reasoned, surely with careful nursing she would have recovered. Now, with his three children beside him in support he was saying his thanks to more than two hundred mourners while trying hard to holdback his tears. The *pibroch* faded and the general rumble of ordinary London street noise once more took over as the piper marched to the left and disappeared round to the back of the church.

Two of the mourners at the thanksgiving service had been Sir George and Lady Matthews, who not only officially represented the bank, but themselves as well, having made certain that their name and title was noted correctly by the official reporters from The Times and Daily Telegraph, who published, at the organiser's expense, a list of mourners ending always with the expression "and many other friends." - Matthews made sure his name was specifically mentioned.

In the ten days since Varlov had produced his astonishing revelation about the diamond Matthews felt that, out of respect to Ishbel, he could not contact Varlov to discuss the proposed bridging loan and sale. Instead, using the bank's resources to their full and coupled with his own initiative, he had acquired from a major brokerage house insurance quotations for the diamond, covering every eventuality that he could think of - from the moment it left the security of the bank's vaults, where it now rested, right up to the time that it would be sold at auction in Switzerland. Then he spoke to a well connected fellow director, now non-executive, of his bank, to ask him to put him in touch with the right person at 'Deermaner', who, without question would be the appropriate people, in his opinion, to give a valuation of the diamond. Never having had any direct experience himself of the diamond business he didn't realise that Deermaner, the world's leading diamond company, might perhaps take a jaundiced view of the appearance on the scene of such an enormous hitherto unknown jewel, when factually until recent times they would have kept track of almost every rough cut diamond as well as helping to guide them towards their destination. This one had appeared from nowhere and would have the doubtful privilege of moving around outside the watching eye of their supposed cartel. Admittedly, the discovery of the Varlov stone couldn't match by a long shot the incredible Millennium Star diamond weighing in at 203 carats, which, Matthews recalled, was so very nearly stolen in 2000 from the Millennium Dome. Clearly, he thought, it was going to take at least six or seven months to get this operation completed. This, he thought greedily would generate a very handsome flow of interest for the bank from the bridging loan, even if competition now obliged them to pare down the rate to just 2% over base. Years of simple and compound interest calculation experience meant that Matthew didn't even need his calculator to come to a figure in the region of £90,000. Getting a share of the fees from the diamond's polishers and cutters was another matter, but splitting a commission with an auctioneer was something they had often done in the past whether in London, New York or Switzerland. That, he reckoned, would be the icing on the cake.

The insensitivity of Lloyd's, although they would of course protest that they hadn't known of Peter Varlov's bereavement, was breath-taking in the extreme. On the day following Ishbel's burial he received, but thank God hadn't opened, service of a Statutory Demand, signed in person by the Head of the Lloyd's Financial Recovery Department, dubbed, fairly or otherwise, by Lloyd's victims and the press alike as the 'Rotweiler'. It had been thrust unceremoniously into the hand of an uncomprehending cleaning lady employed by the Varlov family at their country home, by the very same man in the very same macintosh and brown felt trilby hat, who had so unpleasantly served a writ upon him that evening in September, just six weeks before.

One of Peter's married daughters was staying in the house with him and had carefully gathered all unopened post, which had accumulated in the last ten days - thus sparing her father what she thought would be the agony of reading the literally hundreds of letters of condolence. In fact he found them a comfort with their kind words somehow bringing him closer to his late wife. As they sat together in the drawing room, having driven down from London, they lit the fire and reflectively talk over how the day had gone - concluding their amazement at the large number who had been there, representing all aspects of Ishbel's life, from Dukes and Duchesses to garden helps and odd job men, all united in their affection for the late Princess. It was among the letters of condolence that Peter incongruously found next morning the latest inexorable demand from Lloyd's. With interest accruing at the Statutory rate of 8% the total demand had risen by £23,000 since the original writ and was now edging its way towards the rounded £2.5 million he had talked about. Ishbel hadn't known about the diamond's appearance and Peter decided to say nothing to his family about it either, believing that it would be better to wait until he was totally certain that its value was what he hoped and that his bank had agreed to provide the bridging loan. His children were very aware of their parents' financial problems at the hands of Lloyd's, but never discussed it in any detail being too discreet and in any case pre-occupied with running their own lives. His son, who had followed his father into merchant banking felt upset that he wasn't able to help his parents through this difficulty. Turning to the detailed section of the Statutory Demand Peter read with sudden increased concern that if he wished to avoid a bankruptcy petition being presented against him he would have to pay the debt within 21 days of its service of which already two had   gone by. This was going to mean an almost impossible schedule, but as the adrenalin was ebbing, having flowed so strongly following the death of Ishbel, he now needed the stimulation of a challenge and this could provide it.

Sleeping badly, and drinking too much, hadn't helped Peter get through the immediate aftermath of Ishbel's loss, but he had pulled himself together sufficiently to visit his bank for a third time in as many weeks - this time without the knowledge of Sir George Matthews. It was kind and only right, he pondered, that George had been so solicitous towards him at the time of his previous visit and indeed at the Thanksgiving service when he and his usually socially ambitious wife had seemed to show genuine concern for his solitude. He went, by arrangement, directly to the bank vaults by car - driving his recently acquired hybrid electric Toyota to avoid congestion charges in the West end. He wheeled silently down three levels to the accompaniment of automatically closing security doors behind him and was met by a mystified bank officer and security guard. Within four minutes Peter had withdrawn the diamond from its safety box and was noiselessly spiraling upwards again to reach the daylight.

He drove North and turned left at the end of High Holborn. He arrived in Hatton Garden, the street of the jewellery trade where it is usually impossible to park. Fortunately Peter easily found a National Car Park with spaces nearby. His opinion of London's mayor momentarily went up as he appreciated how the new bus lanes and congestion charges had apparently improved the traffic flow for those who were willing to pay even if he was hurting the Capital's business. Entering one of the featureless glass fronted 1980s office buildings, he found himself in a grey, colourless entrance corridor seemingly devoid of any human life. Facing him was a row of small lifts to the right of which was a panel of numbered call buttons. Pressing one marked 17 he waited for nearly 30 seconds before receiving a reply. Behind him a CCTV camera pointing in his direction moved silently from side to side as it scanned the dark suited visitor. "Prince Varlov for Louis Friedlander", announced Peter using his formal style to avoid misunderstanding. "Take lift number three please and come to the fourth floor where we will meet you." said the disembodied voice from the speakerphone. The elevator was small with two opening doors instead of the more usual one and barely big enough to hold Varlov's ample frame. Silently the lift went up to stop without a jerk at the fourth, allowing the alternative door to open onto an equally diminutive linoleum floored entrance lobby. A glass hatch slid open to reveal a stern faced receptionist unwilling or perhaps unable to smile, he thought.

"Mr. Friedlander is expecting you Prince Varlov, but for security reasons would you tell me your password so that I can complete the usual entry procedure." Ready for this, Peter quietly gave his seven letter code that he had agreed with Louis Friedlander as far back as ten years ago. The door swung open and Friedlander came forward to greet his old friend and business associate of twenty years standing. Louis Friedlander, some ten years Peter's junior was a South African who, having become disillusioned by apartheid and fearing for the future of South Africa, had quit Capetown in the mid seventies seeking his fortune in London through a mixed arrangement of enterprises. His first love when it came to business was doing deals, and because he had boundless energy, a good commercial instinct, and the ability to sell himself, he had rapidly built up an income flow for himself by acting as a 'Runner' or agent and contact man for several smaller fringe merchant banks. Willing both to talk and listen, his knowledge and intuition were invaluable to both buyers and sellers of small companies. When he first met Peter, then an employee of a little known accepting house, he had brought him a deal involving a deferred buy out of a thrusting bureau de change. At the time of the introduction, Louis had set out his terms - they were 5% of the purchase price. No more and no less he asked for, and the only contract would have to be a handshake. At an exceptionally cheap lunch at an East End ethnic restaurant Peter liked the man and he and Louis shook hands. That was the first of nearly eight deals they had eventually done together and never had there been the slightest mis-understanding between them. At any one time he had had at

71

least three potential deals on the go, but that was not enough for Louis Friedlander. With his South African background he was fascinated by the comings and goings of the jewellery traders in Hatton Garden and he was not averse to buying and selling some small single diamonds himself. His skill grew instinctively and his business developed sufficiently until the proud day that he could afford an office. By the time Peter arrived for this present visit he had already been trading diamonds officially for ten years and for the last five of these he had belonged to the prestigious 'Sightholders' club. This made him one of 125 special Deermaner customers, who would be invited ten times a year to 'Sights', which were held in London, Lucerne or Johannesburg thus enabling him to purchase crude diamonds. As a 'Sightholder', along with the other members, he would be offered a quota of stones in a zipped up plastic bag held inside a yellow plastic sack. This was a package deal in the literal sense of the word and he was obliged to buy all the gems offered at the price set by Deermaner. The price was non-negotiable and he could just take it or leave it. Louis Friedlander wasn't stupid and he almost always took it - he was determined to maintain his standing as one of the favoured ones.

Peter, wasn't aware of the restrictions Friedlander acted under, so it came as something of a surprise, when having amazed his friend by telling him his incredible fortune in possessing such an object, the diamond dealer held back in his response. Cautiously, Friedlander explained that Deermamer frowned upon members of the syndicate who tried to go outside the normal rules. Defy these rules and his constant supply of stones would immediately get cut off. The only way that he could help, he explained, would be by guiding Peter unofficially as a friend, to the best and, more importantly, the most trustworthy of the renowned cutters and polishers in Antwerp. This he would be very happy to do for him.

"Thank goodness for London City Airport and cheap commuter flights." thought Peter Varlov a few days later as he and Louis Friedlander, sitting in the front row of the small jet, clipped their seat belts for the short flight to Antwerp. Varlov's bulky frame was poorly suited to the cramped hard edged seating, so much so that he had to apologise to Louis for his bodily overflow - however, the early morning flight was full with its regular quota of businessmen, so nothing could be done to alleviate their closeness.   The name Antwerp always confused Peter as frequently it appeared as Anvers or Antwerpen - in any case it was not a town he knew. Travelling by car in the Benelux countries in the past he had several times got muddled   about where he was going when trying to get from Brussels to Amsterdam, but today was going to be his first real visit to the diamond cutting capital of the world and what would make it interesting was the reason he was there. Peter's head was starting to be swamped with all the gemological information pumped into him from   the   wonderfully   encyclopaedic   knowledge   of   Louis Friedlander. This distracted him from the more mundane subject of planning how to get to the fabled diamond city. Apparently it had only recently become possible to fly direct to Antwerp rather than going via Amsterdam or use the Eurostar train service and change in Brussels.   When finishing their interesting discussion in Hatton Garden, Friedlander had very kindly offered Varlov the use of his company's strong room facility, but Peter, maybe reverting to his Russian refugee origins, declined. Definitely not wishing to revert to the personal carrying methods used in the past, which his father had described, when telling him the tale of his grandfather's visit to Cowes in the Isle of Wight, he had simply kept the diamond in his trouser pocket in the day time, still in its original chamois leather purse, and for the two nights so far that it had been outside the bank vaults, it had lain under Peter's pillow with a piece of string attached to his wrist.

"Wasn't there an enormous diamond robbery here in Antwerp, a little while ago?" queried Peter as they rode in the bottle gas powered taxi from the airport to the 'Antwerp Diamond Beurs'

"You're right." answered Louis. "Not really surprising when you consider the scale of diamond trading that takes place here. Last year alone the annual turnover was measured at near to $25 billion."

"How much got stolen in that operation then?"

"I can't remember for sure, but I think it was in the region of $100 million. The thieves were a very clever bunch. They were so skilful that they got round all the alarm systems and CCTV cameras in the vaults without resorting to the usual technique of hitting someone on the head or shooting them."

"What happened to the loot - do they know?

"Probably, the stuff they stole was all already cut and polished, which would have made it considerably easier to dispose of. To be honest Peter, I just don't know the answer even though the word on the street is that there are at least five firms spread among London, Rome and New York, who have less than fragrant reputations." Peter nodded and said he was getting to see why Louis was so careful to guard his reputation and status as a Deermaner 'Sightholder.'

"We are actually going to see the first stages of a cutting today" Louis ventured as they entered an insignificant black painted door of what had the appearance of a broken down warehouse on Schupstraat in the diamond district. "The craftsmen you'll see here are enormously skilled. Usually there would be no question of us being allowed in to their premises. As it is my 'Sightholder' status got me introductions fortunately to one or two people of influence. Perhaps my obligation to buy $1 million each month from the C.S.O. has helped. Hence the speed with which I have managed to get this set up today."

What took Peter aback was when Louis had told him two days earlier that in the cutting and polishing a diamond could lose up to 50% of its original weight. This, of course made quite a hole in the simple calculations that he and Sir George Matthews had made that day at the bank. Ishbel's death had temporarily removed the numbing effect of focusing on his Lloyd's debt and his opportunity of dealing with it acceptably. Now that her burial and Thanksgiving service were over the crisis remained and he would have to apply all his reasonably active brain to find the best way forward. Turning to Louis he asked him;

"You told me that you were going to 'open the diamond' today - what does that entail?"

"Listen carefully, and I'll fill you in on the steps we'll have to take. First of all a cutter and a polisher will have to polish a facet on the diamond that will let you, me and a professional sorter look inside in order to judge its colour and its clarity."

Standing beside a metal work bench, which certainly didn't possess the appearance or cleanliness of a hospital theatre operating table, was an overalled machinist whose craggy facial features did nothing to allay Peter's alarm. He grunted a few unintelligible words in the direction of Louis, who quickly explained that that was a friendly greeting in Flemish. Peter nervously withdrew the chamois leather pouch from deep in his trouser pocket, where he had been clutching it unconsciously and practically non-stop since getting out of bed that morning. As he passed the treasured content over to the machinist, not a flicker of surprise or emotion showed in his impassive face. Without hesitating he unscrewed the clamps of the 'dop' he used, to the very limit of their opening, and slipped the diamond between the jaws before tightening up the rigid clamp. Unintelligibly still, he spoke to Louis, who translated by saying that they should leave him now for about an hour whilst a grinding process was commenced. This would then reveal the quality of the diamond. Over lunch at a fish only restaurant behind the 'Beurs,' Peter was reminded that they were in the country of the Dover Sole, which the old trencherman had been looking forward to since landing in what the locals insist is Antwerpen. Fried in butter over the lightest of flour dusting, the sole made a glorious contribution to a gourmet's self-indulgence, especially when accompanied by a dish of the world's finest pommes frites. It took more than a good meal to distract his companion from the business in hand and he went on,

"If we assume that the sorter, who we'll meet after lunch." said Friedlander, not being able to avoid belching softly, having sunk his demi litre of beer rather too fast, "finds the diamond to be white, as I expect, flawless as I would hope, and having a good clarity, then we must take the decision of how best to cut it. I hardly need tell you that the art and skill of the cutters and polishers here in Antwerp is second to none in the world, although I must admit that India, because of lower labour costs, is now presenting quite a challenge to their supremacy."

Some hours later, with a simple, but happily conclusive report, hand written on the impressive linen notepaper of Diamants de Vries, for which Varlov had paid a very reasonable fee, the two men were just in time to catch the evening flight back to London. This time there were fewer travellers and they were each able to have the luxury of an empty seat beside them. Re-reading the report for the fourth time, they both agreed that apart from the incredibly unlikely event that it should have turned out to be a 'pink diamond', the result was everything they could wish for. Seemingly, it was graded 'Colourless', which means the purest of white and given the second highest category on a recognised international scale as 'Internally

Flawless'. This should enable the great stone to be cut as a round 'brilliant' with fifty eight facets and finally weighing as much as 150 carats. Alternatively, a less drastic carat reduction might be adopted by cutting it in a more elongated pear shape manner, which although elegant does not have quite the same glamour of a perfect round. That would be for me to decide pondered Varlov to himself, but I'll go for whatever gives the higher value obviously.

"This little piece of paper should be plenty enough to satisfy George Matthews" Peter nearly said aloud, as he worked out his next move. When the plane approached London City Airport he was as uncomfortable as usual at the steepness of the approach and very aware that at either end of the short runway there was a substantial area of water. He had always been a nervous flyer and sitting across the aisle Louis noticed both Peter's hands holding the metal arm rests either side in a vice like grip with his eyes closed at the same time as if in prayer. More disconcerting still was the combination of reverse thrust and heavy braking which made the aircraft shudder violently even after it had landed. Walking through passport control Varlov was thinking that tomorrow or at the latest the day after, he must get insurance cover arranged and the terms of his bridging loan thrashed out and agreed. Only 13 days remained before his debt had to be paid in order to avoid Lloyd's petitioning him for bankruptcy, an action that he was desperate to avoid. If its consequences were not nowadays as dire as would have been the case twenty years before, Peter was old fashioned and had spent his working life in the City when the most serious crime was not to able to meet your liabilities. For him, the stigma attaching to bankruptcy remained the same and included an instant resignation from his St James's Street club - membership of which George Matthews was so anxious to achieve. Modern attitudes might have changed, but his remained very firmly in what he regarded as a far more honourable past.

CHAPTER NINE

LONDON

"Sir George is away from the office until next Monday" came the courteous, but dismissive reply from his secretary, when Varlov rang to fix an appointment with Matthews as soon as possible after his return from Antwerp. 'Things are starting to get very tight' thought Varlov to himself as he counted up the days he had left before Lloyd's did their worst for him.

"Well then please be kind enough to make an appointment for me first thing in the morning of that day - it's extremely urgent and I have to see him as soon as possible." He hoped the desperation was not too apparent in his voice. What the secretary didn't tell Varlov was that her boss George Matthews was actually in Torquay, on a private visit enjoying a Masonic jaunt with Lady Matthews - it was just as well she hadn't mentioned this or she might have been entertained to a flow of sarcastic comments from Varlov about the secret society he had so little time for himself. "That's five more precious days that are going to be wasted" fretted Varlov to himself and wondering how best he could fill the time between today and next Monday. The winding up of Ishbel's affairs was a full time occupation, which he couldn't face on his own and once more he prevailed on his married daughter to come down to the depressingly empty house and help him continue the upsetting task of sorting out her wardrobe and other personal things. Time dragged slowly for him, but eventually Sunday evening came and he went to bed pleased that things would start to move the next day.

Greeting Varlov first thing on Monday morning, Sir George Matthews was even more self important than ever as he spent five minutes dropping the names of the important people, who had been amongst the brethren at Torquay. He just can't help himself thought Varlov but, finally he came to a stop and listened with good grace to Varlov's account of his Antwerp visit and having the diamond examined. The news came as a surprise to Matthews as he had no idea that the stone had even left the security of the bank's safety deposit. He was even more surprised and rather horrified when Varlov told him that he actually had the diamond in his pocket at that moment.

"I really think you should be more careful Peter" Matthew spluttered as he crossly twiddled his gold watch chain. "Remember, it is not yet insured beyond the general cover, which the bank holds for the entire contents of our vaults. Since I've seen you I have taken the opportunity of getting a quote from Lloyd's, with no commitment you understand, for an all risks policy including transit risks, to cover it up to a value of £20 million and I am pleased to tell you that the premium would seem to be remarkably modest, in fact in the region of £2,500 plus of course, the usual insurance tax. Naturally, the conditions would mean all the normal precautions being taken at all times and those would certainly not include you carrying it around in your trouser pocket." Peter reddened a little as he thought of the risk he had taken, but assured Matthews with an innocent smile.

"Well then I had better get the proposal form completed pretty quickly because it may have escaped your notice that I have got less than a week until Sunday 27th November to pay up. OK, that's a Sunday and I feel sure that if the bank has a word with them Lloyd's would grant a short extension of say another ten days or so if necessary if they had your assurance that you were close to completing a bridging loan agreement with me." Matthews liked the implied compliment, but shifted awkwardly in his oversized wing chair and fiddled even more nervously with the gold watch chain bobbing up and down on his paunch.

"I'm afraid it's not quite as easy as that old boy." he said, addressing Peter in a patronising manner. "These things, as you know, have to go before our loan and risk committee and they have already come up with two problems. Unless we can somehow solve them both I'm afraid there is little chance of the committee giving a clearance."

"Christ", exploded Varlov, "you might have let me know a bit earlier that there were problems, instead of swanning off to one of your Masonic jamborees. Meeting your friends on the square, or whatever you call it, is obviously more important to you than looking after your clients." Matthew's already high complexion turned purple before responding.

"That, Peter is one of the more offensive remarks I've ever heard you make. I take very grave exception to it and would ask you to retract it straight away. You ought to know that Masonic meetings have always formed an important part of my charitable work." He invariably resorted to his natural pomposity whenever he felt attacked. Varlov realised he had gone too far and retracted immediately.

"I'm sorry George. You know that I have been under unspeakable pressure of late and I hadn't meant to offend you. You know what I think of the Masons - I've never made any secret of it, but I respect your views are different and we must agree to disagree. Please accept my apology." Sir George was suitably placated by this and with his pride restored smiled benignly at Peter.

"Well, in any case since we met last time these two problems have arisen. The best way I can deal with the first one is for you to have a quick read of this article which appeared recently in the business digest portion of the *Economist*", said Matthews as he pushed across a lengthy article, but with a summary at its foot headed 'Diamond fake fools the experts'. Varlov felt himself, not for the first time developing a cold sweat as he read "Synthetic Moissanite diamonds made of silicon carbide are becoming widespread. The material is so good apparently that the standard thermal conduction testers as currently used by ordinary jewellers cannot tell the difference. What is more the Moissanite stone has a greater density than a diamond and will weigh more than a similarly sized diamond. Hence there is a certain amount of confusion in the trade."

"Our in-house risk assessors have taken the view that for the foreseeable future, loans secured specifically against diamond gem stones are unacceptable." pronounced Matthews with a solemnity, that matched his demeanour. He was enjoying having control over the situation again, having been annoyed by Peter's revelation of his trip to Antwerp. Varlov was very conscious that his good friend Louis Friedlander hadn't mentioned this subject at all in their conversations, but he thought that an almost immediate telephone call to him might clarify the situation from an independent point of view.

"Let me come back to you on that one if I may George, but I would point out that this diamond has been locked in your bank vaults since 1909, so it's hardly likely to be a piece of modern artificial silicon carbide - the bank should use a bit of logic for God's sake. However, in the meantime, get me a copy of that Economist article - I'd like to read it at leisure."

Fortunately, Varlov had the presence of mind not to be thrown by this objection and he reasoned, probably with justification, that it was all just an excuse for Matthews to build up the complexity of the loan for the sake of levering a higher interest rate.

"Now, you take a look at this George." said Peter as he pulled out the stiff white parchment report headed Diamants de Vries. "It isn't an official valuation I agree. That is something that you will obviously want to have done yourselves, but coming as it does from one of Antwerp's most respected diamond analysts you will see that we really are looking at a stone of potentially enormous value. I am sure if you can't help me there are many other banks that will. You may not know that for years I have kept a modest deposit account facility with another bank not situated that far East from here - so I do have other possibilities" Sir George chose to ignore the threat and continued

"I have to tell you Peter, that since   we opened your safety deposit box and you showed me its contents, I have been worrying to some extent about the diamond's provenance, but more to the point, are you able to prove good title to it?"

"That is completely undoubted" Peter protested. "I have explained to you at length how the stone initially came to be delivered to you in 1909 having been brought to England by my grandfather Prince Vladimir Varlov, and how it came to be in his possession before then. The fact that the bank didn't keep proper records is hardly my fault! Indeed this all really irrelevant in any case - the fact that I had the safe deposit key and opened it proves my inherited right – that is your normal banking practice."

"Unfortunately, on that score I'm afraid I've got some rather awkward findings to tell you -   the second problem I mentioned. In the last war, this branch of the bank suffered a direct hit and there was serious damage done to our strong room. You will remember that I told you about that problem with keys when we were endeavoring to gain access to your locker. You also know we had been entrusted in the years, soon after the turn of century, with certain deposits made by the Russian Imperial family at that time. It would not be appropriate for me to go into financial detail, but what we have discovered is some documentation that could relate to the very diamond you now have in your possession." At that moment, if blood could run cold it nearly froze in Varlov's veins. For over a fortnight now he had survived just on hope alone to carry him through both personal tragedy and financial ruin. To get this far and then be obstructed by this over-promoted jumped up bank manager pretending to be a friend made Peter feel slightly sick. On Matthew's desk lay a foxed and spotted sheet of what had once been a cream coloured sheet of linen paper. At its head, still sharp and clear was the insignia of Nicholas II Tsar of Russia. Beneath it was written in a Cyrillic script a paragraph of unintelligible language. The sepia ink with which it was written made it even less intelligible to both Sir George Matthews and Prince Peter Varlov.

"I can't read this, and neither I imagine, can you, but our foreign section had no difficulty whatever in finding an interpreter, to decode it. He has told us that it purports to set out, admittedly quite primitively, the terms upon which a diamond being brought from Cowes, Isle of Wight to our vaults in London could be released. Those terms my friend, I have to tell you, do not apparently include any mention of your family or you." In fact neither man could have possibly known that the paper in question was actually a hurried fraud, written by Admiral Kortaski and sent anonymously to the bank in an attempted revenge against his hated adversary just after the visit of the bank official to Cowes.

"That's not surprising, how could they - I wasn't born when the deposit was made. My name couldn't possibly be in any paper" Peter was getting cross and taunted Matthews by telling him that he was splitting hairs. Both men were beginning to lose their tempers and it was only a sudden fortuitous surge of adrenalin that gave Varlov the idea and speed to do with such immaculate timing what he did next. It was as if some external force had blessed him with an instinct for survival. He rose, almost without notice, and speaking quietly, but firmly, he addressed Matthews.

"Give me that piece of paper please if you would George, my Russian is rusty, but I may be able to understand bits of it." Taking it carefully from Matthews' hand he walked slowly across the room towards the daylight and with his back to Matthews he held the document up to the window and tilting it from side so side he seemed to be searching for a watermark. On the window sill to his right rested a Matthews family treasure, his father's smoker's pipe stand still complete with pipes, cleaners, ashtray and matches. By the time Matthews saw the smoke curling up towards the air conditioning ventilator it was too late.

"My God, what have you done?" roared the puce faced banker.

"That provenance problem is, I believe, now solved - that paper doesn't seem to have existed. Oh, and one other thing George, I wanted to tell you that my club has decided to accept only a very few new members again this year. Conditional upon you still being seconded by the Governor of the Bank of England, as you have so often told me you would be, I will be more than happy to be your proposer. Just think - the next time you and I have lunch there, maybe you'll be allowed to pay!" Despite his pomposity - or perhaps because of it, Sir George knew when he was defeated.

CHAPTER TEN

LONDON

Some days after Peter Varlov had cremated Sir George's little piece of paper, a visitor unknown to either man arrived in a West London hotel, Once again the diamond - released from its dark safe - was destined to bring strange bedfellows together. With a belch loud enough to startle the head waiter, Ajay Jha dipped his manicured finger tips into the rose water bowl provided for his convenience. A gross man, in every way with a soft creaseless skin, he took little exercise or care of himself, so that he looked considerably older than his actual forty five years. Jha was finishing a solitary dinner at his hotel in Gloucester Road. It was the only one in London, which he considered good enough and found sufficiently obliging, to meet his Gujarati tastes. This was the first of his twice yearly visits to Europe and he disliked the March cold of London intensely after the sultry heat of Bombay. To make up for the miserable climate he indulged himself by arranging for the Raj Group of hotels always to keep for him one of their 'Palace' suites and they happily supplied, for a more than handsome price, all his demanding comforts.

Born the eldest son of Praveen Jha, Ajay had been spoiled from childhood, never having had the slightest acquaintance with poverty. He had been raised as a Christian, in a predominately Muslim area, themselves largely deprived of everything except hardship and squalor. His father had started a diamond cutting and polishing business in 1901 in Surat, a town some 150 miles North of Bombay. A place of textile mills constantly belching their yellow smoke into a polluted mustard coloured sky, where workers lived in dismal slums unfit for human habitation. Cows roamed the streets without any hindrance and workers slept, procreated and died alongside their mangy dogs and flea ridden cats. The filth and the teeming population made for an atmosphere so unattractive that it had effectively deterred the white European from visiting let alone

83

setting up in business there. In such conditions it is only natural that with cheap labour and careful training, an enterprise of a different sort could thrive.   There was a time when India mined the diamonds itself, but no longer. All the stones now find their way to India from other countries such as Angola, Botswana, South Africa or Russia - not directly necessarily, but often through Antwerp or Amsterdam, which has long been the centre of the trade. Ajay showed a completely natural affinity for business almost from birth and it was only with difficulty that his father stopped him as a young boy from removing diamond chippings of tiny value from the workshop and trading them for sweetmeats in one of the several Surat bazaars near the factory. By the age of 20 he had already served an apprenticeship in Antwerp with the famous house of Diamants de Vries. As a certificated 'Brillianteerer' he was proud to display the framed parchment credential he'd been given at the time above his desk in what was now his office as the Managing Director of his own company, JHA BRILLIANTS. Following his father's example he had been initiated into Freemasonry soon after his 21st birthday and joined one of the craft's oldest lodges in India, The Provincial Grand Lodge of Bombay established nearly 250 years ago. That will be very good for contacts and business his father had explained to him.

Now in London tomorrow, Jha was to make a formal visit to the City of London, where he would be received with considerable respect by the leading diamond merchants Deermaner's for lunch and where he would have his first contact with Sir George Matthews.   Thanks to his corpulence, the grossly overweight diner slipped awkwardly from his round table having left, as he thought befitted his wealth, a £20 note for the head waiter who, hiding his surprise and disgust at the volume of the belching diner, fawned with the servility more often shown by a Surat beggar. Entertainment of a more private nature was in store for Jha in his Palace suite as the curry filled diamond magnate suite awaited a visit from the sixteen year old olive skinned youth whose company he'd so much enjoyed on his previous visit to London.

The next day a stockbroker, a merchant banker, an auctioneer, a shipping executive, a Shakespearean theatrical knight, Ajay Jha and Sir George Matthews formed a cosmopolitan group of men as they were introduced to each other, each apparently at or perhaps just past the peak of their different careers. No obvious ulterior motive was apparent as the Chief Executive and the Finance Director of Deermaner received their seven dissimilar guests. It was a normal part of the group's public relations policy to have these regular lunches, giving them the opportunity to impress on men and women of influence, the good name of the internationally respected C.S.O. or Central Selling Organisation - by which it was otherwise known. They liked to invite a famous figure from stage or screen as a magnet to ensure acceptance by the other guests. These otherwise sensible men and despite their normal business skills would jump at the chance of later telling their wives they had lunched with some household name from the gossip columns. Seemingly lost on their guests was that their wives would also learn the name Deermaner and henceforth nod knowingly when the subject of diamond jewellery was discussed at any future banquets they might attend.

Matthews always enjoyed being introduced as Sir George and he quickly felt at ease with the grey haired actor, whose name he quickly forgot, but thought he had recognised. The famous actor freely confessed to having no idea whatever why he was included amongst this prosperous collection of guests and cheerfully said that the City was a closed shop to him. Holding his customary glass of tomato juice Sir George was presented more unwillingly, before spotting the table setting, to Ajay Jha. Forcing a smile, Matthews automatically extended his right hand in greeting. The hand that met his surprisingly carried with it an unexpected secret signal - the middle finger of his hand was folded inwards and was very gently tickling Matthews's palm. Routinely, but quite unnoticed by other guests, Matthews's left hand reached forward to clasp the Indian's right elbow. Two Freemasons had acknowledged each other. Not, as both would claim when challenged, a secret society, but a society with secrets.

By the time lunch was finishing Matthews and Jha were on first name terms with the diamond mogul agreeing to visit him at his bank, before returning to India, on the pretext of exploring business opportunities. Sir George's interest had been aroused when Jha had said there were two U.K. acquisition possibilities that he had in mind and they would both require outside funding - one of them was a medium sized retail chain of jewellery stores that had been experiencing recent management difficulties and looked as if it could be ripe for a takeover bid. Matthews always liked to impress people by his status and an invitation to a meeting at his bank was in his opinion a form of patronising flattery. This week he had an additional reason for the over inflated belief in his own achievement by having brought the Varlov bridging loan negotiations to a satisfactory conclusion. The two problems he identified that might have stalled the loan had now been resolved and he had managed to include an increased arrangement fee over and above the interest charged. This, at two over base rate would be making a generous profit for the bank, just by itself, on the near £2.5 million loan.

It was with an almost childlike curiosity that two days after their meeting, Ajay Jha found himself looking around the impressive marble lined reception hall of Matthews's bank. The combination of men walking around in black frock coats contrasted strangely with the golden carp swimming lazily in the mezzanine level lily pond. All this was very new to Ajay as he tried to hide his discomfort. Why this typical example of a British bank manager should want to meet him was far from clear, but contacts or opportunities in business were rarely dismissed without reason by Jha, particularly if they held the prospect of establishing as yet unexplored new lines of credit. Sir George Matthews, at his most condescending, beamed as he welcomed Jha into his office. The formal Freemason handshake once again sealed the relationship for their business talk. The customary Royal Doulton chinaware had been set out with coffee and biscuits and now left alone, the two masons were quickly deep in conversation regarding their respective lodges. Matthews was interested to learn that Freemasonry in its world wide diffusion was particularly strong in India being a leftover from the days of the Raj along with its civil service, legal systems and the railway network. He would impress his dinner guests, he thought, this very evening by repeating all this for their benefit. Using the bank's research facilities Matthews had discovered that Jha's family business was now one of the biggest and most respected firms in the world in the field of diamond cutting, polishing and trading. Jha Brilliants was large and it was powerful, benefiting additionally by it being one of Deermaner's major customers.

Jha couldn't understand why he was being courted so

assiduously by this elderly semi retired banker, who seemed to spend so much time boasting about the quality and width of his social connections. For over half an hour he listened patiently before Matthews built up to what he clearly regarded as one of his finest recent achievements. He inadvertently revealed that he personally had been successful in assisting a member of the former Russian nobility and then quickly changed the subject, having unexpectedly realised his indiscretion. Matthews changed the subject and reverted to questioning his visitor about an issue he had heard was currently plaguing the diamond market. This was the fairly recent arrival on the scene of 'Moissanite' the diamond simulant, which they had only fleetingly discussed at the Deermaner lunch earlier that week.

"To give you an example George, I'll tell you how serious it is." started Jha. "Every year we send upwards of twenty five of our best young cutters and polishers to Antwerp to take part in a tuition course very similar to the 'Brillianteerer' apprenticeship that I did myself many years ago. For these boys it is a hugely exciting opportunity, bringing with it, if they are amongst those who actually achieve the diploma at the end, financial rewards way beyond those of their lowly work mates left behind in Surat." Matthews feigned interest in this not particularly fascinating dissertation before interrupting said,

"What is so special about what you are telling me Ajay?"

"I'll tell you what is special," came the irritated reply. "One of those trainees turned out to be so damned good at what he did that he managed to fool all of us on his return to Surat by bringing with him a twenty carat Moissanite fake blue diamond. Not only had he cut and polished it himself, but had got it out of the Antwerp workshops undetected."

"How did you discover it was a fake?" asked Matthews.

"We didn't - that was the problem. The usual thermal pen testing procedure, which we use, came up with perfectly normal results. The trainee only confessed what he had done when it was discovered and since that day has more or less blackmailed us into rewarding him excessively. I can't sack him - bang would go my reputation, Oh yes, it would be a potentially bad day for the company if he ever left us."

Matthews soon became rather bored and wished he hadn't

invited this big talking Indian to his office. So far there didn't seem to be any sort of business opportunities between them. He impatiently flipping over pages in his desk diary and making grunting noises in mock agreement with everything Ajay had to say. The Indian noticed his rudeness.

"Just in passing George", Ajay smiled and cast his bait, "I might mention that I have been talking to one of your financiers in London about possible funding my company will be seeking if we decide to proceed with either of the acquisitions we are considering. Of course they may not be of sufficient size to interest a bank such as yours, as the smaller of the two looks to be only in the region of £50 million." The atmosphere changed at once and was electric as Matthews hastily scribbled the figure 50 M on his leather blotting pad. Showing his old astuteness, which had helped carry him to the top of his profession, Matthews effecting a bored expression, which belied his real interest, replied glassily

"How kind of you Ajay, to think of us, but I'm afraid it's a bank policy never to consider co-operative financing for customers when there is a competitive interest. We might of course, consider acting as the lead bank, with the others selected at our discretion. The best would be for you to put your proposals in writing - then I can see to it that they receive proper consideration. You can rest assured they will have my full attention"

Pointedly, glancing at his gold watch, Matthews declared that he was afraid he was already running late for his next appointment and displaying considerable lack of grace hurriedly concluded the meeting. He arranged for his astonished guest to be unceremoniously shown out of the bank - not showing him the usual courtesy of descending with him to the ground floor. How very ill mannered and strange that man has been, mused Jha. One moment all over me as a fellow Mason and then a semi rebuttal when I hint at a sizeable business opportunity. I just don't understand him. Jha hadn't realised that he had been the recipient of the long and successfully developed technique of Sir George Matthews, the banker who believed he possessed the ability to build privilege and exclusivity into money lending.

CHAPTER ELEVEN

ENGLAND

It was already six weeks after Ishbel's death and Peter Varlov was gradually recovering from the initial shock of the loss and being alone. The private burial, the public thanksgiving service, the horror of Lloyd's rapacious demands, and the discovery of the diamond had all kept him busy. Each, in its way helped to anaesthetise Peter from the desperate loneliness that was facing him for the remainder of his life. Always a man who needed the company of others it was a prospect he was not looking forward to nor for which he felt prepared. The children had long flown the nest and the home was now far too big for him alone. He loved the county he had adopted and they had both been very happy there for almost thirty years. Even with the likely successful sale of the diamond, a life alone in the Southern English countryside was no way, he thought to survive. He knew it was a problem he would have to face, but for the moment had no idea how he was going to cope. London might be unpleasant in so many ways, but with an infinite variety of distractions, and soon to be accompanied by a healthy cheque book, he could give serious consideration to selling the family home and setting up in comfort in a London flat. Still, he reflected he had time to decide and certainly wouldn't be rushed into any decision and then regret it at leisure.

Shooting as a sport always had a mixed appeal for Peter. He was a more than adequate shot and as such a popular guest gun at friends shoots. However, being unable to reciprocate the generous hospitality he received there was a perennial problem of how to re-pay his hosts and this was a constant embarrassment to him. The only solution, he thought, was to rent a day's shooting and invite his hosts whose birds he'd been bringing down all season. This weekend at a well kept shoot some fifty miles north of London he decided he would broach the subject of possibly renting a day from his host. After an uneventful drive across country he passed the lodge gate and glided almost silently on the downgrade of his friends tarmac drive. He was still fascinated and impressed by the economy of his semi electric hybrid car, which switched off its petrol engine, and slipped noiselessly towards the big house with its welcoming lights shining in the black December evening. He entered the vast listed manor by an unlocked back door carrying his overnight bag and gun case to be greeted by the barking of three friendly dogs each clamouring for attention. Bellowing for quiet, from the dogs, his hostess embraced him with her welcome.

"Peter dear, you must be tired having flogged all this way. I am so pleased you could come. Why not just pop upstairs and relax for an hour or so. No need to hurry your bath as dinner won't be till 8.30 and tonight we are quite informal, so no need to wear a tie. There's just 12 of us this evening, but I think you know everyone. I'll show you up to your room - you've got your usual one."

"How lovely, I'm so looking forward to the weekend." Peter replied.

Later, lying in an enormous round edged Victorian bath, Peter could not help feeling sorry for himself. The room had two single beds, both of which had been turned down by a kindly but unaware housekeeper who did not realise he was now a widower. As the warm water soothed away any tiredness from the drive he found himself reflecting on the almost surreal happenings of the last two weeks.

He remembered with a chuckle how he had outflanked his old friend George Matthews, when he had come up with two semi spurious objections to providing a bridging loan. Would a true friend actually put obstructions in the way he wondered? Anyway he had made the banker look a little stupid over the 'fake diamond' question he had raised. The thing however, that pleased him the most was when he had literally burned the threat of the alleged invalid provenance. George's face when he had offered to propose him for the club was something never to be forgotten as well. He had seen the grin of smug satisfaction which had spread across the man's florid features revealing a set of yellow, slightly crooked, teeth as prominent as their owner's bobbing watch chain. Matthews was unaware however that a system of blackballing was still in practice for the membership election procedure - he wasn't through yet.

What had come as a pleasant surprise to Varlov was how readily the bank accepted the valuation of the diamond as provided by Diamants de Vries. Fortunately they had an excellent reputation in an industry where dishonesty was not entirely unknown. The fact is that they had willingly come up with what verbally they declared to be a modest value of "Somewhere in excess of $40 million," but in writing they were only willing to commit themselves to the figure of a more conservative $30 million. With cover provided of six times, the bank was getting the best of all worlds and Varlov resented the way that Matthews had insisted on taking an arrangement fee for the bank up front of £15,000. However, despite his strong protestations the bank stood firm about this. Arguing about the interest to be charged was as expected and Varlov having checked out the market carefully for the going rate on secured loans was resigned to accepting a far from generous two over base rate for the term of the loan with a savage early repayment penalty in the event of the loan terminating within six months. The bank certainly wanted their pound of flesh Peter thought as he had reluctantly agreed the terms, Insurance was a non event as the proposal form had been accepted by the Lloyd's broker without question once they had had sight of the Diamants de Vries valuation. Varlov himself had written the cheque to the broker for just over £2,000 to provide the wide ranging all risks cover.

Relaxed after his bath and shortly after 8 o'clock, Peter joined the other guests in front of a blazing log fire in the manor's drawing room. His host, unlike his guests was rather obviously wearing a regimental tie and a velvet jacket. Informality of dress never came easily to this Captain of Industry, but his exceptional hospitality was legion in the county, and made any awkwardness over his dress forgivable. Putting down the magnum from which he was dispensing champagne, he gave his guest a bear hug in greeting from which Peter felt an infusion of warmth, sympathy and understanding. The company was good and the food was delicious, but Peter, despite his efforts felt newly strange and slightly uncomfortable as the only single person at the table. As his charming hostess got up and left the dinner table with the ladies, she appealed to the men not to be too long, but her plea fell on deaf ears as the conversation quickly turned to shooting, politics and eventually the Lloyd's debacle. Varlov maintained a stony silence on this last subject. As far as he was aware nobody at the table even knew that he was a member, let alone a major victim of the Lime Street insurance catastrophe. Peter snapped out of his day dream when he heard one of the guests at the other end of the table say that some years back he had been invited by one of the larger Lloyd's agencies to act as a sort of unofficial agent for them with the aim of introducing potential new members from among his many friends or contacts. In return they had offered him an on-going annual commission for each member introduced. Peter looked down the table at the speaker - he was someone he had only a nodding acquaintance with, but he had difficulty in hiding his feelings as the man went on,

"I remember, he was from some Russian refugee family called Kortaski. Born in this country, in fact an old Etonian, but not really an Englishman despite that. To be quite honest I didn't all together like 'the cut of his jib'." said the guest. "Too smooth by half if you ask me. He was very persistent, like all these chaps are, and told me that even a director of the Bank of England was one of his agents, who apparently collected a sizeable annual revenue for his personal account for this sideline."

Now fully concentrating, Varlov managed to keep his silence, but his brain was working overtime. Not only was it possible - no, it was probable - that Anatole had been paying off someone all these years without disclosing it, but the recipient just might have been his pompous banking friend, who had been instrumental in providing his bridging loan. After all it was he, Peter reminded himself, who first suggested him joining and had steered him towards Kortaski when he had decided to go ahead. His mind was also continually turning over the process of the diamond's progress and the essential need for silence on the subject until the sale was arranged was difficult for him to sustain. He was someone who had always been used to discussing his thoughts and business with friends and now he longed to share his problems. Until now he had only talked with George Matthews and to a limited extent with Louis Friedlander, the Hatton Garden diamond trader. Not even his children were privy to his secret - their time would come, and he would enjoy spoiling them and his grandchildren too, when they would all share in the munificence of Tsar Nicholas II.

Good to his word George Matthews had used - and enjoyed using - the full weight of his pomposity when he telephoned Lloyd's. Giving short shrift to the secretary he was quickly put through to the head of the Financial Recovery Department.

"Sir George Matthews here" he announced himself, he had dialled the number himself to keep the call confidential from his secretary. "You are aware, I am sure, that amongst your debtors is one Prince Peter Varlov in a sum not un-adjacent to £2.5 million due to you, as I understand, no later than 27th November."

"That is correct" came the North of England twang from the other end..

"Well, we are Prince Varlov's bank as well as your recognised bank and we would appreciate a ten day stay of execution of your Statutory Demand setting in motion the whole process of a bankruptcy petition. My bank is at this moment finalising a loan facility, which has been agreed for the Prince and I am instructed to notify you that settlement will be made in full by 7th December. I would add that this will be accompanied by a counterclaim against Lloyd's for a considerably larger sum, although I hasten to add that the bank is not a party to that action." Such formality of phraseology was not familiar to the Lloyd's debt collector, who reverted to his earlier clerking origins and mumbled a deferential agreement.

"My bank requires your confirmation in writing within twenty four hours. Please have it delivered to my bank marked for my attention," finished Matthews, as he dropped the telephone handset back into its cradle with a satisfied smile.

Diamants de Vries speedy provision of the valuation to Varlov came at a small price. Instead of charging the normal fee of several thousand pounds for such an important analysis of worth, the venerable firm had asked for and been granted the business of cutting and polishing the fabulous stone.

In a series of telephone calls between Varlov and legal officers of the bank the actual bridging loan agreement was quickly completed and put before the formal loan and risk committee for final approval. It was passed on the nod, but as usual it included a clause whereby the bank retained an absolute charge over the stone until such time as it was either sold or returned to their vaults in The Strand. In addition, the eventual auctioneers would have to sign an undertaking to account to the bank for the proceeds from the sale.

On 7th December a bankers draft in settlement of the debt was delivered to Lloyd's, Room 441, One Lime Street. London EC3M 7HA. At the same time as the motor cycle courier delivered the draft a Securicor Van could be seen emerging from the vaults of the bank in The Strand. It was carrying an embarrassingly small package addressed to Diamants de Vries, Antwerp. Varlov recalled the reluctance with which Matthews agreed to the appointment of the famous Belgian firm as cutter and polisher of the stone. In fact, as Peter pointed out it was really his decision alone, as the diamond belonged to him. Matthews' preference had been for a Deermaner's recommended company in Amsterdam from whom he could have expected to receive an introductory commission in the region of £10,000. Small in relation to the estimated cost of £75,000 for the complete job, but sufficient to pay for the de luxe stateroom on the Caribbean cruise, which Lady Matthews had come to expect as her winter holiday entitlement.

CHAPTER TWELVE

LONDON

"Good Morning Sir"

"Good Morning Stanley" replied Peter Varlov as he settled into the leather seated comfort of the breakfast room at his St. James's Street club. The club servant hovered behind his chair for his order.

"I'll have two eggs with crispy bacon please, and also Stanley, may I have some proper marmalade and not that ghastly peel-less jelly stuff in the tiny pots, which I can never open in any case?"

"Certainly Sir, shall I bring your *Daily Telegraph* as well?" The servant was well used to the petty idiosyncrasies of the members.

Coping with widowhood was proving to be every bit as painful as the bereaved Varlov had feared. Consequently he found himself spending more and more nights at his club where he knew he would find congenial company and avoid the desperate loneliness he felt at home in the country. Inevitably he was drinking more than was good for him resulting in his already sizeable girth becoming more rotundly obvious. All thoughts of the fairly rigid diets that Ishbel had kept him on were now forgotten.

"At least I have the chance of having two time-consuming projects to occupy myself," thought Peter, wiping his lips on the white damask napkin - "so many of my contemporaries seem to have become rather insular after they retired - for them, it seems to be just gardening and golf and waiting for the grave"

For the last month, apart from starting his participation in an Action Group proposing to sue Lloyd's of London, - probably useless he had reflected, but it satisfied his wish to be doing something about getting revenge, he had been spending a considerable amount of time in the evenings studying gemology. He had made his first visit to the Tower of London and saw for himself the Crown Jewels - on one of the centre pieces of which was the Koh-i-Nor diamond set in the Queen Mother's crown. He had been to the British Library to research the history of diamond mining. It was there that he learned how a major part of India's fabulous mogul wealth had come from mining these precious stones from as long ago as the 13th century. To this day the ancient Indian diamonds, known as 'Golconda', are apparently the only ones to possess such a subtle near magical quality of 'luminosity', he read. Peter Varlov already knew from past media publicity that most major jewellery auctions were now held in Switzerland for reasons which he didn't properly understand, but believed were probably to do with the local commissions being payable by both the seller and the buyer. Although this contentious practice was disapproved of and not permitted in other countries, Geneva had somehow still succeeded in practically making this market its own. At the moment Varlov had only the barest descriptive material of his diamond. This consisted of three photographs taken by himself with his digital camera and a preliminary letter from Diamants de Vries in Antwerp describing, in general terms, the rough stone as being white, flawless and weighing around 300 carats in its present uncut state. The photographs showed that because of its elongated shape, the stone might better be cut in a pear shape rather than the more classic circular 'brilliant'. As for the question of provenance, Varlov realised that he might have to rely to some extent on the bank's co-operation when it came to authenticating his truthful claim that the stone had been lying untouched in the bank's vaults for nearly 100 years, having been deposited there by his grandfather. Varlov was also very conscious and rather annoyed that Matthews had already, uninvited, been in touch with one of the large International auction houses with an enquiry about them handling the sale. It was only at a subsequent meeting with a slightly subdued Matthews at the bank that he had made it absolutely clear to the banker that it was he, Prince Peter Varlov who was the owner and vendor of the diamond and it was he who would take the decisions. Furthermore, Varlov was adamant that anonymity should be maintained throughout the sale process, and he pointed out, perhaps too forcefully, that Sir George Matthews was merely representing the interests of the bank. They had admittedly provided a temporary loan of £2.5 million, but against the hugely over generous security of the diamond.

Within strolling distance of his club, Varlov knew there were two well known auction houses. In the past he had enjoyed attending their art sales with Ishbel before taking tea at Fortnum's. He remembered those happy days as he walked towards them. One of these seemed to him to be most renowned for its sales in New York and London of Impressionist paintings together with valuable and rare musical instruments such as Stradivarius violins. The other firm, although having possibly a slightly lower public profile, had recently featured in the news for achieving impressive record prices with its last diamond sale in Geneva. As an older man, Peter Varlov rather liked to give the false impression of being a bumbling innocent - something his appearance supported - rather than open up immediately with all his cards. Making his casual entrance at 10 a.m. to the unassuming, but nevertheless quietly luxurious offices of the first auctioneers, he approached the front desk, where the receptionist, a typical long blonde hair product of some upper class home county family, was working while she searched London for a rich and preferably titled husband. He asked her if he could see one of their senior jewellery experts about the possible sale of a diamond.

"Do we know you? Have you been here before? Do you have an appointment?" fired the distinctly uninterested girl at the desk, shooting off the questions while scarcely managing to take her eyes away from the computer screen in front of her in any gesture of welcome to the grey haired visitor.

"No, I don't think you do and nor do I have an appointment," answered Varlov modestly as he slipped one of his visiting cards across the counter. Disregarding his card, the girl said,

"In that case I'm afraid you'll have to wait until one of our consultant experts is free - that won't be before 11 o'clock."

"I quite understand." replied Varlov, not reacting to the girl's discourtesy, "I'll use the time wisely and walk down the road to get my hair cut, but please be sure to tell your expert that I am waiting. Do you think you can do that?" As he left, the receptionist looked at him with a studied air of superior contempt - why should she care, she thought. She was off to Barbados that evening with her new boy friend. Close to 11.15 a.m. a slim built young man, aged about 35, announced himself to Varlov, who was waiting impatiently in the main lobby, where the receptionist hadn't even invited him to sit down. "I'm Orlando Smythe, I understand you need some help." His dark and expensively cut blue double breasted suit had a rather too obvious pin stripe. It hung well from the man's broad shoulders, but Varlov couldn't help noticing that he had a nervous and deliberate habit of shooting the cuffs of his sparkling white shirt, rather like Prince Charles on a walkabout, he thought, which revealed a pair of diamond and ruby cufflinks in the form of a burgee of a distinguished yacht club. He exuded self confidence, flicking the edge of Varlov's visiting card, as he drawled,

"And how can we be of assistance to you today?"

"I am the owner of a fairly sizeable uncut diamond", Peter began, "which I want to sell. I believe your company handles that sort of thing?"

"Yes we do, but only if we know a lot about the provenance of the stone. Shall we go to one of our waiting rooms and talk about it there. By the way have you got it with you?" the young man's drawl continued.

"Actually no, but maybe you would be interested in these photographs I can show you?" said Varlov.

"Why not?" came the reply - his voice hiding any interest he may in fact have had, "let's have a look at them and at any other papers you may have." An awkward silence was the first reaction to the expert's sighting of the photographs and then in a condescending manner he glanced at the initial report from the famous Antwerp company - holding it slightly away from himself as if it were something suspect. Slowly and deliberately he folded the letter from Diamants de Vries and returned it to its envelope together with the photographs. Equally slowly, stifling a sigh, and with his cuff-links sparkling, he then slid the envelope back across the table in front of him towards the waiting Varlov.

"I'm so sorry to tell you, Prince Varlov, that we are seeing quite a lot of this kind of thing these days." Peter was taking a little objection to what seemed a hint of sarcasm in the young man's voice. "In almost every case the so called diamond, whether clear or coloured, turns out to be a Moissanite fake, although I must admit that I have never seen one being so blatantly palmed off in an uncut state like this one. As for the report by a well known firm like Diamants de Vries, this means very little, or at worst it could be a simple forgery - I just don't know. The only small compensation I can give you is that even as a fake it is of jumbo size and the eye watering weight of 300 carats could make it a record. That might give it some interest or curiosity value at least" Varlov, with a great effort, kept his voice under control,

"Well, thank you very much indeed for your time and expert advice. You have saved me a lot of heartache.   I will be sure to mention your helpfulness and expertise to your Chairman when I see him next for lunch." He shook hands and left - it was only after he was some fifty yards away down the road that he surprised a passing pedestrian by stating out loud what he thought of the young man. Fortunately, the onlooker thought he was speaking on his mobile phone and not directing his invective at him.

It was still only 12 o'clock and Varlov, a solitary figure, wandered absent mindedly down Bond Street, wondering how best to fill the rest of the morning. Over a glass of champagne at the Rivoli Bar he reflected on the rudeness and arrogance of the young man at the auctioneers. Perhaps it was going to be an uphill struggle to get the diamond the attention it deserved without, after all, having to involve Matthews and the bank. Without them behind him, who would ever believe a story like this? He began to despair even though his personal credentials were impeccable, could it be that no one would take him seriously? It was in this mood that he later stepped into the carpeted splendour of the King Street entrance of the second auction house. He had decided to call there after lunch. The contrast to the morning visit could not have been more obvious. The friendly man on the front desk smiled a welcoming

"Good Afternoon Sir," immediately giving him his full attention. Varlov intentionally used the same introduction as he had before in order to test the level of response. "Do you by chance have a visiting card with you Sir?" the reception manager asked - "if you do it makes it so much easier for us to check our data base and be sure we get the right person for you to talk to." In response Varlov handed his card across the counter. The man tapped the details into his computer keyboard and in seconds he had all the information he needed displayed in front of him. He looked up with a beam, "Come this way, Sir. If you wouldn't mind waiting a minute someone will be down to see you at once."   Waiting in a small room just off the main hall, Varlov flipped idly through the pile of glossy auction catalogues left lying around and his eyes quickly spotted a beautifully designed example promoting a forthcoming auction in Switzerland of important jewellery. He was totally absorbed in its glossy pages illustrating a collection of the most staggering pieces from famous names such as Harry Winston, Graff, and Tiffany, when he looked up as the door was quietly opened by a tall blonde woman of immediate fascination. Gliding forward briskly with an extended hand, she introduced herself with a name he couldn't catch and, at the same time handed him her card. Taking this without reading it, he was instantly captivated by a fragrance that was to linger in his nostrils and in his mind.

"I do apologise," she said, "but I must tell you in advance that I don't think I'm really the right person for you to talk to. The most important jewellery is always handled by our office in Geneva where our real experts are based." Varlov, not wishing to show his disappointment that he would not have the pleasure of dealing with this enchanting lady, with her crooked smile and twinkling hazel eyes, reached into his pocket and produced the envelope.

"I know a certain amount about diamonds, but they aren't by any means my speciality" she explained. "Before I open the envelope why don't you tell me something about it and what I might expect?"

"My goodness, what a charming approach to give your prospective clients confidence." Varlov couldn't help himself saying as, almost tongue-tied he was transfixed by the questioning expression in this lovely person's face.

"Perhaps that comes from my television experiences. Trying to relax the owners of the unusual personal treasures that I deal with on the 'Antiques Road Show.'"

"Ah - now I know why your face is familiar," said Varlov, but let me tell you about my stone. In that envelope you'll find three pictures, taken by me, of what is probably the biggest uncut diamond you have ever seen in your life. With them is a brief descriptive letter from one of Antwerp's most famous firms of cutters and traders confirming it as being white, flawless and weighing 300 carats in its uncut state. This is the property of my family."

"Now you've got me excited, carry on and tell me more." she said as her beautifully shaped fingers, with their exquisite lilac varnished nails, slipped open the envelope - he noticed there was no wedding ring. Peter Varlov was a teenager again and completely bewitched.

Scarcely able to concentrate on what she was saying he learned from her card that her name was Suki Bullioni. She worked as a consultant for the auction house apparently in a flexible capacity, but Varlov thought probably in a public relations role. She was very easy to talk to and in the half hour they spent discussing the diamond, Varlov explained its provenance and was intrigued to learn that the appealing consultant had more than a passing knowledge of the Russian Royal family including some startling information about the auction prices achieved for jewellery purporting to have belonged to the murdered Tsarina.

"I think I'm right in telling you that our next major auction of really important jewellery will be in Geneva towards the end of May." Suki said in her slightly lisping speech with its indefinable accent. "Do you think there will be enough time between now, what are we - early February, and the end of May?" asked Varlov. "I don't think the cutting and polishing that is being done in Antwerp will be finished for several weeks yet."

"That's alright - just move as quickly as you can and from our side we can set the ball rolling and easily arrange for the Gemolocal Institute of America, who are based in Los Angeles, to send one of their top people to Antwerp to assess the diamond - that will be necessary I'm afraid. That is, of course if you do choose to give us your full instructions." Varlov, still quite overcome by this woman's gentle approach, quickly nodded his agreement.

"We'll have to prepare a really substantial PR story behind this event. It won't be difficult, but it will be time consuming" Suki went on. "A diamond like this with its special provenance will attract some extraordinary potential buyers. From what you tell me don't be surprised if all sorts, movie stars, Russian oligarchs, Heads of State and even footballers, now they earn such fortunes, will express an interest in this diamond."

"What about the commission you charge?" Varlov semi interrupted as he tried to bring himself down back to earth again and dreaming thoughts he told himself he shouldn't even be contemplating about the fragrant lady sitting opposite him.

"May I call you by your first name Peter?" queried Suki, not waiting for a reply. "I'm not really able to answer that question I'm afraid. It's always a matter of negotiation with my colleagues in Switzerland, but I can promise you that the figures bandied about in the area of 8% reducing as the price goes up, which you've probably read about, don't necessarily reflect reality. This diamond, in my admittedly only partially qualified view, could make a price in excess of £20 million, in which case I suspect the cost to you as the seller would be something comfortably under 2%." Varlov was suddenly fully awake as he heard this astounding figure confirmed for the first time by an actual representative of an auction house.

In the short half hour they had together, Suki herself couldn't help but feel a touch of affection for this smiling, rotund and somehow vulnerable man. She vaguely remembered from the diary and gossip pages of the National press that Peter Varlov had been recently widowed and from what she could tell from talking to him today he lived alone somewhere in the Home Counties of England. Business like she had glossed quickly over the touchy subject of the 'buyer's premium', which starts off at the wickedly high rate of 20% reducing to 12% and lower as the hammer prices rises. Then she briefly mentioned that VAT at 7.6% would be payable on all commissions, but if the diamond was exported from Switzerland after the sale, that could be recovered. Last but not least she explained that insurance was payable as well. But once again the general figure of 1.5% really only applied to items of much lower value - all this could be negotiated.

"When we get those Gemological people over from America to look at it, their opinion as to its earth bound origins will be absolutely crucial. If it's a 'Golconda' and I'm afraid I don't think it is, the selling price could be up to 20% higher."

A little later, walking as if on air, Varlov said his goodbyes and murmured shyly something about possibly having lunch together the following week. Suki left him with her sweetest crooked, but enigmatic smile – his question unanswered.

CHAPTER THIRTEEN

LONDON

"Are they dog friendly?" asked Suki Bullioni when he had summoned up the courage to call her some days later.

"I don't know I'm afraid, why do you ask that?" replied Peter Varlov, not really understanding the strange question. Having dreamed about her, rather like a smitten teenager with a crush, since the moment they had met a week earlier he had decided to invite her for lunch. He was initially frightened of doing so in case of risking a rebuff and also, in the back of his mind, a still small voice telling him that it wasn't all that long since his wife had been buried - in fact only a little over three months. His life in the country hadn't turned out to be as completely solitary as he had initially feared either, as he had been invited out to dinner parties, at least on average twice a week, by all the social hostesses who were only too pleased to have a 'spare man' on their guest list - particularly as he had a title and apparently was wealthy as well. Inevitably he had been potentially paired off at these dinners with some suitable widow or other, most of whom he decided were either, too old, too gushing, too ugly or a combination of all four.

"Peter, I'm afraid I never go anywhere, if I can possibly help it, without my two Whippets - they're like children to me. I usually take them to work with me and most people seem to put up with them. Perhaps the reason for their popularity is, unlike other dogs, they don't smell, bark or lick." Suki laughingly explained in her slightly lisping voice which had so attracted Varlov from the beginning.

"Alright then, I'll ask the restaurant and ring you back as soon as possible" promised the somewhat surprised Varlov. 'That's a bloody nuisance' he thought, after he had put the phone down, 'Firstly I don't much like dogs - any dogs, whether they smell or not, and secondly it will take me an age to find a restaurant in London which doesn't object to the wretched animals.' An hour later Peter was able to ring back to say that he had found another restaurant in Chelsea, which would permit dogs so long as they were properly behaved. Lying through his teeth, Peter assured the manager that the two Whippets were a model of good conduct. When Suki arrived a good ten minutes late for their lunch date, Peter Varlov was already well into his second large pre lunch drink and was feeling at his most jovial best. He was again enchanted by Suki, who was looking every bit as attractive as he remembered, wearing beneath her fur lined Loden overcoat a pale biscuit coloured poplin shirt tucked into what looked like a loose woven cashmere tweed skirt in grey and lilac - perfectly matching her lilac nail varnish. With the shirt she wore a small silk scarf tied lightly round her neck, cleverly giving the impression of being pinned to her left shoulder. Fortunately, as it turned out, Suki had told the truth and the two little animals curled up beneath the restaurant table where they remained unobtrusively throughout the lunch. Suki shyly confessed that she had read up about Peter Varlov since they had first met, as part of her job to help build a good story for the public relations operation by the auctioneers. She had also discreetly learned that following a visit to London by the firm's head of jewellery sales in Geneva, the commission terms had finally been amicably agreed with the total percentage cost coming out somewhat less than Peter had anxiously anticipated.

"I'm sure there's going to be a terrific amount of publicity and interest about this sale in May." Suki started to reveal. "I can't think of anything quite like it since the sale of the Duchess of Windsor's jewellery way back in 1987. I wasn't around for that of course, and in any case it wasn't us who handled the sale, but it is still talked about within the trade in hallowed terms. It must have done a power of good for that year's profits too, particularly as the heavily criticised buyer's premium had already been added on top since 1975."

"Goodness me, do you really think it's going to be that interesting?" a wide eyed Peter asked.

"Yes, I most certainly do," Suki went on. "For that sale, they even had to put up a vast marquee next to Lac Leman in order to cope with the huge numbers of people attending and of course all the press. What's more, they had a semi mirrored version of the sale in New York where more than 600 guests turned up to take part in the bidding. People like Elizabeth Taylor and Joan Collins were all there. Whether or not we'll need extra space I don't yet know, but I am sure that there wasn't a single item of jewellery within the Windsor collection that was anything approaching the size of your diamond although, of course, overall there were very many different lots. From memory I think the total sum raised in that particular sale was of the order of £31 million pounds, which I suppose must be more like £75 million in today's money."

"Well, I'd be happy with that," chuckled Varlov as he poured more wine, "but, forgive me asking Suki, there's one thing that does puzzle me, from where did you get that delicious accent of yours? I thought I had a good ear for languages, but yours mystifies me."

"Don't worry Peter" Suki smiled, "Everyone asks the same question, but you of all people should have guessed it right. My mother was Russian and lived in Paris, but my father, who I never knew, was Italian and I reverted back to his name after my marriage went wrong three years ago."

"Ah yes - I can get that now," answered Peter, "but you've also got a veneer of smart English as well - I'm sorry that sounds very rude."

"Don't worry, I won't take offence. That accent came from the English girls' school my mother sent me to in Wiltshire. She thought that a mongrel like me should be properly educated. So, if you like the result who am I to complain?"

"On that happy note, which would you prefer the Dover Sole or lobster. What can I tempt you with - they both look good?" Peter asked.

"Both are a lovely idea, but if I'm going to get these dogs walked after lunch I'd better hold back a little on what I eat and drink," Suki replied modestly. "I'll just have a salad with some smoked salmon if I may."

"Can I come with you for their walk?" asked Peter a little later, still enraptured by the warmth of her smile, which displayed her slightly inward sloping teeth. Their conversation had ranged broad and wide over lunch, but arrived at the subject of the threatened anti fox hunting bill then working its tortuous way through parliament. Peter learned that, following her divorce three years ago, Suki, in order to have some distraction from her personal problems, had become involved with Whippet coursing, a sport of which he confessed he had only vaguely heard.

"I don't hunt or do any of the normal winter activities like skiing or skating" she said, "but I do love the English country in winter, despite the mud, wind and rain. What's more Whippet coursing has the advantage of not being too expensive like fox hunting, which, as you know, costs an arm and a leg. Sometimes literally," she added with a laugh. As they left the restaurant having enjoyed some delicious cooking and shared a bottle of wine between them, Suki offered to drive Peter in her big four wheel drive to Hyde Park, where she usually walked the whippets. Over lunch they both decried the use by women of enormous four by four vehicles in London and laughed at their nick name of 'Chelsea Tractors.'

"I do think I've got a genuine excuse to have one myself." apologised Suki, apparently hypocritically "and if you like I'll offer you an opportunity to find out why."

"I'd love to know why" teased the now even more captivated Peter.

"You probably know from all the publicity surrounding the banning of hunting with dogs that Whippet coursing is in the firing line as well. This Saturday will be one of the more special of our Whippet coursing meets when the hares will be what is called 'driven' rather than 'walked up.' If you would like to come with me you'll certainly get the chance to see my four by four in its element and being properly used. It's a lot of fun and you'd get to meet some really nice people" said Suki.

"I'm on for that," enthused Peter, "Tell me what do I need to wear?"

"Warm clothes, plenty of them and rubber boots. I'll bring a picnic in the back of the car and we'll need to arrive at the site by 10 o'clock latest, which means leaving London no later than 8 o'clock. You can leave your car in my parking space and I'll drive you down. It's near Bibury in Gloucestershire."

On the drive down on Saturday morning, Suki explained that these meetings, although absolutely legal were held most discreetly so as not attract attention from the increasingly active anti blood sport protestors. There was fortunately very little traffic as they drove down the M40 to the little town of Bibury from where they continued for a number of miles down the twisting and narrow country lanes until they spotted a tiny yellow roadside sign with an arrow pointing to W.C.C. It was then that Varlov realised what Suki had been referring to when she had justified her owning a four by four vehicle. Attempts by non four wheel drive cars to negotiate a deeply rutted muddy track were rapidly thwarted, with family sedans abandoned on the verge amidst jocular references to tractor drivers making a good living from rescue services. Thorn hedging, semi bare in mid winter and dry stone walls edged the field of Cotswold mud and rough edged yellow stone. Partridges and pheasants either strutted or ran whilst skylarks sang their joyful melody having climbed up into the murky overcast well out of sight of earthbound humans.

This was the 1000th meeting and possibly one of the last ever to be held   of The Whippet Coursing Club, which was founded back in 1962.   About fifty members and a handful of guests like Peter Varlov had mostly travelled long distances - Peter heard someone say they had driven from Cheshire that morning - to participate in the centuries old field sport of hare coursing. He read in a magazine someone handed him that this was not, as is popularly believed the traditional miners' sport of greyhound and Lurcher coursing, but only involves their diminutive Whippet cousins. Weighing no more than 12lbs, these affectionate, but somewhat nervous looking family pets are beloved by their mainly female owners and he could see how they were being fussed over after their journeys.

"Some of the owners seem to bear a close resemblance to their pets" joked Varlov out loud and then immediately regretted it in case he might have offended Suki. He did notice though that out of the 28 animals taking part no less than 19 were bitches, although he couldn't work out why this should be. The little dogs, despite being transparently thin and constantly shaking, were amazingly sporting and as Suki reminded Peter, to his relief, they rarely bark.

The adverse effects of the   damp and cold, Varlov quickly learned, as he was introduced to the other participants, who were nearly all elderly, were dealt with by a generous supply of tawny port, fruit cake and maybe the odd cold sausage dispensed generously from the back of the car. The Whippets didn't seem to squabble amongst themselves, but remained loyally close to their handlers. The dogs were uniformly dressed in quilted waterproof coats usually personalised with their owners' initials. The members themselves were dressed in every variety of warm clothing including woolly hats, gaiters, and puffer jackets with Suki sporting a long haired ocelot waistcoat   with a stylish Russian fur hat looking suspiciously like a silver fox. As he finished his third piece of fruit cake a member explained to Varlov that two important officials of the club were known as the Judge and the Slipper. Both he saw, were wearing scarlet coats with shiny buttons. The Judge was mounted on a very fine and beautifully mannered hunter and wearing black boots with white breeches. Peter learned that he was mounted for the simple reason that without the added advantage of height there would have been no way that he could keep up with and properly watch the Whippets as they were running.   The Judge carried in his right coat pocket a huge white handkerchief and in his left a similarly large red one.   The Slipper, a highly skilled man seemed to have copied the Judge and was wearing a white woollen stocking on his right leg and a red one on his left. Peter, being amused by this sartorial imbalance, asked the reason 'why?' The answer was a simple one - he was told that it was just for fun.

A charming gentleman, who said that he had come from Oxford, and was about Varlov's age, explained that today the dogs would be run "two at a time" and before 'The Off' they would be held with a specially designed quick release double collar activated by the Slipper at the critical moment. In addition, today's meeting was to be a 'driven' version as opposed to 'walking up', with some 22 beaters strategically placed by a Beat Master   in adjacent fields. Armed with flags on hand held sticks these energetic people, in the same manner as their counterparts on a pheasant shoot, banged the hedges, stamped the ground and generally made enough din to get the hares to move, if possible in the direction behind the Slipper. Their job was to get the hare to run at speed within fifty yards of the Slipper who was holding two dogs on his special leash. Unlike Foxhounds, neither Greyhounds nor Whippets use any scenting power and merely rely on sight as they spot their quarry moving at more than 30 MPH. Squealing, or as his elderly tutor said 'giving tongue' with delighted excitement, the pair of Whippets are then released by the Slipper, who hopefully, has pointed them in the right direction. For identification, the pair wear either a red or white neck band to enable the Judge to declare in due course which was the eventual winner.

The chase on average seemed to cover no more than one third

of a mile with a strong hare easily outrunning the dogs to reach safety. Furthermore, the hare has the advantage of being able to jinx with the dexterity of a land bound snipe, which the long legged dogs cannot possibly match. His new friend explained that the winner was declared to be the dog that kept closest to the hare and points were also granted for a Whippet which was clever enough to make the quarry turn and remain inside the selected coursing field. Varlov was worried that the Whippets would get exhausted after just one run, but Suki explained to him that in any case, under the rules, they weren't permitted to run more than twice in a day even though they would have loved to do so. Only two out of the thirty running hares flushed out were killed that day and both times the Judge and Steward were on the scene within seconds to ensure a minimum of suffering.

"In actual fact," said Suki, "they very rarely catch the hare, which almost invariably gets away." In addition, unlike Greyhounds, when Whippets lose their quarry, get tired or get bored, they just turn round and come back to their owner. Rough going is no friend to these hawk eyed animals and it was a little distressing for the sensitive Suki to see the cuts, sprains and bruises, which happen all too often to the dogs - Whippet coursing participants are amongst a vet's most favourite customers she told Peter. So friendly and trusting are the dogs that they frequently attach themselves to another owner, or handler, whilst waiting to be restored to their rightful guardian. On a few occasions a Whippet will go back to the Slipper in the hope of getting another run.

Hip flasks of Whisky Mac, the warming blend of Scotch and ginger wine, were circulated freely amongst the members and two slugs of this burning sharpener helped restore Varlov a little. Sadly the conversation among the crowd was largely limited to the subject of banning hunting, which the members naturally thought was dreadful. Views were expressed in typically strong language by many. If the bill was to go through, it wouldn't be easy for any section of the hunting community. Although Whippets weren't living with the threat of being shot, their owners such as Suki would find it harder than the fox hunters to find a legal way by which to surmount the ban.

Varlov wasn't really spellbound by the day's sport, but what genuinely impressed him was the care and devotion shown by all the members to ensure that cruelty was virtually eliminated. Tired and chilled through to the bone, having just survived the near freezing temperature for a long day, which even the offer of free drinks couldn't overcome, Peter was relieved to regain the warm sanctuary of Suki's car. With four more meetings to come this winter, Peter speculated that a little physical discomfort was a modest price to pay to be with the lovely Suki, but if he came to another one he would have to buy some better insulated boots he thought as his feet slowly thawed out from the car's heater.

In near contented silence they drove more slowly back to London. Suki going over in her mind the results of a good day's coursing and Peter's mind inevitably turning to the three month delay before the great diamond sale would happen. "When the sale day eventually arrives." murmured Varlov, as they approached the outskirts of Kensington, I don't know whether or not I will want to be there myself. If I did go it would be wonderful if you would be there with me?" Suki turned briefly from her concentration on the road ahead and, without replying, gave Peter what can only be described as her most bewitching crooked smile. It was neither an acceptance nor a rejection, but just enough for Peter to be able to hope.

CHAPTER FOURTEEN

NAJERA

The whirring of the air conditioning plant had a soporific effect on François' parents as they kept their continuous twenty four hour vigil at his bedside and it was only a slight twitching of one of his feet that re-affirmed that his coma meant life still continued ....
Sitting by a dry river bed the Henke family were idly gathering big pebbles and adding them to small pyramids, which earlier pilgrims had shaped to warn future unwary travellers that flash floods occurred and it would make sense to pitch any form of shelter well above the cones. These curious ancient markings ran for several kilometres in the direction of Santo Domingo de La Calzada from the village of Najera where they had stayed the night before.

"I'm tired Father" groaned Ebbo, "How much further do we have to go today?"

"I don't know son" replied Lucus his sturdy father, "But it shouldn't be more than another six hours walking." The going was stony and there was no question of continuing once the heat of the day got going. Northern Spain, although not distant from Atlantic winds, was in part a barren expanse where once only travellers came through the necessities of trade, but which now saw an increasing number of pilgrims making their slow progress of supplication from Cities as far away as Rome, Paris, Le Puy and Canterbury on route to the shrine at Santiago de Compostela. Shade at midday was vital, plus an adequate supply of water. Fortunately the family had sufficient, carried in a scrip made from a hollow gourd attached to their wooden staffs.

Ebbo at only sixteen years old had been slightly malformed since birth and walked with a pronounced limp. An only child, after the deaths soon after birth of two elder siblings, his head was smaller than might be expected for a lad of his age and still his chin bore only the faintest sign of fluff. Long legged and fleshy though he was, his legs had to support a peculiarly wide mid-riff over which he wore a loose semi-skirt-semi kilt. Naturally devout from childhood he had entered into the idea of making a pilgrimage with enthusiasm even though at this time his unworldly Frankish parents had scarcely a notion of the difficulties involved and were singularly unprepared for making what was a 2,000 kilometre journey. The boy had always been inspired by stories recounted by the local priest of the mighty deeds of St James. Known as St. Iago in Spain, he had performed miracles helping Christians to rid Spain of its Moorish rulers. More than once the priest had said that the Saint had appeared from the sky and single handedly slaughtered the Moorish warriors in battle. No wonder he had become the patron Saint of Spain and nick-named *Matamoros,* the Moor Slayer, for his ability. His fame spread far and wide to France as St. Jacques, Italy as St Jacomo and Germany as St. Jakobus. During their journey Ebbo prayed so devoutly to the blessed Saint each time a hazard struck their path that his parents Lucus and Marta came to believe that their child had semi Saintly virtues himself. They had suffered robbers, witnessed ferrymen turning out to be murderers and become ill with occasional spells of near starvation. They walked for days on end seeing only the rarest of fellow travellers some of whom were delinquents and even some in chains being punished as villains for the act of stealing an indulgence or other such like offence. It was an accepted practice for rich men to pay a poor man 'an indulgence' to make the pilgrimage on his behalf and thus make peace with his maker whilst staying at home and making more money for himself. Indeed there were semi professional pilgrims, who made a living from such activity on behalf of the wealthier but lazier Christians. Once they had to ford a river with their meagre possessions held high above their heads only to be tripped as they stumbled on hidden boulders on the river bed. Fever had caught the two parents as a result of walking in the wet without resource to dry clothing. Appalling attacks of muscle strain had twice laid Lucus immobile for a week with rest being the only sure remedy. It was Marta, with a higher female pain threshold, who displayed amazing fortitude and in her quiet way she provided inspiration for both her son and husband, who unlike the practice of the time treated her with both love and respect.

It was dark as they eventually reached the walls of Santo Domingo de La Calzada, which made the search for a monastery difficult. On finding it they quickly found that, instead of receiving the welcome shelter they expected, they only got a terse and gruff rebuff from a less than friendly monk, telling them they were far too late and anyway there was no room.

"Help us please oh Holy One." pleaded Ebbo's father. The boy meanwhile, having dropped to his knees, was imploring St. Christopher, the traveller's Saint, to aid them in finding rest and food. Begrudgingly the shaven monk indicated that if they retraced their steps a few hundred metres they would find an albergo of poor standing where for a small sum of money they might find primitive lodging. Thus, after eight hours of weary trudge following the route of crude shell-like signals seemingly randomly placed, they arrived at the closed door of a farmhouse with a dimly glowing lamplight above its portal.

Knocking on the door brought no response and it wasn't until Lucus went round the back of the tumbledown building that he found the landlord José in the act of drawing water from an open well. Without a smile the grubby man agreed to take the three pilgrims, but only if they paid in advance for the squalid and primitive excuse for accommodation he could offer. Even for a bowl of water he demanded an exorbitant price and this was insufficient for them to wash off the accumulation of filth, sweat and grime, which had stuck to their weary bodies throughout the day. Explaining that they were on their way to Santiago a small glimmer of welcome made them feel a little better and after they had refreshed themselves with a paid for jug of Rioja Tinto the world didn't seem to be such a bad place after all.

The little threesome had found the transition from Germany and France into Spain a hard one to cope with. Firstly the language was alien to them, secondly after what they were used to the food was basic and poor, but maybe worst of all the hours of eating were impossible. The hardest to cope with was the evening meal taken as late as nine o'clock at night when   the hardy pilgrims had been flogging their way westward for the previous fourteen hours. José and his wife made no concessions to the pilgrims despite their state of weariness. Instead he plied them with further jugs of wine so as to short change them on the meagre supper he was offering. The soup was thin, almost no more than coloured water, soaked up by generous slabs of yesterday's bread. An apology for meat lay greasily on a pottery platter, tasteless, leather-like and of unknown origin.

Portrella served at table, and wearing a simple button fronted cotton blouse, she appeared as wholesome and becoming as her loathsome father José was unpleasantly odorous and unkempt. With long leg of mutton sleeves and only the loosest of button fronting, her obvious physical charms were clearly evident to the pilgrims and other company in the albergo. Throughout the evening Portrella was naturally coquettish as she brushed her way behind Ebbo's wooden bench. On more than one occasion whilst serving at table she felt strangely aroused as her mind had involuntarily returned to the donkey spectacle she had witnessed in the market that morning. With Ebbo the only male present anywhere near her age her choice was limited, but she was more than surprised to notice a manful swelling beneath his casually draped cloth after she had made suggestive eye contact with him several times.

As an escape from the squalor, filth and stench of their surroundings, the pilgrims and other guests in the albergo drank deeply and soon became well and truly boozed. So much so that many amongst them were half asleep and collapsed comatose at the table without having sung the heart lifting songs beloved of hopeful travellers. This seedy state of affairs did not quite apply to Portrella, who with youth firmly on her side and the memory of that morning's happening in the market, was more than happy to make her feelings known to Ebbo. Having already noticed his physical reaction to her presence, she was determined that she would gain his full attention. Although watery thin and poor in quality, the food did have the advantage of lying light upon the stomach and as a result Ebbo, who in fact had had only one beaker of wine, instead of slumping exhausted over the table was as anxious as ever to celebrate his spirituality and found himself being drawn unstoppably to evening prayer. No common language existed between him and Portrella, but the cunning little vixen, sensing Ebbo's wishes saw her opportunity to entice the lad to an enchanting private spot that she knew would please him.

Just metres from the back entrance to the albergo was a diminutive shrine set into a dry stone wall at little more than head height. Lit by the smallest of oil lamps, with wick trimmed low, it faintly illuminated a tiny moonstone figurine of St Iago himself. Clad in the garb of a pilgrim, the Saintly figure wore a rounded hat with an upturned brim at the front, to which was affixed a just visible scallop shell - the symbol of the holy legend surrounding St. James. Using her natural feminine guile but without uttering a single word, Portrella indicated to Ebbo that their devotions could be made together. Ebbo understanding that the time for prayer and supplication was near, without the slightest suspicion, was happily compliant with her entreaties not realising that Portrella's motives were not those of any religious fervour. Quietly, they slipped out together leaving the uncleared remains of the fast congealing and tasteless supper. Holding Ebbo's hand and guided by a dying moon Portrella led the young man to the shrine, where with a gentle tug she brought the spiritual lad to his knees beside her. As the young couple knelt at the shrine it was clear that Ebbo had a great commitment to his Christian beliefs. Noticing his lowered half closed eyes, Portrella couldn't help but lower hers as well, but her thoughts again alarmingly reminded her of the happening in that morning's market. Even with her own eyes tightly closed in attempted prayer, her mind, with a control of its own wandered on to a forbidden subject. After what seemed an age Ebbo ended his prayers to God and St. James and rose awkwardly to his feet. Before turning to walk back to the albergo he felt the warmth of Portrella's body edging closer and closer to him - but this time it was not Ebbo's hand to which she was giving clear guidance. His realisation that in a moment he would be close to committing a mortal sin presented him, for the first time in his life, with an unbearable decision. For three years now he had privately fought this battle with nature, having given himself freely to God and declared that celibacy on the way to priesthood would preclude a form of physical love he would never know.

Without her realising it, let alone understanding why, Portrella's aching heart and body sensed this feeling of rejection. She couldn't understand why she of all young girls in Santo Domingo de la Calzada - the one who attracted more admiring glances than any, she who had so often had to spurn the advances of lecherous men both young and old, had finally found a physical urge for someone and yet was unable to achieve fulfillment. Rejection turned to disappointment and disappointment quickly into anger and resentment. Anger taught her that in itself it could bring no relief except for the ease with which she could absolve herself at her next communion. Revenge, however would bring its own reward and as Ebbo was intending to leave in the coming morning she had little time to act.

Not even drunk, but exhausted from his day's walking and mentally distraught at his obeisance to celibacy he shed a tear, which when seen by Portrella only strengthened her resolve to pay back the wretched fellow for his disinterest. Within minutes the two had parted and Ebbo was asleep amongst the snoring, gurgling pack of sweating humanity stretched out in all manner of careless repose.

CHAPTER FIFTEEN

LISBON

Stanislas had left home at what for him nowadays was an early start. He was dressed smartly, and unusually wearing a suit as he had a couple of meetings in town, one of which was at his bank. The other with a comparatively new contact he had met recently at a local drinks party who had mentioned an investment opportunity in some property development down in the Algarve involving a particular type of holiday complex with golf and tennis - the usual money losing thing he thought, but as he always liked to hear what was going on, he had arranged to meet his contact after he'd sorted out his personal business at the bank. Just after nine thirty he had kissed his wife goodbye and taken the short ten minute walk down to the station at Estefânia to take the train for the quick journey into the centre of Lisbon. He never bothered to drive when he had to go to the city - the trains ran conveniently almost every quarter of an hour and if he took the car, parking was the usual problem common to all big towns. The matters at the bank where he went first were quickly dealt with - there had been a problem when a transfer from his London account had gone astray, and he also had to check some certificates he kept in his safe deposit. Lastly he took the opportunity to pick up his new credit card in exchange for the one that would expire at the end of the month. The manager, who always liked to talk to his international customers tried to keep him for an early drink, but he pleaded another meeting and went on to his friend's office.

Here, he had to sit through a presentation of yet another development he knew would end up well over budget, late and that would be hard to sell. It was difficult for him to feign interest so he was pleased when his friend's secretary finally gave him a folder containing what they had already told him and he was able to say he'd think about it and then leave. He certainly wouldn't be investing in it but politely thanked his friend for asking him and said he'd be in touch. The time was not wasted, he reflected, as unless you kept in touch, real opportunities might be lost. Now, with the rest of his day free he looked at his watch - it was half past noon already. He'd treat himself to lunch he thought at one of his favourite Lisbon restaurants before catching the train home. Walking slowly towards the river side he made his way to the Praça do Comércio idly window shopping and then had an excellent but solitary meal under its arcades at the Martinho da Arcada. Taking his time over the coffee they brought him at the end, he suddenly noticed that for once he had forgotten to switch his mobile back on after reluctantly turning it off when he had been escorted down earlier to the safe deposit at the bank - the clerk had muttered something about the security system being upset by their signals. He tapped in his pin number, his birthday like almost everyone else, and the phone immediately sprang to life. The display informed him that he had had five missed calls. Checking the details straight away, he read that each of these had come from his brother at about ten minute intervals before he had obviously given up trying. "What on earth does he want so urgently," he said to himself as he quickly dialled up the London number. Just three rings and he was talking to his brother's secretary. This time she recognised his voice with a friendly hello, but apologised,

"I'm afraid your brother has left for a business lunch and I don't really expect him back today, although I do know he wants to speak to you. He's in the West End, but he said he'd probably go straight home afterwards - there's a twenty four hour go-slow on the trains here and he didn't want to get stuck in heavy traffic this evening. Can I help?" Stanislas felt frustrated, but thanked her, saying he'd call his brother at home later, and rang off. At once he was trying his brother's mobile, but got the usual disembodied voice saying the phone might be switched off and inviting him to call later. Had it been other than a recording, the owner of the voice would have learned some quite spectacular swearwords - not all in English. He beckoned over the waiter and asked for his bill, which when it eventually came he paid with his new card. He left the restaurant and walked up the Rua Aurea towards the Rossio station to catch his train home. At the station he saw he had just missed a train so would have a twenty minute wait until the next one. He wandered over to the book-stall, "Ah!" he thought, "that's lucky, the British press has just come in." Since they started printing an edition in Spain and

Brussels some little time ago it had been possible to buy that day's English papers in most parts of Europe on the same day and the stall holder was in the middle of putting the new delivery on the racks. Stanislas took a Daily Telegraph from the pile waiting on the floor, but the seller took it quickly back, counted all of them, and then handed the same paper back to his customer. "I'm glad you do your job properly you silly little man," Stanislas said under his breath. On occasions like this he really wished he could speak better Portuguese to tell all these petty functionaires where to go. Instead he bit his lip. He took the paper and, seeing his train about to go, tucked it in with the property folder and took his seat. It was early afternoon and he had the carriage to himself - sitting by the window he watched the passing outskirts of Lisbon brightly reflecting the late winter sunshine. Putting the file on the seat beside him he unfolded the Telegraph and at once realised why his brother had been ringing him. There, on the front page - not the lead, but nevertheless given a very prominent position and headline, he read the news that a hitherto unknown diamond - purporting to have once been the property of the last Tsar of Russia and valued now for at least twenty million pounds - was to be auctioned in Geneva. The article described it as being 'The property of an English gentleman, who wished to remain anonymous.' Stanislas read and re-read the piece several times - he knew who that was, and in his opinion he was certainly not a gentleman, probably not the rightful owner, and even the English bit was doubtful.

As soon as he got home he went straight into his study without saying hello to his wife and picking up the phone he dialled his brother's number. He slammed the receiver down when there was no reply after ten rings. His wife, hearing the house door shut and then the phone bang, came in from the terrace where she had been reading. Pleased her husband had come home early she smiled. "How was it today, dear?" she asked giving him a kiss, "did you get everything done you wanted to?" She had never been absolutely sure about her husband's business interests. Years of training in the City had made him always play things very close to his chest and he rarely discussed anything about his affairs with his wife and she knew better than to ask any questions. "Yes, but something's cropped up and I need to speak to Anatole very quickly - he's not answering his phone, damn him."

"Well he called you three times and I told him to get you on your mobile, didn't he ring? He does want to speak to you - don't worry, darling, he'll ring back later."

"He's taking long enough." Stanislas was never noted for his patience and he was beginning to feel very frustrated. Natasha knew that when he was in one of these moods the best thing to do was just go along with him.

"Go and sit on the terrace and relax - he'll ring - do the crossword or something - it's too nice a day to get all hot and bothered" she said, "I'll bring you a cup of tea, I've managed to get some of your favourite Earl Grey."

Stanislas had just sat down close inside the French windows of the terrace when the phone sounded. He broke all records getting to it! "Hello, hello," he said, "Anatole?" "Yes it's me, Stanislas, have you seen any paper today or heard the BBC news? There's quite a story come out."

"Yes, I've got the Telegraph here and read all about it. I haven't heard the radio yet. It has to be bloody Peter Varlov selling that diamond father always told us about - his story was obviously true - it can't be anything else - it's got to be that. Now we know how he paid the two and half long ones to Lloyd's - he's used it as security for a loan obviously - God, the bastard must be feeling pleased with himself - well over my dead body will he get away with it. We've got to stop him Anatole, we've really got to think."

His brother was more rational. "Look, brother, there's nothing you can do - he's paid his losses, it's him that's got possession of the damn diamond - what can we do about it, nothing? Just calm down"

"I'm not going to fucking calm down - just you wait, Anatole - I'll come up with something - let me think - I'll ring you tomorrow. You want to get even with him as much as I do, don't you?"

"Well only because of what father always told us - I don't have the personal feud you do with the man." They both put down the phone at the same time. Natasha, out of earshot from the phone, called from the terrace, "Hurry up, Stanislas, I've poured you another cup of tea - how was Anatole?"

"Coming in a moment," her husband said as he picked up the phone again and dialled 095 for Moscow. His adrenalin was flowing and he wasn't going to stop now for a cup of tea.

He was lucky, despite it being eight thirty in Moscow, Stanislas found his friend still in his office. He remembered that Boris had always complained about having to work late, because most of his clients were in Western Europe, and thus three hours behind him. This time, unlike his brother's office, there was no secretary for him to get by - just a direct number straight through to his friend's desk. "Dobry vecher," came the reply. Although practically all the business done in Moscow was in English - usually spoken with some form of American accent - Boris liked to answer the phone in Russian just to make the point that he had picked up a bit of the language in the four years he had been managing the broker's branch office there. As soon as he heard Stanislas say good evening back he reverted to English. He knew that his old client spoke fluent Russian - something Stanislas owed to the good sense of his father insisting on speaking it to his two sons when they were children - and didn't want his own inadequacy shown up. Boris Zaneska, although of Russian origins, had been born in Oxford in 1953, where his emigré father was, at the time, a consultant urologist at the Radcliffe Infirmary. His mother, who was Hungarian by birth, had ceased practising as a doctor after the birth of Boris - her second son, His older brother had followed both parents into the medical world, but he was tempted at an early age by the promise of big City money away from any academic career. Working for a firm of stock brokers in London after university, he was offered the chance to build up a Moscow office for them when they joined the general business rush there after the fall of the Iron Curtain. It was an exciting time to be in Moscow and Boris enjoyed it - he was soon accepted as one of the leading players in the new financial business world that was fast developing there. He had met the older Stanislas when he had come to Moscow for a series of company presentations, which had been organised by the broker's London office. Stanislas had personally managed his clients' funds, which were earmarked for the newly emerging markets and, at the time of that first seminar, the whole Russian business had a new frontier pioneering feel about it. There weren't so many experts, and their mutual interest seemed to create a natural bond of friendship between them. Boris had warmed at once to the older mysterious and slightly forbidding fund manager, with his authoritative air, and they had enjoyed a close and mutually rewarding professional relationship broken only by Stanislas's retirement.

"Boris," Stanislas began, "I'm sorry I'm not ringing up with any orders, but perhaps you've seen an interesting item in the British press today?" He knew that the broker would have quickly read through the electronic editions of the papers that morning so he'd always be in an equal position with his clients to discuss any newsworthy matters, and continued, "has there been anything in the local news about a diamond sale - anything about something belonging to the old Tsar?"

"Well trust you Stanislas - I can see you're just as much on the ball as you ever were. It's been in all the local papers - at least all the ones I can read - and I gather the item led the lunchtime news bulletins on television as well. St. Petersburg, apparently, is already demanding its return to the Hermitage," he stopped to cough, "sorry, but why are you calling - its not you that's selling it is it? We could have fun in the market with that sort of money to play with - do I get the commission? God knows we need it at the moment." Stanislas kept his voice casual, "I can see you're still a typical broker - no of course it's not me - I wish it was, but I was just interested to hear what the reaction was. You know me - always keen to know what's going on" Stanislas thought he had said enough for the time being, - perhaps too much, he didn't want Boris to start speculating all sorts of things. He needed to think, but already a plan was beginning to form in his head. He had always been noted for acting quickly and on his own. "Well I'd better go now - you'll be late for your first drink if I keep you any longer - have a good evening and I'll probably ring you soon again if I may."

"OK, of course - any time - it's always good to hear from you - have a good evening."

"Oh, by the way, just one other thing before you go," Stanislas managed to catch him before he put the phone down, "do you still see that drinking friend you thought worked for the FSB? The tall chap with the jet black hair and a fading facial scar - do you remember who I mean?"

"Yes - Igor - he's still around." Boris answered before again saying goodbye and this time ringing off. Strange he thought to himself afterwards, why his caller would suddenly be interested in someone who worked for the Federal Security Bureau - knowing

Stanislas had always been interesting. 'Nothing was ever straight forward with Stan' he said to himself.

After he had replaced the phone, Stanislas went out to the terrace where his wife was waiting. She could tell he was very pre-occupied and always knew better than to try and make conversation when he was in one of those sort of moods. She understood her husband well and the fact that their marriage was such a happy one was due, in no small measure, to this understanding and to her good sense not to ask unnecessary questions. She trusted him - that was all that mattered to her and he loved her in return. He sat down and sipped his iced tea thoughtfully. After a little while he looked at his watch, but saw it was now too late to get any one in their office. He went back to the Telegraph and, trying to concentrate, started the crossword. His ideas were beginning to make sense, but he needed to get hold of the brochure advertising the proposed sale of the diamond in order to have the exact details. He had no doubt whatsoever that it was the one both his grandfather and father had spoken so much about and, equally from their indoctrination, also no doubt that Peter Varlov should certainly have no right to dispose of it especially for his own benefit. He had been very cross when his brother had confirmed that Varlov had somehow escaped the bankruptcy proceedings brought by Lloyd's, but now he had been given perhaps a second chance to carry out what he regarded as one of his grandfather's dying wishes to humiliate the Varlov family. Just as important to him, he now had a chance to get his revenge on Varlov for the wrong he could never forget the man had done him personally in the City all those years ago. His thinking was interrupted when their dinner guests arrived - another ex-pat couple living in the village, that they had owed hospitality to for sometime - and for the next two and half hours his mind was taken off the subject by the usual drivel of polite dinner party conversation.

Lying in bed later, listening to the regular comfortable breathing coming from the other side of the bed, Stanislas himself couldn't get to sleep. The whole business about the diamond kept going round in his head, but the more he thought about it, the more he became certain of his plan of action - he was too excited to sleep. During his whole business career he'd earned a fully justified reputation for complete ruthlessness, stopping at absolutely nothing when it came to beating any competitor or pursuing any deal. Now, he thought before eventually falling into a pre-dawn fitful sleep, he would prove that reputation hadn't stopped with his retirement. He got up the next morning just after his wife and went downstairs to the kitchen for breakfast - the maid, a young girl from the other end of the village, who came over on her bicycle five days a week, was there already busy clearing up the debris from last night's dinner. Natasha gave him a tray she had already prepared for him and he carried his coffee, orange juice and toast out to the terrace. He impatiently looked at his watch and at ten o'clock went into his small study just off the much larger sitting room, switched on his computer and went onto the web site of the main international auction house in Geneva. Flicking through the contact and other routine details he got quickly to the page he wanted. There together on his screen, with the time and date of its sale, was a life size colour illustration of the Tsar's diamond together with all the relevant details such as measurements, weight etc. The details on the next page gave viewing arrangements ahead of the sale and listed the information that any potential buyers would need to provide to prove their seriousness and standing. He printed off two copies of it all and put them in a lockable file in his desk draw. Afterwards he picked up the phone and called Air Portugal at Lisbon Airport. They were unable to help him, but gave him the number of the Lufthansa office which, with typical German efficiency, had answered at once. He made his booking and the girl confirmed it back to him, "You leave here Sir, next Tuesday business class on the 06.30 flight to Munich, a fifty minute stopover and you arrive at Moscow at 16.10 local time, your return is the following Friday coming back through Frankfurt. What about your visa sir?"

"Oh! Damn I'd forgotten that!"

"Don't worry, that's not a problem, we can fix one of the new 72 hour stay visas for you - it'll be waiting for you when you land at Sheramatyevo. Just fax me a copy of your hotel confirmation of your booking and we'll arrange it - I'm afraid it'll cost the equivalent of thirty five dollars on your ticket - there's no way of avoiding that." Stanislas thanked the girl for her help, but before he put the phone down she said, "One last detail for the Visa - you don't have an American passport by chance do you?"

"No, British."

"OK, that's good - no problem then, I'm waiting for the hotel

letter then all's in order Sir. - Thank you for flying Lufthansa."
Stanislas got an unusually quick reply from the Hotel National for
his request for a room for the three nights - he had insisted on a
room in the old wing because, although they were smaller, he liked
their spectacular views over Red Square. Built in 1903 the hotel had
survived the revolution and now there was even a guide to its
impressive collection of antiques, which had been saved from
destruction.   He had enjoyed staying there before and looked
forward to doing so again. He waited half an hour and then called
Boris, who answered this time in English! "Boris, sorry to call you
so soon again, but a bit of private business has cropped up and I
have to come to Moscow for a flying visit next week for three days,
you'll be around I hope?" The broker smiled to himself - he wasn't at
all surprised at the news - after Stanislas's mysterious enquiry at the
end of the previous evening's call he had sub-consciously been
waiting for this one.   "Where are you staying?" he
asked.

"Oh, at the National - they're arranging a car to pick me up at
the airport - I arrive just after four o'clock. I'd like to see you for a
drink Tuesday evening, let's meet at the bar there - say about seven
OK?" Boris pretended to look at his diary before confirming the
rendezvous - he was intrigued and looked forward to hearing what
his old client was up to. Seconds later he was even more intrigued
when Stanislas casually added, almost as an afterthought, "Oh, just
one more thing - if your drinking friend from the FSB, what did you
say his name was - Igor? - is around, it'd be good to see him again
too."

"I'll see what I can arrange - until Tuesday then, I look forward
to seeing you, bye and have a good flight." That night it was a
puzzled Boris who had the difficulty getting to sleep. Stanislas was
looking forward to the action and to setting his plan in motion. With
his arrangements made he would sleep well. Before going out to the
garden he printed off the hotel confirmation and faxed it to the
airline. Natasha was returning to the house from the bottom of the
garden carrying a rake she had been using to clear some old pruning
clippings. She smiled at her husband, who she instinctively saw was
more relaxed than earlier that morning. "Darling come and sit down
and I'll fetch you a coffee," she said, "sometimes I think you forget
you're retired - you're never off the phone. You really should relax

more." Stanislas looked at her and smiled. He felt a small twinge of guilt as he said, "Natasha, something has come up - a rather good investment opportunity in fact. Do you remember that Boris Zaneska who lives in Moscow?"

"The one who had that tall willowy blonde girlfriend, who almost ate him at dinner - how could I forget?"

"Yes that's the one - he's invited me to see him next week - he's got a really interesting proposition about oil in Siberia." I'm flying to Moscow on Tuesday and I'll be back Friday late evening. I'll only be away three days, but I'm afraid you'll have to cancel those tennis people coming for drinks Thursday - make it the week after. I really am sorry but it's a wonderful chance. Can't be helped I'm afraid."

"Are you sure you really have   to go? - I get bored being here alone - it's not much fun without you - Darling - I do miss you."

"Yes, I have to, but I'll be back very quickly" said Stanislas firmly and Natasha knew the conversation had ended.

Stanislas spent a busy weekend - he called Boris again just to confirm that his Russian contact would be able to make the Tuesday evening drink, but he waited until his wife was out visiting her hairdresser - she went regularly every month - before he called his brother in England.

"Anatole, just to tell you I'm off to Moscow on Tuesday - only for three days - but before I go there's something I'd like to talk about with our friendly agent. I normally only ring him at his office, you don't have his home number by chance do you?" Anatole knew at once who his brother wanted to speak to. Over the years they had got used to talking to each other in riddles - a profitable habit they had got into when Stanislas had been working in corporate finance at the Merchant bank - and now it was almost second nature. Both brothers had used this man for various projects that perhaps were better kept out of the usual channels - it was useful that certain matters could not be traced in the normal way.   In any case Stanislas never trusted the privacy of the public telephone system. After he put the phone down from his second call he treated himself to a large whisky - everything, he thought, was falling nicely into place and the old friend he called in London could not have been more willing to help, what was even luckier, with his wonderful contacts on the continent, he was also in an excellent position to do so. He had left no doubt that when the time came he could arrange everything and told his old friend not to worry. Stanislas felt relieved, but nevertheless it had been necessary to stress the need for complete secrecy to the man - he knew from the past that some people occasionally liked to impress others by claiming to know more than they did, but he thought that he had used just the right mixture of threat and promise to make it clear what any lapse in security would involve. That had tied up the end of the operation, he thought - now he just had to wait till he got to Moscow to get the whole thing in motion. He had covered all eventualities as far as he could see and as far as he was able.

He was therefore in a very good mood by the time Natasha returned home and she was pleasantly surprised when he took her down to one of their regular restaurants where they both enjoyed the house speciality - Javali - deliciously prepared wild boar. Monday evening Natasha packed him a small overnight case, - she always did his cases - he was only to be away three nights and he remembered the lengthy wait in the baggage hall on his last arrival at Sheremetevo airport, so was determined to take only hand luggage with him this time. As he knew, basically Moscow has only two seasons - winter and summer - but Stanislas gambled that by the end of March he could leave his really thick stuff behind and thus avoid having a large heavy suitcase. They had a traffic free trip when a sleepy Natasha dropped him off at five o'clock the next morning at the airport and he made his way to the Lufthansa check in desk. He could see the Airbus waiting to return to Munich on the first leg of his trip having arrived the evening before from Frankfurt. The plane was only a third full when it climbed out of Lisbon and headed North-East some fifteen minutes after its scheduled six-thirty time. Stanislas's attempt to sleep was frustrated by the stewardess bringing him a breakfast tray - to kill the time he ate the lot. Some hours later, after his change of plane, he looked out of the window and he could see the forests of fir trees below - they were apparently starting their descent into Moscow and, looking at his watch, he saw they would only be about twenty minutes late. The wait in Munich - an advertised fifty minutes had turned into one of ninety so they had caught up some of the lost time at least. He filled up the two copies of the currency forms in readiness for the Russian customs and watched the pine forests come closer. He was lucky - his visa had been waiting for him in Terminal 2 and not having to wait for his baggage to be off-loaded, he managed to get through immigration in just under forty minutes - almost a record he thought. For his last visit it had taken two hours. He saw a large white placard with his name on and underneath he read his name repeated in Cyrillic scrip. Underneath it all was an expressionless driver looking very bored. The driver became marginally more animated when he realised his passenger spoke Russian and they discussed the recent match between CSKA Moscow and Sporting Lisbon before pulling up in front of the hotel. Taking his case and tipping the driver five dollars he went inside. It was six o'clock, he would register and then have time for a leisurely shower before Boris was coming for a drink at seven-thirty. From his room he looked over towards Red Square - the 400 metre long cobbled space that had seen so much of Russian history through the ages. Looking down at the traffic in the Okhotny ryad he thought how rapid the change had been since his last visit just before the re-election of Yeltsin in 1996 - Moscow was now a bustling modern city. He unpacked the few contents of his case, took out a beer from the mini-fridge and prepared for his shower. He was starting to feel excited - he hoped that in the next three days his plans could be finalised. It was just after half past seven when the phone rang and the desk porter announced the arrival of his guest - he took the lift down into the bar where the women sitting at the far end looked up expectedly at his entrance. He saw Boris sitting alone at a corner table and ignoring their glances went straight over to him. "How are you my old friend?" Stanislas took the seat opposite, "it's good to see you. My God, a lot has changed since we last met - you almost have a regulated market now."

"Yes a lot of the fun has gone, but you can certainly sleep better at night now. How was your flight? Things seem better organised at the airport now - did you have any trouble coming in this afternoon?"

"No - just a bit of a queue to get the rubber stamp that's all, no, no real bother." They ordered two glasses of champagne.

"I see some things haven't changed," said Stanislas, looking at one of the three smartly dressed girls who was still smiling at him from her stool by the bar.

"No, some things stay the same," laughed Boris. "They still catch some poor fools, the other week a young American banker lost all his credit cards when he'd thought he was onto a winner - I don't know what they put in his drink, but he had an almighty headache the next day besides some awkward explaining to do to his head office." Their small talk went on for twenty odd minutes before Stanislas asked,

"Did you manage to get hold of your friend? I'd like to meet him again - I half wondered whether you'd bring him this evening." Boris had been waiting for this question and looked quizzically at him before replying,

"Igor? Yes I saw him Friday and he said he'd try and come this evening - you know the Russians, not very reliable and they're always late anyway – let's give him another half hour. They saw him, his open raincoat revealing a dark well cut suit, enter the bar eighteen minutes later and Boris waved, getting up to greet him as he approached their table. He re-introduced Stanislas, who Igor said he remembered meeting before, asking in English,

"Champagne or would you rather have a Vodka?"

"Vodka please," Igor replied in perfect English, before repeating to Stanislas that it was good to see him again - in Russian. Normal small talk continued in a mixture of both languages, as they finished their drinks - Igor, more voluble than a normal Muscovite Stanislas thought, was talking enthusiastically about the upturn in the Russian economy and the increasing stability that he saw as a result of the Putin presidency. He was clearly a fan of his old KGB colleague, he mentioned twice that he was originally from St. Petersburg so had an additional affinity with him. However, his manner betrayed the fact that he had obviously spent considerable time in Western Europe and that many of its ways had rubbed off on him. Boris confirmed Igor's view of the improvement and the pace of change in Moscow, which had over the last few years taken on all the similarities of any other major European city - indeed, had fast become one of the more expensive ones in which to live. As he proposed another round of drinks, Stanislas turned to call the barman, but Boris interrupted,

"Actually if you don't mind Stanislas, I've got to meet up with some other visitors staying at the Metropol so I'll have to leave you. Perhaps we could meet up later or lunch tomorrow? Tell you what, here's my mobile number - I'll wait for your call."

"OK - thanks Boris, I'll ring you later." That worked perfectly thought Stanislas - exactly as he had asked Boris before the arrival of the Russian to do - so that he would be left alone with Igor. Stanislas thought that the broker had appeared completely natural, but the ex-KGB agent wasn't fooled and dropping any pretence asked directly,

"I believe you want my help - I have limited time so lets get down to business." Looking around him, Stanislas said, "Can we talk here or should we go to my room?" The bar was almost empty - the women who earlier had been looking for an escort for the evening had either found someone or given up and gone to search elsewhere. There were only two other drinkers sharing a table the other end. "No, we can talk here," Igor smiled, "the days of bugs in light bulbs or under tables have gone. Don't worry, I know - I was one of the people who used to put them there!"

"I realise that" began Stanislas I have a very interesting proposition that would suit a couple of your old operatives. It'll be a very profitable business and a chance that I'm sure a patriotic Russian would jump at." The silence seemed longer than its fifteen seconds before Igor spoke,

"If I'm to help you - and, depending slightly on the details, I think I know just the couple who would be good - you'll have to level with me and tell me the whole project - you'll have to trust me."

"I understand that," Stanislas answered, "but on my side I insist on meeting your two contacts first and then we'll go through the plans together - after all, your experience and advice shouldn't come for nothing, should it my friend?" Igor took the bait,

"Give me until ten o'clock tomorrow morning - I'll fix a meeting and ring you with the details." The Russian got up to leave - his handshake left Stanislas's fingers feeling bruised. So far, so good he thought as he went up to his room to let Natasha know he had arrived safely. He watched the mid-evening news before walking past the Bolshoi and joining Boris at the Metropol as arranged. He liked Moscow and still in a strong way he felt proud of his Russian background despite all his life having been lived in the West.

The next morning Stanislas had breakfasted downstairs, but was back in his room when the phone rang at exactly ten o'clock. He picked it up and immediately recognised Igor's voice, without any preliminaries he said,

"All is arranged - we have a meeting at two-thirty this afternoon. Come to the entrance of the Kitai Gorod metro on Lubyansy proezd and I'll pick you up there. We can meet in a nearby bar where it is quite safe to talk."

"OK - that's clear, I've got that. We'll see each other then, bye." The phone had gone dead before Stanislas had finished his sentence. He looked at the map provided by the hotel - going by the underground would mean a change, but he calculated it was just over a kilometre in actual distance, he looked out of the window, the weather was sunny, so he would walk. His watch told him he had some four hours to waste - he went downstairs and out of the hotel. He used the subway to cross the road and, ignoring the souvenir sellers, entered Red Square through the restored Resurrection Gate. He remembered how impressed he was by the gate last time because although it looked as if it had been there for centuries this one was, in fact, only built in 1995 as an exact replica of the 1680 original destroyed by Stalin in 1931. If his father could see Russia now he thought, My God, he'd be happy. Turning left in the square he went into GUM - the old State Department store now transformed and full of attractive well stocked shops and busy shoppers. He walked through the store to the other end and out into the square again. To his disappointment St. Basil's Cathedral was closed - not opening until after lunch so wandering back past the tomb of Lenin he returned through the gateway and went into the adjacent shopping mall and had a coffee at a bar before crossing back to the hotel. He had an early lunch - just a glass of beer and a club sandwich in his room and left just before two o'clock. Walking to his rendezvous he passed the infamous Lubyanka Prison - an intimidating grey building no longer fulfilling its original function, but still the headquarters of the security services. Crossing the square in front, he turned right and arrived at the entrance to Kitai Gorod metro. He was five minutes early.

Just as he heard a nearby clock strike the half hour Igor was beside him as if from nowhere. He gave his fingers more punishment by again shaking hands with him and Igor led him into a bar some fifty metres away. They took a table to the side of the entrance and as Stanislas looked at his surroundings he saw that the place was more or less empty. A couple came in - looked straight at their table - and came and occupied the two spare chairs. Igor introduced them as Eric Nikolaevich and Liza Borisovna. The girl spoke first, "ochen'priyatna," she said smiling at Stanislas. "Very pleased to meet you too," he replied repeating her. She was younger than the man, well dressed with shoulder length blonde hair and thin attractive very long legs. Although her tight mouth gave her features rather a hard expression, her deep brown eyes held a certain sparkle of sexual promise, which her smile emphasised. She was perhaps about thirty two or three and very appealing he thought. The man was in his middle forties, good looking and again well dressed and looking like a reasonably successful middle manager in a bank. They sat down and Stanislas noticing their hands touch got the distinct impression that they were more than just business partners. Not wasting any time on small talk, Igor immediately turned to the man, "Our friend here from Lisbon has a business proposition he would like to put to us." Then turning to Stanislas,

"These two are both operatives and colleagues of mine from the old times - I can vouch for their efficiency, loyalty and experience. For so many of us life has changed since all the reforms, not always for the better, and some of us now - how shall I put it - enjoy carrying out freelance missions, so tell us what you have in mind." Stanislas drew a deep breath and began,

"Well Igor, I met you yesterday and Liza and Eric just now. What I'm going to tell you is very confidential. I hope I can rely on you, but I have no alternative but to put my trust in you. Boris, an old friend, tells me I can - I hope he's right." The three Russians gave their assurance at once.

"I expect you've heard that at around the end of May there is a hitherto unknown diamond - said to be worth more than twenty million pounds - being auctioned in Geneva." All three nodded. "It's said to come from the collection owned by the last Tsar and apparently taken to the west before your revolution and the Royal family were murdered - sorry killed. The present owner - the seller - has not been disclosed, but I know who it is and, let me assure you, it is someone who really has no right to it at all. I therefore have a plan to steal that diamond with your help - it is, as you will have read extremely valuable and I head a syndicate - largely based in Western Europe, who mean to profit from it. You will be dealing solely with me so you do not need to know who they are nor do they need to know you. I stress I will be your only contact. Now some details. I fortunately have the resources to get a perfect replica of the stone made - certainly good enough to fool people before the sale. If you accept - and I'm sure with the sort of value that stone has both intrinsically and because of its provenance you'll not be disappointed financially - you'll be responsible for exchanging these two stones - the false for the real - in Geneva just before the sale and bringing the real one to me in Lisbon. As I plan it that will be the end of your involvement and that is when you will be paid off." Eric was the first to speak.

"How are you going to cash in - it'll be impossible to sell the diamond after any robbery?"

"That, with respect, is purely my affair, but what I will tell you is that the people who are going to make the fake are also experts on the cutting, processing and marketing of shall we say unofficial rare stones and that while any further cutting of this jewel, should that be necessary, the figure will still be enormous." Eric's eyes fixed on Stanislas,

"If my partner and I were to accept your mission we would not be interested in waiting for our money and all that cutting and marketing you talk about would take time - I'm afraid that just wouldn't interest us - How about you Igor?" Across the table Stanislas could see both Igor and Liza nodding. He took his second deep breath of the meeting,

"That is no problem, I propose a fee of one hundred thousand pounds each for the three of you if you accept and a further half million pounds, to be split between you in whatever proportion you decide, on a successful result. Of course all your out of pocket expenses will be looked after during the operation as well." There was quiet for some time, everyone was looking at the other.

"My friend" Igor broke the silence, "would you mind letting us talk for a moment? There's a news stand by the metro station - perhaps you want to go to buy a paper?" Stanislas left them alone. Going out of the restaurant he was suddenly worried - he had just told them what his plan was, they were all former KGB or at least security officers – they certainly did not know him. Their loyalties may still be with the authorities, what if they should just turn him in? He'd been a fool to say so much - he was tempted just to go, but he couldn't back down now, When he took his courage in both hands and returned a quarter of an hour later he was beginning to sweat. They were still there and when Igor started to speak he realised with some relief he'd had no cause to worry. Straight to the point he began,

"We are agreed, the three of us, Eric and Liza will do it with my back up assistance, but only for double your suggested fee." It was nearly six o'clock before they settled on one hundred and fifty thousand each up front and three quarters of a million once the diamond was safely in Lisbon.

"One last point," Eric said, "If it all goes to plan that's all well and good, but what happens if something goes wrong and we get caught somehow ? I'm used to putting people in prison - not going there myself." Stanislas had half expected this question and now he was pleased he had spoken to his old friend before he had flown here.

"Don't worry," he replied, "that has been taken care of - I don't think there's any prison that will be able to hold you. I've got to trust you to get the diamond - you've go to trust me for that." They shook hands, agreed that Igor would meet Stanislas at his hotel the next day at noon, and left. By the time Stanislas had paid the bar bill and reached the street they were nowhere to be seen.

Stanislas woke up in good time - after his successful meeting with Igor and his colleagues the previous day. He had enjoyed dinner later that evening in a new restaurant near the Bolshoi where Boris had insisted on taking him, but now felt happy that he had refused the suggestion to go on to a nightclub afterwards. He was pleased that yesterday's meeting with Igor and his colleagues had gone so well and thanked Boris for arranging things, without disclosing any reason for asking him to do this. Boris knew his old friend well enough not to ask, but couldn't help wondering what it was all about. Having already packed his small case he waited with some impatience for the promised call so that the necessary arrangements could all be fixed up before his return flight to Lisbon at the end of the afternoon. He looked at his ticket and reckoned that if the departure formalities at the airport were still longer than the arrival ones, as they were on his previous visits, he'd have to be checking in about two hours before his five-twenty departure time to be safe. It was fifteen minutes later when the phone rang and Igor suggested meeting for a drink at midday in the hotel bar. Stanislas took his case downstairs and, leaving it with the concierge, he killed time by taking a walk across to the Alexandrovsky Gardens. He was back in the hotel in good time and having settled his bill and arranged a car for the airport later, sat down in the bar to wait for Igor. It was just three minutes past noon when he was joined by Igor and Eric with Liza following almost immediately. After they had greeted each other in Russian and ordered four beers they reverted to English. Igor briefly re-stated the arrangements - laying not only the emphasis on the financial ones, but also on the bank arrangements Stanislas had mentioned yesterday to protect his two protégés. They were obviously an established team. Although they had agreed the day before, Igor insisted that they all shook hands on these again.

"Do you want anything in writing?" Stanislas queried, "I'm not sure that would be a good thing - would it?"

"Most certainly not," Igor and Eric replied, more or less in unison and equally firmly. Igor continued, "I think we all realise what would be involved if things went wrong - for me, your handshake is enough."

"Yes," replied Stanislas and as their eyes fixed each other, the hidden message that each conveyed to the other left no doubt of that in any of their minds. Taking a mouthful of beer, Stanislas started, "As I said I am arranging a copy - a good copy - of this diamond to be made and I plan to have it well before the original will be available for inspection in Geneva by potential buyers. I will bring this to Paris and you, Eric, are to meet me there when I'll give it to you. This should be about ten days before the sale, but we'll fix the exact date and time later. I will be staying at the Meurice - do you know it, rue de Rivoli - that's my usual place?"

"Yes - I know it - for a short time I was in our Embassy in Paris and various visiting government delegations used to stay there in the old days - the two entrances were sometimes useful !" Eric's smile did not reach his eyes and again Stanislas thought he'd rather have him as a friend than an enemy.

"OK, then," he carried on, "once you have the copy the whole operation is in your hands, although I want to be kept in touch as you proceed. You will have to invent some pretext to view the diamond in Switzerland but that won't be difficult. Anyway, that's entirely your job. Perhaps as a potential Russian buyer from St. Petersburg - I don't know - and while doing that you'll make the swap. I'll ask you now one last time - are you confident you'll be able to do this? Now is your last chance to pull out of the whole thing and then we'll forget we ever met. Think hard all three of you before you answer." Stanislas held his breathe during the silence which followed. It felt longer than its actual twenty five seconds. Having exchanged a long eye contact with Igor and then turning to Liza, Eric finally replied,

"We are very confident and you can leave it all to us. I assure you we'll fulfil our part of the contract, have no fear about that - and we'll expect you to fulfil yours and, provide your fake copy at the standard you say." Stanislas relaxed and assured them of this - he felt fortunate that they didn't know he had yet to arrange this, but already he had a promising idea and all he'd need would be a little luck, as indeed the whole operation would. He managed to contain his excitement as he calmly asked Igor how their future contacts should be made.

"Eric and Liza will be carrying out the actual operation," he replied, "so it's best if you now deal just with Eric direct. I am, of course, always available should you need me, but let's keep things as simple as possible. Here are Eric's numbers - the third one is the phone box near his apartment, which you can tell him to go to if you're scared about security." Eric nodded. "It's easier if you call him back there as he'd need an absolute pile of coins himself to ring you in Lisbon! Don't say anything on the other phones you don't mind being public, I still don't trust them at all. We'll wait to hear from you about the exact date and time and other details for the pick up in Paris - if you decide against doing it in your hotel, the Jardins des Tuileries is just opposite and that should be quite safe. Just let Eric know what you want to do - OK?" They all agreed and as Stanislas stood up to say goodbye they shook hands again. "Have a good flight home tonight and I'll wait for your call," Eric's face once more made an effort to break into a smile as he left with Igor and Liza. Stanislas went to the loo and then returning to the bar ordered himself another beer and a couple of sandwiches as he waited for his airport taxi. After another delay during the stopover, in Frankfurt this time, it was nearly midnight before he climbed into bed beside Natasha - who, although half asleep, woke up enough to show him that she was pleased he was home.

"We'll pack for London tomorrow, darling," she said

afterwards, before turning over and falling back to sleep.

"Oh God! The wedding, I'd completely forgotten about that," thought Stanislas, before he, too fell asleep.

CHAPTER SIXTEEN

LONDON

The bride's costume was both generously and beautifully cut. Cream instead of white, with an abundance of spring flowers in her hair and bouquet, the skirt fell classically straight from her thickening waist and did a magnificent job of concealing a pregnancy some five months old. Marriage hadn't really been in the plans of the couple, who had lived happily together as 'partners' for the previous four years, nor had they even discussed it until a slight hint from her uncle Stanislas that she and her future child might be among the beneficiaries in the trust he was setting up. With almost indelicate haste the couple went hurrying to the Chelsea Town Hall Registry Office to formalise their union. As a favourite niece of the childless couple Stanislas and Natasha Kortaski, she had recently become aware that the terms of his will reflected his old fashioned views and referred only to married nieces and nephews.

The Kortaskis liked to indulge themselves and in past years had spent most of the winter in a rented house amongst the Constantia vineyards near Capetown, where they enjoyed the glorious summer climate of South Africa. This year it was only grudgingly that they had foregone warm sunshine to remain in the comparative cool of the Portuguese winter in their Lisbon home. Worse was to come when unexpectedly Stanislas made his rapid visit to Moscow with the near freezing weather in London. Despite his Russian blood, he was thoroughly disenchanted with the Northern Hemisphere winter. It was snowing when their flight from Lisbon arrived an hour late at Heathrow, but not heavily enough to disrupt the expensive taxi ride to their overseas members' club in Chelsea.

"Wonderfully convenient for tomorrow's wedding isn't it?" commented Natasha as they settled comfortably into their usual suite, excited by being back for a few days in her old London haunts and the prospect of the next day's party.

"Yes, but it's a bore having to cart all this wedding gear

around" her husband replied, hanging his suit up in the cupboard, - "if only we didn't always have to be slaves to tradition. I would far rather just wear an ordinary suit instead of this old penguin outfit, which I can scarcely squeeze into any more - it must be at least twenty five years old and looks it I'm afraid."

"Now you know why I try to get you to diet, darling," Natasha responded.

Less than a hundred family and close friends assembled   in Pavilion Road the next day   following the private King's Road Registry Office ceremony, where in the panelled reception rooms they enjoyed some of the best that London had to offer in terms of wedding catering. Left to themselves the happy couple only wanted a quiet family party and would have certainly banned any speeches. They knew that most of the younger guests were not particularly excited by the occasion, and were initially surprised when they got their invitations. The bride and groom were anxious to slip away just as soon was decent. However, the decision was taken out of their hands as the bride's father, Anatole Kortaski, having invited Sir George Matthews and his wife, found it impossible to say no to the retired banker's insistent offer to say a 'few words.' The cake - hardly a traditional wedding one - was decorated with two skiing figures, slaloming down a mountain, was cut amid the usual ribald remarks from the couple's younger friends. Silencing the general reception babble came the stentorian tones of a scarlet coated toastmaster calling out.

"Your Highness, My Lords, Ladies and Gentlemen pray silence for Sir George Matthews, who will propose the health of the bride and groom." All eyes swivelled in the direction of Matthews, who was wearing an old fashioned, rather Dickensian and tightly fitting morning coat. From his local flower shop he had ordered a single rose button hole to wear, complete with leaf backing and a semi disguised water holder. His hair lay flat against his forehead, greased to keep the wave in order and the front curl from springing into prominence. Across his double breasted waistcoat he wore what he regarded as his trademark - a golden watch chain. He stood there for about thirty seconds relishing the attention before starting to speak. His speech, in fact, was mercifully brief and falsely modest, talking more about himself than the bride, but it had achieved for him the dual satisfaction of listening to his own voice and the sense of pride he gained from telling a captive audience that there was a genuine 'Nobleman' amongst them. The nobleman himself, Prince Peter Varlov, didn't even realise that it was he to whom he had referred.

"Thank God that's over," said Stanislas Kortaski to his younger brother. "George Matthews really must be the most pompous arse this side of Christendom."

"You're right - you're absolutely right, - but you've been travelling quite a lot recently, Lisbon, Moscow then back to Lisbon before coming here, all in a matter of days," answered Anatole, "couldn't get hold of you, so I had no choice but to invite him to speak instead, but I must admit there must be some people here who question why he's even included in the guest list. Against that you mustn't forget that I owe just a little of my success to George. I have never much liked the pretentiousness of the bank he worked for, nor regarded them as very efficient, but I'm bound to admit that using them has perhaps lent my firm a certain cachet in some people's eyes and, on top of that, for about thirty years he has been pretty good at introducing customers from the bank to us as candidates for Lloyd's membership, - extra cannon fodder for us, which I needn't explain to you is what makes our bread and butter."

"Apart from everything else it's his ghastly, over upholstered social climbing wife that I can't stand." sniffed Stanislas. "Look how she preens herself as she wobbles round the room" he said as the target of his distaste tottered by with a dripping glass of champagne in one hand and an overfilled canapé in the other. Her grey afternoon costume looked as though it was about to lose the battle to keep her inside it and it was also clear from the way she walked that her shoes were pinching badly. "What's your arrangement with George then? Do you have any formal sort of agreement?" asked Stanislas.

"What a strange question to ask, why do you want to know?" replied Anatole.

"I'm not at all sure," went on Stanislas, "but I have long had a feeling that Matthews isn't quite all he seems to be and maybe he's not playing it absolutely straight with that shit Peter Varlov. Although personally, I'd be over the moon if Matthews did get one over Varlov, after what the ghastly creep did to me."

"Well, it's not anything too significant, no formal set-up, nothing in writing, but now you come to mention it I suppose the commission we send him each year - to him personally, I would add - has added up to a more than reasonable figure over the years." Said Anatole.

"Maybe Anatole, just maybe, you should drop a hint to George that you might have to finish that arrangement - paying all that commission to him. You could always say that the Financial Services Authority were beginning to lean on any kind of third party being paid commission unless the whole thing was made transparent to all the parties concerned. You'd save yourself a bit too and there is bugger all he can do or say about it - the slightest whisper, remember, to the right quarters in the City would be most embarrassing for him."

Anatole completed his duty round of all the guests, refreshing himself generously with his own champagne and enjoying the small talk. In general he was very proud of his daughter and happy that so many friends of both generations had come at such short notice. What slightly bothered him was the way that his brother Stanislas had started hinting that he should put some kind of pressure on Matthews. After all, Stanislas had never been averse to using all his contacts and to getting inside information. Indeed he had paid a heavy price for it when he got caught out some years back. He quite understood why his brother hated Peter Varlov, but didn't realise he had any quarrel with Matthews. He kept wondering to himself and trying to calculate how many introductions Sir George had put his way over the years. It was certainly well over a dozen with at least one of them being here at the reception - Peter Varlov himself.

Anatole's relations with Peter had become distinctly sticky, almost unpleasant, since his Lloyd's debacle. Today he had been studiously avoiding him, as he always seemed to be hovering close by and it was inevitable that he would have to face him sooner or later. His had been an especially unfortunate case, particularly taking into account the death of his wife, but he was by no means the worst hit sufferer within his agency. He wondered too whether Varlov knew that Matthews - he seemed very friendly with him - had been enjoying a little annual thank you at his expense. One of Anatole's favourite sales ploys when he recruited 'Names' was to tell them in supposed confidence that, 'I never put my Names on a syndicate, old boy that I have not joined myself". That always seemed to go down well and gives them confidence. What he never told them was - although the claim was true - just how small a stake he took in order to substantiate this boast. The fact that Peter Varlov had paid up his nearly £2.5 million losses six weeks ago had come both as a huge relief and an even larger surprise to Anatole. Despite their long acquaintance he had no idea that Peter would have been able to write a cheque for such an amount. No doubt Matthew's bank had put up the cash on his behalf, but then surely they would only do so if they were sure of a repayment and properly secured? They had to be holding that diamond as security. Today was the first time he had seen Varlov since the sad day of Ishbel's funeral back in October and he was certain that she hadn't settled his massive losses.

"How nice to see you Peter. How was Christmas and did you stay at home?" came out the Anatole small talk. "I'm so glad to see you smiling again and I can only say that I think you have amazing courage to cope with what has been thrown at you in the last few months. Let's put all that behind us now and try and get some money back."

"Nice to see you too." replied the rotund, and ever cheerful Varlov, hesitating whether he should own up to his potential good fortune with the diamond and of his determined intention to join with others to sue Lloyd's for damages, which most sensible people were saying was foolhardy. The less said of that possible action the better he thought, that way when it became public it wouldn't already be a stale story. Nevertheless, it was only with considerable self discipline that he managed not to talk about it.

Nothing pleased Matthews more than a bit of flattery, particularly if he had enjoyed a drink or two. Now, surrounded as he was by those he supposed to be the upper end of London society, he found magnanimity easy to dispense.

"My dear Anatole," he said. "What a magnificent little gathering." Thus not forgetting to emphasize the small number of guests. "The bride is positively glowing with happiness and her new husband is indeed a lucky man to be marrying such a lovely woman."

"I must say George," Anatole, annoyed by his condescension, forced himself to reply with some irony. "Your observations are most astute."

"It's so nice to be at a wedding amongst friends like these." went on Matthews, wallowing in his post speech pomposity. "I've just been chatting to Peter Varlov. Poor fellow has suffered terribly at the hands of Lloyd's. Happily I persuaded the bank to help him in the short term, thanks to that diamond, which is now getting so much publicity." Sir George stopped suddenly - he knew at once he'd said too much, but after the effect of the excellent champagne his host had offered, he just could not prevent himself. Astonished by yet another example of Matthew's indiscretion, something he was very familiar with, he managed to keep his silence to see what else the man would reveal. Sure enough, Matthews was unable to resist boasting further that by chance he'd been lunching recently in the City and had enjoyed a most friendly conversation with one of India's famous gem stone moguls. 'Enough of this' thought Anatole, 'it's time to tweak his tail a little.'

"In confidence between us George, I must confess that without your friendship and support my own success might never have happened - I've got a lot to thank you for." Matthews beamed, as Anatole continued - a hint of mischief in his voice. "I don't think I've ever quantified it before and certainly never mentioned it, but as you know a good number of the 'Names' in my agency, including of course, Peter Varlov, are a result of your personal introductions." Anatole was enjoying teasing Matthews within possible earshot of his brother Stanislas. "You realise that it all contributes to funding a little bash like this. I know you have profited from it yourself and the benefit is mutual, but nevertheless I wanted to thank you." Matthews's already high coloured complexion turned a shade redder as he shuddered at the thought that anyone might have overhead such a revelation, but at the same time enjoying the inferred praise. Undisclosed commissions, or put more crudely personal 'back-handers, finding their way to bank directors, let alone Central banker's pockets was not a well regarded practice and definitely not a subject for open discussion at a wedding. Just as he was leaving the reception later with Lady Matthews, Sir George felt a hand on his shoulder. He turned sharply to find Stanislas standing just behind him.

"George excuse me, I'm only in London for a few days - I'll be coming in to see you on Monday morning - I'd like to talk about some commission business I've heard about. I'll make it ten o'clock - I won't be late." Before he could splutter about ringing his secretary for an appointment Stanislas was gone. Matthews left feeling impotent and he didn't like that - the remaining hours of the weekend would not be happy ones for him. They couldn't go fast enough for Stanislas. On Monday morning he was his usual punctual self.

"I'm here to see George Matthews - he's expecting me," Stanislas announced to the receptionist just before ten o'clock on the Monday morning. He and Natasha had spent a pleasant Sunday at his brother's house and this morning, having taken the short taxi ride from Sloane Square he was looking forward to his encounter with Sir George with some confidence. After their lunch yesterday while their two wives were walking the dogs and busy discussing the success of the wedding, Anatole had told him quite a lot more of the background of his agency's clandestine arrangements with Matthews. Now he felt he was well prepared for the imminent meeting.

"Could you please sign in, Sir, its just for security, and then I'll see if Sir George is ready for you," the young girl passed the register over, together with a pen and began to lift up the phone.

"No need for that," interrupted Stanislas, "we have a private meeting and, don't worry, he's most certainly expecting me I assure you. Just tell me where his office is and I'll go up." Taken by surprise the receptionist said without thinking, that it was room 312 on the third floor and then immediately regretted it as Stanislas turned at once and disappeared into the lift before she could do anything.

"Oh God!" thought the young girl, "this isn't a good start." She had only joined the bank that morning and her more experienced colleague, who was meant to be showing her the ropes, had said she would only be five minutes in the loo."

"Don't worry," she had added, "there're no visitors listed until eleven o'clock - just hold the fort and answer any phone calls and I'll be right back." Upstairs Matthews was sitting at his desk not looking his usual confident self - his secretary had been surprised to see him enter the office without warning about an hour earlier - normally his first appearance of the week was about eleven o'clock on Tuesday and today was only Monday and only ten o'clock. She had to look at her desk diary to make sure.

Matthews had passed through her office hardly acknowledging her presence and gone straight through to his, shutting the door behind him. A little later when she had put her head round and tentatively proposed a cup of coffee he had told her very abruptly that he didn't want to be bothered. He'd had an interminably wretched day of waiting yesterday - the more he had thought over that short conversation he'd had with Anatole at the wedding and the completely one-sided one later with Stanislas on Saturday, the more apprehensive he had become. Perhaps it was his old banker's intuition, but he most certainly had a feeling that the meeting this morning with the elder Kortaski brother, he had never been able to get on so well with him as with his younger sibling, was most certainly not going to be just a routine one. His reflections were interrupted by a commotion outside. He heard his secretary's voice raised,

"No sir, if you wait here I will see if Sir George is in." This was at once followed by one he recognised as Stanislas Kortaski's

"There's no need, I know he's here and he's expecting me - I'll just go in - thank you young lady." With that his door was opened and he found himself face to face with Matthews. Before either could speak, his phone rang,

"Sir George - it's reception here, I'm afraid a visitor asking for you refused to go through the normal signing in and now seems to be on his way up to your office - I'm very sorry , sir, but I really couldn't stop him, I'm alone on the desk at the moment. Do you want me to warn security?"

"No, its all right, he's here - he was expected in any case - I'll talk to you later." Matthews put the phone down and did his best to smile a welcome, "My dear Stanislas, what a pleasure to see you again, do sit down. We so much enjoyed the wedding on Saturday - everything went so well don't you think and the bride looked beautiful - how are things in Lisbon, a beautiful city, you're so lucky to live there. You'll have some coffee won't you?" Without waiting for a reply he got up, opened his secretary's door and said,

"Fiona, some coffee and biscuits please," before returning behind his desk and sitting down again. The long suffering girl raised her eyebrows and went off to the kitchen. Stanislas thought he'd wait for the coffee to be brought before dropping his bombshell. For the moment he went along with the small talk.

"Yes - the wedding did go well - she's a lovely girl and I have always been very fond of her. Good collection of guests too - it was nice to see so many old friends - Anatole managed it very well. I was a bit annoyed by seeing Peter Varlov there though, I would have thought he'd be licking his Lloyds's wounds in private - glad his luck ran out - can't stand the man." Matthews felt uneasy - it's difficult being on both sides he thought.

"Well I've always got on quite well with him, I think he'd like to think he is more a friend of mine than he is but, of course, I have always seen his faults and after you told me about your experience with him I've managed to keep my distance." 'Like bloody hell you have,' Stanislas said to himself, 'everyone knows what a two timing little greaser you really are, my friend, always running with the fox and hunting with the hounds.' Actually aloud Stanislas said,

"I know you have, George, it must be difficult in your position to do the right thing always. I suppose your business loyalty to the bank must always come first."

"Absolutely, Stanislas, absolutely," Perhaps this meeting wasn't going to be so terrible after all he thought. Matthews stopped talking as Fiona brought the coffee tray and placed it on a side table to the left of Sir George. There was silence as she poured their coffees before smiling at Stanislas and leaving them alone.

"Now Stanislas," Matthews nervously restarted, "how can I help you? You mentioned some business involving commissions - I'm sure the bank would be happy to listen to any proposition from you, - after all the association between us goes back some while now." Stanislas looked straight at Matthews and saw a mixture of fear, apprehension and doubt in his eyes. He is just a blustering bully and coward he thought - years of cross table direct negotiation, probing and investigating with financial directors, brokers or analysts had given him an excellent extra intuition that had never left him.

"No, George, I am not here to talk so much about my business but rather more to talk about yours. First let me say, I know your bank has lent Varlov the money which he owed for his underwriting losses, and I also know what security the bank holds for this loan and how it's going to be repaid." Matthews butted in,

"I cannot possibly comment on that - you know full well I can never discuss one customer's business with another." Ignoring the interruption, Stanislas continued,

"I also know that it was you who introduced Varlov along with several other of the bank's customers - I emphasise all people you have only met by virtue of your position here - to Lloyd's membership via my brother and that the annual commission for these, amounting to a more than reasonable sum my brother tells me, has been paid to you personally, or rather to your private account in Luxembourg." Even a shocked Matthews couldn't miss the sarcasm now entering Stanislas's voice, "No doubt the Inland Revenue has approved this scheme, and I am equally sure that you have informed your employers here of this other account and the commission arrangements - you will be aware that this is a standard requirement of your compliance rules and as a much respected member of the financial establishment I am certain you would never want to break these requirements either in spirit or fact"

Matthews, his normal ruddy complexion having turned several shades paler, slumped in his chair but managed a smile as, thinking fast, he spoke,

"My dear friend, the arrangements with your brother were made many years ago - I had almost forgotten the details. Remember before 1979 the top rate of tax here was up to ninety eight per cent - everyone had there little dodges going on - I bet you did yourself. You can't blame me - you really can't - I was then merely a young manager trying to get on. I helped your brother and he helped me - the whole thing was mutual. I meant no harm"

"Yes - you're right - we all had our arrangements and, your whole thing was mutual, but the difference is that what he did was legal - what you got up to was illegal and underhand - perhaps more important when regarding your present position - for a banker totally unethical. If you disagree we can ask your chairman for his opinion - he and I used to belong to the same golf club - I know him well - shall we do that? Let's ring him now." Matthews slumped further in his vast leather seat - by now any colour in his cheeks had disappeared entirely and for what seemed like five minutes, but was only thirty seconds, remained silent. He wished he knew more about Stanislas's affairs, but they were never his main bankers - and there were no useful threats he could think of to use against him. He tried to start speaking twice before any sound came, when it did his voice had lost its usual deep resonance and took on an almost Uriah Heep cringing quality,

"Stanislas, I have always regarded you and Anatole as two very good friends. I know you dislike Peter Varlov, but he is a customer of the bank and that's the only reason I keep up with him, really you must believe me."

"George - please don't go on digging your hole deeper - you are a two timing social climber who would sell his grandmother on e.Bay if there was a profit in her - so shut up and listen, OK?" Sir George fiddled with his watch chain and looked out of the window - he was furious at being spoken to like this, but felt utterly powerless to do anything. He had to admit to himself that Kortaski had him firmly over a barrel as he quietly asked,

"All right - what is it you want?"

"That's better," Stanislas allowed himself a smile, he almost felt sorry for the deflated Matthews, "I shall tell you. First, as I said, I know - or rather can guess - what arrangements the bank has made with Peter Varlov over his loan. The sale of the diamond - I can only congratulate the bank on the level of their security - has been announced and it's expected to fetch in excess of twenty million pounds. Presumably you will have free access to the diamond or be actually holding it here before it is shipped to Geneva just before the Auction date. Am I correct?" Matthews - who'd already had a nasty thought of his knighthood - precious to him, but far more so to his wife - being stripped away should his past conduct come out - nodded. "OK then, there are, I expect you know as well as I do, excellent methods nowadays for making exact replicas of precious stones good enough to fool all but the very top experts. While the diamond is in your custody, or at least under your control, and before it goes to the sale, you will arrange for such a model to be produced and to be handed to me in Paris before the original goes on display at the auction house. Is that clear?" Matthews shifted uneasily in his seat. He was beginning to sweat,

"How can I possibly do that? You're asking too much, you really are."

"I am sure that among all your many contacts there'll be someone you can think of to help you - aren't all your fellow masons meant to support their brothers in trouble?"

"That's a cheap remark - I really can't, no I won't do it."
Matthews was beginning to get his fight back and colour was
returning to his cheeks. Both soon went again as Stanislas stood up
and stabbing his finger for emphasis said,

"All right, my dear George, don't do it. However what you
should remember is that unless that replica - a perfect one, don't try
any funny tricks my ammunition is always fresh. Unless that copy is
in my possession before the original is in Geneva, your Chairman
will know everything we've discussed this morning. *The News of the
World* pays well for these sort of stories and knighthoods have been
taken away for less - it would be a pity to have to reprint your
visiting cards - Sir George." Matthews looked as if he might faint,

"But that's blackmail," he whispered.

"Exactly," said Stanislas as he shook George Matthews's limp
hand and left his office. "Could you take your boss a large whisky
please, I think he rather needs one!" he said as Fiona smiled
goodbye. Five minutes later as she put the drink down, Sir George,
not turning as he gazed out of the window quietly told her,

"Cancel any other appointments for today - I have to go out."
An hour later Lady Matthews was a little annoyed to have her lunch
with friends interrupted. However her annoyance turned to anger as
her husband slammed the door and went straight to his study
without acknowledging her or her guests. He remained in solitary
isolation for the rest of the day. Stanislas himself enjoyed his lunch
at the Connaught with Natasha and two old friends before they left
for the airport and the evening flight to Lisbon.

CHAPTER SEVENTEEN

LONDON

Lady Matthews was so disturbed about her husband's state of mind that she insisted he see a doctor immediately.

"Honestly George, you were as white as a sheet when you came home early yesterday and all my luncheon guests commented at the way you slammed your study door in my face, let alone not giving any greeting to my Hurlingham Club Croquet committee members."

Matthews had stayed in his study with the door firmly shut until well after his normal bed time before he had crept upstairs to his dressing room. Unable to sleep and having had no dinner, his problems just went round and round in his head getting worse as the night went on. The consequences of his exposure would be nothing short of complete disaster and he was incapable of getting them out of his mind. Starting with the loss of his treasured knighthood, there would be an investigation by the Inland Revenue, forced resignations from all his non executive directorships including, of course, that of the Bank, with the obvious loss of all the not inconsiderable directors' fees, a humiliating appearance before his fellow 'brothers' at the Masonic Lodge, having to leave the International Bankers Club, perhaps a possible threat to his pension arrangements, in fact complete professional and social disaster. The list was too awful to contemplate, but his worst terror was having to face Lady Matthews and tell her everything - she regarded her imagined social standing in South West London society to be of the highest importance and unassailable.

"Thank you dear, I'll be alright, don't worry – I'll be alright" Matthews said in a less than convincing tone, but clearly with no intention of explaining his recent behaviour. "We've got some problems at the bank, which they've asked me, as usual, to try and sort out. Therefore, forgive me dear if I leave now and for once we forego our usual after breakfast chat - I can't be late."

He was delayed by some signal trouble on the District Line on his journey to the office, so he had extra time to think about his plan of action.

"Fiona, would you immediately try to get me that Indian visitor on the phone I had here a few weeks before Christmas. You remember I asked you to take some notes about our conversation including the possibility of a loan facility available for his company if he was to proceed with a takeover in the U.K. Ajay something I think he was called." George Matthews brusquely demanded of his secretary at the bank, as he swept past her desk, forgetting his usual morning courtesies. "You may need to use his mobile phone - the number was written on his card I remember. I've no idea where he'll be at the moment." Minutes later his secretary came in to tell him that she had called all his numbers including his 'mobile' which was provisionally switched off and she had left a message. However, luck was with Matthews for once that morning and within half an hour his secretary buzzed through to say that Mr. Ajay Jha was holding on the line from Antwerp. He snatched up the phone quickly,

"How are you Ajay, I thought maybe you would be back in India by now. It must be pretty nasty in Antwerp if the weather is anything like London?" Matthews said, recovering his normal manner.

"Actually, I'm going back by Air India tonight from London taking the 2130 flight, which let's me have a decent sleep in one of their new aircraft with the full length beds."

"I don't know what time you are due at Heathrow, but could we meet there late this afternoon - I need to see you urgently before you go back?" asked Matthews.

"Certainly we can, but please can't you give me some idea now what it's all about?"

"Sorry Ajay, I don't have time to go into it now, I have an imminent meeting with some long established customers of the bank, from Kensington Palace," he lied. "It would be totally inappropriate for me to keep them waiting. I'll transfer you to my secretary, who will sort out with you a suitable time and meeting place at Heathrow." Showing the same brusque manner as when he had dealt with Lloyd's, Matthews quit the phone and left the arrangements to his secretary.

The time available was short - actually limited to forty five minutes, when the two fellow Freemasons finally met in the clubroom lounge of the Sheraton Hotel at the airport. Cutting straight through the pleasantries and small talk, Matthews went direct to the subject, as a curious Ajay slowly manoeuvred his huge frame forward in his bucket chair which was uncomfortably gripping him tightly on either side.

"Since we last met at my office" began Matthews, "there have been marked changes in money market conditions, which means that my bank is now in a position, quite fortuitously, to give favourable consideration to the proposal you put to me." Ajay made no response and waited for the pompous banker to finish his presentation - wishing he would speak in plain English that he could better understand. The habit of English business people always talking in riddles both puzzled and irritated him. Matthews went on at length to say how credit easing, subsequent to Britain's unforeseen exit from the Exchange Rate Mechanism, admittedly some years back, was proving very beneficial to Sterling based operators such as themselves. "My bank" said Matthews, lending as usual his full weight to the emphasis on the word 'my', "Is currently able to borrow in the International Market at quite exceptionally favourable rates. While it lasts we can use this for the benefit of our special friends among whom, my dear man, I hope I can count you." Not a glimmer of interest showed on Ajay's smooth skinned features, as he wondered why he was getting this offer, after all if Matthews's bank was behaving like this why shouldn't any other bank do the same?

"You may not know George," responded Ajay after a long uncomfortable period of silence, "that the gossip in European financial centres including Antwerp has been about nothing else for the last few days except the future of the Euro. There actually seems to be some real doubt its survival with at least one member country already having broken several of the single currency rules. When I was with the old firm Diamants de Vries they were positively full of it and worried what the future would hold."

Sir George didn't give up,

"Obviously, I can't bind the bank to any final terms for a loan that we might discuss here this evening, but I can tell you that the rate would be a very commercial one that your own finance director at Jha Brilliants would find most attractive."

"I must admit that does sound quite appealing George and I

really do appreciate you not having forgotten the little chat we had at the end of last year - I thought you might have done. Yes, we are still considering that takeover of a retail jewellery business and I will, of course, hand on your comments to our finance director." Ajay grinned for the first time since they met that evening, dipping his bejewelled fingers into the peanut bowl "You may not be aware that the second most talked about subject inside Antwerp's diamond Beurs is the cutting being done at the moment of an apparently incredibly large diamond that has suddenly appeared from nowhere. I was wondering if, by chance, there might have been any connection between the assistance you mentioned when we met having given some ex Russian nobleman and the massive, I'm told 300 carat, specimen being worked on at De Vries?"

"How on earth could you possibly think that?" exploded Matthews, utterly taken by surprise - he'd forgotten his indiscretion at their first lunch. Revelling in the shock he'd just inflicted, Ajay dealt a master stroke as he explained

"You see George, I have since a boy, been a fan of Sherlock Holmes and I have been able to learn that this huge diamond is not, as perhaps one might imagine it to be, a 'Golconda' from Eastern India. That apparently became obvious from the first viewing of its colour and clarity inside the face of the stone I'm told. Almost the only other country from which diamonds of such a weight and of this type have been discovered is Russia. So, as Holmes would say, 'Elementary my dear Matthews.'" His laugh reverberated through his rolls of fat.

Doing everything he could to disguise his dismay at the news that the diamond cutting was now public knowledge, Matthews's vanity inevitably got the better of him and he spotted his opportunity at the same time. He replied.

"Prince Peter Varlov is a very long standing and special dear friend of mine and I can tell you, but keep it in the strictest confidence, that it was with considerable pleasure that through me the bank were able to help him with his unfortunate set of rather serious financial problems resulting from his membership of Lloyd's of London, the Insurance Market you know. The poor man has suffered terribly in other ways in the last six months. Not only his huge financial losses, but he lost his dear wife Princess Varlov as well - she was also a special friend of ours of course."

"So then I'm right that the big diamond does come from Russia?" asked Ajay.

"Yes, I think you can say that its origins are connected to the last Tsar and Tsarina of Russia, but you wouldn't expect me to disclose any details I know regarding Prince Peter's private affairs."

Matthews's circumstances were desperate and the threats surrounding him were still pounding relentlessly in his head as he sought to find an equally desperate solution. Now was his chance. For years, although he had enjoyed his company, he was very well aware that Stanislas Kortaski was a ruthless operator, certainly never given to idle threats. He had firmly ordered Matthews to provide him with a copy of the diamond and what was worse he had put a deadline on him to do so. Sir George was thinking fast and his excuse was feeble, but it was the best he could think of quickly, and he could see no alternative except to float it now before the meeting finished. Taking a deep breath and tight control of his shaking voice, Matthews appealed

"I really shouldn't tell you this, but within our brotherhood certain confidences under pain of expulsion, can be exchanged. As you have cleverly Holmes-like deduced, my dear friend Prince Peter is indeed obliged to sell the diamond in order to meet the losses I have just told you about and the act of doing so is naturally proving to be unbearably distressing to his pride and sense of family loyalty. As a pathetically small compensation and to help him bear his loss I should like to present him, at my own expense, with a replica copy of the jewel when it is finally cut as a keepsake."

How very strange this man is, thought Ajay, now realising that he was effectively trapped within the confines of his bucket chair. He could neither reach forward once again for the peanuts nor find a means of release without assistance.

"I presume you are talking about a proper copy, a really first class job and not just a cheap glass bauble?" asked Ajay.

"Oh yes, I want it to be virtually undetectable by the experts, as near to the original as possible" Matthews replied, "I remember you told me quite a lot about this new simulant they call Moissanite - could that be the right material do you think? – you're the expert."

Ajay gave a forced smile.

"If you will help me part company with this ridiculous hotel chair my dear chap, I will think about it and let you know.

Meanwhile, you must excuse me my check in time has almost past. I must go or I'll miss the flight." The chair audibly groaned with relief as Sir George pulled Ajay upright.

The huge frame of the Indian mogul squeezed through the inadequately narrow revolving doors of the hotel and Matthews collapsed pale faced back into his own chair - the prospect of facing Lady Matthews with even half the truth did not bear consideration. However, perhaps he was lucky this time and he had found a way out - he knew he was facing a difficult few days before he'd hear from Ajay Jha, but at least now he could hope.

The relief felt by Matthews was almost tangible when after an interminable three days of silence his office phone rang at 10 a.m. sharp with a call from India. It was Ajay Jha to say that at a board meeting of his company it had been decided to proceed with a cash and stock offer for the whole of the issued ordinary share capital of Britain's number three retail jewellery business. It would involve his company needing a cash facility of £45 million for three years, repayable at the end of the term by another public share issue or failing that a re-negotiation of the present loan. Astute and quick witted though he was, Sir George Matthews was so bound up with his terror of being exposed that he had almost forgotten having more or less pledged the Bank into providing Ajay Jha with an over generous facility - what if this did not pass his loan committee without some other sweetener? - That would be another problem for him. Instinctively Matthews hesitated in replying in any detail, but invited him to submit a formal written proposal for the bank's consideration.

"And by the way Ajay" asked a trembling Matthews, trying to make it sound like an afterthought "While you're on the phone - what's your position regarding the diamond copy we discussed?"

"Oh my God, I nearly forgot to tell you" came the sing song reply. "I have been having a bit of a problem with the young apprentice cutter I told you about - the one with the astonishing skills. He is demanding a hefty reward of £15,000 to do the job in Antwerp, where I would have to send him. You don't want to spend that sort of money do you?"

"But can he do it?" panicked Matthews, giving his position away.

"Oh yes, he can do it alright, but he is demanding the fifteen grand cash plus his expenses - all payable up front. This means you finding a sum in the region of £17,000 immediately, which I told him is out of the question as far as you are concerned just for a gift"

"Let me think about it overnight Ajay. It does sound a bit steep and more than enough to fork out for a present." bluffed a fearful Matthews, regaining his composure, but knowing full well what his answer would be tomorrow - he would have been willing to pay that and a great deal more to save his skin and especially not to have to face an angry Lady Matthews. Cheap at the price he thought to himself if I'm saved that problem.

Meanwhile back in India, Ajay replaced his phone and smiled with satisfaction as he sat back behind his desk. Relative to its size and importance within the Indian economy, the head administrative offices of Jha Brilliants in Surat were comparatively unimpressive. Age old grime coated the bare concrete walls and the rusting window frames effectively disguised the fact that the turnover of the company, now employing nearly two thousand largely low paid workers, was in excess of £500 million a year. Inside the diamond factory the conditions showed no improvement as Managing Director Ajay Jha had no intention whatever of providing his employees with anything other than the strict minimum obligation - thereby maximising the profits and the payouts which would all accrue to him. To be fair, Jha's own office too, was spartan and tatty, sporting an ancient and noisy wall mounted air conditioning unit that squeaked and wheezed as though its end was near. An enormous, well worn leather chair, its springs broken and split with the stuffing showing through, was the command throne of the company's head man placed behind a huge Victorian partners' desk that was actually bereft of its leather top. Any personnel summoned there were favourably impressed by the frugal nature and modesty of their chief.

Jha didn't giggle often, but when he did his whole massive frame - resembling the old advert for Michelin tyres - heaved about like an uncontrolled balloon straining at its moorings. The cause of his present merriment was the telephone call he had taken earlier that afternoon, the day after the previous one from Sir George Matthews. The self important banker had telephoned him from London to say that he had been thinking hard about the substantial cost that he'd been quoted by Ajay for making a copy of this exceptional Russian diamond. He had told him that he would only accept the terms on condition that the work would be completed and the copy delivered to him in Paris by early May. What made him laugh out loud was not the £15,000, which after all he knew was mere bagatelle to either man, but the reason he had suddenly thought of for why Matthews had this curious and apparently compelling reason for wanting a copy. 'Perhaps' Ajay thought, 'Sir George has got a secret French mistress I suppose - she must be pushing him pretty hard if she's in such a hurry. I hope she's worth it!' With a little ingenuity he would be able to use such information to black-mail Matthews gently into improving the terms of the loan his bank seemed so keen to offer his company. Shouting through an open wall hatch to the next door office Ajay demanded the immediate presence of Praveen, his star apprentice who the firm had already sent to Antwerp last year to increase his experience.

The young man was an exception to the general show of modest frugality, having been chosen for a diamond cutting and polishing apprenticeship with Diamants de Vries in Antwerp, because of the extra promise he had shown over the others. While there he had gained an insight into the Western world and a love for its way of life, which remained foreign to his fellow Indian workmates. Showing fine prescience, his parents had chosen the name Praveen in hopeful recognition of what their firstborn son might achieve - the Sanskrit meaning of the name was most appropriately 'Expert'. He shared this name with Ajay Jha's father, which gave him an added advantage and just a touch of superiority in the eyes of his employer. This was the third time he had been called officially to visit the Managing Director's office. The first was to notify him of his acceptance as an Antwerp apprentice. The second was on his successful return from Diamants de Vries clasping his diploma award certificate as prize winner of the year. It was then that an alarmed Ajay had discovered that Praveen's skills extended well beyond the mere cutting and polishing of precious stones to removing them as well unnoticed from their proper home.

As the young man knocked on the door, Ajay Jha showed no hint of respect for his employee, but kept him standing for twenty minutes outside his office and repeated his discourtesy when eventually he was invited to enter.

"I have arranged, Praveen, for you to return to Antwerp in order to carry out an urgent copying job for me. Diamants de Vries are in the process of cutting and polishing a very large diamond, which will finally weigh, I believe, well over 150 carats."

"But boss sahib, it is not possible for me to go to Europe at this time, because next week I am having the big happiness of my sister's wedding. I have to be there" whined the startled Praveen."

"Don't worry about that young man - this is far more important and I will pay you £10,000. Imagine all that money for you after just three or four week's work." Overcome at the prospect of such an unimaginable reward Praveen quickly forgot his protests.

"Though how can I copy it boss, if the original is not yet finished?"

"That is a good question. Leave that to me. I will make sure that you arrive in Antwerp just a few days before its completion. During the time you are there you will be able to take all the precise details of the cut from the designer's drawings and you will make a study of the diamond itself so that you can then select the perfect piece of Moissanite for the copy. Then it is simply a matter for you of cutting and polishing the copy so that you have a perfect replica. Just one other thing - this is for a private collection, there is no need for anyone to know what you're doing. Do you understand that is important?"

"Yes, but you make it all sound so simple - I hope you're right." He turned and left the office.

Travelling economy class from Mumbai, as people were getting used to calling Bombay, to Paris was not a very pleasant experience, but still exciting to Praveen. By the time he had taken two different trains from Paris, through Brussels, to the provincial Belgian town of Antwerp, he was far too exhausted to set about presenting himself to the Managing Director of Diamants de Vries that evening although that had been organised by his boss Ajay Jha he could wait until the morning. There were a few weeks in which to do the job and as he settled into a meagre two star hotel in downtown Antwerp he looked forward with some relish to the task ahead and rubbed his hands at its spectacular cash reward.

Security at the diamond factory, surprisingly, turned out to be far less stringent than Praveen had expected. He was a likeable and plausible character, who made friends easily. By asserting his privileged visiting rights, using this personal charm as well as his sponsorship by the De Vries chief executive, and his previous intimate knowledge of the internal arrangements of the company, it only took him a day to gain access to the designer's drawings of the diamond. Using a three dimensional holographic imaging camera, he was soon able to produce working drawings that would be perfectly adequate for 90% proof cutting of a copy. The remaining 10% of the work would need hand finishing - a talent for which Praveen possessed equally or even better than a lot of the senior 'Brillianteerers' some with more than twenty years experience. When accepting his instructions from Ajay Jha he had insisted on being funded properly in advance for his expenses and these included the sourcing and purchase of a suitable piece of Moissanite, the essential simulant he would need before he could make a start on the actual copy. Also known as silicon carbide, this synthetic material, although not quite as hard as diamond itself compares excellently in terms of colour and clarity with the real thing. In fact to the naked eye, it appears indistinguishable to anyone except a true expert and even then further tests are needed. With the right connections and credentials it can be obtained from semi conductor manufacturers reasonably easily. Praveen had carefully researched just such a facility during his earlier apprenticeship when he'd had some wild ideas of mass-producing tiny fakes himself for flooding a gullible market waiting out there to be fleeced. He had discovered that £1,000 placed in the right hands in an Antwerp bar would result in a sufficiently large 'preform' chunk of Moissanite to be discreetly delivered to him at his hotel within a week of his arrival and, importantly, with no questions asked.

CHAPTER EIGHTEEN

BELGIUM

Praveen had last been to Antwerp in summer, but now in a cold spell before spring had properly arrived it was a completely different and rather unpleasant place to be. It was also unfortunate that the diamond business district, where Diamants de Vries was situated, was located near the town's railway station. This in common with most other cities, was an area associated with the dross of society - beggars, no hopers, prostitution and other examples of human misery. Antwerp was now the second major port of Europe, after Rotterdam, so crewmen from every part of the world tumbled ashore from their various tankers and container ships, and vied with each other to sample the dubious pleasures available in the seedy fleshpots of the City's red light district. For an Indian like Praveen, who had benefited from what its diamond expertise offered by teaching him and developing what were now his quite exceptional skills, the town held little attraction. Brussels, just fifty miles away, with all the draw of a cosmopolitan capital city, was far more appealing. Its reputation for night life and café society spread far and wide and as the centre of the European Union offered a sophistication hitherto unknown to the Indian. He was a bright young man, with a good education, having attended a school back in India at the famous hill station of Ooty. At 7000 ft up in the Nilgri hills, in a cold intemperate climate, his formative years were spent under the relatively severe discipline involved in the religious and educational instruction given by his schoolmasters, the Irish Christian Brothers with their strong work ethic. These dedicated men ran the college with a policy based on threats or demonstrations of inflicted pain - Praveen had often suffered from the strap, which was an everyday instrument of chastisement and used with lightning speed at any sign of concentration lapse. Although he did well in his exams, this success wasn't achieved without cheating, which unfortunately seemed to come as second nature to him and eventually led to his parents politely being asked to find him another school. Slightly built and noticeably shorter than his fellow South Indian compatriots he made up for this lack of height by cultivating a waggish, even old fashioned manner, more associated with a senior Indian army officer than a modern young jewellery specialist. His moustache was curled up at its extremities and although he never knew its value it was sure that everyone noticed him in a crowd - the black whiskers bristling on his upper lip.

Using the laptop, provided for him by his employer, to investigate the more titillatingly explicit web pages on the subject of serious fun in Brussels, led Praveen to a brightly lit bar just off the 'Grand Place'. Called 'DIALLO', its main difference from a dozen other similar establishments was that all the tables, some with two seats, some with four, had hanging above them a different number ranging from 25 to 125 encased in an illuminated pink globe. On each of the tables, he noticed there was an old fashioned telephone. At the far end of the spacious café, which was decorated in a false art deco style, and held more than fifty tables, was a long bar and Praveen uncomfortably squeezed himself onto a bar stool between two men so engrossed in telephone conversation that they made no effort to make room for him.   Like the rest of the café, the bar had some twenty telephones along its length, each with a number prominently placed in front of them. With what looked like a capacity crowd of mostly young people, the café was filled with a hubbub of clinking glasses, jangling telephones ringing and the general buzz of suggestive merriment.   The illuminated numbered globes kept flashing on and off in time with the ringing of the telephones underneath. Praveen ordered himself a whisky based cocktail off the printed list from one of the smartly dressed attractive barmaids, who were busy scurrying around, and asked her to explain what the telephones were all about.

"You see your place number is 47 and that refers to this telephone here - that's all. If you're patient for a while you'll probably get a call. Meantime just look around the room yourself to see if there is anyone you'd like to speak to." she explained. "If there is, just dial the number you see over their table."

"Tell me, what do I say to the people I call and what happens then?" queried a still rather puzzled Praveen.

"That, my friend is entirely up to you," the girl smiled. "You make your date - we only provide the lubricant." Sitting next to him now was a young man, about his own age, who was very busy dialling a whole series of numbers one after another. When he got an answer, he just repeated the same words each time.

"Hello, I'm François and I am sitting at number 48. Would you like to have a drink with me?" Seeing that he didn't seem to be having very much success, Praveen broke in as he finished one of his calls.

"It doesn't seem to work very well" he observed casually to François.

"Oh! don't worry," was the immediate answer, "it's always like this to begin with. What happens, you see, is that the girls always say 'No' at first, but at the same time they write your number down. Then, when they have had the chance to look you over they decide if you're worth a re-call. Come on, why don't you try ringing a few yourself?" Success came quicker than either expected and within fifteen minutes, and another cocktail, the two young men had both made good progress with two girls at different tables and had agreed to join up with them for a drink. Praveen, with his old fashioned ways, was surprised to find that the two girls regarded themselves on equal terms with the boys as they established immediately that they would maintain their independence and pay their way drink for drink.

"We're going Dutch in Belgium," they joked by way of explanation. Praveen didn't understand. The four had an amusing evening, eventually ending up in a jazz club off the 'Rue de la vierge noir' where, encouraged by the combination of low lights, modern music and too much drink, the two couples made positive progress towards a multi racial union. François, rather superior in his Gallic manner, told his new found friends that he was working in Brussels with the French Trade Commissioner specialising in the reconstruction of the inter community wine growers associations. After a little digging, Praveen learned that this was a slight exaggeration of his actual status which was in reality that of an intern completing a six month work experience course arranged by his college back in Lyon as part of his study of European Union systems assimilation.

Smoking cannabis at Praveen's mountain school had been a fairly relaxed experience as despite the strict anti drug regime imposed by the Irish Christian Brothers there had not been a great deal of attention paid to the actual material being smoked by the pupils of the sixth form. Along with many others, Praveen could have been seen many evenings at the back of the main building contentedly puffing at a junior size water pipe or hubble-bubble, as it was known, in the bowl of which would be a little piece of glowing charcoal usually sprinkled lightly with chopped up tobacco, but occasionally with the chopped leaf of Mexican Gold, if it was available. In the open air, the smell of cannabis freely dispersed and unless a more attentive Brother wanted to investigate and demanded to know what was being smoked, the senior boys were left in peace. Only once did Praveen get caught out and that was by an over zealous teacher, whose sexual preferences were not only towards young men but were plainly stimulated by sadism. The severe thrashing that he received as punishment for smoking pot, gave the Brother a thrill quite inappropriate to his calling. Now, quite unabashed, although fortunately discreetly, he rolled himself a spliff. He was surprised when neither of the girls nor François accepted his offer of a 'drag' and indeed made their disapproval very clear. The combination of drink and cannabis made him far more loquacious and expansive than his normal slightly reserved manner. Over confident and eager to show off his importance in front of the girls, he invited François to come to Antwerp in the very near future where, he said he would give him a personally conducted tour of the diamond factory. Boastfully, he claimed to be a senior Brillianteerer with overall responsibility for designing, cutting and polishing one of the world's most impressive stones. Oddly, Praveen didn't extend his invitation to the girls, who showed far more interest in seeing the priceless products than François. However, the young Indian was insistent and the Frenchman, though bored by the idea, found it impossible to say no.

Back in India Praveen had already shown no compunction in removing small diamonds from his employer which Ajay Jha had quickly discovered. To fund an increasingly ambitious lifestyle he continued this practice and removed the tiny off cuts and chippings for which he had, on his previous visit, discovered a ready market in the back streets of Antwerp. Now, emboldened by his assumed promotion as the copier in chief of one of the greatest diamonds the world had ever seen, he began removing much larger chippings that would inevitably only lead to his discovery by the security division of the Belgian firm and to his subsequent disgrace.

The day that François arrived for his promised visit to Diamants de Vries turned out to be an eventful one. Firstly under the supervision of a De Vries Director, but with Praveen himself doing the talking, he was shown the finished diamond, revealed for the first time, although admittedly, not properly lit or presentation mounted. To François, it looked nothing special - just like an outsize stone lying on the Brillianteerer's workbench. However, his visit coincided with one of the regular snap raids and routine full body searches of the personnel - plus any visitors present like François. Moving with the practised speed and cunning of a lizard, Praveen had, without the slightest difficulty and with absolutely no feeling of dishonour, slipped the tiny pouch containing his day's haul of chippings, into the back trouser pocket of the unsuspecting François, who felt nothing. Within minutes the unfortunate visitor was searched with the inevitable result and was unable to explain the contents of his pocket, which were as much a surprise to him as they were evidence to the security staff. Thinking fast, he claimed diplomatic immunity by showing his security pass of the French Trade Commissioner's office in Brussels. By giving an undertaking that he would return, François managed to escape the threatened immediate arrest by the Belgian authorities. Instead, as he volubly continued to protest his innocence, he was escorted off the premises by the security guards having given this and a further written statement about the purpose and circumstances of his visit. He was also instructed to fetch his passport and to surrender it to De Vries.

After his failure to return two days later, the subsequent enquiries to both François's residential and Trade Commission addresses met with blanks. From that moment it really was as though he didn't exist. De Vries themselves were unwilling to pursue the case too deeply for fear of the resulting publicity and the exposure to the outside world that their security was not nearly as stringent as might be expected. Praveen may have suspected his whereabouts, having talked to him during their initial evening meeting in Brussels. It was then that he had heard François talk vaguely about wanting to undertake a lengthy Catholic pilgrimage through France and Spain. Within a few days of François's mysterious disappearance, Praveen had a phone call from one of the girls, whose company they had so much enjoyed that evening at the 'DIALLO' café in Brussels. She had fallen for the young Frenchman and that night they had already established an intimate relationship.

"I have telephoned the little flat he has rented in Brussels and even been round there, but there is absolutely no sign of him. You must help me - he wasn't the type just to leave like that." pleaded the distressed girl.

"I think I may know where he has gone, but I can't tell you the reason." replied Praveen without explanation, thinking quickly how to prevent this outsider from getting any ideas and these being passed on in some way to the police. To his enormous relief, so far De Vries had kept the matter of the stolen diamond chippings strictly as an 'in house' enquiry and Praveen was most concerned that it should stay that way. "Did he not ever talk to you about going on pilgrimage?" ventured Praveen.

"Yes, I think he did." answered the uncertain girl, grasping eagerly at any kind of lead.

"Well, I shouldn't be surprised if he hasn't set off on foot and all alone to walk to Santiago de Compostela, which as you may know is far away in North West Spain. The problem is," Praveen was thinking fast now, as he went on with his explanation. "He will, as a religious person, be travelling as a true pilgrim - not wanting any contact with the outside world. I'm afraid you have little or no chance of contacting him as he trudges alone from monastery to convent and from hostel to refuge on his lonely trek. He certainly would not wish to be traced. His journey takes him over desert, mountains and rivers for something over a thousand miles - searching, all the time as he goes, for the spiritual truth." I should almost be a poet the Indian thought as he finished. The poor girl sobbed her broken hearted goodbyes. Praveen felt reasonably assured he had spun a good yarn and stopped her having any idea of trying to search for François. He would, with a bit of luck, be unlikely to hear from her again for at least another six months, by which time he would have long been safely out of touch back in India.

Later that week a little brown parcel, tied with string and sealed with red wax, was lying in his pigeon hole at Praveen's hotel when he came back from the diamond factory after another frustratingly idle day. All the time since his arrival from India he had had to act out a pretence to the Diamants de Vries management that he was busy collecting sufficient research material from his visit to write a thesis intended for publication in India, which he hoped, he explained would become the eventual standard authoritative work for future Indian students preparing for their apprenticeships in Antwerp. The influence of Ajay Jha, and his company Jha Brilliants as one of their foremost international customers, was such that De Vries, in their position as his sponsor, felt they were more or less obliged to give Praveen the same security privileges they extended to Ajay himself although they were not normally granted to staff members at his level. The cutting and polishing of the great Russian diamond was nearly finished. At this stage, and though Praveen had already surreptitiously obtained the necessary accurate drawings of how the finished piece would appear, he was blocked from making any further progress until he had got hold of, from his outside source, the substantial piece of Moissanite he needed. Now three days later than promised, with the arrival of the parcel he thought his wait was over. He carried the little package to his room and with trembling fingers broke the seal and cut the string before tearing open the paper covering to reveal a lump of heavy stone-like material measuring approximately 2 inches square. Its finish was a smooth opaque grey entirely devoid of surface scratching or colour variation. 'One thousand pounds well spent' contemplated Praveen as he began his plans for starting the cutting process in the next two days. During his previous apprenticeship he had befriended one or two of the cutters in the factory so he had little problem in arranging to work alongside one of them with the full use of his duplicate, and often under-used, set of cutting tools. He knew that in all these sort of operations the initial cut would be by far the most hazardous part of the process. Praveen was frightened that during the initial cleaving of the synthetic material an irremediable fissure might appear. His fears in this respect proved only too well founded and within two hours of him starting the night long procedure, the cutting machinery had automatically ceased to work, leaving a terrible and very visible double fissure, which ran horizontally right through the piece of now useless material. Time was now very limited as the real diamond itself was due to be completed within a week or so and he was faced with the unpleasant prospect of having to admit to Ajay the failure of his mission. His boss would, no doubt, demand all the money back - that thought alarmed him. Praveen had been aware that the simulant supplier he had used, because his price was the lowest, certainly had a somewhat dubious reputation and it was more than possible, he surmised, that what they had supplied him with might well have been stolen itself as well as being internally flawed. They would, of course, blame him for mis-handling the cutting and would naturally refuse to supply another piece for fear of repetition. Given the nature of the transaction he had absolutely no comeback with them. Thus Praveen had only one desperate option left that could possibly meet his time restraints and this was to steal directly from the raw material strong room of De Vries.

Only the size of a small cabin trunk, the gem repository was built into one of the walls of the chief executive's office. Praveen's keen eyes had noticed during one of his few visits there that when the director was in his office it was his normal practice to leave the safe door slightly ajar, only closing it fully when he left the room. An automatic floor pad alarm under his carpet warned him if by chance he should attempt to leave the room without first closing the safe door. Always devious by nature, Praveen knew that all he needed to do was to disconnect this primitive pressure pad beneath the carpet and somehow arrange for the unsuspecting man to be distracted into leaving his office in a hurry. Next morning, despite having no excuse for being in that part of the building, he casually walked past the head man's office and quickly bent down and slipped his pocket knife beneath the carpet edge where it met the door sill. With a quick deft wriggle of his wrist he had located and then in no time snipped the thin wire leading from pad to alarm switch. After achieving this he retraced his steps to the end of the corridor. There he waited until the director approached from the other end and met him by the door - his mobile phone held in his right hand.

"Mr De Vries, excuse me barging in but, I have an urgent phone call on my mobile for you. I don't know why, but my Indian boss is calling from his car on his way home and says he needs to talk with you about something urgent. I've noticed that the phone only gets a strong signal outside - I don't know why?" lied Praveen. "Come out this way, Sir and I'll give you my handset. He says it's private so I'll leave you alone and wait by your office for my phone" As he left him in the open air outside the side door of the factory building, he heard him vainly shouting louder and louder into a non-responding mobile

"Ajay, Ajay are you there? I can't hear you - if you can hear me ring me in my office - Hello? Hello?" It took Praveen just thirty seconds to select a suitable piece of untouched Moissanite from the cabinet, put it in his pocket and return to stand innocently by the open door. The director handed him back his mobile - he abruptly explained the line was impossible and said no doubt Ajay would call him later if it was important. A relieved young man went back to the working area and could not resist a smile as he felt the square shape securely in his pocket.

Five days following the afternoon of Praveen's theft a cleaner reported she had noticed a piece of what looked like an electric wire projecting from the edge of the C.E.O's office carpet just by the door. Later - a testing of the alarm showed it to be faulty, and after the subsequent check of the raw material cabinet's contents one piece of Moissanite was found to be missing. By now however, as a result of working very long hours, Praveen had finished the construction of a practically perfect replica of the awesome original. It would only require him to place the original stone and his copy facet to facet to prove the success of the cloning, and his job would be over. He was feeling relaxed again.

Meanwhile, on schedule and in accordance with the instructions of Sir George Matthews, the Varlov diamond left Diamants de Vries bound for London and once more the strong room security of the bank. Matthews had left instructions for the security department to notify him the moment the diamond was safely received by them. Within an hour of its arrival having been announced Matthews called security and asked to come down to see it within the confines of the strong room area. Displayed alone, resting on crumpled tissue paper and still in the simple cardboard box in which it had journeyed from Antwerp, his first impression was how small - even insignificant it looked compared to the last time he had seen it in its still uncut state. The overhead strip light did nothing to help in reflecting the luminosity in the stone and for a moment Matthews felt a wave of disappointment. Nevertheless, the shrewd ex banker in him had not forgotten to carry with him from his office the set of Victorian letter scales on which he had originally weighed the stone those weeks before. Using a cloth duster hurriedly borrowed from one of the members of his staff present, he carefully lifted the diamond from the box and noted immediately that it had been cut in neither the classic round shape of a 'brilliant' nor the pear shape, which he had anticipated. Instead it was an almost symmetrical oval, obviously chosen to achieve the minimum wastage in the cutting process. Gently and almost reverently he placed it on the scale before methodically adding the small weights measuring the ounces and fractions of ounces. The swinging needle steadied after several mis-alignments, leaving Matthews the simple task of counting up the value of the little weights. The total came to just under 1¼ ounces. This was, in jewellery terms 37 grammes, the equivalent of an astonishing 185 carats. His reverie ended with a bump as he slowly placed the enormous jewel back into its modest container and remembered his unpleasant meeting with Stanislas. He only now had three weeks in which to get a copy made and delivered by him in Paris.

He hadn't heard a single word from Ajay Jha since his telephone call accepting the Indian's conditions and terms for doing the job. His worries were to be further exacerbated the following morning. Before that he characteristically proved himself quite incapable of keeping his association with the diamond confidential. He boasted to Lady Matthews how, totally thanks to his skills, contacts and experience, he now virtually held under his control an exceptional piece of Russian Royal memorabilia of major historical importance. Lady Matthews, also noted for her indiscretion, thought this would be something she would enjoy re-telling to her fellow croquet committee members - they would be very impressed she said to herself. The next day before Matthews could call him, Ajay rang from Surat to sort out various clarifications of the loan terms and conditions his company was being provided by the bank. He ended the conversation to the horror of Matthews by saying
"Oh! I almost forgot, by the way, George, I am afraid to tell you

that something has cropped up and there could be a little delay in getting that diamond copy for you. Sorry"

"What do you mean some delay?" gasped Sir George, desperately trying to hide his concern.

"Oh nothing really serious, I hope, but I learned the other day that there's been a bit of trouble with what they politely call 'Gem mis-appropriation' at Diamants de Vries. I think that my so called star apprentice, whose honesty I'm afraid I have always suspected a bit anyway, may have been involved in something stupid - the silly young man. Anyway they have, I think, provisionally taken his passport away. The copy has been made, but this may stop him from travelling to Paris or being able to get it out of the factory."

"But you made a promise." yelped Matthews - now unable to hide his panic, "that you would definitely have that diamond delivered to me in Paris by the first week in May. I relied on you - you gave me your word."

"So I did old boy, so I did." and the phone went dead - as Matthews almost wished he was as well!

CHAPTER NINETEEN

NORTHERN SPAIN

Nursing staff at the Najera hospital were kind to François' parents and ensuring that they were made as comfortable as possible with two collapsible metal beds, placed in the room where he lay in a coma – they continued to watch him anxiously as his facial expression betrayed no hint of the dream going on behind ....
Portrella worked out her way to grab a hasty and lasting sweet revenge for what she regarded as her humiliation. In a flash she remembered at the market that very morning the self important figure of the Magistrate Raimondo, who so crudely but clearly had made his obscene wishes obvious. If she could just think of a way to incriminate Ebbo for a minor crime, then he would come before the twisted and dis-figured Magistrate, who no doubt would punish the innocent lad. It didn't take long for her to work out that if he was convicted of a theft, the punishment – almost certainly a flogging - out would do the job to her perfect satisfaction. The Depotillo family weren't the owners of any valuable bric a brac and the only thing the now spiteful wench could find was a pewter mug of little value, but nevertheless great sentimental worth to her father. It had been left to him, or more likely misappropriated by him, when a pilgrim returning from Santiago had got too drunk and pledged it in payment of board and lodging. It was a paltry thing, but small enough for her to remove it easily from its present resting place and to conceal it in the sack containing Ebbo's worldly goods including his treasured Bible and Rosary. There was

no problem in carrying out the vengeful act as in almost total darkness she stowed the household object deep into his canvas sack.

Come morning, but late in accordance with Spanish custom, the three pilgrims set off without so much as a backward glance, little knowing that Portrella was about to alert the Magistrate, and he in turn the town militia that her family had apparently given succour last evening to a set of thieving villains.

Sufficiently refreshed by their stay in the Santo Domingo de La Calzada albergo despite its discomfort and unpleasantness, the Henkes quickly made good the distance to the village of Belorado - a humble hamlet if ever there was one. Here the only accommodation was a half built cave, where the only ventilation was a doorless entrance and the hole in its turf roof. Newly built, the giant mole hole had plainly been dug out by troglodyte farming folk to provide a shelter both from the heat in summer and the freezing cold of winter. Furthermore it acted as a haven from roving bandits, who would not hesitate to kill for the sake of stealing even the minimal possessions of unsuspecting travellers.

As the three lay exhausted from the 30 kilometre walk, slaking their thirst with brackish water from the River Oja, or what remained of it during the summer drought, Ebbo became aware of his name being called in a questioning tone. The walk had taken the family over varied terrain including the beginnings of the Meseta or Spanish desert. Wildlife was mostly reptilian with frequent snakes and lizards basking in the sun. Lidless eyes revealed the narrowest of sinister black slits that almost closed entirely as the sun penetrated their unprotected lenses. The creatures usually scuttled or slipped away rapidly as the walkers approached. Overhead the occasional kite would circle and for some inexplicable reason a Linnet- like little bird decided to adopt the family for several kilometres. Skipping from bush to tree the brown flier seemed to lead them in an ever westerly direction. Whether it was seeking companionship or food was a question that vexed Ebbo, who kept on experiencing a sense of spirituality radiating from the tiny feathered creature. The noise of calling voices drifted nearly through the afternoon haze and after some minutes its clarity was sufficient for him to recognise for certain that it was indeed he who was being sought.

Ebbo stumbled only half awake from the cool and darkness of the earthwork shelter and innocently shouted a reply of greeting to the approaching voices. To his surprise he saw two rather alarming semi uniformed ruffians appearing. One armed with a spear and the other carrying an evil looking club.

"Stay where you are Ebbo - don't move", screamed the club bearer "and you won't get hurt". Ebbo, now trembling with fear fell to his knees in alarm and replied,

"Who are you and what do you want from me?" By this time his mother and father had also quit the primitive shelter and came anxiously forward to join their son. In seconds, the ruffians had grabbed hold of Ebbo and threatened to kill all three pilgrims unless he revealed the contents of his pathetic sack of personal belongings. Language comprehension between them was near to non-existent, but their intentions were clear as the two similarly dressed aggressors manhandled the little family into the mouth of the underground shelter. Seizing what possessions they could find they emptied the pathetic contents onto the sun baked earth outside. A pair of badly worn sandals, some coarse material under garments, a knife, a pottery mug and bowl, a leather flask containing water, a bible and a few scraps of writing vellum. What aroused their fury was a pewter mug of no significance.

"Thief, thief you have stolen this most precious object from José, the albergo owner in Santo Domingo de La Calzada." Spluttering, and blubbing, Ebbo protested vehemently that he had never seen the object in his life before, but all to no avail. The spear carrier, with his companion's assistance, lashed Ebbo's wrists behind his back before flinging him to the ground with such force that he was rendered momentarily unconscious. Totally without ceremony like a hunted animal he was dragged inside and tied tightly to the stump of a small tree, which formed the centre piece and table of the troglodyte dwelling.

Next morning, even before the sun had risen and the two men having blocked the entrance during the night for fear that Ebbo's parents would escape, the family were cruelly forced to start walking back in the direction from whence they came. They had no understanding of what was happening and just imagined they were victims of local brigands out to rob them of their money. A blindingly painful march ensued as Ebbo and his parents were prodded, jabbed and sworn at by their captors. Finally near collapse from thirst, hunger and exhaustion the three eventually reached Santo Domingo de La Calzada at dusk where, still without any explanation, they were thrust forcibly into a cell of the town jail. Three metres square and two metres high gives little space for human survival, and even though a ceiling grill permitted a borrowed form of daylight from the adjoining passage it was scarcely sufficient to let the prisoners breath. The straw covered unswept mud floor was damp and stinking from decaying human excrement leaving barely a patch untainted for them to lie on. Bread and a pail of water was provided, but nothing else. The only explanation for their incarceration were the oft repeated taunts of "Thief" that blasted their suffering ears making any sleep impossible.

At daybreak the family were hauled physically from the cell, dragged to a neighbouring courtyard and lashed to wooden scaffolding fixed to the wall for the very purpose of tethering animals and humans alike. By noon the now totally confused and terrified family had a charge read to them and interpreted from Spanish to a semi intelligible Frankish tongue, which was just sufficient for them to understand that they jointly stood accused of stealing a pewter mug, the property of José the inn keeper, and that they would appear before the town Magistrate that very afternoon to answer this charge.

CHAPTER TWENTY

HARLEY STREET - LONDON

There was neither a whiff of antiseptic nor any other hint of medical practice, just a grand high ceilinged room with its Adam fireplace. Two comfortable three seater sofas, four reproduction Chippendale chairs and a central coffee table made up the only furniture in the heavily curtained, slightly overheated room in which Sir George Matthews sat alone nervously paging through the latest edition of *Country Life* he'd picked off the pile. His eyes rested momentarily on a 'for sale' advertisement for a white stuccoed mock Spanish style Villa in South West London. He nodded sagely as he recognised the property as that of a near neighbour and grinned with self satisfaction that the asking price was not shown. Instead, 'Price on Application' graced the advertisement - a sure indication of its superior value. His satisfied contemplation of the value this implied for his own residence was broken by the entrance of a white coated receptionist announcing,

"Mr. Greysdon is ready for you Sir George, would you like to follow me please?" Matthews walked behind the receptionist up the mahogany banistered staircase for two floors before she swung open some double doors exposing a grandiose 26 ft long drawing room furnished with what looked like the entire collected works of England's greatest equine painter George Stubbs. Matthews noted that there must have been at least ten horse pictures hung on each wall, giving the place an impression of being more the London office of Tattersalls, the famous bloodstock auctioneers, than the consulting rooms of one of the more reputed brain surgeons in London.

Mr. Greysdon, a diminutive and dapper little man, prematurely grey, rose from behind a massive partners' desk, put on his half moon glasses and came forward hand outstretched. Dark suited with a spotted bow tie, the eminent consultant, often referred to by his medical peers as a 'Top Man', realised, sub consciously, that there was a certain similarity with him, the neurologist now at the peak of his profession, and his patient the self important Sir George Matthews. Both were proud to show off the various trappings of their status. Never was there any question of Mr. Greysdon visiting a patient, nor would Sir George ever consider visiting a customer - both were far too important for that, they felt. These were men, who by their own specialised achievement, sat proudly in their sumptuous surroundings creating self-justification for their inflated fees, together with their equally inflated egos - the consultant in Devonshire Street and the banker in his parlour in The Strand.

"What a marvellous collection of paintings." began Matthews, noting that the consultant made no response to his customary masonic handshake.

"I have to tell you alas, Sir George, they are not originals - I wish they were - but if I say it myself the fact that they are all more than one hundred and fifty years old and defined as being 'In the school of' gives them a recognition value, which is hard to equal - in any case I like them" said Greysdon. "I see that you have been referred to me today by my good friend Dr. Hallet - I don't think we have met before have we?" the consultant began as he returned behind his fortress-like desk and started looking at his notes. He didn't wait for a reply. "I understand you have been suffering from depression, eating disorders and slightly uncontrollable finger quivering. Would that be an accurate assessment of your symptoms?"

"Yes, I think that just about sums them up - it seems to cover everything. I'm afraid I'm in a position as a senior director of the bank, where I am constantly making far reaching decisions and in the last few weeks I have been particularly under pressure," replied Matthews, who was quite determined not to reveal any hint of the actual reason for his medical condition. The real reason, he could only admit to himself, was his downright fear of the future and the accompanying sheer panic at the possible consequences. Sleeplessness, the inability to keep down his food and blinding headaches were all understandable results of this state of mind.

"I quite understand your problem Sir George," went on the soothing consultant, working out in his mind how he was going to be able to justify a substantial fee note while recommending merely a simple palliative, or even just a placebo. At the same time he was hardly able to believe the sheer pomposity of his patient - in that he is in a class of his own, he thought.

"Let me examine you, but probably we ought just to try some mild medication to start with. I will suggest something along these lines to your Doctor Hallet. That should do the trick for a man with your heavy responsibilities. He hoped his patient didn't detect the note of irony in his voice. "If this doesn't succeed, I can tell you now, although it would need some further expansive tests before I could recommend it. I am at the advanced stages of developing a Deep Brain Stimulation capability that has achieved astonishingly successful results already. The treatment involves the insertion of an implant electrode into the subgenual cingulate region known as Cg25 of the brain. However don't worry, we are far from suggesting that yet in a case like yours."

"That does sound very interesting, but as you say, let's hope that nothing so drastic or mysterious will be needed." answered the now terrified Matthews as he took off his shirt, went over to the medical couch and laid down at full stretch.

Afterwards, as he walked from the Devonshire Street consulting rooms, he made a quick mental analysis of what options were open to him. The visit to the consultant had forced Matthews to concentrate his mind on what action to take over Ajay's unwelcome news that there could now be a delay over the delivery of the diamond copy. He had several options with the first one perhaps being to beg Stanislas for more time. This he dismissed at once. In quick succession followed the ideas of going to Antwerp himself to plead with De Vries, possibly offering to pay Ajay a higher price to use his influence and thirdly, declining to finalise the loan terms to Ajay's company, despite them now being virtually agreed. It was the last solution which had the most appeal and, he thought, the greater chance of success.

Immediately he got back to his office, Matthews summoned the bank's head of corporate lending to come up, bringing with him the complete files on the Shah Brilliants loan deal including the company's latest report and accounts and the most recent unaudited management accounts they had just received. He rapidly scanned through the figures with an expertise that surprised and impressed the senior loan officer.

"I observe," said Matthews finally, "that there is a considerable discrepancy between the Gem stock valuations of both India and Antwerp in the latest published accounts, signed off by the auditors, with the much lower current figure shown in the management accounts. Surely the difference should be reflected in the 'work in progress' figures - should it not?"

"Now you point it out I must agree. That is perfectly true Sir George, but what would you propose we do about it? You did say that you wanted this deal to be agreed as quickly as possible - I was only following your instructions." The manager thought he had better cover himself, "you see here ....."

"That's as maybe, but I never said jeopardise the bank's position" interrupted Matthews quickly. "Send an e-mail, straight away to Mr Ajay Shah, the Managing Director of Shah Brilliants, pointing out that certain small technical deficiencies in the accounts have been observed and that pending an investigation and an acceptable explanation of the gem stock certification, the bank's loan committee would be reluctant to formally authorise any facility. Be sure to e-mail it immediately and then confirm by registered post." ordered Matthews, showing a hidden streak of ruthlessness in his desperation. He couldn't resist adding,   "I am due to give an address tomorrow to the Institute of Fiscal Studies and it will prove an excellent example of a warning about the dangers involved in cross continental stock valuations. My speeches are usually picked up and reprinted in most of the professional accountancy journals."

"Yes Sir" replied the bank official, hiding a smile at yet another example of the man's famed self importance and pomposity. 'That should make sure that the banking intelligence services put out a warning sign about Shah Brilliants he thought vindictively.

His visit to the neurological consultant had worked enough magic for Matthews to feel that the undoubted enormous fee he would soon be called upon to pay had been justified. As the weekend was approaching he suddenly suggested to his mystified wife that they spend it relaxing at a health farm not too far from London. Although refreshed by the end of the two days there, Matthews remained in an alarming state of mind as he was forced to wait for a full week before he heard any word from India. After Ajay's last call which had ended with the phone going dead, all attempts by Matthews to reach him had failed. He had been fobbed off by various excuses - Ajay Sahib was absent from his desk for private business, at other times he was in a meeting not to be disturbed, or had just left for lunch and would ring back - he never did. Matthews was counting the days between now and his scheduled meeting with Stanislas and time was fast running out. At last it was an e-mail message which re-opened communication between the two masons as Ajay demanded to know why Matthews's bank had suddenly adopted such a manifestly ridiculous position over the accounts of the company. With temporary superiority on his side, Matthews eagerly responded that the matter was out of his hands, showing improbable modesty he explained that he was only a pawn in the final decision making process. He could however, influence the loan committee to some extent and it would be helpful if in turn Ajay could bring some pressure to bear on De Vries to release   the diamond copier's passport.

"Why are you so worried old boy?" queried the Indian in his high pitched voice. "I know now why you were so anxious to get that copy made - and now it looks as if you think you can hold me to ransom over the bank loan."

"What do you mean by that Ajay, of course not, I told you the reason when I first asked if you could do it? The bank loan has nothing to do with the copy." Matthews was now very worried that perhaps he'd gone too far.

"Yes, you did tell me some cock and bull story about wanting to do something for a friend, but I never believed that, and don't ever forget that our lodge has connections spread far and wide. I have heard that certain disclosures about you might be imminent. You are playing funny tricks about my bank loan, but remember two can play at that game."

"What disclosures? - I don't know what you're talking about. What rot is this?" Matthews was sweating and now very anxious indeed.

"Oh yes you do old boy. Don't you remember that when we first met in London at that lunch in the City you boasted of your Royal connections and how you had helped one of them with an introduction to Lloyd's of London?" asked Ajay with an alarmingly precise recall. "Well I leave it to you to decide who's blown the whistle on you, but meanwhile let me emphasise if you don't stop sabotaging our loan facility with your bank I'll see to it that the copy actually is delayed - for some considerable time at that! The ball is in your court I think Sir George." Matthews knew he was beaten - he capitulated at once and the next day the head of the bank's corporate lending department was not a little confused to be told abruptly to rubber stamp the loan agreement for Shah.

CHAPTER TWENTY ONE

NORTHERN SPAIN

François' parents spoke no Spanish, which made any detailed communication between them and the Medical staff in the hospital difficult, but it was clear enough to both of them that so long as his breathing remained even there should be no deterioration in his condition. They continued their anxious vigil – both wondering what thoughts lay behind his expressionless face..........The courtroom was a dismal sight comprising a raised dais with a crude wooden chair upon it set behind a massive oak desk. Here the Magistrate himself would sit and usually entirely regardless of the truth or any explanation, would dispense his personal favourite form of justice, which extended from just time spent in the stocks with all its attendant humiliation right up to execution. Thirty lashes to the back and buttocks was a standard punishment for such minimal offences as drunkenness or work time sloth - for this reason he was much feared by the local peasants. Dressed in a bottle green damask robe, the puce faced magistrate entered, wearing, despite it being mid-summer, a fur trimmed headgear and a full sleeved billowing shirt. Scarcely stifling a garlic smelling belch as his grossly swollen thyroid gland visibly pulsed, the petty tyrant dropped heavily into the chair pompously demanding from a court orderly a cushion for the comfort of his ample backside.

The magistrate, never at the best of times known for his patience, was brief, perfunctory and non-caring as he demanded the details of the charge brought against the family to be read. Cunningly led by a senior town militiaman, the albergo owner José repeated the evidence that the pilgrim family had robbed him the night before of his most treasured possession - a pewter mug. It was bright, it was loved and it was symbolic, explained a suitably distraught José. He explained that on discovering the theft he had immediately sent two uniformed law enforcers to hunt down the villains, who he believed had committed the crime.

When the magistrate heard that the stolen item had indeed been recovered from Ebbo's sack, he did not hesitate to flex his disproportional powers and refused to hear any word from the boy or his parents - he knew where his duty lay he pronounced.

"You shall be punished by death this day by hanging from the neck in a public place." The loving father Lucus offended the court by attempting to offer his own life instead of his much loved son, to which the magistrate threatened to hang the three of them, the boy Ebbo for theft and his parents for contempt of court. All protests stopped.

There were only eight people in the courtroom apart from the pilgrim family and one of these was Portrella, who had merely expected that the magistrate would punish Ebbo by humiliating him with a spell in the stocks, a whipping or the pillory for a day so she could taunt him with her coquettish behaviour to make him realise that any rejection of her favours was not a folly to be undertaken lightly. When she heard the actual sentence she uttered a scream of anguish so piercing that the magistrate ordered her to be removed from the courtroom by force, not before thinking that this might provide him with an opportunity to visit her in a cell. Portrella had unintentionally caused her potential lover to be sentenced to death - she sobbed silently in her impotent dismay.

CHAPTER TWENTY TWO

LISBON

He must have fallen asleep lying in the sunshine and it took him a few seconds to react to Natasha's call.

"Stanislas, you're wanted on the phone - it's George Matthews," adding unnecessarily, "he's calling from London." He got up slowly and went towards the house. He hadn't heard a thing from the banker since that meeting with him on the Monday morning following his niece's wedding. During that time he had left two rather cryptic messages with the secretary - largely, he admitted privately to himself, out of spite - that he was looking forward to seeing Sir George' in Paris again very soon and that he hoped everything was going well with him. He picked up the phone and to his surprise, and perhaps disappointment, found Matthews to be in his usual confident and rather condescending form.

"My dear Stanislas, it's good to hear your voice. I got your message and am so sorry not to have been back to you before but I have been working so hard on your behalf and am very pleased to tell you that now I think I'll probably be able to help you with your little problem. As you know here we usually manage to solve our customers' difficulties for them." It was as well that they were only talking on a long distance telephone and weren't in the same room - Stanislas swore to himself that he'd have hit the pompous idiot had they been so. Unaware of this, Matthews carried on, "I hope to be coming to Paris for a weekend with my wife around the beginning of May and perhaps we could meet then? I'll let you know my programme so we can fix something. Things all right in Lisbon, old boy?" Faced with the sheer bluster of Matthews, it was a few seconds before Stanislas recovered his composure. When he did, he shut his study door before answering in case his wife was in the hallway outside.

"Sir George - I use your title just in case the next time we speak it isn't appropriate - let me remind you of our arrangement and some facts you appear to have forgotten. You seem not to appreciate how delicate your position is. You will produce what I have asked for to me in Paris before the tenth of May. It is not a question of you letting me know your programme - I will tell you all the details of our meeting and you will do exactly as I say. Do you now understand that? Can your obviously thick head register that? I would hate your trip to be delayed because of any interviews you might be asked for by the Inland Revenue or perhaps even News of the World correspondents - I don't think you'll have to visit the Palace though to give up your knighthood. Now is everything clear and are you confident that you will be able to do as I wish?" George Matthews's shaking arm almost dropped the phone. He was too deflated even to try to fight. Before replying he took a gulp of water from the glass on his side table. Now, in contrast with his opening remarks his voice was strangely contrite, almost two tones higher,

"Yes, I promise you all is arranged, please believe me - just tell me where you want to meet - really it'll be fine, there's no need to threaten me, you know we are old friends. We go back a long way you, your brother and me - please - doesn't that count for anything?" Stanislas ignored his wheedling tone,

"OK, I'm glad to hear you've managed it for your own sake - I will ring you at home tomorrow evening and give you all the necessary instructions - remember, these you will follow to the letter or you know what I will do - let me check your home number again?" Matthews repeated his number, but then had an awful thought, "Just one thing, my friend, should Lady Matthews answer the phone, I just want to point out that all this is very strictly between you and me. Please don't say anything to her." Stanislas couldn't resist a final barb, "You mean you don't want me to talk about the Luxembourg account with her - surely she has a signature on that one? You are a secretive fellow - you shouldn't hide things from your wife! Till tomorrow evening, 'Sir' George, bye!" It was as well that Stanislas couldn't see Matthews's face as he put down the phone - perhaps he would even have felt sorry for him. Afterwards Stanislas remained in his study and checked his watch - it was five o'clock - eight o'clock in the Russian capital. Taking out the card with Eric's numbers - he dialled his flat. Four rings and he recognised his voice and immediately asked him to go down to the call box and wait. He gave him five minutes to get there and dialled its number - he was lucky it must have been empty and Eric picked it up on the second ring. Not wasting time on any small talk, Stanislas explained that all was arranged for the copy to be available as planned in Paris the first weekend of May, that he would be staying, with his wife, at the Meurice and that he would see Eric on the Saturday morning - they would fix the exact details when they arrived in Paris - he should ring him at the hotel. Eric listened silently and for a moment Stanislas thought the line had gone dead, "Hello, hello, did you get all that?"

"Yes, I'm still here, but there's just one thing we should clear up before all this - you mentioned an early payment and there'll be expenses, travel etc., to think of as well. I'd like that cleared before I leave."

"Yes, don't worry - I'll sort that out this week - with you or Igor?"

"With Igor - he'll tell you where we want it."

"What about your hotel in Paris - it's not a good idea for you to stay at the Meurice where I am - shall I book you another?" Eric was almost abrupt,

"No thank you - we'll handle all that, you don't need to know where we are, do you?"

"Well I'll need to ring you perhaps? Anyway can you confirm those dates now?" Eric gave his agreement and before ringing off told Stanislas that he would be arranging a local mobile phone in France, so he'd give him that number as soon as he got it. After pouring himself an early vodka and tonic, Stanislas e.mailed the Meurice and reserved a double room at the back, away from the noise of the rue de Rivoli for three nights. Over dinner later that evening Natasha was very touched and pleasantly surprised to learn that he was taking her for a romantic weekend to Paris as a delayed birthday present.

Largely to keep his victim sweating, Stanislas waited until after nine o'clock that evening before dialling the Matthews's house. What he couldn't have known was that Sir George was so anxious that his wife shouldn't answer after his parting remark yesterday that he had been home waiting for the phone to ring since just after four o'clock. As bad luck would have it, Stanislas finally came through at the very moment when Matthews had gone to the loo - something he had uncomfortably delayed for some time.

"Hello, Lady Matthews speaking," his wife began as she heard her husband shout something indistinct from behind the door at the far end of the hall, "can I help you?" Stanislas resisted a very strong temptation to carry out his threat and instead simply said his name and asked to speak to her husband. He did just allow himself to mention, to her complete puzzlement, that he hoped she would enjoy her weekend in Paris. Sir George, fiddling with the front of his trousers, arrived a little breathless at the phone. Before she passed it to him Stanislas smiled, as he heard her ask her husband what was all this about a trip to Paris and then telling him he'd caught his shirt tail in his zip. Ignoring this, Matthews roughly grabbed the receiver from her,

"Hello - can you hold on a moment, I'm going to take this in my study." He went quickly to the other room, picked up the extension on his desk and then went back to the hall to make sure his wife had replaced that one. Making an effort to sound normal in case his wife could overhear, Sir George began, "Now, my dear Stanislas, tell me all the arrangements - you know I am only too happy to help." Like hell thought Stanislas as he instructed Matthews to take a Eurostar to arrive in Paris just after noon and then take a taxi to the Hotel Luxembourg Parc where a double room - he mentioned he had made it a twin-bedded one - was booked in Sir George's name for two nights.

"What about the object I've arranged?" Sir George interrupted. "It is going to be given to me while I'm in Paris." Stanislas hadn't realised this but immediately went on;

"In that case the kind present you have promised me should be delivered to you before three thirty that afternoon. I will contact you at four o'clock and we'll take a little walk together in the Jardins du Luxembourg - just opposite your hotel - it's very pleasant there in the late afternoon and not very crowded. Is everything now clear to you? - I would get extremely nervous if there were any hitches?" The menace in Stanislas's voice was unmistakeable and Sir George could not help shivering.

"Oh yes, quite clear - really quite clear, thank you. I promise it'll all be OK. Nothing will go wrong."

"As long as that's so - I hope so for your sake - then I'll let you go. Oh! by the way - a happy coincidence, I'm playing golf tomorrow with your Chairman - he's over here for a long weekend with his wife - they're arriving from Luxembourg - probably been staying with his banker friends there - they've most likely been talking about foreign accounts! Shall I give him your regards, George?" After he'd rung off, Sir George poured himself a much larger than usual whisky before telling his excited wife that he was taking her to Paris for an early fortieth wedding anniversary present. He swallowed his drink as quickly as his wife swallowed his story, and then poured himself another.

For once everything had gone well. The early morning Air France air bus from Lisbon had landed some five minutes ahead of schedule, their luggage had been the first to appear on the carrousel and the little traffic their taxi encountered on the way in from Roissy hadn't delayed them. Thus just less than forty minutes after landing Stanislas and Natasha were being helped out of the cab by the door porter at the Hotel Meurice.

"Bonjour Monsieur Kortaski, bonjour Madame, bienvenue à Paris." He took their cases and led them through to the front desk. The receptionist smilingly booked them in,

"It's a pleasure to have you back with us, Monsieur Kortaski, it's been a long time since your last stay."

"Well I am just an old retired man now," laughed Stanislas, "can't afford to come to Paris that often nowadays, but we're here to celebrate my wife's birthday - thank you for your welcome, it's good to be back." Handing the electronic key to a porter she smiled at Natasha,

"Edouard will show you up to your room and I'll have your baggage sent up straightaway. I hope you enjoy your stay." Without changing her professional smile she turned to deal with the next couple. Up in their room Stanislas looked at his watch, and said,

"Come on, its twelve fifteen, we'll walk up to the Crillon and have a glass of champagne before we decide where to lunch." In the end they went to the Hotel Costes - somewhere Natasha didn't know and where she pretended to be a little jealous of her husband admiring the collection of very decorative models who appeared to be regulars.

"Don't worry, darling, I'm at least as old as their grandfathers - I don't think they'd be interested in me," joked Stanislas. After lunch they walked back into the Rue de Rivoli and, turning left, window shopped as they strolled to the Louvre. Taking the escalator down they wandered round the subterranean shopping precinct - known as the Carousel de la Louvre. While Natasha was queuing to pay for some post cards she had picked from the rack, waiting outside the shop, Stanislas heard his mobile sound in his pocket, looking at it he saw he had received one message. He read it quickly - it merely told him that 'E' had arrived in Paris and Stanislas should call the number listed tomorrow lunchtime. As Natasha joined him he smiled and began,

"Darling, I'm sorry I'm going to have to leave you just for a short time to call someone from the hotel - there was a little thing I didn't have time to finish before we left and I promised I'd deal with it today. Why don't you take a stroll round the Louvre - there don't seem to be too many people waiting at the moment - and we can meet back at the hotel. Look, it's three thirty now - shall we say six-thirty. That'll give you enough time for some shopping afterwards if you like."

"I thought this was our weekend - can't your business wait until we get home?"

"I'm really very sorry Natasha, you have a look round here and then the shops and we'll have the whole evening for dinner just by ourselves - I promise." Stanislas kissed her cheek, squeezed her hand and turned away. He found a call box a little way down the road on the other side near the Palais Royal and using the phone card he bought in the Tabac on the corner, dialled the number of the Hotel Luxembourg Parc.

"Puis-je parler à Sir George Matthews s'il vous plaît?" he began. Recognising his Anglo-Saxon accent the voice at the other end replied immediately in English,

"Certainly Sir, I'll put you through." He waited perhaps ten seconds and then Matthews was on the line.

"Hello, Stanislas, you got us a very good hotel - we arrived about three hours ago, some hold up in the tunnel."

"Right - have you brought what I need with you?"

"Yes, that was waiting for me here. All is well my dear friend, don't worry." Stanislas gave Matthews his instructions,

"In twenty minutes you are to enter the Jardins du Luxembourg - turn right out of your hotel and enter by the gate beside the Art Gallery. Turn left once you are in the gardens and walk up past the Orangerie until, just after a fountain on your left a flight of steps goes up to a memorial to some resistance fighters who were shot by the Germans - I will meet you there. Is that clear?"

"Yes, yes that's quite simple, I'll look forward to seeing you." Unctuous as ever Sir George looked at the time, "twenty minutes from now you said?"

"Yes - and George - don't forget to bring the little present with you."

"Of course not," finished Matthews looking at the package which two hours ago the young Indian employee of Ajay had brought him. He'd had the embarrassment of having to introduce him to his wife and offer him a drink downstairs in the public lounge. He had drawn the line when the Indian had suggested they go up to the bedroom to inspect the object. He had taken a chance and done that later when he was by himself - thank God, he swore to himself, it looked perfect to his admittedly untrained eye. Sir George put the phone down.

"Who was that, George, no one knows we're in Paris? Let's go for a little walk before having a tea somewhere - it says in this guide that St. Germaine is just down the road, we can have a little stroll round there, dear." Matthews tried hard not to panic -

"Darling," he lied, using the term of address he only used in emergencies, "that call was just for an important customer of the bank. I happened to mention we were coming here the other day at lunch and he asked me to do him a favour and bring something over for his son who's at college here. I'm just going to meet the boy now for five minutes so it's done - then I can forget it - I'll come straight back and we'll go out." Lady Matthews was cross,

"What is going on, George, first you have some wretched Indian boy come to the hotel as if you've ordered a takeaway curry and now you - a director of the bank - have to do the job of a messenger. Really you let people use you far too much, you're too kind - I've always said you're far too conscientious."

"Yes dear," Sir George said as he picked up the parcel and left the room. Three minutes later, and after being very nearly mown down by a bus when he forgot to look left instead of right crossing the road, he passed the fountain and went up the stone steps. He saw Stanislas waiting for him, sitting in the spring sunshine. He got up as Matthews approached and shook his outstretched hand looking at the package in the other one.

"Have you checked it - can you guarantee that the thing is good enough?" he asked.

"Yes, I promise you, it's been copied by the best Indian diamond expert, I told you I could arrange it - here it is. Take it." Sir George was almost truculent - his relief was evident.

"Well I'll check all that later - well before you leave Paris so should there be a problem?" He seemed to pause and he pointed to the memorial on the ground, "I often think it awful how those poor resistance fighters were shot without any mercy right at the end of the occupation....." his voice faded away but Matthews understood its tone and shivered despite the warm sun. Stanislas looked at his watch - he had an hour or more before he said he would meet his wife back at the hotel. Although Natasha wasn't an extravagant person he slightly tremored at the thought of her alone in Paris with the credit cards and then smiled to himself when he thought that in his pocket now he was carrying something that could earn him many millions of dollars. She could buy what she liked the he thought. "I'll walk back with you to your hotel, George," he said feeling almost a tinge of pity for the pompous little man now that he had fulfilled his task. Sir George felt uneasy, he didn't want Stanislas meeting his wife, but couldn't think how to put him off without looking suspicious.

"I'd ask you for a drink but we're going out with...." he began, but to his relief was interrupted by Stanislas,

"That would be very nice but I must get back - don't want to interrupt your weekend too much. You've got a lot to discover I expect - this is a fascinating City." Matthews objected to being talked to in this condescending tone - he wanted to say he had been to Paris before, but for once prudence overcame his pride, and he remained silent. As they reached the Luxembourg Palace, neither of them noticed a young black haired Indian man with a drooping moustache following some thirty metres behind. He was carrying a small digital camera. Had Sir George turned and seen him, he perhaps would have remembered his face from the delivery made just a few hours before. Leaving the gardens they crossed over the rue Vaugirard and said their goodbyes. Opposite two members of the Garde Républicaine, on sentry duty outside the entrance to the Senate, had watched uninterestedly as the young Indian took a photo of the two men shake hands before crossing the road himself and following Stanislas. Holding the package in his pocket, Stanislas thought he would go back by foot to the hotel - he had plenty of time and he enjoyed walking round Paris. His route took him past the Musée d'Orsay and he thought perhaps he'd bring Natasha there before they left. Taking the footbridge across to the jardins des Tuileries he reached their hotel bedroom room five minutes before Natasha entered with three rather large and expensive looking carrier bags. On her way in she had slipped and dropped one just by the hotel's revolving doors and she had thanked the polite dark skinned young man who had helped her pick it up. Before she arrived her husband had had just enough time to call Eric and tell him that all was in order and announce that he had the replica safely ready to give him the next day. Eric had been rather short with him, cutting him off by saying he'd call at eleven thirty tomorrow and they would meet just after that.

"Have you had a good afternoon, darling?" Stanislas asked his slightly breathless wife. Natasha smiled and answered with a kiss,

"It's so lovely to be in Paris and you are really wonderful to arrange all this just for me." He looked proudly at Natasha - how beautiful his wife was, he thought, and being some twenty years younger than him he felt a lucky man to have married her. He smiled,

"I've booked a table tonight at Le Dôme for dinner - I haven't been there for ages and you love fish. For tomorrow evening the concierge is trying to get us tickets for the opera." She kissed him again. Later after they had showered and dressed for the evening, a taxi took them to their dinner. The next morning, unusually Natasha was up first, but Stanislas soon followed her and they rang down to room service for breakfast. She only wanted a coffee and perhaps a croissant, but Stanislas couldn't resist asking for two poached eggs as well - they were a weakness of his and he remembered the hotel did them particularly well.

"That's just sheer greed darling - after last night," Natasha complained, "you'll have to play more golf when we get home. I don't want to lose that athletic energetic man I fell in love with do I?" They waited in bed for the food to arrive. At the same time as room service tapped on the door, the phone rang - Stanislas picked it up, but as he said hello all he heard was a click and someone hanging up. He looked at the time - a quarter past nine - that can't be

Eric he thought, perhaps it was a wrong number. He picked up the receiver again and dialled the hotel operator.

"Did you just put a call through to this room?" He asked as he acknowledged the bonjour of the breakfast waiter with a nod.

"Yes Sir, there was an outside call for you, but they seem to have been cut off. As soon as they ring back I'll re-connect you."

"Thank you - please ask them who they are first, I don't want to be disturbed on a Saturday." Natasha noticed his slight unease,

"What is it, dear, don't worry, come and have your eggs - they'll spoil if you wait." He sat down opposite his wife and together they enjoyed their breakfast. He was fortunate - Natasha wanted to go back to one of the shops she had visited yesterday and then was going to have a quick lunch with an old friend who had married a Frenchman and lived at Neuilly.

"I'm sorry, Stanislas, but I haven't seen Felicity for ages and I just told her we were here for a quick visit. It was either a lunch today or she really wanted us both to have dinner with them at their flat."

"No, you go for your lunch, don't worry. Thank God its not the dinner - he's a frightful bore, thanks for getting me out of that one. Do you need some cash?"

"Thanks darling, give me just a few notes in case, but I've got my card." Kissing him she left and he waited impatiently for the call from Eric, whiling away the time zapping through the various television channels, eventually settling on some old travelogue extolling the virtues of St. Petersburg. Exactly at eleven thirty the phone ring startled him - picking it up Stanislas waited for the caller to speak.

"Hello, Mr. Kortaski?" It was Eric.

"Yes - sorry not to have spoken, but I'll tell you why when we meet. How do you want to do this? I have everything here for you." Eric was very short and to the point,

"Go into the Tuileries Gardens just opposite your hotel. Turn right on the central path towards the Place de la Concorde until you reach the pond. On your right you will see the Jeu de Paume and on the side towards that there is a statue of the Chat Botté - I will meet you there in thirty minutes. Is that clear?"

"Yes - Oh by the way..." Stanislas began to answer, but the dialling tone already showed that Eric had gone. He took the small package that Sir George Matthews had given him the afternoon before and while he waited could not resist taking another look at its contents. Using a handkerchief to hold the replica he was amazed by its beauty - there was no other word to describe it - he was sure this would fool all but the very top experts. Putting it back in its wrapping he went down to meet the Russian. Waiting for the green light to cross the road he didn't see the small Indian man hidden from his view behind two slightly larger Japanese tourists.

The other side of the road Stanislas entered the gardens. It was a typically beautiful clear May lunchtime and he was as impressed as any of the tourists there by the view stretching from the Louvre behind him, up the Champs Elysée past the Arc de Triomphe to the skyscrapers and Mitterand's Grande Arche at La Défense. Slightly to his left he could see the Eiffel Tower pointing up to the cloudless sky and for a moment he almost forgot his immediate business as he took in the whole scene. He certainly didn't notice the same Indian from yesterday following about twenty five metres behind. He reached the pond and looked over to the right - there he could see Eric, standing alone by the statue - he felt disappointed as he had half hoped to see Liza again - but as he approached he was greeted by the thinnest of smiles from the Russian. They shook hands in silence before Eric spoke,

"Igor has told me all is well with the initial payment - the correct Zurich account has been credited and all can go ahead." The rigid formality and impersonal manner of Eric both impressed and at the same time slightly unnerved Stanislas - he could never imagine this man as a friend – he was a complete professional. He held the package in his pocket as Eric told him to go with him across to the other side of the gardens towards the river. He saw there was some maintenance work being done in the area and with this discouraging the tourists and the workers off for lunch it was far more deserted than where they were. They stopped under the shade of a tree.

"Right, I have the replica - to me it looks perfect for our purposes. Here it is." He handed the wrapped forgery to Eric who, hardly looking at it, immediately put it into his jacket pocket before replying,

"Right - you can leave everything to us now. It's probably best if we don't communicate again very much except in an emergency until we meet in Lisbon. I will, of course, report progress every so often to you. Liza and I will be in Geneva fairly shortly, but just one detail - to avoid detection I think the closer to the Sale date we can make the exchange the better so you'll probably not see us in Lisbon until after the Auction. I'll keep you informed one way or another, but remember call boxes are far less traceable than mobile phones"

"Thank you Eric - can I offer you a drink or something before we part?" They walked to the centrally placed café and sat at a table in the sunshine as they ordered two beers. Eric looked round and then turned back leaning slightly closer to Stanislas. "Have you brought anyone with you - a bodyguard or something?"

"Absolutely not - why do you ask such a strange question - why on earth would I do that?"

"Well I noticed as you arrived just now you had a young chap following you - he looks rather Indian - with a moustache, certainly Asian - and since we've been together he's followed us, seems to be busy with his camera too. I don't like it. Look round casually and he's just over your left shoulder." Stanislas took some beer and waiting a few seconds before pretending to turn to watch a pretty girl walk by - he saw him at once.

"That's the Indian who opened the door at the hotel for me last night - what on earth is he playing at - I'm going to ask him." Half getting up Stanislas was pushed back into his seat by Eric,

"No you're certainly not. We'll carry on pretending we haven't even seen him. Don't worry I'll easily find out what he's up to, if anything, after you've gone - remember I've got some experience of that sort of thing - if he is doing something he shouldn't I promise you he won't be doing it for long. He'll not worry you again." Stanislas looked at Eric with a certain amount of respect - it took one professional to recognise another - even so he couldn't help slightly shivering. "Again I repeat don't expect us in Lisbon until after the Auction. We will be in touch, but as I said never forget that call boxes are far less traceable than mobiles phones."

They finished their drinks and Stanislas went back to the hotel after saying goodbye to Eric. On his way he went into Smiths, the English bookshop, to waste some time. He bought the newspaper and then picked up the latest copy of Country Life and flicking through its pages he suddenly saw a special article talking about the forthcoming sale of the 'Tsarina's Diamond.' Closing the magazine he went to the cash desk and bought it - he'd read it properly later but he thought at least the Auction House's publicity machine is working well. After Natasha returned to the hotel from lunch with her friend just before three o'clock they decided they'd take the metro down to the Bastille and have a walk round the Place des Vosges - the beautiful square built by Louis X111 where Victor Hugo lived - and then have a tea somewhere before coming back to get ready for the Opera. Stanislas was very happy and impressed as ever that the Chief Porter had worked his usual magic and conjured up two rather good seats for that evening's performance. He even thought the inflated price not unreasonable given their gold dust like quality. They walked across the road and went down into the Metro. As they put their tickets into the barrier to pass through they were stopped by a gendarme.

"There's been an accident, Sir, and the service is temporarily suspended - could be for some time I'm afraid, where do you want to get to?" They mentioned the Bastille - "In that case your best way is to walk down to the station at the Chatelet - they're turning the trains round there." Behind them a crowd was beginning to build up, Stanislas heard someone say to one of the officials,

"The usual reason, I suppose, unusual on a Saturday afternoon though!" He remained rooted to the spot when he heard the reply,

"Yes - it's a tourist we think, looked like a young Indian, seemed to fall straight in front of the train. Killed instantly poor chap."

"I'm not surprised, these platforms are too narrow when they're full with all the foreign visitors like today - everyone pushing and shoving - specially on this line. People will stand so close to the edge in the crush - its all too easy - poor devil." Stanislas took Natasha's hand as he turned and led her out back into the open air.

"Are you all right dear?" she asked, "you look a bit shaken."

"It's nothing darling, really nothing, I just suddenly felt a bit claustrophobic with all the people down there - don't worry - come on, we'll take a taxi, there's one over there outside the hotel." Later back in their room Stanislas watched the regional news while changing for the evening. The fourth item was about the earlier accident. A photograph of the victim was flashed up on the screen together with an appeal for anyone who might recognise him to come forward. Apparently no identity documents were found on him

- his digital camera had been squashed by the train wheels. Although perhaps not surprised it was still rather difficult for Stanislas to hide his shock as he found himself looking at the same Indian who had been in the Tuileries earlier. It was lucky Natasha was still in the bathroom taking a shower. Across the river in their own hotel Sir George and Lady Matthews were already for the evening and enjoying a half bottle of Champagne between them in the lounge. In the far corner some other guests were casually watching the news waiting to see what the weather was going to be the next day. Rather ostentatiously sipping her champagne Lady Matthews glanced over at them - as she saw her husband's visitor of yesterday staring at her from the screen, with the appeal for witnesses to come forward sub-titled across the bottom, some champagne unfortunately took the wrong route and went up her nose. Her noisy snort brought the waiter rushing over with a glass of water.

"George did you see that - on the television? I'm sure it was your little curry messenger man from yesterday - he's been killed." She was trying to whisper, but her remark was more like a stage aside and several other guests turned to look at the Matthews.

"Nonsense dear - I didn't see it, but they all look the same. In any case he was just a messenger - don't know where he came from." Fortunately Matthews hadn't seen the photo on the television and didn't give it another thought as they enjoyed their dinner at La Coupole. When they returned to the hotel afterwards the night porter had a message for him. It simply said please could he have a word with the manager tomorrow morning before leaving. He nodded, thought no more about it and had a good night's sleep despite his wife's wine induced snoring. The next morning they packed their cases to pick up later when they took a taxi for their four-thirty something Eurostar. As Sir George approached the reception desk to settle his bill, a young man, dressed in the regulation black jacket and pinstripe trousers of an Hotel manager, came out of the room behind and in near perfect English asked Sir George if he could spare him five minutes in his office. Matthews nodded, told Lady Matthews to wait for him in the lounge and followed the manager.

"How can I help you?"

"Please sit down, Sir George, I am very sorry to trouble you but it is perhaps a slightly delicate matter - I don't quite know how to put it!" the manager began, rather wishing it hadn't been him on duty that particular Sunday, "but last night on the television news there was an item about some poor Asian man killed on the Metro and asking if anyone knew who he was."

"What on earth has that to do with me young man - why do you tell me this? We're only visitors here for the weekend you know." The young man shifted uncomfortably and tried to ignore the question. He continued,

"Well I understand someone called for you at the hotel yesterday morning, I don't know more as I wasn't on duty myself, but our door porter says it was the same man he saw on the television yesterday evening as having been killed. I just wondered if you could tell me more about him and whether you think you could help the police trace who he is? - he was carrying no papers." The manager was clearly embarrassed as Matthews replied,

"Someone did bring round something for me, that's right, but I have absolutely no idea who he was. He was just some young delivery chap I suppose - must have worked for a courier firm. Of course I'd like to help if I was in a position to, but really it may not even be the same man. He was here only for a very short time and I'm not sure I'd recognise him again."

"I hope you don't take any offence of my asking, Sir George, but I told the porter I'd have a word - he was feeling quite anxious about it. Please think nothing more about it and in any case we have your address should, by chance, we need it." Matthews did not like the implications of this last remark, but managed to hide his feelings as he replied,

"My dear chap, I quite understand, you did right to mention it to me. Don't be angry with your porter - he must see so many people its very easy for him to make a mistake." The manager ushered Sir George out,

"Thank you Sir, I do hope you've enjoyed your stay with us - come again before too long." Matthews rejoined his wife, but did not tell her any of their conversation - instead implying that the man wanted some introductions to London hotels for a job in England.

"People can't resist asking me to help them," he told his wife - "such is leadership." The manager looked at the duty roster - he would have to wait until tomorrow morning before he could tell the porter the result of his chat. It was only later that he realised that he had forgotten to ask Sir George Matthews which firm had made his delivery, but then he reflected the whole thing was actually none of his business.

CHAPTER TWENTY THREE

NORTHERN SPAIN

It was now nearly thirty six hours since François had been brought to the emergency wing of Najera's ultra modern hospital. Thanks to the efficiency and dedication of the staff his condition remained stable. His twitching suggested that beneath the coma his dream continued..........Weeping and wailing, the grief ridden parents left the gibbet site without a backward glance as the body of their only child swung silently in the evening breeze. Ebbo's remains were not a pretty spectacle, as his flesh changed from pink and white to black and purple. His already scant clothing had partially uncovered a dead body swollen with gasses and as the coarse linen of his skirt fell untidily, two mange ridden dogs vied with each other to tear the remains from off him. Supporting each other Lucus and Marta slowly crept away in the direction of the cathedral where to their relief they found an open transept door. Inside they collapsed to sleep. They were penniless, hungry, thirsty and cold. At Belorado, the two militiamen had robbed them of everything they had, even what small items of spare clothing they possessed had been snatched away. The stone on which they lay gave sparse comfort, leaving only their utmost faith in the goodliness of Saint Iago, to whom devotedly they prayed till the morning light enabled them to crawl away seeking a pauper pilgrim's charity from the monastery. A distant bell clanged from behind the massive door of the Santo Domingo monastery. Built nearly thirty years before, it harboured some 150 monks whose supposed purpose was, apart from praying, to give succour to weary pilgrims, who in ever increasing numbers were beginning to visit Santo Domingo on their way to Santiago de Compostela 500 kilometres to the West.

"Who are you and what do you want?" barked a surly member of the brotherhood.

"We are poor pilgrims from Worms in Germany" replied the pathetic couple.

"You ought to know then that we never open our doors to pilgrims earlier than 2 o'clock in the afternoon." It is a fallacy to imagine that a hood covered shaven head, a long brown cassock, sometimes a corded belt and usually crude leather footgear always indicate a warm and generous personality. Like any group of people there are some brothers naturally blessed with normal goodness and others are an example of utter brutishness - the duty brother doorman was typical of the latter kind. Lucus and Marta explained their plight, to which the Monk, recognising them from descriptions he had heard from ghoulish spectators at yesterday's hanging, took fright that he might become linked with associates of a recently condemned man. So, with a resounding thud he slammed shut the massive oaken door.

"We are doomed, we are worse than doomed, we will die of starvation or thirst or cold. What are we to do? Soon we'll be dead like Ebbo" howled Marta clinging to her husband. "We are outcasts nobody will help." Lucus was a strong man, who loved his wife and with his arms surrounding her he explained that he was not prepared to surrender so quickly to such an undeserved fate for either of them.

"If we have to, we will steal food ourselves and at

least if we get caught and punished it will be justice for a sin, unlike poor Ebbo, who has lead a blameless life and was completely innocent till the moment he died." With those words the hapless couple shuffled away to find any kind of crowded place where traders might be selling edible produce, which they could pilfer.

Thus in just over a fortnight Ebbo's tragic parents, having regained their strength, reached Santiago de Compostela having at least found some true Christian charity along the way. Nobody came after them to demand the return of the few pieces of fruit and loaf of bread they had stolen in Santo Domingo de la Calzada. On reaching the Galician countryside they became overwhelmed with spiritual zeal and experienced an inexplicable but nonetheless real magnetism leading them towards the tomb of the saint - one of the first apostles of Jesus Christ. Here they hoped to find a place of worship and some shelter. In fact they found a glorious site dominating a hilltop surrounded by rich forests of Holm Oak and scented Eucalyptus trees. The church was in an advanced state of construction containing at its heart the very sarcophagus of Saint Iago. Over a period of a thousand years this holy place had become the third most popular pilgrim destination in the world after Jerusalem and Rome. More than one hundred thousand faithful each year were walking, riding or sending other's in their stead to venerate the dusty bones buried deep beneath the floor of the cathedral. Spiritually refreshed and now thankfully physically restored, Lucus and Marta began making plans for the long trek to Worms - returning more than 2,000 kilometres and still with no funds with which to pay for any accommodation or provisions. The intensity of their prayers to Saint Iago were so impassioned that they convinced themselves that they should allow themselves to be born homewards to safety by the apostle himself. They had no fear that they would find adequate provision. Their deep faith was well rewarded when on the third day of the return march they saw approaching from the East, a small figure walking along the very path they had followed in the opposite direction a few days earlier. He was aided by a wooden staff a good deal taller than its carrier. As he approached they were enraptured to see beneath a large round brown coloured felt hat, the kindly face of a bearded man of diminutive stature. In fact he couldn't have stood more than 140 centimetres, wearing a well worn brown cassock on which were clinging a multitude of scallop shells. On his round hat too, with its upturned frontal brim, he wore another scallop shell. They hailed him joyfully as he approached within twenty metres, but despite his kindly smiling visage no sound of reply came forth. Instead they both smelt the unmistakeable tang of the sea, the salt, the brine, all fresh and clean. The figure walked on passed them and just as he appeared from nowhere he vanished in the same way. Shaken, but certainly not afraid, Lucus turned to Marta and said

"That figure was surely none other than St. Jakobus." Marta, who was quaking with emotion like Lucus fell to her knees and implored the vanished figure to give them a sign or symbol before tearfully turning for reassurance to her husband. His response came quickly enough when he said

"Look Marta, one of his scallop shells has fallen from his cassock and is lying in our path. What does that mean?"   This time it was for Marta, the knowledgeable one, to say.

"My Dear Lucus, have you forgotten that Saint Iago was ship-wrecked off the Spanish coast of Galicia, and when his body was washed ashore it was covered with scallop shells." As in a trance she continued "Saint Iago himself has blessed us in God's name by giving us one of his everlasting shells. We must wear it ourselves and guard it with the utmost care so that in turn it will guard us." Without fully understanding what had happened or how the nights and days had passed, they arrived only eighteen days later at the gates of Santo Domingo. They hadn't realised that with pilgrimage their visual appearance had changed for the worse and they were unrecognisable as the parents of Ebbo the long dead thief. This time their arrival at the monastery was without a problem and they were even granted the comfort of a cell each in which to rest and pray. Grieving doesn't carry a given span, but rather more its desperation gradually dwindles unless re-kindled by events. The little brown cassock clad figure was never far from their minds and it was thoughts of him that gave them the courage to re-visit, broken hearted, the site of Ebbo's hanging. Enquiries concerning the actual burial spot of the supposedly guilty boy were not forthcoming and Lucus feared that the body would have been cut down and taken away for dumping in an open pit. Nevertheless, holding tight to Marta's hand, at dawn next morning they walked trembling in the direction of where they remembered the gibbet had stood. What they saw was so incredible it defied all belief. There, still hanging by the neck from the gibbet was their son who they believed was dead. The faintest glow of a smile played round his lips and his eyes instead of shut were glittering. As if from Ebbo's mouth came words, perfectly clear, saying,

"Father, Mother, you have seen Saint Iago, who appeared to you in acknowledgment of your prayers. He has been beside me now these thirty six days and all the while he has let me stand upon his shoulders whilst he fed me and sponged my face with water. You prayed to Saint Iago just as I did. Hence he visited you on your return journey from Santiago de Compostela and helped you to come back here safely to find me. Now cut me down dear parents, and you will find me well and unharmed by this experience." Ebbo's parents dropped to their knees and crossing themselves they exclaimed in unison "We have truly seen a miracle."

CHAPTER TWENTY FOUR

GENEVA

Although it was over two months since the initial announcement of the sale had been made, the auction of what the press described as 'The Tsarina's hidden diamond' was still attracting a great amount of publicity - both locally and around the world. When Eric and Liza arrived in Geneva in the middle of May some two weeks before the date when the hammer would fall, the press were still giving it front page prominence. The gossip columns were having a field day speculating on which film star or footballer would try to buy what would be the ultimate status symbol for their wife or girl-friend to flaunt. One paper had David Beckham as 'definitely' prepared to bid, another apparently had 'inside knowledge' that it would be Catherine Zeta-Jones who would be wearing it, while a third 'knew' that the Prince of Wales was determined that his long term mistress Camilla Parker-Bowles should be adequately rewarded for her years of waiting before he would finally get around to marrying her. The Hermitage Museum had apparently announced their interest and hoped that it would return there as part of the history and heritage of Russia. There was an unsubstantiated report that Oleg Grodientov, one of the senior curators of the museum, had flown in from St. Petersburg and was due to be one of the first to be allowed to view it when the Auction house put it on display for the two weeks before the sale. The international press had been invited to a view the day before prospective buyers would start to see it and this achieved even more publicity for the sale. Speculation as to the possible price ranged from rather a conservative seventeen million dollars to perhaps a rather over optimistic forty million dollars, but as far as the Auctioneers - and the unknown 'gentleman' who was the seller - were concerned this was all only excellent coverage, which continued to create an enormous interest in the whole business. There had been, also, a lot of speculation about the identity of the seller ranging from the few remaining living relatives of the old

Russian royal family through a list of other possibilities from a very senior member of the House of Windsor to perhaps a descendant of one of the revolutionary gang who had murdered the Tsar and his family and had stolen it at that time. The Auction house had a list of twenty potential bidders who had asked to be able to view the stone - all had had to satisfy the company that they were serious contenders supplying the necessary information about their various backgrounds and financial resources. Although this information was in any case kept strictly confidential, most potential bidders were sending their experts and agents to do the viewing on their behalf. All this secrecy only whetted the appetite of the press for more gossip and apart from the names originally talked about there was also press conjecture about at least twenty five other possibilities such as Bill Gates, the Grimaldi family and the Rothschilds. All were avidly discussed, only to be eliminated by some, confirmed as certain buyers by others, or to be discarded when more possibilities joined the field. There were even some minor show business celebrities and second rank business people from various countries who carefully let slip that they could be interested in the hope that some of the fervent publicity would rub off on them - the business men hoping their rivals, and their banks, would believe that they could afford such a purchase. A newspaper reported with some satisfaction that this had rebounded already on a French business man running his own company from Marseille, when the tax authorities had asked him why his previous tax returns had ignored any possible liability to the wealth tax, and that if he was thinking of buying a twenty million dollar diamond perhaps he might be liable for this. After this article appeared there was less interest shown from that particular section.

It was in the middle of all this speculation and publicity - willingly fuelled by the hard working public relations team at the Auctioneers - that Eric and Liza settled into the small two roomed apartment in Carouge on which a 'Mr. Everly' had paid a deposit and a months rent in advance to the agents at the end of April. 'Just as well they gave me the key then', thought Eric to himself, 'they might not have recognised me again without the moustache, blonde hair and glasses.' It was rather a hot and humid early evening, so Eric and Liza were pleased to have arrived at their apartment in the

Rue Ancienne and relax after their three and a half hour journey in the train from Paris. Eric had chosen to travel by train as the entry formalities at Cornavin Station were usually less stringent than the more security conscious Cointrin airport, and he was simply carrying the copy of the diamond in his jacket pocket. Earlier he had met Liza as arranged at the Gare de Lyon where they'd had just enough time to catch the TGV. After he had left Stanislas in the Jardins des Tuileries he had made his way slowly on purpose to the Metro where the platform was five or six deep with tourists taking the line down to the Louvre or the Bastille. It was more his sixth sense than anything else that told him that the Indian he had pointed out earlier was still just behind him. At the moment a train entered the station he moved to the platform edge and a split second later turned and, with no perceptible movement noticed by anyone, simply pushed his totally unprepared stalker by the elbow into the path of the train. No one had seen the quick movement nor noticed him leave in the ensuing commotion and he quickly regained ground level where he soon found a taxi to go and meet Liza. He was quiet on the train, but Liza thought this was merely a result of the late night they had enjoyed the previous evening in Montmartre.

Settling into their temporary home they watched the early news on the television - the last item was of another American film star expressing interest in the diamond sale, probably for a fee from the public relations people Eric thought - before walking to the Place du Marché at the end of the street and eating an excellent steak in the restaurant on the corner. For just a short moment Liza thought they could be mistaken for any normal couple in love and on holiday together as they sat finishing their bottle of wine.

The next morning Eric prepared his papers - Igor had produced a false letter of introduction purporting to come from the Armoury, the magnificent museum inside the Kremlin which houses the opulent collection of treasures accumulated over the centuries by the Russian Orthodox Church and the State, which stated that a Mr. Gregor Ivanowitch - one of their senior fine stone experts would be requesting a view of the diamond being offered for sale and requesting that the Auction house give him every co-operation. The letter added that by way of identification Mr. Ivanowitch carried his Russian passport number ZAM 65294/KL and detailed its date and place of issue. They also requested that, because of the acute rivalry with the Hermitage in St. Petersburg, the visit and interest of their representative be kept strictly confidential and secret. As he read these documents Eric's admiration for Igor's forgery skills only increased - even the passport had a well-used look and contained several interesting visa stamps. A similar one had been provided for Liza.

He waited until eleven o'clock before he rang the Auction house. The telephonist had a little difficulty understanding his effected heavily Russian accented English, but in the end he was put through to the director, who, she told him,   was in charge of arranging the viewing of what she described as the 'Tsarina's diamond.'

"Ah - yes, Mr. Ivanowitch, we received yesterday a letter from your Direction in Moscow, I have been expecting your telephone call - welcome to Geneva." He sounds very friendly thought Eric, thankfully realising that for once the Russian postal service had worked and Igor's letter had arrived in time. The voice the other end continued, "When would it be convenient for you to visit us, Sir, I presume you'd like to come as soon as possible?" Eric broke in,

"Yes - I would be grateful - there's a lot for me to appraise before the sale date in assessing what our bid should be and you appreciate that while my advice is the most important, the final decision will be made in Moscow following my report."

"Yes, of course, now let me see," Eric could hear the man shuffle some papers, "would eleven-thirty tomorrow be convenient for you?" After what he thought was a reasonable pause Eric confirmed that would indeed be convenient. "Good, you obviously have our address, so I'll expect you tomorrow - have you visited us before?"

"No, this will be the first time I'm afraid, but as the letter you have received says I will be bringing a copy of that together with my passport."

"Oh, Mr Ivanowitch all that is quite in order, don't worry - we are very much looking forward to someone from the Armoury coming here - it will be a pleasure to see you - no, all I was going to say is that you come to our front desk in the normal way and ask for me - Jonathan Hamilton-Gray - I will tell my staff to expect you."

'There's no need to ask whether you're English,' thought Eric to himself as he noted the name, before adding aloud,

"Just one thing you should perhaps know Mr Hamilton- Gray, I will be bringing my assistant, Anastasia Votrikova, with me - she'll have her passport as well - I hope that is all right?"

"Absolutely no problem, Sir, we'll await your visit tomorrow - in the meantime I hope you have a good day in our City, till we meet then, goodbye Mr. Ivanowitch." Eric put down the phone and told Liza what the arrangements were,

"Tomorrow we start to earn that lovely fee – it's really good to have something to work on again, I sometimes miss the old days!"

Eric put away the false papers before he and Liza left the apartment and took the tram into the centre of town to have lunch over-looking the lake.

"Just think, Liza, tomorrow we will be handling something the last Tsar probably handled himself, it's quite a thought isn't it?" After lunch they did not go straight back to the flat, but walked passed the Auction house where Eric noted the buildings either side and worked out the quickest route down to the jetty on the lake. He and Liza also looked at the on-street parking arrangements and checked the position of the various CCTV cameras in the area - a little later he bought a small spray can of black paint just in case he needed to put a few of them out of action quickly. Eventually, satisfied that they had seen all they needed before their first viewing tomorrow, they watched some water skiers taking advantage of the early season sunshine before catching the return tram to Carouge and another excellent steak later in the evening. Afterwards back in the apartment, they both, despite their professionalism, took some time to get to sleep as they anticipated the events of the next few days. Although after Liza rather easily persuaded Eric to help her relax by the way they both preferred, they both slept soundly until the radio alarm woke them rather sharply at seven-thirty - they had four hours before their appointment.

They took their time showering and dressing and then had a leisurely breakfast before they got ready for their eleven-thirty appointment the other side of town at the Auctioneers. In his role as a senior member of the curatory staff at the Armoury, Eric decided to wear a suit and put on a pair of heavily framed glasses which helped to give him an extra air of seriousness. Liza dressed in the international uniform of jeans, tight enough to show off her long legs, and topped by just a white cotton blouse - the summer weather had already arrived in Geneva. They left the apartment just before eleven o'clock and, after waiting five minutes at the stop, sat at the back of the tram, which took them across to the other side of the Rhone commencing its journey down to the Mediterranean. They arrived outside the Auction house some ten minutes early. Without waiting they went through the double blackened glass doors into the air-conditioned luxurious comfort of the rather grand oak panelled and marble floored reception hall. To their left Eric noted that there were two lifts, although the old styled building was only four stories high, and straight ahead he saw a very impressive double staircase leading to the gallery style first floor. The whole scene spoke of wealth, discretion and taste. Turning to their right they approached the smiling receptionist sitting behind an impressive antique oak reception desk.

"Good morning Monsieur, Good morning Madame – it's Mr. Ivanowitch and Madame Votrikova isn't it? Welcome to our offices." Eric was a little surprised by the efficiency of the reception - the girl had taken out the letter of introduction which Igor had sent them and asked them both for their passports as she said, "Purely for routine you understand, so I can note your visit in our records." He was even more surprised by the apparent complete lack of security although he was sure there were cameras recording the whole process hidden somewhere in the wooden panelling. The receptionist dialled a three digit number on the desk telephone and Eric and Liza heard their arrival being announced after her call was answered immediately. "Mr. Hamilton-Gray is coming down straight away, Mr. Ivanowitch, please take a seat while you wait," the girl said, as she replaced her phone. They moved to the area just beyond the reception desk where there were two large black leather chairs accompanied by a matching settee. Before they had a chance to flick through any of the glossy catalogues lying on the glass coffee table the lift doors opened and a well dressed - good looking although typically English, Liza thought - man of about thirty five with longish wavy brown hair approached them with his hand outstretched.

"Mr. Ivanowitch, Madame Votrikova how do you do. I am very

pleased to welcome you to Geneva - at least you avoided the thunderstorms of last week." He had an assured confident calm and smiled as he caught Liza's eye. It was Eric, who smiled in return as he replied,

"It was good of you to arrange our viewing so quickly - you appreciate that this has to be done with the greatest discretion and secrecy as in no way does my museum wish for its interest to be known before the auction. That would make it very difficult for me and of course for my colleagues back in Moscow. You can imagine the rivalry going on between the various parties involved in Russia because of the immense historical significance of this diamond and any talk of our possible intervention could seriously damage our chances. Perhaps I shouldn't even ask you the question, but may I have your assurance on this point now?" The auctioneer, who had been discretely inspecting Liza, hid his annoyance at what he regarded the Russian's impertinence and replied that, of course, Eric could have his absolute assurance and guarantee on this point - he couldn't help adding that his company only enjoyed the excellent world-wide reputation it did because of very many years of proven reliability in such matters. Mr. Hamilton-Gray ushered his visitors over to the lift and took them up to the second floor where his office overlooked the gardens at the back of the building. Without him having asked for it, his secretary brought in a tray of coffee together with a selection of mineral waters - Eric and Liza nodded when she offered them the coffee as they sat down opposite the auctioneer. Liza smiled warmly at Hamilton-Gray as she slowly crossed her legs in her chair. She saw his eyes lower as he watched her jeans tighten over her long thighs and kept his gaze there for some seconds. As she leant forward to put her coffee cup down on the table she allowed the unbuttoned top of her shirt to fall open just long enough for him to catch a glimpse inside. She caught his eye and again smiled back holding his gaze until he seemed to redden slightly and quickly looked away. Eric watched this apparent accidental exchange and said to himself, 'Good, Liza's got his attention - he's taken the bait.' Liza began the real conversation,

"Please tell us about the sale arrangements, Mr. Hamilton-Gray, we don't want to waste your time."

"You appreciate that this wonderful diamond has only just been put on view," Hamilton-Gray began, "and we are expecting a really great amount of interest from all parts of the world. You may have seen some of the publicity going on in the western press as well as in your own country since the announcement of the sale and we have had more enquiries already about this item than any other I can remember for a very long time. It really does seem to have captured the imagination of a whole lot of potential buyers." While they finished their drinks Liza thought Eric managed to cover quite well with some vague generalities when, to their alarm, the auctioneer started to discuss the items in the Armoury and the other museums after mentioning that he had visited several when he and some friends had spent a long weekend in Moscow some fifteen months before. At last, thought Eric, as Hamilton-Gray eventually suggested they go down a floor where they could inspect, as he put it, the object of all the interest. This time they ignored the lifts and walked down to the floor below.

"Just one thing, Mr. Ivanowitch, perhaps you could take these gloves in case you need to handle the diamond," he handed across a pair of white cloth gloves as he spoke. Eric took them but replied,

"Thank you, but today I want, if I may, only to make a preliminary inspection - thorough, of course, but looking at the quality, the colour, the cutting etc., - you know the sort of thing - and then, after I have discussed it with my colleagues back in Moscow, come back again with your permission, to make a final appraisal and then I will appreciate, with your permission of course, being able to handle it and get what I call the feel of it. It is then I will be deciding what our final bid should be."

"Well Sir, you're the expert and it's for you to say how you want to do it. I'll arrange things entirely as you wish - I'm here to facilitate matters so just you let me know what you want." With that Mr. Hamilton-Gray, taking a key from his pocket, opened the end door in the corridor, stepping aside to let his visitors enter first. The two Russians couldn't help gasping with an unwilling intake of breathe as they came face to face with a hitherto hidden part of their nation's history. The stone was sitting by itself on a small purple velvet cushion in the centre of this smallish room - it had a sheen and a beauty that spoke for itself. Eric went through the motions, looking at the diamond from all angles first with his glasses on, then with a magnifying glass and finally with his naked eye. He gambled that the auctioneer couldn't speak Russian and pretended to point out various things to Liza in their native tongue, who made notes on the clip-board she had produced from the small document case she was carrying. At one stage he handed her his magnifying glass to look at something he was emphasising - she looked and nodded her agreement before giving the eyeglass back.

As Hamilton-Gray was talking to Liza, Eric looked round the room. He could see a CCTV camera focused onto the diamond and another above the door. No doubt that was also alarmed as well but there were no windows for security to worry about. In all they spent just over thirty minutes in the diamond's company before thanking their guide, who locked the door and escorted them down to the entrance hall. Eric shook hands and confirmed that he would be in touch soon about his second visit and repeated that he would appreciate a more detailed examination then. As they walked down the street outside Eric turned to Liza,

"I really can't believe they have so little security - could you see anything except those CCTV cameras and obviously some alarm system on the doors? There must be something we missed"

"I think there were some pressure pads under the carpet round the display table, I could feel them as I walked around it and I did notice what looked like panic buttons under the reception desk and in the office up stairs. Also that mirror at the end of the Entrance hall, it looked antique with its gold leaf, but it was almost certainly a two way one - I had that funny feeling I used to get in the old days that we were being watched down there, funny how some instincts stay with you." They walked on towards the lake in silence before Eric spoke again,

"Well - I thought that went very well - in any case with how we are planning to swap the diamond their security won't be a problem. For our plan it's very helpful to be dealing with an old fashioned gentleman - I saw how he looked at you." He playfully slapped Liza's bottom before she replied,

"He might be old-fashioned but he was extremely good looking!", she laughed.

Eric left it a full week before ringing Hamilton-Gray to arrange his promised second visit to the auctioneers. The time dragged slowly for the two Russians despite the tension building up as the sale date approached. There was certainly no let up in the media coverage of the event - if anything it increased, feeding itself on increasing rumour and gossip, as the auction approached. One of the wilder stories printed in a very down-market French publication was that the real seller was Queen Elizabeth, who wanted the cash to build a new Royal Yacht to replace the one denied her by her government! In another magazine - published on the same day and belonging to the same group - she was determined to buy it and would 'definitely' be the highest bidder! In all this frenzy no one had remarked that perhaps it was strange that there still had not apparently been any public reaction shown by any of the authorities in Moscow. The interest of the Hermitage Museum in St. Petersburg was known, but that seemed vague, and several of the mega-wealthy 'new' Russians or Oligarchs, were mentioned, but any official government reaction had neither been reported nor even suggested.

Eric and Liza spent the seven days almost like normal tourists, one day they walked all the way down to the lake, crossing the bridge in front of the Jet d'eau pumping its five hundred litres of water a hundred and forty meters up towards the sky every second, to the Quai du Mont Blanc, where they took the morning boat down the lake to Thonon-les-bains, had an excellent lunch and returned on the afternoon ferry.

"It's a pity they don't run one at night," said Eric looking at the timetable by the ticket hall, "it may have been an easier way to leave town - it was worth looking at, but it's no use to us in fact. I'm afraid there's no choice - we'll have to use the car Igor's arranged from here. I'll ring him this evening just to check things."

"Well, in a way it's a pity, Eric, but I agree the boat does take two hours for what is only just over thirty kilometres - that could be a great disadvantage." Liza responded, looking at the map above the timetable. The evening before he rang to arrange the viewing, they went up to Cologny and dined on the terrace of the Lion d'Or with its sweeping view over the lake and the city of Geneva.

"Sometimes an assignment has its advantages," Eric laughed, "All this goes down on expenses - I feel just like a western business man - not bad for an ex-party member."

The next morning he dialled Jonathan Hamilton-Gray's direct number and arranged the meeting.

"Well, Mr. Ivanowitch, are you sure you're not cutting it a bit fine - if you can't come tomorrow you'll only see the stone just over twenty four hours before the sale, will that give you enough time?" Eric seemed to hesitate before replying,

"I agree it's not ideal, but strictly in confidence there are unfortunately two factions arguing back in Moscow and they've told me to wait until the last possible moment before swinging a decision on them - that way the doubters won't have a chance to question my advice and it'll be fait accompli!. Russia may be now an official democracy, but we still have our internal politics, I'm afraid. I'm sure in your business you have the same thing?" The auctioneer laughed,

"God yes - don't tell me about it - OK - we'll see you in two days time at three thirty, until then - goodbye." Eric and Liza spent the time in between rehearsing their whole scheme - very simple in its conception, but relying on two essentials - absolute split second timing in their liaison and with them both having complete confidence in the other. There could be no second chance if either failed. Unfortunately their practising was made rather harder by not having a third person with them to act the part of Hamilton-Gray. They could only hope that their first impression had been correct and he had the normal male weakness for a pretty girl. Luckily on the day, the weather remained warmer than the May average and there was no problem for Eric to wear the loosely fitted linen jacket he had brought specially - it had been cleverly cut, so that when he had it on the extra material on the inside was unnoticeable and as he put the false diamond in the side pocket, to the observer it would still looked empty. Neither of them could eat much lunch before they again caught the tram into town and entered the Auctioneers just before three-thirty. They were greeted by the same receptionist although this time she was flanked by two large, crew cut, dark-suited individuals who, Eric knew, were most certainly not just fine art experts.

"Good afternoon, I hope you both have been enjoying Geneva," the receptionist began, "Mr. Hamilton-Gray is expecting you so I'll just let him know you've arrived. Do please take a seat while you wait." They both moved over to the leather seats as the two security men watched. Eric could see that they were wired with radio equipment and one had a distinct bulge by his hip which didn't need any imagination to guess what was underneath. He could feel the inside bulge in his own pocket and, although an agnostic, offered up an involuntary prayer to some God or other that the Moscow tailor had properly performed what he had promised. Both Eric and Liza were having the same thought, puzzling about what they should do if this time the security men accompanied them up to the diamond. Everything they had planned had been based on the experience of the last visit - they looked at each other, but without being able to discuss it they both realised there was little that either could do. It was a long five minutes for them, as they waited anxiously, before the lift doors opened and a smiling Jonathan Hamilton-Gray was shaking their hands.

"Please excuse me, the phone rang just as I was coming down. The television people want to film the diamond this evening before their coverage of the sale tomorrow night - I didn't really want them to, but they offered a good donation to my Chairman's favourite charity, so it wasn't my decision in the end." He smoothly guided Eric and Liza towards the lift before continuing, "So I had to arrange it all - it's meant having to get the security boys in at short notice to accompany the television people all the time they're in the building, but don't worry, we'll have plenty of time - they won't bother us - they are not due until five o'clock. If you watch later you'll see me being interviewed," he said looking straight at Liza. He turned and called across to the receptionist, "Bridget - get the two chaps a drink or tea or something. I'm sure they could do with something while they're waiting." He nodded at the two men. Going up in the lift Mr. Hamilton-Gray didn't see Eric's and Liza's relief as they smiled at each other. This time they went straight to the room where the diamond was displayed without first going to the private office. As they entered Eric carefully put on the pristine white gloves that Hamilton-Gray had handed him - again they were both very impressed by the sight of the gleaming stone sitting on its velvet cushion reflecting the focussed spotlight beaming down from the ceiling.

"May I this time have your permission to pick it up for a closer inspection?" Although he knew the answer, Eric felt he had to ask.

"Certainly but just one second," the Auctioneer went across to a panel they hadn't noticed before in the wall beside the door, "I'll just switch off the pressure pad under the cushion - we don't want to wake up the whole building!" Eric watched intently as he opened the panel and Liza saw his hand go into his jacket pocket - even with all her past experience she could feel her heart begin to thump - 'God is he going to risk it now,' she thought to herself. For a second Eric was tempted, but Hamilton-Gray flicked the alarm switch almost automatically, hardly looking away. "O.K., now - you can pick it up!" He gave Eric the go ahead.

What he was looking at straight after, however, was the miniskirt which only hid a small part of Liza's long tanned legs and the almost transparent linen top under which he could see the smallest of lace bras which hid nothing. Liza approached him as Eric, following the nod from the auctioneer picked up the stone. He placed his magnifying inspection glass to his eye and began a detailed look. Liza standing behind him against the wall slightly tapped Hamilton-Gray on the shoulder and he turned at once. With a smile she passed him a small piece of paper - as he took it he looked at her and she leant towards him as if to whisper something in his ear. It was probably only fifteen seconds that he found he had an ideal view down to her waist through the inside of her shirt, but that was long enough for Eric. All their rehearsals had paid off - their split second timing perfect. As Eric brought his inspection to an end and replaced the diamond onto the cushion he turned to Hamilton-Gray,

"Thank you very much, don't forget to switch the alarm back on - with the TV people coming you can't be too careful." Going down in the lift the bulge in his pocket felt exactly the same against his side - he offered up another prayer to the same God as before - if this continues I might almost believe, he promised himself. Later, after the two Russians had left, Jonathan Hamilton-Gray took out the small note Liza had given him - on it was written a number of a Russian mobile with a drawing of a heart underneath. He spent the next half hour looking out of his office window holding the paper and daydreaming. He was brought back to earth when the receptionist rang to announce the arrival of the television crew. Slightly adjusting his trousers, the bulge in them subsided.

CHAPTER TWENTY FIVE

GENEVA

Hardly speaking, they made their way back to Carouge and their temporary home - the pent up excitement following their success gradually abating. The whole switching of the diamond had gone as well as they could have possibly hoped. Now even Eric - the veteran of many years of dangerous cold war spying activities - couldn't help trembling a little as he thought of the ancient diamond, worth at least twenty million dollars, and of its historical connections to the turbulent past of his country just resting unwrapped in his jacket pocket.

"It's lucky we're in one of the safest cities in the world," Liza said smiling at him, "now would definitely not be the ideal time to be mugged!"

"Don't even tempt fate by joking about it - God, that Auctioneer chap was so laid back - the randy little sod, I just couldn't believe it would be so simple. What number did you give him in the end - not your own I hope?"

"No - I do believe you're getting jealous, Eric - I gave him that new one I took out anonymously. My sister in St. Petersburg has got the phone, I hope she'll know what to say if he does call. Don't worry nothing can be traced back here." They got off the tram two stops before their own one and walked the rest of the way, crossing the bridge and stopping for a last coffee in the Place du Marché. Eric's mobile rang just before they reached the apartment. As he stopped to take the call Liza walked on ahead and she was already at the entrance of their flat when Eric rejoined her. Neither of them noticed the man watching them intently from the other side of the road as they had approached their front door. Liza was just putting her key into the lock when they both turned with surprise as they heard footsteps behind them and a voice,

"Mr. Ivanowitch, one minute if you please, I would like to speak with you." In the comparative gloom of the entrance hall Eric blinked - momentarily blinded - as the flash bulb went off just a couple of metres in front of his face and then he had his first view of the fresh faced young man of about twenty five in rather creased jeans and blue striped open neck shirt emerging from behind the flash. He resisted what would have once been his almost automatic reaction to grab the camera, tear out the film, and break it on the ground - something he had done countless times in his old profession. Instead Liza was surprised to hear him ask almost politely, but at the same time in a tone that made his displeasure quite clear,

"Who are you and what is it you want? - Perhaps the police will have something to say about you taking unwelcome photos? This is a private building"

"Please let me explain - I don't want any bother - look here's my card. I am Christophe Guedot from the Antique and Auction Newsletter - I'm sure you've heard of us. I understand, Mr. Ivanowitch that you are here with your assistant on behalf of the Armoury Museum in Moscow to bid for the Tsarina's diamond at the sale tomorrow - all I want is to ask you a few questions?" Eric swore silently to himself, thinking how it must have been the Auctioneers - or their receptionist - who had tipped this man the information. Liza looked at him anxiously, but making a supreme effort, he managed to control his temper as he replied,

"I am not prepared to say anything to the press - you will appreciate that nothing has been decided and there is no useful information I can give you. Just one little thing - it's strange your editor didn't telephone Moscow to ask for an interview. Just turning up on my doorstep uninvited and unannounced is a little odd to say the least. May I ask how you knew I was in Geneva and at this address?"

"I'm sure you understand that I cannot really tell you that Sir, - you wouldn't expect me to reveal my sources, but really I don't see why you can't tell me anything about your bid now I'm here. You've seen all the press coverage the sale has had already - I just want something general as background. My piece will obviously only appear after the auction and should your museum be the successful buyer surely you will welcome the publicity?" Eric was wishing he could apply some of his previous dissuasive tactics used during his KGB days. He was fast running out of patience and with the diamond now feeling heavy in his pocket, he was anxious to get inside. Speaking slowly and deliberately he shut the man up as he told him,

"Mr. Guedot, please listen to what I am going to tell you - no do not write anything down - you are to forget we have had this meeting. We are going to destroy the photo you've taken and then I will not take any action about you invading my privacy. At the Armoury we know the owners of your magazine very well and I would hate to suggest they had a reporter too many on their pay-roll. Perhaps after the sale I will be able to let you have something, in return, on an exclusive basis but, trust me, we Russians can be good friends, but very dangerous enemies. It's for you to choose which you want me to be so now give me that camera please." The implication was clear and Guedot saw the menace in Eric's eyes and also noticed that Liza had shut the door of the flat, blocking any escape. He handed the camera to Eric, who quickly took the film out and exposed the whole reel. As he started to put the camera back into the journalist's case he noticed a picture of the receptionist from the Auctioneers in one of the side pockets, "That's a pretty girl who's that?" asked Eric innocently.

"Oh! That's my girlfriend," said Guedot at once and rather proudly, not realising, until too late, exactly what he had confessed.

"You're a very lucky man, Mr. Guedot. Anyway, thank you for your co-operation, I'll look forward to talking to you after the sale - lets hope you'll have a scoop, but remember absolutely nothing until then, right?" The handshake he gave the young man was very firm and one he was unlikely to forget.

"Mr. Ivanowitch, you have my word."

What a stupid fool Eric and Liza both thought to themselves and smiled as the frightened reporter left. Going into the sitting room Eric poured himself a beer and Liza had an iced tea. Eric took the diamond - kept hidden deep in his pocket while Guedot had been there and, still being careful only to handle it with the same kid gloves he had used previously to handle the fake. He placed it on the small coffee table in front of the sofa and sat down beside Liza as they took their drinks. They were both mesmerised by the sheer beauty and luminosity of the magnificent stone.

"Why don't we leave now?" asked Liza a little later, "we've got the stone, now all we've got to do is get it to Lisbon and the money's ours - what are we waiting for?" Everything had gone so well up till now she thought and her training had taught her always to conclude matters as quickly as possible to avoid other risks. Eric was silent for some time before answering,

"The call I had, just before that idiot came barging across with his camera, was from Igor. He's arranged with a friend working in the Consulate for him to leave a Mercedes parked outside the Richemont and the envelope with the papers and keys left for Mr. Ivanowitch with the porter's desk tomorrow just before the sale - for some reason he can't do it before - I asked why, but he couldn't tell me. For a reason I don't understand the car's also going to have a Turin registration. As this is now all arranged I think it better if we don't risk starting any suspicion by not turning up to the auction - we can leave immediately after it. What we'll do tomorrow afternoon is to buy two tickets for the boat across to France and we'll casually drop the receipt for these - I'll pay by this false credit card to buy our seats in case a decoy trail is needed." Liza looked worried,

"Don't you think the faster we put the most distance between us and Geneva the better - aren't we running a risk staying here? Look at this reporter man this afternoon - we don't want any more complications Eric."

"No, trust me, it really will be better my way," Eric insisted, "if we're not at the sale your lover boy will notice you not being there. He's very anxious to see you and he might use that phone number. Supposing your sister's out and someone else answers or he discovers it's in Russia some other way. No, let the poor man fantasise about your body one more time - in any case it'll be interesting to see the auction and who goes to it. I might even bid myself to get you a Christmas present - do you think there's a limit on this card Igor had made for us? Trust me everything's going to plan." Eric put his arm round Liza and drew her closer for a preliminary kiss. Later, as she slowly organised some food for dinner, Liza thought it's not very many couples who have made love in front of a twenty million dollar diamond. Perhaps that is something she'd be able to tell her grandchildren. Sometimes she wished that her relationship with Eric was just the normal humdrum one of an average couple back in Moscow, but she really loved him and part of the reason for this, she thought, was the mutual excitement of the life they led. Take that away and we'd probably part within a fortnight, she said to herself.

Eric had followed Liza into the shower after their love making and took his time, while she prepared a cheese omelette and salad in the kitchen. Opening the last of the 12 bottles of Chablis they had bought just after they had arrived, she carried the whole lot into the small sitting room and put the tray down on the coffee table in front of the sofa. The diamond was still sitting there looking somewhat incongruous on the cheap Ikea furniture. Eric had not bothered to dress after his shower and was sitting down in his bathrobe. He took a white handkerchief from his pocket and, without touching the stone directly with his fingers, he wrapped it carefully and put it back into the specially tailored pocket of his linen jacket. Before they started to eat, Liza switched on the television and they found themselves watching the exact replica of the diamond Eric had just put away.

"Tomorrow evening, probably shortly after eight o'clock this diamond - once the property of the last Tsarina of Russia - will change hands for something in excess of twenty five million dollars here in Geneva," the commentator was in full flow, "we have become used to some magnificent fine art sales taking place here over recent years including the still very much discussed sale of jewellery, some years ago, belonging to the late Duchess of Windsor, the American divorcee for whom a King of Britain gave up his throne, but even that has surely been eclipsed by the romance and perhaps the intrigue and mystery behind the secret story which lies hidden in the deep lustre of this wonderful stone you see on your screens now. If it could speak - what tales it could tell!" The camera panned round the Auctioneer's room, which Eric and Liza recognised from that afternoon before zooming in showing a close up of the replica the Russian had placed there some three hours earlier. Eric couldn't help smiling as he said to Liza,

"If the story is hidden inside it, then thank God it can't talk!" They watched as the presenter interviewed Hamilton-Gray about the age and quality of the stone. He then turned to an American, introduced as one of the foremost world experts on precious stones, who spent some time rather repeating what the previous speaker had said before speculating on the probable buyer.

"Of course, apart from the States and the Middle East, there'll be tremendous interest from Russia itself about this - remember, since all the changes, there are even several individuals there for whom a price of around twenty five million dollars to own such an important part of their country's history is just small change. Museums from all around the world will be competing and, I dare say, quite a few people from the west - I could name many with that sort of money from Bill Gates downwards - would be eager to have the prestige and publicity of owning such a prize." The television presenter - showing the typical aggression of his trade - interrupted and turned to the Auctioneer,

"In your catalogue you describe this stone as being 'The property of a 'gentleman', can you enlarge on that description at all? There has naturally been much speculation since the announcement of this sale about the possible owner - can you confirm that, at least, it's neither the Russian government nor any member of the British or some other Royal family?" Mr. Hamilton-Gray smiled rather resignedly,

"I've been asked that a lot in recent days - I'm afraid we cannot enlarge further on what the Sale Catalogue already says, it is the property of a gentleman and, again I'm very sorry, no amount of questioning or pressure will get us to add anything more or to give any further information. I simply have nothing more to say on that subject. The seller has requested absolute anonymity and he, she - or they - have a perfect right to do so. It is one of the main conditions of sale and I stress their secret is safe with us." Eric turned to Liza,

"That may be true, but the secret of who a buyer might be wasn't particularly safe with their receptionist" The presenter looked cross as he continued,

"I understand your position, but I'm afraid I must press you a little further - you say that this stone was once the property of the Tsar and Tsarina of Russia before their deaths in the Revolution?"

"That is correct."

"Then may I ask, do you have real and solid proof of that and are you happy that whoever the seller is he has a proper legal right to sell it?" The interviewer sat back in his chair, a satisfied smirk on his face. The Auctioneer reddened slightly, taking exception to the inference implied in the question,

"I can assure you and all your viewers that we have done our own thorough research and we are entirely happy on all counts. I have to say I do not like the tone of your question. I would hope that the long reputation and high standing of a company like ours - established over many decades - would speak for itself on these matters." Not to be outdone the presenter rashly tried another attack,

"Nevertheless the commission on a sale of this magnitude must be very tempting...." Hamilton-Gray butted in,

"Sir, I must say now that I take great offence at your remark and must ask you to withdraw it. We gave you every facility for your programme at short notice, but I'm afraid I am now going to end this interview. With the attitude you have taken perhaps its better if your cameras are not at the sale tomorrow." He strode out of the room leaving the television crew in the company of the security men. It was only their producer who followed him.

"I do apologise, Sir, he was going quite against what we had agreed - I promise you. I'll have someone else - more experienced - do the broadcast tomorrow" The Auctioneer knowing that they needed television coverage for the sale, looked straight at the worried producer and said,

"OK, let me have a full written apology for my board and then we'll forget the matter, but I don't want that man any where near the sale." Eric switched off the television just as the Swiss version of '*Who wants to be a Millionaire?*' was beginning. He teased Liza about how strong her new boy friend was - he was sure this assertiveness had turned her on. Although he was laughing, he was quietly pleased when she said that his own was quite enough for her. Eric looked at her - he was very lucky he thought, to be able to combine such pleasure with his business. For him, she was really an excellent companion in every way. He poured them each another glass of wine as they finished their food.

"Tomorrow evening we'll get to the Richemont fairly early and then enter the auction with the crowd. Hamilton-Gray gave me these special passes so we should be all right to get in, but I'd like to locate the car first - we'll leave just before the end and get across into France quickly before we swap the number plates."

"What?" Liza asked.

"Yes" Eric said. "Igor has arranged a second set of numbers - I didn't tell you. The car is on local Geneva plates at the moment so any border check will not be very much - once we're out of Switzerland we'll be driving as Italians! How do you feel about some dolce vita? Let's walk down to the corner and have a coffee before watching the late news and going to bed."

The insistent ringing from his mobile woke them both up. It was nine-thirty and they had overslept after talking late into the night. Both had retained a little of their somewhat jaundiced attitude acquired during years of service with the KGB during the Cold War - they had each for part of that time, although at different periods, been attached to the Russian Embassy in London, where their English nick-names had initially originated and where they had also acquired some of the typical English love of understatement and lack of any show of emotion. Nevertheless neither could help the excitement they had felt the day before when the substitution of the genuine diamond had been successfully made and the flow of adrenalin had made sleep slow in coming. They had both been a little surprised after all the years of their indoctrination by the Communist regime, that once free from its controlling yoke, how their emotions had been deeply moved by holding this impressive evidence of their countries past. Eric saw Igor's name show up as his caller.

"Hello, Aleksei here," for once Eric used his real name, "All is in order - we're going to attend the start of the sale later and then leave here. Could you tell Lisbon that we expect to be there in two - three at the maximum - day's time? I won't call you again unless there's any trouble." Liza couldn't hear Igor's answer before Eric quickly said goodbye and rang off. He turned to her in the bed,

"Larisa," he started, now using Liza's full name, "we'd better not waste time. Let's get up and once we've got our things ready we'll take them to the car so they're in the boot well before any action at the hotel. We'll leave as soon as the agent comes to check the apartment and get the keys."

"When did you arrange that? Is it OK that they see us leaving?" Liza looked slightly anxious.

"Don't worry," Eric replied, "I wondered about that, but finally I think it better they just see us check out normally - we only booked the flat until today in any case and we don't want to start any suspicion. I'll make sure the agent sees these false Easy Jet tickets to London - I must hand it to Igor, he thinks of everything." They showered, dressed and used up the last of their Nescafé as a breakfast. Later, just after eleven o'clock, their small cases were already packed and sitting by the door when the young assistant from the letting agents knocked. He made the usual cursory inspection of the rooms, checked the various meters, signed the release forms and handed back the deposit Eric had left with them originally. They all left the flat together,

"Can I give you a lift to the station Sir," asked the agent, "I'm going that way and could drop you off for the airport train - what time's your flight?" Eric smiled,

"That would be very helpful - I think we take off at three o'clock - don't we darling?" Liza mumbled her agreement, "Yes but we can always have a quick lunch while we're waiting. It's very kind of you." The young man was even more pleased he had made the offer as Liza got into the front beside him and stretched her long legs while she settled into her seat. He was annoyed he was too shy to offer her any help doing up her belt! The lunchtime quiet had begun and there wasn't much traffic - they reached the station in just over ten minutes. Getting out of the car, they thanked their chauffeur and he watched as they carried their cases up the stairs and wheeled them towards the platforms. He was rewarded by Liza turning and giving him a farewell smile. They waited for fifteen minutes inside the station before coming out again and crossed the tramways before walking down the Rue des Alpes towards the Richemont Hotel. They found the car exactly as planned, got the keys and papers from the concierge and left their luggage locked in the boot. Eric looked at his watch - it was half-past midday, just under eight hours before the Auction would commence he thought. Already outside the famous old hotel any passer by could see that some important event was about to take place. There were three large vans with impressive satellite dishes sprouting from their roofs and a little further up the road three police vans each with six rather bored officers playing cards inside. Eric and Liza dodged quickly behind one of the vans when they saw Hamilton-Gray, accompanied by an efficient looking blonde lady carrying a clip-board, coming out through the main doors of the hotel. They watched from their hiding place as they got into a top of the range 4X4 BMW and drove away.

"Let's go down to the lake and have some lunch over the other side. There's nothing we can do this afternoon and heaven knows if we'll be able to eat anything this evening - we could well have to sleep in the car!" Eric looked at Liza as his hand checked for the umpteenth time the safety of the small package inside his jacket.

"You know you really are taking a risk if you go into the sale with that in your pocket - do you want me to stay with it in the car?" asked Liza.

"I've thought of that, but whatever we do is a problem. I really think the less risk with all these police and other people around is to leave it locked in the car. No one'll attempt anything around here this evening."

"No one except you, Aleksei," laughed Liza.

"There's an exception that always proves every rule my darling little Larisa," smiled back Eric, patting her on the bottom. He remembered with glee, it was the sight of her bottom covered in some very tight trousers, which had first attracted him when he had luckily been standing behind her at a medal presentation by Gorbachov in the pre-glasnost days. They had lunch sitting on a terrace just down stream from the Jet d'eau - fortunately there was no wind so they were spared any trouble from the spray - and then, both conscious that they had a long afternoon ahead of them before they could go back to the hotel, lingered over their coffees as long as they dared before paying the bill and walking round the old city.

Meanwhile, back in the Richemont Hotel, preparations for the sale were nearing their completion. Hamilton-Gray returned from his lunch with his assistant to find the ballroom covered in the cables and other paraphernalia of the television networks covering the event. Hotel staff were beginning to set out the seating under the banks of arc-lights which were more-or-less ready in place and were being tested. The room was hot, but the air-conditioning system was beginning to win its battle against the heat they were generating. In the middle of a temporary stage covered in rich red carpeting was the stand from which the Auctioneer would be conducting the sale. On each side of the dais there were a series of telephones set on tables in front of two long pew-like benches and set high up either side of the stage were two large electronic screens, like scoreboards at a tennis tournament, showing various currency conversions together with the times in Moscow, Geneva, London and New York. An engineer was busy testing the sound equipment and, as he counted 'one', 'two', 'three' etc., 'testing', Hamilton-Gray whispered to his assistant,

"It won't be very long now - hopefully, I'll be counting out the millions like that later!" The banks of flowers, largely white and blue, decorating the room almost made it look ready for a wedding reception as no effort or cost had been spared in its preparation. Although this large ballroom had seen many big and important functions before, there was no escaping the atmosphere already building up that this particular evening was a very special one indeed. Finally at just after five o'clock the hotel manager, Monsieur Nielson, approached Hamilton-Gray who was talking with his colleague, Keith Johnson and a second man who the manager didn't recognise. He coughed in the discreet manner all hotel managers have when they need to attract someone's attention,

"Excuse me, Mr. Hamilton-Gray - good evening Mr. Johnson, how nice to see you - my staff tell me that everything is now ready."

"Thank you - you've done your usual excellent job, the Auctioneer replied" - "it all looks splendid. Just one small thing, you've forgotten the small table on the stage where we'll place the diamond. We'd better have a place for that I think." Without hesitating or smiling, the manager said,

"I'll have that done straight away - I assume you'll provide the security case."

"Yes - it's in a bullet proof glass display case and being brought here at seven-forty five," Hamilton-Gray turned towards the third man, "Oh! Monsieur Nielson, may I introduce Maître Petelet - our notaire - I don't think you've met before, who will be officially attending this evening's sale."

The Auctioneer looked at his watch - only two and a half hours to go. He took a small piece of paper out of his pocket and dialled the number he read on his mobile. The number rang five times before he heard a recorded voice say something in Russian he took to be the usual invitation to leave a message. Walking away slightly, so he was out of earshot of the others, Hamilton-Gray identified himself before leaving an invitation on the tape for a late drink or perhaps dinner after the Auction and saying how much he would like to see Liza again before she left Geneva. He returned and joined the Notaire, who was still talking with the Hotel manager. Together all three made a final inspection of the room as the television crews continued setting up their cameras.

The Auctioneers had arranged a room off the right hand side of the stage for their staff to use as an office, while everyone waited for the sale to commence. Direct video telephone links with their offices in New York, London and Paris had been set up for the sale and were being tested together with a fourth which was with an associated company in Moscow. Typically, the shortest distance one to Paris was causing the most problem. Two secretaries were checking through the list of people expected to be there in just under two hours time - it read like a gossip columnist's dream and, indeed, their profession was well represented among the press invitations that had been issued. Earlier that day Hamilton-Gray had received a call from London confirming that the owner - Peter Varlov was never mentioned by name in any of their correspondence - would not be there. Instead, while all the sometimes frenetic preparations were being made, he remained quietly in his house in the English countryside, with his children.   The London office of the Auctioneers had arranged for him to enjoy a private direct television link as an extension of their own. He poured himself a decent sized whisky and water as he watched the test pictures coming through - champagne was resting in his fridge for later. He was sad that his wife would not be there to share this solution to his problems, but he was surrounded by his children and for the first time for many months he was feeling relaxed and confident about the future - all was no longer black, he felt.   He'd had a phone call earlier from George Matthews to wish him luck for 'our' sale. His own private boasting of this at home had led his wife to insist on holding a small dinner party where she thought her husband could suitably impress her guests when the sale was shown on their satellite television. Although technically the auction was a public event, open to everyone, the Auction house had issued a number of specially embossed invitations and the first ten rows of seats had a cordon across the aisle reserving them for the special guests they were expecting. Well before seven, the bar set up in the ante-room was filling up and, with most of the ladies dressed as for an evening of high society and the men similarly attired, the sense of occasion was almost tangible as the noise level of background chatter gradually increased. Aleksei - as he was Mr. Ivanowitch for the evening he was using his proper name which had been printed on the gold edged card the Auctioneers had issued him, and Liza went first to the car and left the small package safely locked in the boot behind the spare wheel. So far, the last of the many bizarre places this precious, historical, but above all very valuable geological object, had found itself during its long story. Fortunately no one had noticed Eric and Liza as they had opened the boot, but Eric was relieved that the car was just visible to the police vans - now grown to eight - parked round the hotel. It was seven-fifteen and together they went through the doors into the front hall and made their way into the bar. Despite the vintage champagne and other drinks being offered, they both took a simple plain orange juice. Standing in a corner rather enjoying watching what was almost a cabaret of people all trying to impress the others, Liza felt a tap on her shoulder.

"How are you?" Hamilton-Gray was smiling, as he put his arm casually on her waist. "I can't stop, I must get straight back, but just wanted to make sure you got my message earlier - is dinner possible?" To his obvious annoyance Eric stepped in,

"Hello, how are you? I'm afraid that this evening I'll have to claim Liza's help - I'm expecting a long conference call from Moscow later after the sale." The Auctioneer's smile only half hid his disappointment, but he leant forward and whispered to Liza that he would call her the next day to celebrate. She felt his lips gently touch her ear as he did so.

Despite the personal setback, walking back to the temporary office, Hamilton-Gray was feeling a mixture of elation and nerves as the adrenalin began to flow. He had over fifteen years experience since he started with the Auction house straight after coming down from Cambridge with a highly respectable 2.1 degree in history, but this evening would be, by far, the most important of his professional life. Even his widowed mother had rung from the old family home in Wiltshire proudly saying she had seen him on television. Outwardly he appeared his usual confident, assured self, but inwardly there were one or two butterflies beginning to flutter as he glanced at the digital wall clock and saw 19.35 staring back at him. Not long now, he thought. People were starting to take their places in the main room and the bar, as in a theatre, was emptying fast. Suddenly a hush took over, followed by a collective intake of breath, as everyone watched six armed security men gingerly carry a two foot high glass display case covered in a small Russian flag and place it carefully on the small round table now standing just to the right hand side of the Auctioneer's rostrum. As the flag was removed and hung behind it, people, many with opera glasses, strained to view the shining lustre of its contents. From their aisle seats near the back of the room Liza could not only see at least five members of various European Royal families, but enough heads of Industry to form a Stock Exchange index all by themselves and certainly recognised enough representatives of the acting profession to cast any Hollywood blockbuster more than twice. In amongst them were some of the more heavily sponsored sportsmen and the daughter of a recently deceased tycoon, sitting beside her new boy friend, probably eager to spend some of her recently acquired huge inheritance. The seats in front of the telephones either side of the rostrum were now taken by the staff from the Auctioneers, all checking that the connections were up and ready with their potential buyers at the other end of the lines.

Eric looked round, but couldn't see any obvious presence of the Russian government or the museums - perhaps they were the telephone bidders he thought. There were however two men who he noticed, sitting some four rows in front of him to his left and, although he didn't recognise them, both looked as if they might be there from Moscow. Sitting there he could only see the close cropped back of their heads, but there was something unmistakeable about the suits they were wearing and how they were speaking to each other, although they were out of his hearing, that instinctively told him they were Russian.

With most people now seated the buzz of excitement could be heard above the background music - in respect to the diamond's origins they were playing from Borodin and Eric whispered to Liza,

"I'll tell the boss back in Moscow when we get home, this piece is from Prince Igor!" The television arc-lights were switched on giving the small object of all this fuss an extra gleam in its glass prison as Hamilton-Gray, accompanied by two fellow directors, his assistant and Maître Petelet, appeared from their small office and, as these others took their seats on the side, he took his place behind the rostrum. He received the go-ahead signal from the television producer at the back of the hall and there was complete silence as he began to speak.

"Your Highnesses, Ladies and Gentlemen, on behalf of my company I welcome you all here to Geneva this evening. I also welcome the many others who are joining us from the other major world centres either by video or telephone link." He indicated the big screens above his head and the two benches of telephones to either side. "I am sure I speak for all my colleagues that we regard having been asked to handle this sale to be one of the highest points in our company's long history. It is indeed a great honour." He paused and took a sip of water from the glass in front of him and then went on, "You will have all read by now the truly romantic story behind this most magnificent diamond. I will only add, it is, without a doubt, perhaps one of the most important of its kind ever to be presented at a public auction. We are happy to have Maître Petelet here," He indicated the lawyer seated behind him on the stage, "with us this evening, and his Cabinet is holding all the background documents and other details, including the all important legal verifications of this diamond by two of the world's acknowledged experts." As he said this Eric squeezed Liza's wrist and smiled at her as she turned towards him. The Auctioneer continued, "The conditions of sale are clearly laid out at the back of the sale prospectus and, I have to point out, in any dispute that it is Swiss law that will prevail. Have I missed anything, Maître?" The Notaire looked at the camera and saw he had the red transmitting light glowing on top before he smiled straight into it and slowly shook his head. His wife and children watching at home had instructed him to do that and they would be happy now with his five minutes of fame. Hamilton-Gray looked round the room thankful he was wearing his tinted glasses against the bright television lighting but blinking a little nevertheless, as he concluded his introduction, "Before I begin the actual sale are there any relevant questions from anyone?" He listened as the audience looked uneasily round the room at each other, rather like a wedding congregation, waiting for any objection, but in fact no one spoke. The Auctioneer sat down, took another sip of water, refilled his glass from the carafe beside it and paused dramatically for some fifteen seconds before standing up again, holding his gavel slightly aloft and saying, "Now who will start me at ten million dollars for this diamond?"

Hamilton-Gray looked expectedly out on his audience, waiting for some reaction to his invitation for bids. His colleagues, holding their phones on the two sides, remained silent and people in the front few rows strained round to see if anyone behind them was responding. If such a thing were possible, Eric sensed an almost silent buzz of excitement and anticipation envelop the room. This silence probably only lasted for about twenty seconds, but to Peter Varlov watching from the comfort of his armchair at home in England, it seemed to be a great deal longer - by Sir George Matthews, sitting in his suburban home some miles away, it was hardly noticed as he kept interrupting the television commentary to boast about his part in arranging the sale, to his wife's gullible guests. The Auctioneer completed his survey of the room before continuing, "Five million to start surely? - come on Ladies and Gentlemen," he smiled at the audience, "don't be shy, someone's got to begin - who's going to have that honour?" There was a further short pause as the potential bidders showed the traditional reluctance to start the ball rolling. Finally someone, Eric couldn't quite see who, over on the far side and nearer the front, held up a numbered identity paddle, one of the ones which had been given to bidders by the auction house at the time of their registration. At the same time he heard a woman's voice clearly say,

"Four million."

"Thank you Madam, Ladies and Gentlemen I have four million to start us off." There was a ripple of rather nervous laughter coupled with a little applause as Hamilton-Gray added, "I think that may be just for the ten per cent deposit. Come along now, I'll take the bidding in quarter of a million steps if it helps you." Two different paddles went up, more or less simultaneously, from the middle of the room, "I have four and a half million, OK - five million, thank you sir." The silent anticipatory buzz, which Eric had sensed earlier was now becoming audible as three more bidders responded, quickly taking the price to seven million, and a fourth entering for the first time bounced it straight up to eight. For the first time one of the telephone bidders - the third from the end on the left hand side - held up his paddle with a bid of eight and a half. "I have a telephone bid of eight and a half million dollars from New York," announced Hamilton-Gray. This was quickly followed by a bid from London for nine million from the other side, capped by one of ten from the most recent bidder in the hall. The Auctioneer took some water from his glass and wiped his face quickly with his handkerchief - the heat from the television arc-lights was beginning to defeat the air-conditioning and he was feeling warm - without stopping he took his jacket off and put it on the back of the seat behind him. He acknowledged another telephone bid of ten and half then two more from the body of the hall and another buyer calling in from Moscow with one of twelve million. Eric couldn't help noticing one of the two men he had thought earlier were almost certainly Russian, put his mobile phone to his ear before whispering something to his companion, and together they both quietly, and practically unnoticed got up and left the room through one of the side doors. This manoeuvre could have only taken a couple of minutes, but when Eric re-concentrated on the sale he heard Hamilton-Gray saying "Thank you, I have sixteen million from New York." A gasp went round as the newly rich heiress slowly, but deliberately put up her numbered paddle, "Seventeen million." However her bid only stood for a few seconds before the assistant handling the calls from Moscow quickly stepped in with eighteen million and a second from the same city capped it with a bid of nineteen million dollars. The heiress smiled as the television camera focussed on her again and she turned to kiss her boyfriend whose bewildered expression betrayed his shock. "Ladies and Gentlemen, I have nineteen million dollars," another sip of water, "Do I have any advance on nineteen million dollars?" The silence would have enabled the proverbial dropping pin to be heard throughout the room. People began to look round at their neighbours, searching for a sign that someone else was going to come in.

"Twenty million!" the assistant on the phone with the previous under-bidder from Moscow almost shouted and there was a small ripple of applause from the audience as yet again the electronic screen recorded the higher price.

"Thank you, twenty million, Ladies and Gentlemen - this is a unique stone with an impeccable provenance - is there any advance on twenty million dollars? It must be worth a lot more than that - come on Ladies and Gentlemen, don't miss your chance." Hamilton-Gray waited, now thoroughly enjoying this drama in which he was the chief player, he looked straight into the camera pointing at him and smiled - his years of experience handling high value sales told him that there was certainly another five or ten million dollars out there ready to bid. It was for him to drag out the bidders, but before he could start talking again he heard a strange collective murmur coming from the audience - and at the same time felt someone touch his elbow from behind.

He turned to find his assistant handing him a folded sheet of notepaper - her whisper telling him to read it urgently was picked up by the microphones before he reached forward belatedly to turn them off. The audience were beginning to shuffle in their seats and the low initial murmur was fast becoming a general hubbub of talk. Hamilton unfolded the small piece of paper as his colleague and the Notaire seated behind him rose and joined him at the rostrum. He read it, and passed it silently to them, before switching the microphones back on.

"Your Highnesses, Ladies and Gentlemen, I'm afraid that I will have to ask your indulgence. An urgent matter has just been brought to my attention and I must ask for a brief interval before we proceed with this sale. Do not worry it is just a minor technical problem we have had brought to our attention and I hope to be able to resolve it very shortly. In accordance with the general conditions of the sale all bids still stand and remain effective. May I invite you to take the opportunity of refreshing yourselves with another glass of champagne in the meantime and we'll resume in, say, half an hour."

The waiters were already uncorking the bottles in the bar at the back as Hamilton-Gray joined his colleagues in the side office.

His co-director re-read the notice. It was on headed paper from the Russian Consulate in Geneva accompanied by a photocopy of a legal looking deed. The notaire began explaining,

"It says here quite clearly that the Kremlin, the very top of the Russian government it emphasises, is disputing the ownership of this diamond and denies that the present seller has any rights whatsoever to offer it for sale. Unfortunately the Consulate here has succeeded in getting a temporary injunction against this auction taking place - there is nothing we can do but halt the whole thing. I'm sorry, old boy, but you'll have to just go out there and explain. What an unholy bloody mess." Eric and Liza left before Hamilton-Gray had gone back into the hall and finished his explanation - there were a few rather rude questions and comments from the other clients, but mostly a stunned silence as the news began to sink in. The television commentator was already interviewing some legal expert, who was self-importantly going through the different permutations he thought possible, and some people remained in the hall excitingly discussing the news among themselves. Just as she was leaving, Liza noticed the same security men, who had earlier brought the diamond to the sale carry it out, but this time they were accompanied by three members of the Swiss police. As Eric started the Mercedes he handed the small package he'd taken from the boot to Liza.

"It's your turn to carry it now," he said as he edged the car past the crowd of journalists pushing into the hotel.

"It's not the first hard thing from the Kremlin that I've held!" Liza laughed, "but more seriously I bet it's Putin whose pushing for it - he obviously wants St. Petersburg to have it and doesn't see why they should pay. They want it back free. In a way I do understand him - it did belong to the Russian nation really in the first place."

At Peter Varlov's house the champagne remained in the fridge, but the whisky bottle emptied fairly rapidly - when his phone rang neither his daughter nor he answered. After seven rings Sir George Matthews hung up and went slowly back into the sitting room to face the ridicule of his wife and the contemptuous looks of her guests.

CHAPTER TWENTY SIX

GENEVA

The ballroom at the Richemont was slowly emptying with the stunned guests leaving after Hamilton-Gray's embarrassed announcement that the auction would be delayed. Hopefully, this would be for only forty eight hours as when he had studied the documents handed in from the Russian Consulate with his co local director, David Johnson, and Maître Petelet, one of them pointed out that the interim injunction gained by Moscow was for only twenty-four hours thus giving the seller an immediate opportunity to answer the charges. The little office provided by the hotel was packed with everyone talking at once. Standing near the door Jonathan Hamilton-Gray moved quickly to one side as someone pushed rather roughly to enter. Had Eric been there he would have recognised the fellow Russians he'd seen earlier leave the auction as the two men introduced themselves to Hamilton-Gray.

"Good evening Sir," began the slightly shorter, thicker-set, but better dressed of the two men in perfect English, "I am Andrei Malnikov - the Russian Consul here in Geneva," he held his arm forward to shake hands with the auctioneer, "and this is Mr. Mikhail Kazakov, who arrived from Moscow this morning." The second man, taller and thinner than colleague, gave more an impression of a University professor or some such academic with his wavy grey hair, half moon steel framed glasses and slightly dishevelled clothes. "Mr. Kazakov," the diplomat continued, "at the risk of embarrassing him, is the internationally recognised leading expert on precious stones and, in particular, those and other jewellery which were once in the collection of the Tsars and the old Russian Imperial family. He is the Curator at the Vystavkaa Almaznogo Fonda - I translate for you its English title, 'The Diamond Fund Exhibition' - housed in part of the Kremlin and where, you may be aware, most of this ancient royal collection is now kept …."

Hamilton-Gray shook the second man by the hand, but at the same time interrupted the speaker,

"Mr Malnikov we have received your interim injunction halting the sale on the grounds that you contest the seller's right to his ownership of this diamond. So we therefore have no choice other than to suspend proceedings." He looked towards Maître Petelet and received his signal to continue, "However, you will appreciate that, on our side, we, in liaison with the owner's bank, have done our complete due diligence and are equally satisfied of the bona fides of the seller and his proper legal title to this stone." The Consul whispered something to his companion as Hamilton-Gray continued, "Therefore you will appreciate that tonight, as I said, we are merely suspending the auction. Indeed we have to do so under the terms of this temporary court order, but if necessary, I am sure, the owner will fight this very strongly. May I suggest the best thing is that we all meet calmly tomorrow morning in our offices, when we can have a proper discussion - entirely without prejudice to either side's case - and I will arrange for the relevant interested parties in the United Kingdom to be present through a telephone-video conference link? Then we can see if we can't resolve the matter in some mutually satisfactory way, without recourse to further legal action and too much delay, which would be bad for everyone. I must confess however that that seems to be highly unlikely this evening. I am sure you understand, and Mr. Kazakov too, that tonight we are not prepared to talk any further before taking advice from our lawyers, and with them present at any discussions. So far we have only had the benefit of advice from Maître Petelet who is our notaire." He smiled at the Consul before finishing, "May I suggest ten-thirty tomorrow morning gentlemen - that will be nine-thirty in England and my assistant will have hopefully been able to make all the necessary arrangements by then." Standing just behind him she was already making some rapid notes on her clip board. Mr. Malnikov, nodding at the Curator, agreed but added, "We will both be there of course, but also so will my Ambassador who is arriving here from Berne about now and will be attending himself."

Hamilton-Gray whispered in his assistant's ear through her blonde hair,

"Make sure the Chairman's there for God's sake then. I'm sorry, but tell him he'll just have to leave his mistress in St. Tropez by herself for a day and fly up here," before opening the door and beckoning a waiter over with a full tray of drinks. Some thirty minutes later with and at least a bottle of champagne inside him the Consul said goodbye,

"Thank you, Mr. Hamilton-Gray. That was an excellent drink. You understand, I hope, that I am merely the agent in all of this - as indeed is the Ambassador. Our instructions have been coming from a very high level indeed back home. It is all out of our hands," the museum curator quickly nodded, "Good night and I look forward to our meeting in the morning." Jonathan Hamilton-Gray left just after, but before he went to bed he re-tried the number written on the scrap of paper lying beside his phone, but again there was no reply.

On her way home, his assistant passed by the office, where her call to Sir George Matthews received rather a grumpy answer - she wasn't to know it was interrupting Lady Matthews in full spiteful flow. His temper was further tested after she told him that the conference call for the meeting would be starting at nine o'clock the next day - thirty minutes before the Russians arrive – so he would have to be in his office by then. Just before Hamilton-Gray went to sleep he realised that during their conversation the second Russian hadn't spoken a single word - perhaps at the meeting they would need an interpreter. He phoned his assistant just as she was undressing for bed and another detail was added to her clipboard notes.

Everything was ready before nine o'clock in the large pine panelled board room on the top floor of the Auctioneers' offices. From an internal windowless wall, the portrait of a patrician figure looking down with an expression of disdain was of a former Chairman, painted by the eminent artist George Bruce. On the table, in front of each chair, was a dark brown leather bound blotter, a foolscap notepad and an accompanying pencil. In the centre was the telephone receiver for the link with London wired to two auxiliary units holding speakers each end of the table. Either side, raised up against the wall, were two screens which were to receive the video conference links. A small bottle of mineral water and a glass stood beside each blotter. Harriet, Hamilton-Gray's assistant, made one last check round the room before going to her boss's office and telling him all was prepared.

"Good, thank you Harriet, I want you to take notes of the meeting for me so I have a record of my own, independent of the lawyers. Has Thomas arrived yet by the way?" Hamilton-Gray was referring to Thomas Warderby, their local Chairman, who ahead of his retirement due in about eighteen months time was more and more a part time one.

"Yes Jonathan, he's in his room - he arrived about half an hour ago, but I warn you, not in the best of tempers, He flew up very early this morning in a friend's plane from La Mole, the exclusive private airfield near St. Tropez - he looks a bit rough - probably had no sleep last night!"

"OK, I'll pop along and see him - I'd better brief him as far as I can, then we'll have a coffee and go through my notes back here - the Russians will be arriving at ten thirty so tell everyone to be in the boardroom by ten and warn London we'll connect up then. Oh, Harriet, I almost forgot - get hold of the company in Antwerp just in case we need any expert advice - they wrote the initial report, which we have a copy of in our file. Keep that handy thanks." At ten o'clock the board-room began to fill up as Hamilton-Gray and his assistant were joined by David Johnson and their sun-tanned Chairman, quickly followed by Maître Petelet, who was accompanied by two partners of Ponsonby and Allen, the major international law firm of which the Auctioneers had been an important client for very many years. "Maître Lebaille, Mr. Varley, how good of you to come at such short notice," Hamilton-Gray welcomed them. "I think you know everyone here. Let me stress that we have made it quite clear that the meeting this morning is without prejudice so you could easily find yourselves in court later today on the owner's behalf, but last night the Consul - Mr. Um..." Harriet showed him her pad, "Malnikov, thank you Harriet, Mr. Malnikov seemed anxious to have a discussion, but I wasn't going to do anything without you gentlemen present." The two lawyers smiled and, taking their seats, opened their notepads. At the same time a small light flashed on the centre receiver and the television screens came to life. There gazing at them from London - it was clearly his office - they saw Sir George Matthews with a second man seated just to his right. Hamilton-Gray began, "Good morning Sir George, I am Jonathan Hamilton-Gray and, for the record, the others round the table are my Chairman, Thomas Warderby, and my fellow director David Johnson, each man acknowledged his name by nodding at the camera. Going on round the table from him are Maître Lebaille and Mr. Varley from the Geneva office of our lawyers, Ponsonby and Allen, and next to Mr. Varley is Maître Petelet the notaire, who was at the attempted sale last night." Sir George nodded and introduced his colleague as Ian Challiner from the bank's legal department. Somewhat to Hamilton-Gray's surprise he added that Peter Varlov, who he had finally managed to contact much earlier that morning, had just joined him, but would stay out of camera view and merely wished to observe events. The minutes up to ten-thirty seemed to drag, but the two Russians arrived exactly on time and a secretary showed them into the room together with their Ambassador, a small dapper well dressed man, who offered his firm handshake all round and then immediately left the talking to his Consul. Both sides made their cases and it was clear fairly shortly that no compromise was going to be reached.

"If what you say is correct, Consul," Maître Lebaille said, "my client - and I must confess, myself - cannot understand why you left it so late to raise these objections. There has been almost non-stop publicity for a long time about this diamond sale…"

Sir George Matthews butted in anxiously, "a diamond which my bank is satisfied, from all our records and documentation, and they go back to when it was first given to us for safe keeping very many years ago, well before your revolution I would add, is the rightful property of my, I mean, our customer and he has a complete right to sell it if he so chooses. I am Sir George Matthews and have personally verified everything." Before the lawyer could resume the Consul answered, "And my government, Mr. Sirgeorge," he clearly knew nothing of the English honours system, "is equally determined that any property coming from the ex royal family in Russia has always remained State property." The Ambassador nodded. Sitting all those miles away Peter Varlov, hidden from the camera, was looking anxious and Matthews himself was beginning to sweat.

"If I may finish my point without further interruption," Lebaille continued, looking at the camera hoping it would transmit his annoyance to Matthews, "your action, delayed or otherwise Mr. Malnikov, seems even more surprising given the two inspections made, and the strong interest they showed in bidding, by the Armoury Museum. Indeed, they may have already entered the bidding. Given the semi-official status and position of this museum in Moscow I cannot believe they would have sent one of their leading experts and his assistant to Geneva to spend nearly two weeks here for the sale without at least the tacit approval of your government."

Malnikov looked stunned, he turned to the Ambassador and the again silent Mr. Kazakov and spoke rapidly in Russian, before reverting to English.

"May I ask who came from the Armoury Museum? To Mr. Kazakov's knowledge, and he naturally liaises very closely with them all the time, indeed they are even housed in the same building of the Kremlin as is his own museum, the Armoury has shown absolutely no interest in acquiring this diamond for itself at any time since the sale was announced." Hamilton-Gray looked at his assistant, who scribbled something on a piece of paper and handed it over, reading it he said,

"It was a Mr. Ivanowitch and a Madam Votrikova - they came twice and I saw them again last night at the hotel just before the sale. They were both there." He felt he shouldn't admit that he still had her mobile number in his pocket.

"May we have a twenty minute break please, we would like to confirm something." For the first time it was the Ambassador who spoke.

Without waiting for a reply the three Russians made for the door and Harriet hurriedly showed them into a side room.

"Please, if you want to use the telephone that one is a direct outside line." She said pointing to the corner. No one said very much while they waited for the three to return. After about twenty minutes absence they re-entered and sat down in silence, this time Hamilton-Gray was surprised that the hitherto taciturn Mr. Kazakov was their spokesman saying, - in perfect English

"Gentleman - I knew before we requested this short interval, but now I have the absolute confirmation from Moscow - no one called Ivanowitch or Votrikova works or has ever worked in recent times at the Armoury Museum. I wonder, Mr. Hamilton-Gray, whether in your and the lawyer's presence I may inspect the interesting object we are all arguing about?"

The auctioneer gave some instructions to his assistant, who got up and left the room. As the others waited a secretary, unaware of the drama which was fast developing round her, served coffee and left two plates of biscuits either end of the table - these were left untouched. Had they been watching they would have seen a similar operation going on in Sir George's office and just the shaking hand of Peter Varlov coming briefly into view as he lent forward to take his cup. There was immediate silence as Harriet returned followed by three security men one of whom placed a small metal safe box in front of Hamilton-Gray. Without pausing for effect he opened it at once with a small key. Then he took out the leather bag together with a pair of white cloth gloves, got up and walked round the table to place both in front of Mr. Kazakov. The tension was almost tangible as the others watched him put his small inspection magnifying glass to his eye and make a long detailed and silent examination of the diamond. After what seemed like an age to Matthews staring at the screen with growing apprehension, the Russian expert deliberately placed the stone back into its leather purse and put both back into the safe box, before looking slowly round the room. Pausing for effect he said,

"Gentlemen, you will appreciate that I cannot, without making some more detailed tests, be absolutely sure, but from this initial inspection and, I would add with all my experience, I am ninety nine point nine per cent certain that the diamond I have just examined is a fraud."

Back in London poor Peter Varlov dropped his coffee cup and slumped back in his chair - in Geneva Hamilton-Gray told his assistant to call the police at once and then get him an urgent call through to Antwerp.

From his seat beside a speechless Sir George, Ian Challiner calmly leant forward and, after telling Hamilton-Gray that he or one of the bank's other lawyers would be in touch with him later, switched off the video link with Geneva. Looking at his two companions it was difficult to judge which of them had been more stunned by the Russian's announcement.

"Sir George," he asked, "has there ever been any doubt expressed before in any of your reports on which presumably your offer of a loan to Prince Peter Varlov was based as to the authenticity of the Tsarina's diamond? The loan committee told me that finally it was only your strong personal recommendation and assurances that ensured their positive, and I would add, unusually speedy reaction to the request against what I understand was their better judgement." Matthews was nervous now and began to bluster,

"Absolutely not - I'm not taking responsibility if that's what you're hinting, Challiner, I just passed on the documents Peter provided, isn't that the case Peter?"

After all the build up of excitement and anticipation ahead of the sale, the huge disillusion and disappointment of the actual event and now this impossible news today, Peter Varlov had had enough. However, some fight remained and as his eyes narrowed he looked at Sir George,

"George, you know I left all the negotiations to you, you agreed all the arrangements, I was merely guided by you for everything. That's what you seemed to want." Ian Challiner smiled to himself as Sir George squirmed at the unexpected onslaught. The bank had their scapegoat if they needed one.

CHAPTER TWENTY SEVEN

NORTHERN SPAIN

If only the poor boy's parents had been able to find out why someone had attempted to murder their son in a church, but so far the police had been incapable or unwilling to offer any form of explanation and all they could do was wait and pray – he slumbered on with only an occasional muscular twitch revealing some unknown thoughts........Raimondo, the magistrate was stout, and although only 40 had the appearance of a man at least fifteen years older. A florid complexion, gained from many wine devoted years, with wispy thinning hair which scarcely covered a heavily freckled dome. An unexplained scar on his left cheek and some missing teeth did nothing to improve his looks and indeed the few he had remaining protruded in a most unattractive manner. These unsightly features were as nothing compared to the glowering goitre swelling on his neck, which gave the impression of having a life of its own and always to be in imminent danger of bursting. He had lied and cheated his way to an office way beyond any merit or ability of his own, arriving at the post of magistrate some two years before. Not surprisingly un-married, he was accurately described by his many enemies as a slothful, unsuccessful and repulsive lecher. Raimondo compensated for his physical shortcomings by dressing in a bizarre array of fancy costumes that he falsely imagined portrayed him as a man of many facets including such things as hunting, prowess with a cross-bow, musicianship and even academia. Today, being a Sunday, this thoroughly unappealing man had been, as usual, to morning mass at the cathedral. He went, not out of any Godliness or devotion, but for self aggrandisement. Reserved for the gentry, such as they were, of Santo Domingo de la Calzada, there was a boxed off portion of the nave and within its confines the pews were slightly raised. This privileged enclosure was not, as Raimondo would have liked at the Easterly section of the nave, but close to the West portico and hence discreetly out of view of ordinary worshippers. Today, he had dressed himself in the extraordinary attire of what he believed reflected the perfect image of a senior law-enforcer. Under a black frock coat he displayed a flamboyant un-buttoned white lacey jabot tapering down to breeches quite brazenly showing off a girth more befitting a drayman. His legs, the shape of cucumbers, were quite unsuitable for the wearing of black silken stockings, but these he chose for sensual rather than sartorial reasons.

As the mass ended, the magistrate, with an unnecessarily exaggerated genuflexion, walked self consciously alone down the nave and out into the heat of the Sunday sun. The market was in full swing and looking out from the cathedral's prominent clock tower the chief bell ringer was enjoying the colourful sight of dozens of stall holders' awnings beneath which the simple country produce on sale was displayed. The vain law enforcer strutted, peacock-like, through the aisles - with his usual air of self importance, as he greeted those he regarded as his social inferiors. He was actually talking to a senior Brother from the monastery when his eye fell on the familiar shapely figure of Portrella, the pimento selling daughter of the albergo keeper, who he had had removed from his court a few weeks earlier for causing a disturbance with her shrieking. With a quickening of his gait he reached her stall just behind some other would be shoppers, and with an ill mannered shove he got in front of them before sweeping his three cornered hat ostentatiously from off his dappled pate.

CHAPTER TWENTY EIGHT

GENEVA

When Eric and Liza had left the hotel, their departure unnoticed in the general hubbub which was then taking place within the auction room, instead of turning right to enter France by the usual route near the airport, they headed more to the South and crossed the border taking a minor road near St. Julien-en-Genevois. Here a cheerful but bored douanier waved through the first car he had seen since five o'clock that afternoon. Once over the border they kept to the old route nationale rather than risk the possible controls at the toll entrances to the autoroute. Some fifteen kilometres into France Eric pulled into a lay-by secluded from the main carriageway by an apron of fir trees. Quickly checking that there were no other vehicles parked there, he took off the local Geneva number plates and revealed the Italian ones already fixed underneath. As they sat there checking the map both jumped as Eric's mobile suddenly rang. He looked at the display, but the number showing meant nothing to him, without actually speaking he pressed the button and, with some relief, heard a voice he recognised as Stanislas's saying good evening. The news of the abortive sale had already reached Lisbon. Briefly, Eric brought Stanislas up to date and managed to assure him that all was well - as they were speaking, he told him not to worry, he, or rather Liza, was holding the genuine article and they could be expected in Lisbon within two days. Stanislas gave him yet another telephone number on which he was to ring him for the rendezvous details in twenty four hours time. Until then they were only to ring this number in any emergency, not otherwise. Eric gave Stanislas his agreement and rang off. He started the engine and once more drove off into the night. Distracted by Stanislas's call Eric had forgotten he had left the Geneva registration plates lying in the dead leaves of the lay by where he had put them down beside the car to answer the phone. Some thirty kilometres on as they neared Nantua, they rounded a bend and Liza clutched at Eric's upper thigh, her heart almost stopping as they were whistled into the side by two blue uniformed gendarmes.

"Good evening, Monsieur, just a routine check - please could you present your car papers, insurance and driving licence? Please switch off your motor." Eric turned off the ignition and fumbled in the side pocket of his door, praying that Igor's normal standard of organisation hadn't failed. He handed over the documents to the officer and noticed that his colleague was making an inquisitive inspection circuit round the Mercedes. Both men walked some way off still holding the papers and Liza saw one of them speaking into his radio.

"Do we make a run for it?" she hissed to Eric not moving her lips. Eric remained silent and apparently relaxed behind the wheel, but she saw his right hand go towards his trouser pocket. "My God," she thought to herself, "he'll shoot them if he has to and then bloody what?"

The young officer, not realising the danger he could have been in, leant down to Eric's open window, smiled and said,

"Thank you Sir, all seems to be in order - bon route." The Russian took the papers back with the same hand that would have willingly shot the gendarme dead had it been necessary, re-started the engine and drove on into Nantua. They were lucky and found an all night routier café where two steak-frites helped to restore their nerve. They discussed whether to spend the night in one of the bedrooms in the same establishment, but finally decided to drive on. It was three o'clock in the morning as they took the road round the south of Lyon and crossed the Autoroute du Sud where some early departures were already making their way down to the Mediterranean. They headed South West as their cross country route took them south of the Massif Central and through the Dordogne. They stopped near Figeac and, after filling up with petrol, spent some ninety minutes resting beside the river - both dozing off for what was their first sleep for over twenty four hours.

They woke up, took a coffee in a nearby bar and continued their journey. Although Liza offered, Eric insisted on driving. Unlike the border leaving Switzerland, as they eventually crossed into Spain at Hendaye, the traffic did not stop and the unmanned border posts were beginning to show an air of neglect and disrepair. Such is the benefit of the European Union, thought Eric. They had a last meal in

France just before the border and, with both now starting to feel tired, drove on in silence.

"Christ, be careful - what the hell are you doing?" Liza screamed, suddenly horrified, as Eric just managed to pull back to his side of the road out of the path of an oncoming lorry. "Now you really must stop, Eric, you're tired and a bloody danger." He pulled into the next parking area provided on the recently rebuilt road and they both took another coffee from the mobile bar set up in one corner. As they got back into the car, Eric again looked at the map - he glanced at his watch before turning to Liza,

"We are obviously not going to make Portugal this evening, we'll have to stop the night somewhere. We're here," pointing at the map, "let's get on a little further and find somewhere to sleep for the night." To keep him awake Liza talked almost non-stop until just over an hour later they thankfully pulled into the riverside parking at Najera. Getting out they noticed what appeared to be two hikers walking across the bridge looking up at the storks circling above - relieved at their safe arrival and with her tension slightly abating Liza gave Eric a kiss.

CHAPTER TWENTY NINE

GENEVA

Immediately the three Russians had left the boardroom, Hamilton-Gray sat down with his two colleagues and the lawyers. The hint contained in his suggestion, that, possibly the Notaire would like to leave if he had other important matters to deal with was not taken and Maître Petelet remained determinedly at the table - his wife would love to hear the gossip over dinner that evening he thought. The Auctioneer began,

"I do not want to go into too much detail before the police representatives get here - it looks to me quite frankly as if we're in a bloody mess. Harriet has telephoned the FCP..."

"The what?" interrupted Thomas Warderby, who was finding his concentration suffering after his pre-dawn departure earlier from St. Tropez and his continuing hangover from the evening before - his full retirement couldn't come soon enough, he thought. The Auctioneer glanced a little angrily at Warderby before continuing,

"The Federal Criminal Police - and they have immediately despatched one of their senior Investigation Officers by helicopter from Lausanne. He should be here shortly with the junior chaps, who are joining from their office here. In the meantime I'm going to telephone the Antwerp people to see if they can throw any light on this matter, but after what the Russians said I must confess it looks as if we've been the subject of a very serious hoax. No, that is wrong - we're the gullible victims of a huge criminal deception. And we'll be the laughing stock of the fine art world if this all gets out."

"Have you still got the introductory papers that allegedly came from the Armoury about the two visitors from last week?" Mr. Varley, the Geneva lawyer asked quietly, looking up from the notes he was making.

"Yes of course," Hamilton-Gray turned to his assistant beside him, "Harriet, please ring down and ask Beatrice to make a dozen photo-copies and bring them up here at once. Also make sure the closed circuit television tapes are available covering the time of their visits for the police to see. Do that first, then I want to see our insurance file - you'd better check through that, Maître Lebaille, as soon as you can."

The police eventually arrived about two hours later and helped by his colleagues, Hamilton-Gray soon gave them all the available information he had. Led by an impressive Inspector Weilder, whose German accented French gave away his Zurich origins, the police moved both efficiently and quickly. In routine questioning. the receptionist confessed to having told her boy friend - a young journalist - about the interest and visit of the Armoury and Christopher Guedot was immediately called out of his office to give such information as he could. This led them to the exact apartment used by Eric and Liza and they soon learnt from the agent how he had dropped them off at the station en route for the Airport and an Easy Jet flight, he thought, going to London. It was easily established that neither had boarded any plane that day, but as Hamilton-Gray told the Officer when he announced this, that was known anyway - he had seen them at the sale in the evening!

It was then that the investigation had its first piece of luck - a Police patrol making a routine tour in the almost no man's land round St. Julien-en-Genevois stopped when one of them had an urgent call of nature. Standing behind one of the fir trees gratefully answering this, the officer looked around. On the ground just beside him, only half hidden by the overgrowth, were two Geneva Registration plates. After the details were radioed through to both the French and Swiss police, they were identified as those of a Mercedes which the CCTV cameras outside the Richemont showed being driven away a few minutes before the Auction had broken up the night before. An immediate alert was put out for patrols to check all Mercedes saloons on roads leading away from Geneva and a Gendarme in the Nantua district spotted this order by chance just five minutes before he was going off duty. Taking the details from his log he went to see his superior. An item on the French Television early evening news brought in a report from a hotel owner of a couple being spotted sleeping near Figeac, in a similar car, although he hadn't noticed the registration plates. A routine check of the hidden cameras still operating at the border showed a Mercedes crossing into Spain later in the day, but with its Italian number clearly visible.

In view of the publicity, the involvement of the Russian Government and the value and importance of the stolen property, the police forces now of three countries were each pulling out all the stops, and although co-operating closely, each hoping they would have the prestige of actually solving the case. The final clue that evening came from an irate lorry driver pulling into a café's parking area where he was heard complaining loudly about a near head-on collision with some madman in an Italian registered Mercedes. The Café owner had seen the news earlier and phoned the local police - the lorry driver benefited from a free meal as he waited to make his statement. Thus Eric and Liza, parking the car in Najera a little later, were blissfully unaware that at the same time the Spanish police were studying large scale maps of the area including a list of the stages making up the Pilgrims' route.

Meanwhile, back in the Auctioneer's offices in Geneva, Maître Lebaille and Mr. Varley had read the small print of the various insurance policies the company held. A similar action was taking place almost simultaneously at the bank in London with an anxious Peter Varlov demanding to know the position and at the diamond cutters in Antwerp as a precaution by them.

"There is no doubt, Mr. Hamilton-Gray, that your policies, with the additional security that they are underwritten at Lloyd's, fully cover you against any theft or fraud," began Maître Lebaille, "up to a maximum value for any one single item of fifty million dollars."

"Let's cut out all your legal crap," Thomas Warderby, bored by all the hanging around, said, "just tell me - if we have been conned by these bloody people are we liable and will the insurance pay? That's all we're interested in!" Mr. Varley placed a hand on Maître Lebaille's arm before replying himself,

"Providing you can prove you did proper due diligence of all the details and have taken reasonable measures at all times to ensure normal security, the answer, in my opinion, is yes."

"Right then," said Warderby," you'd better start claiming Jonathan - now can I get back to the South?"

CHAPTER THIRTY

NAJERA - NORTHERN SPAIN

While Eric and Liza were finding a room for the night and picking a restaurant for a meal, another diner - some two hundred metres from where they were sitting - was coming to the end of his supper in a relaxed and almost jocular atmosphere. However, to Wilhelm, with his Teutonic temperament, there had been no doubt what the Bishop had meant and that he had been serious. No doubt whatsoever.

"Capture the chickens and bring them to me here. Do this and great will be your reward," he had said somewhat theatrically before he blessed the room and smilingly wished a general good night. Wilhelm and his walking companion were also spending the night at Najera, the ancient capital of Navarra, but they were in the monastery founded in 1032 by King Garcia on the spot where a vulture and a partridge were said to have guided him to a statue of the Blessed Virgin - hence its name of Santa Maria la Real. Liza had pointed out the entrance to Eric as they had looked for their hotel.

The dinner the two pilgrims had shared with the monks and the visiting Bishop had been good, but nothing special. The thick vegetable soup had been followed by some sort of fish casserole - it was a Friday - hunks of bread and a local goats' cheese of unbelievable odour. All had been washed down with a local wine, which promised more a headache tomorrow rather than a pleasant feeling tonight.

Arriving here before the expected hospitality of Santo Domingo de la Calzada, where the food, wine and bed was said to be far superior, it had been immediately clear that this community was very much a poor cousin. The church although once grand with its famed cloisters and containing Garcia's tomb together with that of his family and descendants, was now run down. Although there were still visitors coming to see the cave where the Holy statue had been found, the generally neglected fabric was witness to the lack of both funds and worshippers, who preferred the weekly drive to the animated liveliness of neighbouring Santo Domingo, some 20 kilometres away, with its cathedral, its market, its crowds and its pilgrims - all wearing the white feather plucked from the miraculous cockerel whose direct ancestor had attracted such prosperity and fame to the town. There were no more vultures or partridge to keep the interest at Najera.

Yes, the Bishop had been right thought Wilhelm - how could the pious but poor community of Najera compete with such an attraction.

"It's that cockerel," the prelate said, warming to his subject and not realising that he was being taken seriously by the young man, "get that here and then we would see a difference, then we'd see who got to the Sacred College first." It was true that he had been excited by at least a chalice full of the local wine - his face was becoming more the colour for a Cardinal rather than his cap - but to Wilhelm sitting beside him the proposal was mistakenly taken almost as a command and as clear as Henry II's had been to his knights about Thomas à Beckett. "Capture the chickens and bring them here. Do this and great will be your reward." The Bishop looked around the assembly and only the monk sitting opposite him saw his wink. Wilhelm immediately began thinking, he liked the idea of a reward, and he enjoyed action. Looking to the far end of the table where his walking companion appeared to be in deep thought. "I wonder," thought Wilhelm to himself, "things would be easier with two - but a shared reward is only a half of a whole one - I'll try to keep this to myself, but he'll be useful I'm sure!" It was as well the Bishop had retired for the night - thought Wilhelm and he wanted to keep his planning to himself. The Prelate might have spoken to François as well.

At the other end of the refectory table, François had enjoyed his meal - although the food was certainly basic and the wine felt as if his head would pay for it in the morning. The genial company of the monks around him, with their easy conversation and their obvious concern to prove their hospitality as good as anyone's, helped his recovery from the exhaustion induced by the 25 kilometres he and Wilhelm had walked together that day. In all it was good to relax in friendly company and he had enjoyed the general banter of the light hearted conversation.

Being lost in his thoughts and nursing a generous goblet of the home distilled digestif which his two neighbours had pressed on him, François was feeling relaxed, happy and at peace with himself and with the world. The sixth child and the third son in a family of eight children, François had always felt attracted to the religious life and at the age of 21 now was the time he felt he should commit himself to the church should it become clear to him that his vocation was real. This was why he was largely under-taking the ancient pilgrimage to Santiago de Compostela after his unnerving experience in Antwerp at the hands of Praveen. Finally, starting from his home near Lyon, to where he had fled after leaving Belgium he prayed that during the course of his journey he would receive guidance as to his future by retracing the steps of past generations of believers. Admittedly the experience of being cheated by Praveen in Antwerp and the subsequent clash with the authorities had precipitated his decision to make the trek, but to do so had always been in his plans.

He could never forget that autumn morning some seven years before when the actual idea of the pilgrimage had first come to him - he had been alone on a slight rise of land in his father's vineyard between Mâcon and Lyon watching the sun rise with the promise of another golden day for the vendange, when his gaze had been captured by something shining on a rocky outcrop not far away across the small valley. Afterwards he thought perhaps it had been just the trick of the rising sun, the sleep in his eyes or the morning mist dissipating ahead of the midday heat, but however he tried to explain it, he couldn't dismiss the feeling of peace and calm that the apparition had engendered in him. The form it had appeared to take was of a young, but somehow radiant female person with an air of utmost holiness coming from her. He remembered above all the immediate inner sense he had that he was being called by a power he didn't understand to a life he hadn't yet contemplated - a still small voice speaking to him of certainty where before he had had doubt. Quietly sipping his digestif, he remembered that morning as if it was yesterday and realised his life had been changed from that moment. On the pilgrimage he had met up with Wilhelm some seven days ago at Ronçevalles, his entry point to Spain, and they had walked together since then. It had been good to have company for both young men and while the spirituality of the one was balanced by the more worldly, even cynical attitude of the other, they had got on well enough. They conversed in adequate English, with which their respective schooling had left them, and the week had passed agreeably enough for both of them.

The pleasant dreamy mood induced by the convivial dinner, the wine and the digestif and his sudden remembering of that life changing experience in the Beaujolais countryside some seven years before was broken and François sat up abruptly. He overheard the Bishop and Wilhelm seeming to discuss the proposed theft of the mystical chickens from Santo Domingo, which he had read about, and his travelling companion negotiating a reward if this were done. Surely the Bishop had only been joking, but his companion apparently was taking it seriously.

The next day's walk together would be very interesting. Both men went to bed that night in their individual cells, but sleep was a long time coming for them as they each made their plans. Although unrealised by either, those plans would have effects way beyond what they could imagine. In the morning they were woken by the crowing of a lone cock.

Getting up early, François said his morning prayers by himself - not, for once, choosing to join the local monks in their Chapel - and met an already dressed, and François piously suspected, an unprayed Wilhelm in the refectory for a breakfast of very black coffee, fruit and toast. Entering the room he received a monosyllabic grunt as greeting from Wilhelm, whose head was suffering from both the quality and quantity of last night's wine, and a rather heartier one from the few monks who remained before going off to start their daily tasks.

By seven o'clock they were both ready to leave - taking the advantage of the comparative cool of the early morning to tackle the hot, sandy and deserted trail, which lay ahead of them to Santo Domingo de Calzada. A path which although a comparatively easy 25 kilometres didn't offer much shade from the piercing sun nor much chance of diversions through meetings with the local population.

Saturday morning saw the street market come to Najera before travelling to its Sunday bonanza at Santo Domingo. Wilhelm and François walked around the stalls and profited by buying some saucisson, bread and fruit for their mid-day stop. They were also careful to replenish their water containers, despite this adding extra weight, as they would have a strenuous walk ahead of them. Taking the path west out of Najera both men were happy to walk in silence up the initial climb through the woods before reaching the open country. Both had much to think about - the one plotting the kidnap of the mystical chickens they had yet to see, but whose existence would now have such a profound influence on both their lives, the other hardly believing that his friend could have taken the suggestion of the Bishop seriously and feeling - again that still, small voice was speaking to him as it had over the years since that Autumn morning - that he was somehow put there to stop whatever stupidities would occur. It was Wilhelm who eventually broke the silence.

"That was an interesting evening last night - but tonight, my friend, we'll be eating and drinking better. I don't know about you but my diary tells me that I'm ahead of my planned schedule and I think I'll stay a few days at Santo Domingo and have a rest. What's the point in getting to Santiago de Compostela too soon and while Burgos may be fun, Santo Domingo will be cheaper."

"What changed your mind? Yesterday you said you wanted to press on so you aren't late back home for your sister's wedding." asked François.

"Oh! I'm not bothered about three or four days and in any case it's not me that's getting married - I only have to turn up at the church 5 minutes before!" After this burst of conversation they walked on in renewed silence - the trail dropping down to cross a boulder filled dry river bed then rising the other side made them concentrate on their footing. François thought now it's obvious, he's determined to carry out the Bishop's plan - he does take it seriously! Perhaps it would be better for the moment to play ignorant, to go along with his companion's ideas and to have a bit of fun at his friend's expense before considering how he should react. Delay sometimes is good, but this time it would lead to repercussions so severe for both men that had he known, perhaps François afterwards would wish he'd dismissed it all and changed things there and then. This time François spoke first:

"Don't you think we should press on to Burgos before taking a break - it's a bigger town, there'd be more interest there and more to do?"

"You can if you want, but look at this beautiful country, don't you think a few days resting in this peace will be good? No, I've decided, I'm staying at Santo Domingo - the place has always appealed to me. I hear the refuge is comfortable, the old buildings fascinating, the local girls pretty and the wine is good. No hard feelings if you go on alone, but I'll miss your company - why don't you stay?" Wilhelm said, as he looked almost pleadingly at his friend. François waited, he didn't want to appear too easily swayed - and another five kilometres were added to the day's total before he spoke up again.

"OK, I've been thinking, I've been on the go more or less every day since leaving Lyons. "You've got a good idea - I'll treat myself to a break and stay with you."

"That's wonderful," Wilhelm replied and sounded almost sincere. It was now coming up to 11 o'clock and the sun reaching for its highest point was burning down on both young men. Sweating under their sunhats they both slumped under the meagre shade of one of the sparse trees which dotted the landscape. Opening the food they had bought earlier that morning they began to eat.

He saw them coming a split second before they hit and instinctively ducked down to his left. There had been some movement by the road, at this stage only about twenty five metres from where they were sitting but slightly hidden by a rise in the land, and he had turned to look in that direction. One stone fell harmlessly a little distance past them, but the second, about the size of a flattened golf ball, caught François on the top of his right shoulder.

"What the hell was that," said Wilhelm. "Is there some bird after your food?"

"No - it looks as if someone's throwing stones at us. If it was deliberate, their aim was bloody good." François rubbed his shoulder where the bump was now the size of a second squashed golf ball. After the initial shock they both ran towards the road and reached the top of the small rise hiding its view from their picnic spot just in time to see the back end of a large bluish car disappearing fast round the bend in the direction of Santo Domingo.

"Someone apparently doesn't like pilgrims," said Wilhelm, "don't take it personally."

"It's not your shoulder that hurts - whoever threw that meant to hit us."

"Oh - I don't think so, why would anyone do that - it was just kids throwing stones." They returned to their food, but suddenly Wilhelm spoke again.

"Come to think of it did that car look familiar to you? I'm sure I saw it in the parking at Najera last night when we arrived there. There weren't many in the square. I bet that was the one."

"I don't know - I only managed to see it was blue, I didn't even have enough time to see what sort of car it was, only some big saloon - a Peugeot or Mercedes, they all look the same, but the whole thing did seem deliberate."

"Why on earth would anyone stop in the middle of nowhere to throw stones at two walkers they couldn't have known were there in the first place?" asked Wilhelm. "Be logical, now you're being paranoid - it was probably tourists with a couple of children stopping for a pee."

As they carried on eating, François wasn't so sure - he couldn't get rid of that feeling he had had all morning, a sort of sixth sense, that they were being watched. He was too embarrassed to tell Wilhelm, but he definitely felt uneasy - for the first time since he left Lyons he didn't feel secure and he'd be pleased when they were safely at Santo Domingo.

"Didn't you see anyone with that car you saw last night in Najera? There weren't many people around." He asked.

"No," said Wilhelm, "I just noticed it had Italian plates and a nasty dent on the driver's door. If it was that one it wouldn't be hard to identify. Forget it, they probably were just throwing stones at random and didn't even see us. It's like when they're on the beach - people just pick up a pebble and throw it."

They sat slightly apart, but not so far that they were out of the tree's shade as they finished their food. Both were tired after the morning's exertions and lost in their thoughts - it was some time before either spoke.

"It's only about another nine kilometres to Santo Domingo - it'll be good to get there early." said François, "we'll be able to find a place easily."

"Oh! I'm told that there's plenty of room there according to the pilgrim's guide, so no worry about a bed," answered Wilhelm, "we'll have a scout round before eating, the guide books also say that Saturday nights could be quite lively there before the market - let's see" His shoulder still throbbing, François collected his things together, if it was just chance, he thought, why stop there, why only two stones and why such good aim. The more he thought, the more deliberate it appeared. He couldn't get the incident out of his mind. Lifting his rucksack he said

"Come on let's go. I could kill for a nice cold beer."

With that happy prospect they both resumed their journey. As they trudged up the side of yet another dry river bed - how they would have appreciated a swim in the hot sunshine had it been full - the ringing of Wilhelm's mobile interrupted the quiet. He answered it quickly, moving sharply away from his friend, rather pointedly making clear he didn't want to be overheard. His curiosity roused by this, François tried to listen but could only hear

"Yes.......yes......act quickly..... Burgos ...when? .... I'll text you with what we'll ....500 Euros .... No, I'll need more please" François turned as Wilhelm returned - looking slightly uneasy François thought.

"Who was that - no problem I hope?" he asked.

"No - only my sister, it's her birthday today and she was just thanking me for a card I'd sent her - at least the post works from here, that's something." They walked on, each concentrating on the track, with neither feeling any compulsion to carry on the conversation in the heat. François couldn't explain why Wilhelm had obviously lied to him about the phone call - in any case whoever it was who rang it was absolutely none of his business - perhaps he was only asking his father to send him some money. He had only asked to be pleasant and couldn't really care less who it was although he was rather curious. The fact that he had obviously lied made the whole thing very intriguing - particularly after he'd overheard the Bishop's offer last night. Had Wilhelm already hatched a plan and was he calling in help?

"What does your sister do?"

"She's a secretary in some lawyer's office - going to marry - a nice chap, an engineer, who was at school with me funnily enough."

"Just the two of you in the family?"

FORGOTTEN DIAMOND

"Yes - you're asking a lot of questions. "

"I'm sorry," laughed François, "everyone tells me that - I'd better shut up, curiosity killed the cat they say!" Little did he realise that curiosity would possibly kill more than the cat before too long. They walked on covering the rather uninteresting last few kilometres to Santo Domingo more or less in silence, broken only by the leading arrivals of tomorrow's market happily hailing them from their trucks as their pilgrims' path re-joined the road for the final reach into town. They easily found the *Casa de la Cofradía del Santo Albergue de Peregrinos* and fixed up their sleeping arrangements in the ancient refuge. Then sitting in the square outside the church, drinking what they thought was a well earned beer, they didn't notice the interest being taken in them by the couple having a similar drink on the terrace of the equally ancient, but now rather grander Parador on the other side. Somewhere in the distance they could hear a cock crowing. At that very moment François saw a man turning the corner into the square and without being able to explain it he seemed to feel a shock of instant recognition as the blood drained from his face.

"What's the matter?" asked Wilhelm, "Are you feeling O.K? You look as though you've seen a ghost"

"Don't worry it's nothing." Luckily their attention was immediately diverted as the church tower seemed to stir and the bells started ringing. The doors flashed open and a newly wed couple - surrounded by laughing friends - stepped out into the sunshine. There would be a good party in the square tonight! The couple from the Parador terrace briefly looked at the wedding party before turning their gaze back to François and Wilhelm - and then slipped unnoticed into the church.

They finished their beers in silence in the late afternoon sunshine - both tired from the day's walk and, although not admitting it to each other, both still slightly worried by the unexplained stone throwing episode at lunchtime. Perhaps it was all just a bizarre coincidence after all - but the whole episode had been unsettling and left an uneasy feeling. Anyone who could deliberately throw stones like that couldn't be totally pleasant, thought Wilhelm. It was about half past five and the square was beginning very slowly to show the start of some activity with people setting up tables, music apparatus and all the other paraphernalia, which the wedding party would be using later. They were both feeling a little hungry, but knew that here in Spain it was no use expecting dinner anytime before nine at the earliest so contented themselves by finishing the rather dry peanuts which had been unwillingly provided with their beers and only then when they had been asked for.

"I think I'll have a wander around just to see what the place is like," Wilhelm stood up, "do you want to come or are you going back to that book you've been reading ?"

"No, I think I'll come with you - let's take a look at the Parador and see how the rich travel." They walked slowly round the square, bumping into the stall holder who had sold them their saucisson that morning in Najera, who suggested they would have been better hitching a lift with her.

"Thanks, but I think that would be rather against the spirit of our pilgrimage," answered François laughing, "in any case the walk has built up our appetites so we'll probably be customers again tomorrow"

"If we get any sleep with the wedding party going on," interrupted Wilhelm, "they look to be preparing quite a do." Priding herself on always knowing the local gossip, the stallholder volunteered the information that the bride was none other than the daughter of the refuge owner where they were staying, and suggesting that if they played their cards right they'd get an invitation to the evening's fun.

"Most of the town'll be there so two more won't make any difference," she said, "it'll help your Spanish to dance with a few of the local young ladies - I wish I was twenty years younger myself and had left him behind - I'd show you a few steps." She pointed at her husband, who appeared to be having a late siesta stretched out on one of the benches and whose snoring didn't need help from any of the sound equipment being set up for the evening to be heard. "She's married the son of one of the local farmers - I don't think her parents will have to wait overlong for their first grandchild either from what I've been told - there was more than the two of them in the church by all accounts - but I shouldn't spread gossip or her father'll run me out of town - he's a pious one." They left the woman, who had turned to talk to three other customers and went towards the Cathedral.

This is named after the hermit Dominique and contains his tomb, where he rests under a Gothic canopy added in 1513. It was Dominique who, in the eleventh century had lived here and built an inn, a hospital - now the parador - together with a bridge over the Rio Oja and a pathway to help the pilgrims on their way to Santiago de Compostela. Although largely built in the early 1500's, the Apse shows its Roman origins, and the ancient fortifications around the Parador were built in the fourteenth century. The whole place had an air of history and romance. After deciding they were a bit scruffy to enter the Hotel they approached the Cathedral passing the front of the Parador. Both were too impressed with the sight of the magnificent Gothic façade with its Baroque bell tower and the large classical entrance door from which the newly married couple had emerged earlier, to notice the dusty dark blue Mercedes with Italian number plates and what looked like a nasty dent on the driver's door parked in front of the hotel beside a Renault Clio. They entered the Church through the cloisters on the left. As they went they picked up a multi language descriptive leaflet giving some explanation about the chicken legend. It was only a few steps across the nave before they saw the actual gilded cage positioned about ten feet off the ground opposite the Saint's tomb. Almost at the same moment that they saw the illuminated interior of the cage they were nearly deafened by the shrill of a crowing cockerel which was clearly visible, with its white mate behind the bars.

"That will bring us luck." exclaimed François fervently. "According to the legend any pilgrim who hears the cockerel crowing is blessed by Santo Domingo himself." In silence, they read the leaflet between them and learned that in the year 1090 a little family of pilgrims consisting of a 16 year old boy and his parents had arrived at Santo Domingo de la Calzada just as François and Wilhelm had done today. Because the boy had spurned the amorous advances of the daughter of the albergo owner where they were staying, she had angrily sought her revenge by hiding a silver jug in his knapsack and then accusing him of stealing it. He was soon arrested and at a summary trial was found guilty and hanged the same day. About a month later his parents returning from Compostela found him on the scaffold still living and proclaiming that St James had looked after him. The amazed parents rushed to the local magistrate's house where they begged him to come and cut down their living son. The magistrate's response had been incredulous as he swore,

"If he's alive, then so are those two chickens roasting on the spit for my Sunday lunch." Whereupon the two fowl sprouted white feathers and flew off from the spit. Much impressed by this extraordinary legend, Francois's faith was heightened to a level he had not known since the vision he had experienced seven years before and again he had that strong feeling that he was somehow reliving history of which he sensed he was a part.

CHAPTER THIRTY ONE

NAJERA

Before Eric and Liza themselves had left Najera that same morning and, with the diamond almost throbbing in the side pocket of Liza's jeans - placed there so she could keep her hand on it quite naturally without any suspicion - the two of them decided, like the two pilgrims, to buy a picnic lunch in the market. They would, they thought, then travel on, hoping to make Lisbon quite easily before the end of the day. Indeed it hadn't even been their intention to stop the night at Najera, but with Eric insisting on doing all the driving and the unplanned delay in Figeac, fatigue had dictated a night's stop rather than risk a further accident. Their journey was also made longer as they preferred to use the smaller country roads to avoid any possible police checks by the main routes. They queued patiently at one of the market stalls to buy some of the local ham and saucisson they would eat with the juicy local tomatoes they had already got from its neighbour.

Ahead of them two local wives were discussing some village gossip no doubt with the market seller in what they assumed to be Basque, but as they waited, their attention had been naturally drawn to the two young pilgrims standing behind them who were talking in more understandable English.

"I'm sure the Abbott was serious about the chickens - I read up the story last night in my guide - and it would be rather fun to bring them back here, it would do no harm and he did say there'd be a reward !" one of the pilgrims was saying.

"How'd you get them out of the Church unseen and back here? - This I must see. In any case I'm sure the Bishop was pulling your leg - he couldn't have been serious," the second pilgrim replied, "what I am certain about anyway is that the locals do take this sort of thing very seriously and they certainly wouldn't see the joke !"

"Oh François, you really are an old prude sometimes - unwind a bit - it's not going to do anyone any real harm and the whole story is only a silly legend anyway - come on it'll be a laugh" Looking at each other Eric and Liza smiled, the conversation made absolutely no sense to them as they reached the head of the line and bought their ham.

"There's a rotisserie over there - I'd have thought the Abbott could get all the chickens he needed from there," laughed Eric, "why would he give a reward to those two for bringing him some others?"

"Perhaps they're the ones that lay the golden eggs," chuckled back Liza as they took their purchases back over the bridge to the car park. By now the market was in full swing and Eric was conscious of the long distance they still had to drive. As they approached the Mercedes its lights gave the usual momentary flash as Eric automatically opened the doors.

"Oh God! Eric look at this," Liza cried as she went round to the far side, "some bastard has dented my bloody door." Eric came round and saw the damage - it looked as if a heavy motorbike had driven or fallen against it leaving a nasty deep dent, but worse than that it was stopping the door from opening or closing properly.

"Blast, we'll have to get that fixed before we get too much attention. - it's not really safe - the police are bound to stop us if they see it." Eric looked at his map - "We can get to Santo Domingo by using this old road here," his finger pointed out the way to Liza, "it looks to be largely the old pilgrims' route but quite driveable. Let's hope there's a garage there that can do us a quick repair job - come on, jump in and whatever you do don't lean against the door."

Although it rattled as they climbed the same dust track followed a little earlier by Wilhelm and François, through the forest out of Najera, the door fortunately held closed. Liza still had one hand on the diamond against her upper thigh and the other holding the handle. Out of the forest they crossed the pleasant open country with the distant mountains still showing remnants of some late snow on their tops and they began to feel relaxed at last. They passed the odd pilgrim - sometimes alone, often in groups of two or three - all making their slow progress on foot towards their eventual target of Santiago de Compostela. Suddenly there they were, the two who had been behind them earlier in the market, sitting some thirty metres from their track half hidden by a rise in the land.

"Let's have some fun and give them something to think about apart from chickens," Liza said, "just stop for a moment, I need a pee anyway!" The wind was in their favour and the two pilgrims obviously hadn't heard the car pull up. Liza did what she had needed to for the last few kilometres and then each of them picked up one of the many smooth squashed spherical shaped pebbles from the side of the road and threw them - whoosh! Liza's stone hit her target and Eric's was close enough to alarm him as they jumped back into the car and left quickly - both laughing rather too much, as the nervous tension, which had constantly been there since the exchange of the diamond, dissipated a little more. It was a childish thing to do thought Eric, but it helped us to lighten up a bit, and they hadn't seen the car he was sure.

Arriving at Santo Domingo they had no option but to book into the Parador, - a one time hospital refuge for pilgrims, but now a luxury state owned hotel. They left the car parked outside as they went up to their room. Coming down stairs again having left their luggage, the receptionist gave them directions to a local garage where thankfully they later left the car with a promise, induced by the exchange of a 100 euro note, that all would be done by the morning. In the late afternoon sunshine they began the walk back to the hotel. Liza was still holding the diamond in her pocket as if her life depended on it - as indeed in a very real sense it did. The chicken story was everywhere in the town - no traveller could miss it.

"Now I know what those two idiots were talking about this morning," Eric said, "come over here and read this." Liza read the sign Eric was standing by,

"That never happened to any of the chickens we had through the factory when I worked there temporarily," laughed Liza.

"I'd forgotten you had done that work in the experimental chicken farm - how long did you stay there, nine months I think you told me?" Eric asked.

"Yes, about that - long enough to know all about the inside of a chicken at any rate. In the end the KGB never did implement that bird flu virus infiltration scheme in the West. So my research was wasted." replied Liza, "but I'm your trained fowl expert if you need one! Come on, let's go and have a beer." She continued, "You'd better ring Lisbon, as agreed, to warn of the slight delay. We don't want him getting nervous - I've heard what he does in a temper, so better not to provoke one!"

They were walking down the *Calle Mayor,* and passing the Nunnery church on the left, and had almost reached the *Casa de la Cofradía del Santo Albergue de Peregrinos* the pilgrim's refuge - when they heard them. Turning, all they saw were two large determined looking men carrying heavy sticks running as fast as they could towards them shouting in a language they didn't understand.

"Christ! is that the bloody Spanish police? Perhaps they've traced the car quick, quick, in here. Stay calm, but follow me." said Eric. He grabbed Liza and all but threw her into the large entrance hall of the refuge. Without stopping they rushed through the reception vestibule and into the large dormitory area behind where two somewhat startled pilgrims were laying out their mattresses for the night, and then into the garden courtyard at the back. Looking around they saw this was lined with a series of numbered hen coops each containing a fine pair of pure white chickens. Hearing raised voices from inside the refuge asking excitedly in about four different languages what the hell was going on they hardly waited to think.

"We daren't risk being searched and the diamond found." said Eric, "Where can we hide it until we can see who those two men were?" Liza opened the first coop and without hesitation, or saying anything, and as expertly as if she was back in her old research job, she smoothly pushed the priceless diamond into the egg producing cavity of a rather surprised chicken and an equally astonished Eric. Its mate began to crow as she quickly closed the coop's door. Relieved for the moment they made their way quietly out of the refuge, but as they passed, trying to be invisible, through the reception area they saw their two 'Spanish policemen' innocently booking in for the night after their days pilgrimage. They overheard them telling the receptionist how they always ended their day's walk with a friendly race over the last 100 or 150 metres just to see who would buy their first beers! Eric and Liza were sweating as they thought about the necessary call to Lisbon - the chicken would most definitely not be mentioned. They realised they couldn't go back now for the diamond as the Refuge manager was blocking the door to the dormitory talking to two new arrivals. They would have to return a little later.

Leaving the refuge, where fortunately the sudden arrival of six more dusty pilgrims had diverted the attention of the reception staff from their rush into the back courtyard, Eric and Liza could only return to the Parador to plan the recovery of the precious stone.

"At least," said Liza, "from my experience I am sure that the hen will retain the stone for some time - they only normally lay once a day and I noticed an egg already in the coop!" More or less as an afterthought she added, "Don't worry - just pray." Back in their room they made the call to Lisbon, explaining to Stanislas the damage to the car and the delay of twenty-four hours, rather over emphasising that the accident happened when the car was parked and that they most certainly had not been involved with any police over it. With his fingers crossed Eric also assured Stanislas that the 'package' was entirely safe and in a place where no one would think of looking for it! Nevertheless, he was mystified as Stanislas mentioned something about having made some contingency plans to cover such a delay and its possible eventualities. Eric, although not understanding Stanislas as he told him not to use any heroics if the two of them were unfortunately confronted by the police, mumbled his agreement,

"I always look after my friends," Stanislas had said as he put the phone down. It was now about half past seven and Liza rightly thought that most of the pilgrims would be too busy quenching their thirsts built up during the dusty day's walk to notice them and after changing their clothes to help avoid, as far as possible, any instant recognition, they returned to the Refuge determined to recover the diamond. Arriving at the hostel they entered confidently in through the large doorway and were just about to slip as unobtrusively as they could through the reception hall and dormitory into the courtyard, when the door was pushed open and the rather gruff guardian appeared,

"Stand aside a moment," he more shouted than said, "and hold that door open for me - can't you see I've got my hands full?" Both Eric and Liza gave involuntary gasps, their eyes, as they looked at each other, holding the same mixture of fear, horror and despair. The Guardian was carrying the hen coop - the number 'one' showing very clearly - and was obviously leaving the refuge with it. Eric and Liza were struck to the ground and could only watch helplessly as he placed the coop containing the two chickens, but more importantly the diamond with them, onto a small trolley and began to push it towards the *Plaza-del-Santo*. Eric and Liza followed at a safe distance, their hearts beating somewhat faster than was good for their blood pressure and their palms sweating more than was pleasant. Although their training had accustomed them to facing difficult situations, the thought of losing that precious multi million dollar piece of Russian history when their mission was so close to success was a severe test to their composures. Reaching the Plaza they watched as the guardian stopped by the *Santa Iglesia Catedral*-and took the coop off the trolley before carrying it into the church through the small aperture, which formed a part of the magnificent Great South door of the Cathedral. Quietly entering themselves, they were just in time to see him open a small doorway cut into an internal stone wall of the church. Now, out of view he must have climbed an internal curved stairway, which gave access to the elevated and ornate cage they could see about ten feet above the ground, inside which two other white chickens were clucking loudly. All they could do was to watch from behind a pillar as the Guardian swiftly and with an ease, borne of many years practice, exchanged the two pairs leaving in the cage 'their' hen and 'their' diamond. It was probably nerves, but Liza began to laugh.

"What the hell's so funny?" said Eric, "We're completely fucked, the diamond is locked inside the bloody chicken inside the equally bloody cage and all you can do is laugh. What the devil are you thinking? Come on we've got to do something quickly."

"I'm sorry," said Liza, "but I was just thinking, I bet all those years ago when the Tsar gave the stone to Prince Varlov, no one thought it'd end up in the egg hole of a white chicken locked in some Spanish church in the back of beyond!"

"We'd better think fast," replied Eric, although he couldn't help half smiling himself, "let's go back to our room and we'll sort out a plan. Something not so funny Liza, remember if we don't get that stone back pretty bloody fast we could end up much further beyond the back of beyond ourselves and it won't be inside a chicken!" In their room they ordered a bottle of Rioja and sat on the terrace drinking as they planned their action. "We'll get into the church just before it closes and grab the hen - those locks on the doors looked pretty old and feeble to me. If I hold the wretched thing can you easily get the diamond out or will I have to wring its neck?" asked Eric.

"No problem," answered Liza, "I'll just need to buy a small

bottle of olive oil and some rubber gloves from that shop over there and it'll almost be like picking cherries if you see what I mean!" As they waited, their bottle of wine gradually emptying, Eric suddenly started,

"Look, look Liza over there. There are the two pilgrims from this morning who were talking about stealing the two bloody chickens for the Abbott of Najera" They both dropped their wine glasses as they watched the two pilgrims enter the church through the cloisters by the west door in the *Calle del Cristo*. Without speaking they immediately left the hotel and entered the cathedral through the same way. There were three groups of tourists going in ahead of them and they were held up slightly as these bought their postcards, but when they got inside they could see the two young men on the right hand side of the nave near the chickens' cage. The normal silence of the church was broken by the sudden crowing of the cockerel - once, twice but the third time appeared to be slightly muffled and hearing footsteps, Eric and Liza hid behind a pillar. They emerged in time to see one of the pilgrims leaving the church through the south door carrying what appeared to be quite a heavy knapsack. They looked at his companion as he crossed the nave, turning to genuflect in front of the Altar crucifix before entering the far side of a confessional tucked against the wall of the north-west chapel. Eric was thinking quickly - his mind in overdrive. "If he makes his confession and tells the priest about the plan to take the birds then they'll probably remove them to a safer place and we'll get no chance to get the stone back," he whispered to Liza, "we've got to stop him somehow."

Approaching the confessional they couldn't help noticing the picture hanging opposite. They read the caption, it was the Apostle St. Bartholomew who, in what was probably the first example of ecclesiastical sick humour, became the patron saint of leather tanners after being flayed alive. This picture gruesomely portrayed his death and the chapel was dedicated to his memory. Looking at the picture Eric realised what he had to do. Stepping quietly up behind the kneeling pilgrim, he picked up the boy's rosary he had left on the seat beside him and whipping it quickly round his neck pulled it tight, held it for some seconds as his victim struggled, and then for certain he pulled it tight once more. They turned to leave just as they heard the footsteps of the priest coming to hear the evening's confessions. Without speaking they quickly crossed the church, but finding the south door now locked went down the steps to the crypt and hid under the tomb of Santo Domingo watched over by the statues of St Peter and St Juane. It was cold down there but their shivering wasn't only caused by the low temperature.

Fr. Fernando didn't much care for Saturday evening confessions. It was always stuffy in the enclosed stall despite the cathedral being the coolest summer spot in Santo Domingo de La Calzada. What's more his obligation to wear a fairly heavy black cassock for the duty was a personal penance he resented having to perform when he was the one meant to be asking others to do theirs! A white cotton cassock would have been a much more suitable garment for the hot summer weather. In any event today, after a siesta interrupted by the noise of the party preparations just outside his window, and perhaps a glass too many of wine with lunch, he was feeling distinctly uncharitable.

There are four separately sited confessionals in the cathedral and the one he'd be using that evening was on the North aisle just past the chapel containing the famed fifteenth century Flemish reredos - the ancient screen that used to shield the altar - and which fortunately benefited from a little shade. The atmosphere was heavy with the lingering smell of incense, candle smoke combining with that of the stale garlic which had accompanied his lunchtime gigot. Fr. Fernando shuffled a bit as he walked, the result of his arthritis, which as a seventy five year old he realised would only get worse. In his younger days he had always been a supremely fit cleric - at one time well known in the cycling world of Northern Spain as the "yellow pedalling priest"- an allusion to his youthful prowess as a frequent wearer of the coveted yellow vest when he was an often successful participant in various cycling events. Approaching the confessional he noticed that one side of it was already occupied by a kneeling figure devout in pray. A pity, he thought, that he would have to start work so quickly as the doze he was looking forward to would have been far more agreeable. The only parts of his would be Penitent which he could see were a pair of hairy tanned brown legs beneath khaki coloured shorts and a pair of stoutish walking boots with deeply indented rubber soles. On the floor beside the kneeler was a brown beret on which Fr. Fernando noticed the rounded half of a scallop shell, pinned to its leading edge. From past experience Fr. Fernando knew that before any confession he would have to listen to the usual tales of woe from a walking pilgrim en route to Santiago de Compostela. He liked pilgrims, if only for the single reason that they were normally un-pretentious. Anyone foolhardy enough to set off as a matter of choice to walk hundreds or thousands of miles following a medieval trail across mountains, rivers and deserts, either must have some sort of moral fibre or be crazy he thought. Furthermore, the only reward at the finish was a spiritual one and a paper certificado - rather like a tourist souvenir - written in Latin stating that they had duly reached Compostela, the resting place of Sancti Jacobi. What he could never understand was why pilgrims almost always asked him if he knew a cure for, or a protection from blisters.

He thought the answer should have been obvious. "Get a good pair of walking boots," was the down to earth advice he always gave them. He never ceased to be surprised by the number of them who seemed quite ill-prepared for their ordeal and had put so little thought into their training.

The elderly priest opened the wooden grill and, entered the claustrophobic little booth gingerly lowering himself onto the bench within. Then carefully laying down beside him his prayer book and the latest copy of "Cycling Monthly" he switched off his mobile phone, before composing himself with silent prayers for pilgrims, coupled with a   heartfelt plea for a speedy completion of his hour long stint. He crossed himself and then began.

"My son," croaked Fr. Fernando, clearing his throat. "I am now here and ready to hear your confession." The silence which followed the priest's invitation was complete. Earlier, the peace of the church had been broken only by the nearby sound of the two chickens crowing and cackling. From the ornate gilded cage on the South aisle of the cathedral the two white birds had been clearly showing signs of considerable agitation with wings flapping and beaks pecking vainly at the metal bars of their prison. Nobody really knew why, but these two famous white domestic fowl, traditionally the current descendants of a long line going back to the eleventh century, only raised their voices at the prospect of feeding by their keeper or a pilgrim. The rest of the time they scratched and poked about in the straw and shavings clucking contentedly the while. "My son" repeated Fr. Fernando, "Can you hear me or are you deafened by the unaccustomed silence of this Holy place?" Earlier Eric had noticed that the chicken crowing had increased to a crescendo before stopping abruptly.

The silence continued from the other side of the grill and more out of curiosity than anything else the arthritic old priest laboriously got up from his seat of duty and stepped out of the confessional to speak in daylight to his waiting penitent - perhaps he wants to meet before he makes his confession he thought. It was however, obvious from his bowed head and folded hands that the pilgrim was deep in prayer. As the kindly priest touched the shoulders of the kneeling figure, in what was meant to be the gentlest of greetings, he was frozen to the spot and would never forget what happened next. Moved by his touch the penitent in prayer became a fallen body lying motionless on the stone floor half out of the confessional. Face upwards, his staring eyes bulged, apparently lifeless, looking as if his death had occurred by strangulation. Around his neck was strung a rosary, the cross still suspended from the ligature of murder. For the first time in his priesthood Fr. Fernando swore in church.

"Bloody hell," he blasphemed - before hurriedly crossing himself for a second time.

CHAPTER THIRTY TWO

SANTO DOMINGO DE LA CALZADA

Wilhelm had been lucky. As he left François near the Chapel of St. Bartholomew to wait for the priest to hear his confession, he had crossed to the other side of the Nave and was looking at the impressive tomb of St. Domingo. Out of the corner of his eye he saw a person he recognised as the guardian of the refuge, enter through the south door carrying a heavy box. With this he went straight to the small door giving the access to the stairway leading to the raised cage, which was such a feature of the Cathedral. The guardian put the box down while he opened the door and Wilhelm could see that it contained the two chickens destined to start their week of duty. Immediately he realised that by a lucky stroke of fortune he was presented with the chance he was after. As the guardian picked up the box and with what seemed some effort began to carry it up the narrow stairs, Wilhelm slipped through the open door and was able to conceal himself behind it in the tiny space between the stone wall and the door. Hardly daring to breath and praying he wouldn't sneeze from all the accumulated dust, he heard the man grunting as he manoeuvred the box with the chickens squawking inside as he made the exchange.

"Ouch, you bloody little devil," he heard, as one or other of the birds, apparently complaining more loudly, had pecked some part of the man. The guardian came carefully back down the darkened steps carrying the same chicken coop with its new inhabitants, and went out through the door pulling it shut behind him. It took Wilhelm's eyes some minutes to acclimatise themselves to the comparative darkness - rather like entering a cinema after the film has started, he thought - but when he was able to pick out the details he was relieved to see that from the inside, the door was opened by a simple push-bar - clearly done so that someone having left their keys outside would not be trapped. Thank God for that, he thought to himself - his method of exit hadn't been something he had thought of a few minutes earlier when he had impetuously entered and hidden

280

behind the door! Taking out of his knapsack the small bottle of ether and the cotton wool he had bought in the pharmacy at Najera he climbed the stairs. The two white birds were busy eating the grain, which had been left them, and seemed to ignore his arrival behind their cage. The back door of this was kept shut merely by a simple piece of wood pushed through two round hooks. He slipped this out and opened the back. Taking a thick wedge of cotton wool he doused it with the ether and grabbing the hen bird, which was the nearer of the two, he held it firmly round its face. It didn't take long for it to take effect and he dropped the limp bird in his haversack. After a similar operation, which took slightly longer, as the Cockerel put up more of an objection than its mate, both birds were safely unconscious in his sack. He went down the stairway, gently pushed the bar and sent up a quiet prayer of gratitude when the door opened silently. He stepped out into the church once more and shutting the door as quietly as he could went towards the exit. He could see across the other side, the back of François kneeling in the confessional and vaguely noticed two other visitors near the chapel as he left the building. Tourists, he thought as he could hear them talking in what seemed some Eastern European language. Leaving the church he turned left and then straight away right as he strode purposefully down the Calle Mayor. The knapsack on his back was heavy with the two sleeping birds, but he wanted to get them to their temporary home as soon as possible. He wasn't sure how long the effect of the ether would last and he certainly didn't want to attract any attention.

Overnight he was going to leave them a little grain he had managed to drug with some old sleeping pills he had brought with him and just hoped that they would have an equal effect on the chicken that they had on him. He didn't want them advertising themselves by crowing away in the morning! It took him just over seven minutes to reach the little chapel at the near end of the bridge over the somnambulant Rio Oja. Without too much difficulty he was able to open the simple lock and get inside. He put down his knapsack and spread the doctored grain on the floor together with some water in the base of a plastic bottle he cut open, and then almost tenderly he placed the two dreaming chickens on the floor beside it. He would be back first thing in the morning he thought, and with a bit of luck they would be quite unnoticed until then. He shut the door and started back to the town centre. Again he was lucky he thought. There was no one by the bridge and he was only watched by three storks idly flying overhead. As he neared the *Plaza del Santo* - still busy with the preparations for the wedding party that night - he was stopped by two policemen, who blocked his path and told him to go round the other way.

"There's been an incident in the church and we're closing off the whole area," he was told in answer to his question, "You can't get through this way. Go round the outside." His face went white - they can't have discovered the chicken's disappearance yet surely, he said to himself not entirely convinced. He was starting to shake, but then he heard the siren which preceded an ambulance leaving at high speed with a police outrider escort. Outside the church he saw an old priest surrounded by a crowd of inquisitive villagers all talking at once. Standing at the back of this throng he was just able to make out the priest saying that he was about to start his confessional when he found a strangled pilgrim kneeling in the booth -

"I did all I could," the priest was saying," but I can't believe he'll survive. The medics said he was just breathing, but he'll need a miracle - nothing less. Who knows what happens in life - who can foretell tomorrow - I go into church to hear confessions and instead have to give the Last Rites to a young man who had all his life ahead of him. Pray for him, my children, pray for him." Several villagers - most in a state of shock - crossed themselves as they stayed in groups of threes and fours, all talking at once. Their shock was certainly shared by Wilhelm. He didn't need to add two and two together to realise that the victim was François.

"What the hell can I do?" he murmured to himself, "it can't be true, it just can't be true." He approached one of the police officers standing near him. "Can you tell me where they have taken the victim, I am certain he was a friend of mine and I must know."

"Come with me, young man," the Policeman said, and seeing how upset Wilhelm was, and then sympathetically led him towards the Church and to another man, who although in plain clothes was clearly a detective. "This man says he's a friend of the victim, Pedro, do you want to talk to him?" He patted the young pilgrim gently on the back in a gesture of kindness.

"First of all from his identity card he had in his pocket his name is François Dubarry. He's French from somewhere called Vaux-en-Beaujolais - I gather its just north of Lyons - is that your friend?" What little hope Wilhelm had had, vanished,

"Yes," he managed to say.

"When did you last see him?"

"I left him in the church just under an hour ago - he wanted to make his confession and I said I'd see him back at the Refuge. We're staying just down the road there. We met a few days ago somewhere before Najera and have walked together since then. How is he, where have they taken him, can I see him - please I must know?"

"Hold on, my lad, hold on," the detective was writing in his note pad, "they are taking him to hospital at Najera - he was just holding on apparently, when they took him, but I don't have too much hope. If we need you again where are you?"

"I'm on pilgrimage," Wilhelm repeated, "and as I said, staying at the Refuge just down there." He refrained from adding didn't you listen the first time?

Wilhelm rushed back to the Refuge and running through the door almost knocked over Maria, who worked part time there. She was the pretty friend of Sophie, the guardian's daughter, whose wedding was to be celebrated that evening. Maria looked worried,

"What's the matter with you?" she asked "you look ghastly." She had noticed and rather fancied Wilhelm when she had booked him in the day before. She was at a loose end at the moment deciding whether to go to teaching college or not and had this temporary job helping out at the refuge. She enjoyed it - meeting a wide and varied set of people was interesting. She had liked the look of Wilhelm as he came in yesterday. Although Wilhelm had been rather dishevelled after a day's walking, it was the twinkle in his eyes that had first attracted her. With some relief to have someone to talk to, Wilhelm told Maria all about what had happened to his friend. The words came tumbling out although he still couldn't really take the whole thing in and was in shock. Maria made him a cup of hot sweet tea and sat him down in a quiet corner. "Now think practically," she said, "do you know where his home is?" She had always been sensible and she was certainly not a character to let any situation panic her.

"No," Wilhelm replied, "all I know is he's called François

Dubarry and lives in somewhere called Vaux-en-Beaujolais. He told me his father has a vineyard."

"OK, - that's enough to go on" she said.

Maria straightaway went to the phone, "I want the telephone number of a family in France, yes, what, Vaux-en-Beaujolais. No I don't know what department, but the family name is Dubarry. That's D-U-B- A- R- R- Y, got it?" Wilhelm listened as Maria waited. After a couple of minutes she took a pencil and scribbled down a number, "Thank you very much, bye." She put the phone down and handed the piece of paper to Wilhelm. "Here's their number - now ring them. You do 0033 for France and leave out the other 0." Feeling sick Wilhelm began to dial. The call went better that he hoped - he had got Monsieur Dubarry straightaway - a lot easier he thought than having to tell François's mother - and briefly explained as well as he could what had happened. It was strange, he thought that the police hadn't appeared to make any attempt to contact the family and he pictured some country Gendarme quietly cycling through the Beaujolais countryside not thinking to use the phone! François's father was shocked, but seemed to be a practical man and soon recovered enough to sort out what he would have to do. He would leave with his wife and another of their sons that night, to come to Najera. Trains were completely impracticable for such a cross country journey, so he would drive, he'd said. They would leave after they had phoned the hospital and he swapped mobile numbers with Wilhelm. He politely thanked Wilhelm for calling and rang off.

"God, I'm pleased that's over," Wilhelm said to Maria, "the father sounds a very capable man, but it must be absolutely dreadful for them, poor devils." Wilhelm broke down - all the emotion, the stress, even his conscience after stealing the chickens at last got the better of him and he wept in Maria's comforting arms.

They were sitting quietly in the square outside the Refuge and he was feeling better.

"Listen," Maria started, "I'm going to Sophie's wedding party this evening - the whole thing's arranged and still going ahead. She's my best friend and I'm sure she'll let me take you with me. You need something to take your mind off things for a while and it'll do you good. You must come. Please."

"I'm not sure I'm up to it after all that's happened - besides I've only got my shabby walking kit to wear. - No, I think I'll have an early night although I don't suppose I'll be able to sleep. Thanks though, for the idea." Maria, as well as being attractive with her dark hair and deep brown eyes, was a very determined girl and being attracted to Wilhelm - she wasn't going to let him escape so easily.

"Don't be silly, you've done all you possibly can for François for the time being. His parents are on the way and we'll ring the hospital later to see whether there's any news. What more could you do by moping around here and it'll be bad for you to be by yourself tonight? That certainly won't help your friend François will it? As for clothes, that's easy, you're about the same size as my brother and he really won't miss a pair of his jeans and a shirt. I'll go and get them now. No question - you are coming." With that Maria went off to her apartment and was soon back with a set of clothes. Seeing her walking towards him with her beautiful eyes fixed just on him, Wilhelm decided not to protest any further.

He took a leisurely shower, changed into the borrowed jeans and shirt and went downstairs to wait for Maria in the cobbled entrance hall. She arrived some fifteen minutes late smilingly making her excuses.

"I'm sorry, I've kept you waiting," she said, "let's go." Finally Wilhelm was pleased that Maria had persuaded him to accompany her to the wedding - she had been right, all the distraction had put the worry he had for his injured friend to the back of his mind as she had said it would. He was going to enjoy this evening he thought as he took her hand and they began the walk towards the obvious sounds of the wedding party. "Sophie is my oldest friend," Maria explained, "we went all through school together and now she's married the boy she always wanted to - they've been going out together for more than five years now."

"What does he do?" "

"His family have a vineyard not far out of town - it's been theirs for generations - and he'll take over from his father soon. Their wine is some of the best in the area now, so we should drink all right tonight," Maria went on, "it's funny Sophie and I always used to argue about which one of us would marry first - well she's won that race now." They reached the square which was already full with a mixture of local townsfolk and other wedding guests from further afield all self-consciously eyeing each other and congregating around the long buffet tables laden with food and drink. In the corner by the clock tower, where an improvised stage had been set up on which stood an upright piano, a five man band was already beginning to perform. Maria got Wilhelm a large glass of red wine from of a barrel on one of the tables and he took a first sip - Maria hadn't exaggerated he thought, it was very good. She took his hand again and pulled him behind her as they approached the newly married couple. "Sophie," Maria said kissing her friend on the cheek, "wasn't it wonderful - the service today - you looked so lovely." Her friend blushed as Maria went on, "this is Wilhelm - the boy I told you about, Wilhelm this is Sophie."

"Congratulations," Wilhelm said, "to you both."

"Oh! I'm sorry," interrupted Maria, "this is Jaime - he's the lucky man," as she kissed the bespectacled man standing just behind Sophie. "We're both very happy that you're here," Jaime looked at Wilhelm, "Maria told us it was your friend in the church this afternoon - a dreadful business, have you got any news? We're both so sorry - anyway, you relax and enjoy yourself - I am sure your friend is in good hands at the hospital." Wilhelm smiled his acknowledgement, but before he could reply others came up to claim the attention of the bride and groom. He walked round the small Plaza with Maria, who introduced him to several friends whose names he immediately forgot - the place was now really quite full - but she was proud to show him off. The evening was well under way. Time went on, the band encouraged people to start dancing and as the wine began its inevitable effect more and more couples joined the floor. Wilhelm held Maria tightly as they danced to some ancient Sinatra number - at least something he recognised among what he assumed to be all the Spanish favourites they had been playing. Maria's head fitted snugly into his shoulder. After some time she imperceptibly led him behind clock tower and round into a sheltered courtyard. As the music played on in the background she lifted her face and with her dark eyes penetrating into his she kissed him passionately and deeply.

"I've wanted to do that ever since I first saw you," she said, "now come in here and no one can see us." They made love urgently as if each was giving to the other the comfort both needed. They fell silent as they re-arranged their clothes after what they had started with a kiss, but realised had ended with something much more significant. With their arms round each other they made their way back to the now less populated dance floor. No one seemed to have noticed their absence until Sophie sidled up behind Maria and whispered something in her ear. "Don't you dare," was a blushing Maria's response as her friend winked at Wilhelm. People were leaving and he vaguely heard the clock tower was striking half past midnight. He suddenly remembered that he had to be up and at the small chapel by the bridge early in the morning and reluctantly mumbled to Maria about having to go back to the Refuge. She held him for just one last dance - a very slow number - and as their bodies swayed, confident together in their new found unison, both were too pre-occupied to notice an older couple walk across the Plaza, help themselves to a couple of glasses and some leftover food and disappear into the Parador. Tonight Wilhelm was feeling very good, as indeed was Maria as she kissed him goodnight and arranged a morning breakfast rendezvous.

CHAPTER THIRTY THREE

NAJERA

François' parents, between dozing and drinking endless quantities of fruit juice, had spoken to a friendly family doctor from their home town in France and he had told them that within a matter of hours now they should probably know whether their son would survive or succumb, but meanwhile he remained as before keeping any dream well hidden .... Gasping and incoherent with joy, but hardly able to understand what they had witnessed, Lucus and Marta ran from the scene of the hanging. Indeed they ran so fast that one of them fell over on the rough stony path leading to the Court building in Santo Domingo. Being so ecstatically happy with their discovery, they had overlooked the fact that it was Sunday and the doors to the Court Offices were closed. Instead they fortuitously knocked on the door of the magistrate's residence adjoining the Court.

"Who are you and what do you want - making such a dreadful din on the Lord's Day?" demanded the unfriendly crone, who pulled open the lynch-gate.

"We must see the Magistrate" screamed the pair in unison. "Our beloved son is alive and well, despite being tied to the gibbet where the hangman left him over five weeks ago."

Raimondo,   was going through his usual ludicrous preening display for   Portrella's benefit. He adjusted his hat, and flicked his lace handkerchief at an imaginary speck of dust, in the conceited but vain attempt at making a favourable impression on the young girl. As always she made it obvious that she didn't welcome his attentions and treated him with copious scorn. Had she known at that very moment Ebbo, the subject of her thieving accusation, was close to safety, she might have been less confident about putting such an important town official in his place. Instead, she laughed aloud at the puffed up fellow and even went as dangerously far as to hint that the tightness of his breeches did nothing complimentary for his manhood.

"Be on your way Sir, and be sure your constables catch any more villains like the one who stole my pewter jug." were her final words shouted after him as he headed home for Sunday lunch. The magistrate's lodgings were comfortable thanks to the energy of the peacock like character who lived there. Expensive draperies imported from far off countries and wood carving that bore more resemblance to Moorish tradition than Christian elaboration furnished the few rooms. These rooms surrounded an open courtyard for which they acted as a shelter from the wind. In the middle were its principal features, a well and a cooking spit. Still following Moorish custom a pit had been dug beneath the spit into which green branches, when available, were laid on kindling. Since dawn two massive logs were glowing lower down and the resulting smoke was giving off a pungent, almost choking, aroma. Raimondo was not a mean man, so long as any acts of generosity helped his uncontrolled need of showing off. This particular day he would be entertaining other dignitaries of the town and it was only right he thought that they should realise the honour they had been granted in receiving an invitation to share in the splendours of his Sunday table. Whether by design or by deformity at birth his chest extended unnaturally forward, so that when he boasted or feigned self deprecation, his buttons almost burst with pressure from underneath. Clucking to himself with self importance he gently prodded the roasting meats and fowl that were being turned slowly over the fire by the village lad employed occasionally for that and other similar menial tasks. Suddenly, his self satisfied peace was disturbed by shrieks and bellows coming from the direction of the lynch gate. In a moment he was confronted by two emotionally hysterical pilgrims, who he afterwards recognised as the parents of the boy he had condemned to death a few weeks earlier.

"Ebbo, our son, who you wrongfully sent to his death on the scaffold, is alive and well and we demand that you come immediately to cut him down." implored the near demented couple.

"Are you crazy or are you trying to make a fool of me?" retorted the magistrate, angry at being disturbed in his home by these less than fragrant pilgrims.

"No Sire, we are completely truthful in our claim and we insist that you come and cut him down." Rather than call the constables to remove forcibly this disturbance to his Sunday lunch, Raimondo, utterly incredulous of what Lucus and Marta had told him, thought to deride them straight away for their stupidity and at the same time get rid of them quietly least they proved an embarrassment in front of his expected guests. With an explosive roar Raimondo sneered,

"Have a good look at those chickens and those portions of lamb roasting on the spit? Well, let me tell you, you simple travelling peasants, that if your son Ebbo is alive as you claim then those chickens are just as fit and well and in a moment they will re-grow their feathers and fly off."

CHAPTER THIRTY FOUR

SANTO DOMINGO DE LA CALZADA

When they heard the old priest shuffling towards the confessional they had quickly crouched down, hardly daring to breathe, behind the tomb of Santo Domingo with the stony eyes of St. Peter watching them. There was a complete silence and then they heard the priest open the swing door of the confessional and move to the side where they had left the penitent kneeling. They heard his shout as he discovered what they assumed was the dead body. He seemed to be bending over it and making some effort to resuscitate the man and then they heard him calling the emergency services, literally shouting into his mobile phone. Keeping down as low as possible behind the tomb they looked at each other.

"The police and ambulance and all the rest will be here very quickly - I saw where their depot was just the other side of the school behind and then all hell will break loose," whispered Liza, "they'll make a thorough search and they'll catch us. We've had it unless we do something fast."

Eric's eyes did the answering as he looked first at Liza and then around to see what hope of hiding they had. He was going through his old procedure - first calculate the situation, then decide on an action and do it. He had noticed them very briefly earlier but now luckily remembered the two bench seats just above them - perhaps there was something there he thought. The sirens preceded the arrival of the ambulance and it was far too late for them to move. They could only remain in their cramp making crouched positions while they waited anxiously. As the medics busied themselves round the young pilgrim prone on the ground, their talk - in very excitable Basque - was completely lost on Eric and Liza.

At last they more sensed than actually saw the body of the pilgrim, wrapped in a protective gold sheeting, being placed on a stretcher and to their temporary relief, and surprise, carried out escorted for the moment by everyone - including the priest. As they all left the nave, Eric grabbed Liza and quickly helped her to climb over the railings into the small side chapel set aside for private prayer. There he thought his own prayers had been answered as the two side benches he had remembered did have hinged seats with enough room for a person to lie comfortably flat inside. They each got into one and waited. Sure enough they could both hear a noise which they assumed to be the police start making a search. This time they were speaking in Spanish and Eric was able to understand a little of what was being almost shouted.

"There's no one in the crypt," the first voice said, "how about the side chapel - shall I get the key and look there?"

"No, don't bother that's locked from the other side and no one could have got in there - no, I'm afraid whoever it was must have left before Father Fernando came in or he'd have seen them. There's no one in the Church. Come on we'd better start a search around the town before they can get any further. Damn there goes my free Saturday evening."

Liza held her breathe in the stuffy space - her heart was thumping and she badly wanted to sneeze from the dust. After what seemed an eternity she smiled as Eric lifted the seat and helped her out of the temporary coffin.

"We got away with that," he said, "but they've locked the church so we're stuck here at least until after midnight - we can't break out with that party going on. We'll go down to the crypt again and wait there until its quieter outside and then get the diamond back and leave for Lisbon straightaway."

They were getting bored and cold. Now it was dark their only light was from the shadow coming through the windows higher up and not much penetrated its way down to the crypt. They could hear the clock tower opposite chime the quarter hours, and they could also hear the music from the wedding party, which appeared to be going at full strength in the square.

"At least we wouldn't be getting much more sleep even if we were in our room over the way," said Liza, "they all seem to be having rather a good time."

"That was eleven thirty it sounded just now - I reckon another hour or so and we'd be safe to get out. We'll go straight to the garage and pick up the car - the owner said he would leave the keys hidden above the front wheel, as they don't open on Sundays. I paid him in advance. I hope the bugger has done it OK or we'll give him a little visit another time!"

"What about our stuff at the hotel," Liza asked, "we'd better just pick that up if we can and pay them to avoid any suspicion. We can always say we were dancing all night at the wedding - God, I'm cold!" She huddled on the flat top of the tomb and Eric looked at her just as a ray of light crossed her features. She was attractive in that Slavic, leggy slightly mysterious way which, seemed to be the trademark of so many young Russian girls since the fall of the iron curtain. Their relationship - starting in their days as KGB operatives, when her job was to compromise visiting western business men in Moscow and he was there to take the photographs and do the blackmailing afterwards - had been purely professional to begin with. However, it hadn't been so very long before Eric got rid of his wife of twelve years - she had been rather drab - and they had become lovers. The first time they had made love was in the shadows of St. Basil's Cathedral in Red Square where the risk of being caught had made the actual act far more exciting and memorable for them both. Indeed, Liza particularly seemed to be really turned on by danger, and Eric used to joke that there was only one way to release her nervous tension. He was always a happy man to help her do it. As he watched her profile in the dullness of the crypt she unconsciously stretched her legs and slightly writhed against the rough stone top. Eric felt a familiar desire growing from the base of his stomach. Despite their present circumstances, with the need to recover the diamond, to get out of the church, to find the car and to get to Lisbon before being caught - this was something even he with years of KGB training behind him just couldn't control. Moving towards Liza he held her face firmly in his hands and kissed her - deeply and strongly as his tongue explored her moist open welcoming mouth. She kissed him back with at least equal passion, her tongue doing its own exploration. They remained like this for what seemed ages, both holding each other as tightly as if their lives depended on them not letting go, both gasping for breathe as their tongues sought even greater depths under the intensity of their embrace.

He brought his body alongside hers and his hands left her neck and began their familiar welcome exploration downwards. "I'll keep you warm my darling," Eric's voice was hoarse with passion and lust and his erection beginning to hurt within the tight restriction of his trousers. He found the buttons of her cotton shirt and almost tore them off in his haste - the shirt fell to the floor just at the feet of St. Peter and, as he released her breasts, her bra fell next to St. Juane on the other side. His kiss left her mouth and moved to her right breast where her firm nipple was raised willingly ready for its treatment. He sucked it hard - something she always loved. Liza was now beginning to moan and fearful of someone hearing he had to put his hand over her mouth to quieten her. During this time Liza had not been idle - she had, with a skill learnt at one of the best spy schools in the old Russia, taken off his shirt and undoing the front of his slacks was skilfully massaging her lover to new heights of his trembling manhood. Eric slid Liza's trousers off passed her ankle with the string slip she was wearing quickly following. Now with nothing between her naked bottom and the cold rough stone of Santo Domingo's tomb she felt strangely sensuous and pleaded with Eric to enter her. Despite being more than ready, Eric hesitated and turned his body to kiss Liza between her legs - his head was trapped by her thighs crossed strongly round his neck as she reciprocated in kind - her gently biting teeth dangerously increasing his excitement. The music from outside in the square was building up to a crescendo of noise and hid their groans as they both turned back together. At the same moment as Eric finally entered Liza.   Using arts learnt at that same spy school, he brought them simultaneously each to a shattering climax. Outside they heard the clock strike half-past midnight - time to leave Santo Domingo to his peaceful sleep, take the chicken and go, they felt ready to face anything.

Both savouring, despite their austere surroundings, that warm afterglow which follows satisfactory love making, they dressed quickly and silently in the darkened crypt. The celebrations continued on the other side of the wall and the music now seemed to match their mood in its sensuous slowness. They could imagine the young couples, just the other side of the wall, wrapped round each other and moving together to its suggestive rhythm. Spain had moved fast after the death of Franco and the young were now the same as anywhere else in Europe - gone forever was the old age of strict morality and chaperones Eric thought, not dissimilar to the Soviet Union becoming the far more licentious Russia after the fall of the Iron Curtain.

"Ready?" asked Eric, "make sure you don't leave anything -

let's go." With that he held Liza's hand as they climbed the steps out of the crypt reaching ground level just opposite the raised chicken cage. With a facility gained by much past practise Eric easily broke the small lock in the doorway of the stairway leading to the cage with the small screw driver he took from his knapsack and climbed up. Liza watching from below suddenly heard Eric swear and then almost fall out of the door. Despite the gloom she could see the panic and horror written in his expression. "They've gone, the bloody chickens have gone, and that first fucking pilgrim boy must have taken them! What the hell do we do? If we loose that stone we're dead."

"Stay calm - we've got to find him," Liza whispered back although now frightened herself. "Let's get out of here and watch the refuge - that's where he was staying."

"Don't be stupid, he won't have taken the chicken there - that's where they belong, he'll have hidden them somewhere else." Eric snapped back, "Oh God!"

"Of course he'll have hidden them, but if we get him in the morning we'll be able to get their whereabouts from him - he'll not take too much persuasion. We'll nab him as he gets out of the Refuge - it'll be just like old times in the Lubyanka - now come on and get us out of here. It's not like you to panic."

Working their way round the north side of the church they found a small door in the exterior wall of the cloisters and again Eric's well used screwdriver did its magic. They were in the street and walking hand in hand as if they were just ordinary lovers on the way home after a Saturday evening out. Wandering through the square where the wedding party was starting to wind down, they picked two glasses of wine left on the buffet table plus a couple of tapas each and made their way up to their bedroom. They didn't see in the shadows Wilhelm and Maria, tightly entwined, enjoying a last smooch before the music stopped. Safely back in the hotel they set the alarm for five thirty and exhausted, both fell asleep before either spoke again.

CHAPTER THIRTY FIVE

SANTO DOMINGO DE LA CALZADA

The first ring of the alarm and Eric was immediately out of bed - Liza took a little longer to realise where she was, but then soon followed him. They took a lightning shower, dressed and left the hotel walking past the front of the Cathedral and through the untidy evidence of the wedding party, towards the Refuge where they assumed their quarry was still asleep. Eric was furious, largely because he knew he had only himself to blame. More delays meant more awkward explanations, more questions to be answered and, of course, more dangers for the two of them. After more than ten years as a senior KGB operative he thought he should have reacted better to apparently being chased the day before. He didn't need any imagination to tell him what could lie in store for them should they fail to complete their contract to deliver the diamond safely to their employer in Lisbon. Eric blamed himself for behaving like an amateur and for his panic the day before, which had led to all this trouble. For him to have confused two oddball pilgrims running down the road for some form of authority chasing them had been quite ridiculous. After all his training and experience that had taught him never to panic it was almost unforgivable he told Liza.

"I'm really out of touch," he said again and again more or less to himself, "a beginner's mistake and I have to make it - God knows why"

They reached the door of the Refuge and Liza's watch told her that it was just twenty minutes to six. Everything was still firmly shut and they sat on a bench in the little square off to the right.

"We can't have missed him," she whispered, shivering slightly in the early morning freshness, "all we can do now is wait. Don't blame yourself - we'll sort it all out now."

"You leave everything to me and just carry out anything I tell you to do," Eric spoke sharply. He was operational now and Liza simply his assistant. As they sat there in silence she couldn't help thinking how far away his comparative tenderness of last night felt.

She looked sideways at him and saw the old expression of emotionless determination, which had been so familiar to her in the past. It was just as if they were back in Moscow waiting to drag some unfortunate in for questioning, torture or worse in the days before perestroika.

The nearby clock tower struck six o'clock and almost simultaneously the large impressive old doors of the Refuge were swung open by the same man who had taken the chickens down to the Church the evening before. Three pilgrims left almost at once obviously wanting to be well on their way before the sun had any heat in it and to get to the next refuge in good enough time to be sure of getting in - two of them were the ones that had run down the road towards them yesterday and Eric quietly cursed them under his breath. Liza tried to talk to him, but he shut her up - just like the old days when they were on a job she thought. He wanted no distraction - his mind was totally professional and there was no side-tracking him when he was working. Eric suddenly broke the silence,
"I want you to be waiting nearer the door and when our man comes out you are to approach him with some query or other. Then walk with him in whatever direction he goes - at the same time try and look at whatever he is carrying but I am sure he won't have the chickens with him, he couldn't have taken them into the refuge so they must be hidden not very far away. Just keep him distracted and I'll do the rest - understand?" Liza nodded and moved nearer the door pretending to take an interest in the adjacent notice board - the clock struck the half hour, they waited and seven o'clock sounded. "Christ, are we going to have to be here all morning," Eric thought, "please God he didn't leave last night."
His past training had taught him to have self-control at all times and he put the desperation he was beginning to feel straight out of his mind although he was still kicking himself for forgetting that lesson the day before. Then suddenly, almost like a magician appearing on stage, Wilhelm came out of the Refuge and turned towards the Church.
"Good morning," Liza said approaching him from behind, "do you know where I could get some bread on a Sunday morning here?"
"No, I'm on the pilgrimage and only arrived yesterday, sorry."

Wilhelm smiled and continued walking. Liza seemed naturally to fall in step behind him. As they passed a closed bar and just before they would have entered the *Plaza del Santo*, Eric came up behind the pilgrim. He left Wilhelm no doubt that it was a very sharp knife that was digging into his left side rib-cage just below his heart.

"If you let out one single cry you're dead, just carry on walking and no heroics - dead heroes may get medals, but they don't live to wear them." He whispered into the pilgrim's ear as his other hand firmly held his collar.

It had all happened so quickly. In a state of shock Wilhelm just walked zombie-like between Liza holding one arm and Eric the other side keeping the knife in dangerous evidence. They guided him straight past the south front of the church and continuing down the *Calle Mayor*. With a lack of logic, perhaps induced by his fear and shock, all Wilhelm could think was that he would be late for his planned breakfast with Maria! "Get in here" Eric almost barked the order, "its the old abattoir - you know what happens in abattoirs? That's why I've got this knife my friend." Eric was enjoying himself. They pushed him into the bleak bare room and sat him on the only furniture there, an old wooden chair. Quickly and efficiently Liza taped his mouth and Eric tied him to the chair with the thick cord he had produced from the small haversack he was carrying. They emptied the bag Wilhelm had been carrying on his shoulder, but it only contained his few bits of clothing, his papers, mobile phone but certainly no sign of any chicken let alone a priceless diamond. "Listen and listen carefully," Eric began, "I'm going to ask you some questions, if you answer them to my satisfaction then you'll be OK - if not, or if you try anything clever, like shouting or something, then things will be different. Remember your friend in the church - I don't think his prayers helped him very much" Wilhelm struggled with the cord, but quickly realised that it had been tied too well for any hope that he could work it loose. He was scared, as was evident from a damp patch beginning to show on the front of his shorts, but at the same time his natural German obstinacy produced a determination in him to resist. This couple had clearly been the ones who had attacked François, he thought, and now was his chance to trap them. "What the hell do they want?" he asked himself but couldn't think, "why me? - I've got nothing they could possibly want."

"Now," began Eric, "I shall ask you what we want to know and you will signify by nodding if you will tell us. Here is a sheet of paper and a pen so you write the information on that. If I need you to speak my partner will remove the tape from your mouth. Don't try to shout because, believe me, I am very quick with a knife and you'll find it difficult to speak again without a tongue. Is that understood?" Terrified, but with his determination and natural obstinacy increasing, Wilhelm didn't move.

"I asked whether that was understood?" Eric repeated. Again Wilhelm didn't move. He did after Liza reached from behind and, despite that damp patch, twisted his genitals through 360 degrees both ways - the metal cooking tongs she used to do this saved her hands from getting dirty. Wilhelm's eyes rolled with pain and he felt instantly sick. "Now, my friend, again is that understood?" Almost blinded by the tears rising in his eyes this time Wilhelm nodded. "That's better," said Eric, "it's quite simple what we want to know - yesterday you took the two chickens from the church, where are they?" Whether it really did come from his German background or just his general approach, Wilhelm had always dug his heels in against any form of authority and even at school he had been noted for fighting against anyone who tried to control him. After the initial shock, even after the sickening pain still throbbing in his groin, Wilhelm thought to hell with these people. He took the pen and wrote "Fuck off!" He heard the swish before he felt the pain. With a flash of the knife Eric had cut open the whole front of his clothes from top to bottom leaving nasty open slashes on his chest, left thigh and calf. After many years of disuse blood started to drip once more onto the floor of the old abattoir. The tape stopped him shrieking, but the look of terror in his eyes told Eric all he needed to know. Quietly, as if he was merely asking him whether he took sugar in his tea, Eric repeated, "Please tell us where you have hidden those chickens." Wilhelm remained in shocked silence, he closed his eyes and thought of Maria from the night before and how she would be waiting with breakfast for him. He soon stopped thinking of anything as Liza's cooking tongs repeated their action. Wilhelm's head rolled back, his body slumped forward - or as far as it could in its restraints - and he seemed to be fighting for breath.

"Be careful," whispered Liza to Eric, "he's no good to us dead."

"I know, give me that horsewhip. We'll see if that can jog his memory" They turned Wilhelm round and even with the tape covering his mouth the shriek as the first cut of the whip bit into his back was shattering. Eric continued the scourging with the same dedication for which he had always been noted - the volume of Wilhelm's reaction increased. Eric sensed that the fight was going out of his victim and was sorry he had none of the electrical shock equipment his old Soviet bosses had provided. Swift, clean and excruciatingly painful, particularly on wet flesh, that had been the surest way of getting difficult confessions and he had been one of the experts in its use. He had enjoyed that.

Both Eric and Liza were too busy watching their victim to notice Maria looking horrifyingly through the small fanlight, which although being glazed with frosted glass had a small corner missing. Earlier she had waited with breakfast all ready on the table for Wilhelm's promised arrival - he had said about seven fifteen. The evening before was one she knew she would remember for a very long time. First the desperate rush to the hospital at Najera with Wilhelm to see François - she had been particularly touched by how much Wilhelm had been affected by his friend's probably fatal accident and how he had gone out of his way to find and to phone his family in Lyons. At least François's parents were on their way, but it seemed as if there was little or no chance of him making even a partial recovery. The full investigation could wait - she had been determined that Wilhelm should have a comforting and enjoyable evening to help him relax from the ordeal. She had arranged for him to come to her friend's wedding party with her - perhaps it was the atmosphere of this or the amorous qualities of the Rioja or even just their personal chemistry, but they had become lovers before the end of the evening. She was therefore more than a little upset when Wilhelm - who had seemed as genuine as he was passionate the night before - had failed to arrive as he had promised to do in time for breakfast this morning. After waiting thirty minutes she had phoned her friend, who was on duty at the refuge, and he told her that Wilhelm had left at about seven o'clock, but was due back sometime for the rest of his things. Worried that he might have misunderstood where they were to meet Maria went out looking for him. After going round the town looking at the likely bars and cafés she was rather despondently walking down the *Calle Mayor* towards the Cathedral on her way back to her apartment. As she passed the old abattoir, a place that always upset her when she thought of the animal suffering that had gone on there, she heard a sort of shriek that sounded really neither human nor mechanical. "What the hell was that?" she asked herself. She resisted the impulse to run back to her rooms. Again she heard it and not really believing her courage she stepped gingerly up to the little fanlight through which the noise seemed to come. One quick look was enough to tell her all she needed to know. She had to get out and get help immediately. Running round the corner into the Plaza del Santo she bumped into two friends of her father just coming out of the corner bar.

"Quick, quick - my friend's being murdered in the abattoir, for God's sake come now," she broke down in the arms of the first man. Hearing the shouting two more came out of the bar and the four of them followed the distraught girl round the corner. Liza heard it first and Eric almost immediately after - the four men running and shouting just gave them enough warning to escape through the back of the abattoir leaving Wilhelm tied in the chair. Maria's dress was soon covered in blood as she held his head to her bosom. Wilhelm just managed to whisper,

"I told them nothing," before he fainted.

Maria had managed to clean up Wilhelm a little before the police arrived soon after they had been called by one of his rescuers. He was able to give them a good description of his attackers, but professed complete ignorance when he was asked what sort of information they had been seeking, neither could he offer them any motive he could think of for their attack. The Inspector's instinct told him that the German pilgrim was holding something back for some unknown reason. He had clearly suffered a most horrible experience, but appeared not to know why or even what information his captors had been after.

"Can't you think of any reason why these two people should have singled you out like this? Any reason at all even if you think it absolutely irrelevant? They were clearly waiting for you specifically. They must have asked you some questions. Think again, this is very important and time is not on our side. These two could be the same people who attacked your friend in the church yesterday - indeed they almost certainly are. They're clearly very dangerous people and we have to catch them." The policeman hesitated as Maria gave Wilhelm some warmed brandy trying to calm his nerves, he was still extremely shaken. The inspector spoke calmly, almost father like,

"Listen, you say you don't know what their motives are, but it appears they've attacked at least the two of you - perhaps they have a general grudge against all pilgrims, it's a possibility, and there are certainly plenty in this area who could be very vulnerable targets. They have to be caught, and caught soon before they strike again," he added as the German sipped his drink. There was silence for some seconds and then Wilhelm spoke.

"Yes I understand all that, I'm afraid I have been very stupid and I have to confess to doing something I now regret very much."

The Inspector watched him closely, He thought of his own son, not far off Wilhelm's age and felt sorry for him. Quietly he said,

"Tell me everything, Wilhelm, I'm sure whatever you did, it didn't deserve this sort of beating. Don't worry, I have a son of my own, I'm quite used to hearing anything."

Wilhelm held Maria's hand as he told of the conversation during the dinner some days before at Najera. How he had been silly and taken the Bishop seriously, perhaps after too much wine, and how he had childishly gone on to steal the chickens from the church.

"It was where I had hidden these birds that those two wanted to know, that was the only thing they asked, nothing else. Well, once I had taken the birds out of the church I hid them in that little chapel on this end of the bridge. As far as I'm aware they must still be there, although I can't think why these two should be so interested in this. I don't know where they're from but they both seemed to speak with some Eastern European accent. Thinking about it, although I can't prove it, they were probably the same two who attacked François and me on the way here...."

"Tell me about that," butted in the Inspector, "that could be very important."

Wilhelm recalled to the policeman how they had stopped to eat their picnic lunch, roughly half way from Najera, when two people had stopped their car on the nearby road and thrown the stones.

"I think they were driving a Mercedes, I caught just a glimpse as they drove away, I think it had an Italian number, but really I don't know," he added.

"A Mercedes, Italian plates - you're sure?"

"Not certain, no but I think so." At once the inspector gave some quick instructions to his assistant who immediately left the room - the alert, broadcast earlier throughout the whole region had specifically mentioned a couple travelling in an Italian registered Mercedes. Any sighting of this car was to be reported at once to the region's incident centre set up in Bilbao. The Inspector received his instructions very quickly. They were to wait for the arrival of two senior officers from Bilbao who would be coming by helicopter accompanied by two visiting investigation officers from Switzerland. In the meantime no one was to be allowed anywhere near neither the little Chapel nor that part of the bridge. Road blocks were to be set up on all the exits to Santo Domingo. The policeman looked kindly at Wilhelm and smiled,

"Don't worry about taking the chickens, son, you've been punished enough for that already. It seems there's a much bigger egg involved in all this than any you had in mind."

Later, after the arrival of the officers from Bilbao everyone was ready for action. Despite Maria's objections, Wilhelm had agreed to help in the plan proposed by the Swiss officers. The Mercedes had been found quickly, but purposely left untouched by the police, and from this they knew that the probability was that the two attackers were still hiding in the area. Wilhelm was to make his own way down to the chapel and recover the chickens - he'd be closely shadowed, but the hope was that his two assailants might be watching as well and would follow him.

"We'll do a house-to-house search if necessary later," the inspector explained, "but this way we might just flush out our quarry quicker."

"Well it was my stupidity taking those wretched birds that's led to all this, and to poor old François's death. I'm responsible. I'll do anything to help, don't worry, Maria, I'll be all right - please understand, I've got to do this." He explained to his worried girl friend.

Hidden behind a builder's rubbish skip, Eric and Liza saw Wilhelm pass the church on his own and turn towards the bridge. A few minutes earlier Eric had finished his mobile phone call to Stanislas and was briefing Liza.

"Do you understand all that? Stanislas has fixed it with his chap in Switzerland, so we don't have to doubt him. He says it will all only take something under six months. You understand the part you have to play?" Liza nodded, but held Eric's hand very tightly. "OK, here he is - come on and good luck," Eric kissed her as he withdrew his hand. They let him get some thirty metres ahead before leaving their hiding place and following. They didn't look back. but they realised they had an equal thirty metre lead over six other men, two of whom were leading very alert looking German shepherd dogs straining at their muzzles. As Wilhelm reached the small chapel and opened the door Eric caught up with him - in the struggle the now very much awake and extremely excited chickens fled down to the dried up river bed squawking and flapping their wings. Liza made a dash and tried to catch them, but was soon trapped by one of the dogs before its handler produced a pair of handcuffs. As she was led back up to the bridge she looked back to the chickens and saw the hen appear to lay an egg on the river bed - in its excitement it has produced the desired result despite her not being able to reach it, she thought. Eric held Wilhelm strongly in front of him with one arm whilst the other held a small gun to his throat.

"Release the girl or I shoot him" he shouted at the surrounding cordon of police, "I'll count up to ten!" Liza shrieked,

"Aleksei 'No'" as he began counting

"Adin.......Dva......Tri......" lapsing into his native Russian tongue. For perhaps only three minutes or less everything seemed to be a mad turmoil of excited activity. The marksmen lowered their arms, but unluckily Eric didn't see the dog leap from behind the chapel until it was too late. He felt a pain as its teeth sank into his arm and there was a crack as his gun fired harmlessly into the air disturbing the audience of storks circling overhead. Afterwards, the guardian from the refuge, the local police had asked him to be there, easily captured the two chickens and expertly put them into the carrying cage he had brought for the purpose and then placed it on his trolley.

Eric, the pain beginning to throb in his arm, stood   beside Liza as, handcuffed, they both looked down from the bridge. She whispered something to him and without anyone noticing pointed down to the river bed. In the cracks of the dried mud Eric saw the glint as the strong sunlight reflected off an unmistakeable stone lying caught inside the decaying body of a dead fish. They watched in silence with a mixture of relief, admiration and disbelief as one of the storks swooped down to the river bed, leaving its companions still wheeling above the whole dramatic scene. When it rose up again, in the direction of its nest perched dangerously high on the roof of the church, the reflection had disappeared together with the body of the dead fish. Nothing remained among the caked mud of the river bed. As the police were checking the inside of the chapel he attached Eric and Liza to the nearby railings with the handcuffs. While they were waiting there Eric was able with a little difficulty to send one last short message from his mobile before dropping it over the bridge into a pool of the river.

CHAPTER THIRTY SIX

NAJERA

The shafts of bright sunlight penetrating through the cracks of the blinds almost hurt the tired eyes of François' parents as they maintained their ceaseless vigil, now well into its fourth day. Although the clinic had made a room available for them near their son they hadn't really used it and lack of proper sleep only increased their sense of unreality, hopelessness and despair. The young man remained lying death-like on the bed, with only the occasional movement of a muscle - the doctor said it was probably only an involuntary reaction - and the bleeps from the various monitors showing there was still some minute sign of life. Outwardly François appeared peaceful, but his parents knew from what the medical staff told them he was more dead than alive and they feared the worst could happen at any time. One of the nurses came in and gently sponged his face before straightening the sheet and putting his arms outside the covers down by his side. His father left the room - he wanted to telephone his other children at home - but his mother remained, holding his hand tightly in hers, talking to him and willing him to show some sign that he knew she was there for him. Eventually she must have dozed off into a light sleep for a while, but was roused suddenly by a change in sound from one of the monitors.

The oscillations showed his dream continued. The doctors said his mind appeared to have been constantly dreaming since his admittance. They said that this was not unusual in cases of severe shock when the patient remained in a long coma. The parents watched anxiously as the occasional irregular stirs made by their son seemed to correspond with the larger variations of the wavy yellow lines monitoring his brain activity........... François looking around - saw that a white mist had started rapidly to fill the courtyard, rising like steam from the well - it was warm, it was damp, and somehow its purity was comforting.

Even in the heat of a summer day it steamed as it overflowed the rim. Spreading quickly around the courtyard it rose to cover the humans, the spit and its roasting meats. In minutes everything was enveloped in mist. It carried with it a luminescence that painlessly semi blinded the five witnesses to the extraordinary happening. Apart from the creaking of the turning spit a total silence embraced the courtyard as from nowhere the air became filled with feathers. François thought he was going to sneeze, but couldn't move, White feathers of differing sizes gently floating down to land on the heads and shoulders of all the company before settling as a soft white carpet underfoot. With the mist subsiding, the strangest of all sights was revealed. There, strutting slowly and proudly was a beautiful pair of chickens - a pure white cock and a matching hen.

"This is another miracle we have seen" exclaimed Lucus and Marta in unison, falling to their knees.

Stunned, but still aware of his dignity, Raimondo acknowledged that they had just witnessed something quite outside even his comprehension. He was forced to accept Ebbo's parents claim that their son was alive. The chickens willingly allowed themselves to be gathered up by Lucus, and the townsfolk saw the unusual spectacle of two loudly clucking and crowing birds being held aloft and carried reverently across the market square into the West door of the cathedral. All the while a small crowd was gathering as they were intrigued by the procession lead by the Magistrate praising the Lord this day for his great kindness. The Bishop himself became involved as he learned of the amazing happening. When asked for an explanation by Raimondo he could only exhort them to pray. He suggested that they and as many others as wished, should make haste to the gibbet for the purpose of cutting down the poor young man, who, he said had clearly been blessed and saved by the intervention of the good Saint Iago. Shortly, the Magistrate and the Bishop saw for themselves as they approached the scaffold, that indeed Ebbo was alive and well. Within minutes he was brought down and was seemingly completely unscathed from his ordeal. The chickens were left in the care of a servant of the cathedral and many people picked up white feathers from the ground and stuck them in their hats. The Bishop blessed the birds with holy water from the font and ordained that they should from henceforth be kept within the church as a living reminder of the wonderful miracle of Saint Iago. The news of this miraculous event spread rapidly from town to town. Within twenty four hours piety and curiosity had brought many visitors to Santo Domingo de la Calzada hoping for a glimpse of the living Ebbo and of the chickens.

The machinery of justice sought a culprit for Ebbo's suffering and the finger of guilt pointed at Portrella herself and her parents. After all it was she who had demanded Raimondo to capture the villain, alleging that he had stolen the pewter jug and now there was unchallengeable proof that Ebbo had been wrongly condemned. In his courtroom later in the week the magistrate had no difficulty in extracting from the girl an admission that it was she who had so wickedly planted the jug in Ebbo's knapsack. Swiftly, the law enforcer concluded that Portrella with the connivance of her father

José were guilty and should be hanged forthwith from the very same gibbet from which poor Ebbo had been dangled. By the end of the week José had been hanged, cut down and buried, but Portrella pleaded that her father, whose loss she certainly did not regret, had forced her to commit the crime and had compelled her to make a false admission of guilt. This was just the opportunity Raimondo had been waiting for as he had slightly different and more personal plans in mind for the young girl. It was also very clear that she had never had much love for her father, who, she revealed with sobs of grief, had already had indecent knowledge of her by force. He now told himself that this was the very chance he had been waiting for when he too could satisfy the craving he had held so long for the girl. He could explore the coquettish girl in a manner pleasing to him and his devious habits. She would now be his to possess and do with as he wished and he planned to waste no time in doing it. He reminded her,

"Do you remember Portrella that not so long ago I said to you that an evening spent with me at the court house would be one you would never forget?" In his dream François helplessly saw the girl as she was led crying to the magistrate's house and somehow he couldn't move to save her however hard he tried.

His distraught mother saw there was just a small drop of moisture on François's upper lip just below his nose and wiped it softly away with her white linen handkerchief - soon after she noticed a single tear drop from his closed left eye fall onto the pillow.

It was all very hazy, the light shimmering through a white mist, and nothing seemed to be in focus, he tried to move his body again. He wanted to scratch his nose, but something was stopping his right hand from moving. Everywhere there seemed to be a moving sheet of white feathers, he shook his head to stop them going up his nose and in his eyes, he felt one gently brush his mouth, and then his eye, and thought he was going to sneeze. Briefly, trying to open his eyes he was conscious of a face staring at him - a face he thought he vaguely recognised, but whose it was he couldn't think. He seemed to be back as a young boy in Beaujolais looking at his vision. Then he heard a voice, his mother's, and more noise as others were rushing at him through the wall of feathers. He tried again to open his eyes and gradually the room, his mother, his father, a grey haired man he didn't know in a white coat and a nurse came into focus. He looked slowly round as he began to take in his surrounding,

"Where is this? Where am I? Where have all the feathers gone?" His parents stood either side of the bed holding his hands.

"Just rest for now, my darling François," implored his mother with emotion, "We'll tell you everything later." Then turning to her husband they both looked at their son, "We've just seen a miracle," they whispered together. Just before his eyes closed his father heard François whisper to himself,

"So there were no feathers - I dreamed the whole thing, but I'm sure I did see and hear those chickens"

CHAPTER THIRTY SEVEN

LISBON

It was now the middle of September and Stanislas had been very busy in the four months since he received that last cryptic message from Eric after his arrest. That evening he had watched the news and seen the report of the dramatic arrest in Northern Spain of two suspected Russian 'criminals' fleeing from Switzerland following the theft of the 'Tsarina's diamond' at the sale in Geneva. The reporter had emphasised that unfortunately the actual diamond - again its historical importance and provenance was explained - had not been recovered and that its whereabouts remained a mystery. Immediately the bulletin had ended Stanislas had rung the London number his brother had given him some time back for his old contact only to have an answering machine give him another number to try in Berne. Dialling this he had managed to speak to the man and gratefully received all the assurance he needed. He had passed on the information which Eric had told him and was instructed not to worry and was assured that 'all would be taken care of.'

Two days later when he was out playing golf his wife answered the phone and was a little surprised to be given a message for Stanislas. She was to tell him that 'the ice had not melted, but was back in the fridge and that spring would be early'. The caller, who did not give his name made her repeat the message twice. Later that evening Stanislas just laughed when Natasha had relayed this exactly, telling her that it was only part of a continuing old joke old joke from one of his erstwhile City colleagues. She still remembered this now, four months later, when Stanislas told her that another business friend had invited them to Geneva for a few days holiday and golf. The summer had indeed seemed very long and been insufferably hot in Lisbon, which easily persuaded her that a few days further north in the fresh mountain air would do them both good. They stayed in their friend's chalet in a charming village several hundred metres above Geneva. On their first morning Natasha was interested to see a large black limousine - locally registered - draw up in front of the heavily geranium decorated chalet. Two men, identically dressed formally in dark suits with white shirts and the same crimson ties, got out. She saw her husband go out to meet them, smiling and shaking hands with both. He talked for a moment before coming back into the chalet where he told his wife he just had to go into Geneva to talk about a possible property deal. These men were from an *agence immobilière*, he explained, and he'd be back towards the end of the afternoon. She was a little annoyed to be left alone but, kissing her, he promised the rest of their stay would be uninterrupted. As he walked back to the car she was surprised to overhear him speaking to one of the men in Russian. Natasha spent the day relaxing with her hostess - someone she had not met before, but who struck her as very friendly - on the terrace of the chalet. Despite her pleasant day she was more than happy when she saw Stanislas arrive back, this time alone, just after tea. He was in buoyant mood and Natasha and his friends pulled his leg saying that his deal must have been very successful and profitable! He confirmed to his wife later that everything had indeed gone very well and now he could just concentrate on her and the golf.

A week after they had returned home to Portugal he settled down with his usual evening whisky to watch the news on the BBC World Channel. Had Natasha been watching him, instead of being in the kitchen preparing dinner, she could have seen that he showed no surprise - merely a satisfied smile - at the third item in the bulletin, reporting two simultaneous and equally daring prison escapes in Geneva. One apparently involved a bogus refuse lorry and the other a micro-light powered glider. It was reported that the two Russian thieves, both described as 'infamous ex KGB operatives', who had recently   been convicted of stealing the 'priceless Tsarina's lost diamond' when it was being auctioned earlier that summer in Geneva had been simultaneously sprung from their prisons. The Swiss authorities hinted darkly that the clearly professionally organised operation had been planned with inside and possibly foreign assistance. One reporter even suggested that the Russian Ambassador was being called in by the Berne Authorities for urgent consultations. This was later strongly denied by both sides. Next day the news contained a follow up report of the discovery of a badly burnt out Mercedes containing the charred remains of two incinerated bodies. Although they were completely unidentifiable, fragments of prison clothing found in the burnt out wreck, the police said, linked them to the two Russians. A further support of this theory was the coincidence that this car had been found in the same lay-by where the diamond thieves had earlier discarded two Geneva registration plates during their drive away from the auction all those months before.

Natasha called from the kitchen, "Dinner'll be about fifteen minutes - anything on the news, darling?"

"No, nothing surprising," Stanislas answered, "nothing unexpected at all!" The report ended by saying that the Swiss police were taking DNA samples found on the burned remains of the prison suits and they expected these to match those of the two Russians. Stanislas turned the television off. He could relax now - all was well and he could look forward to the visit of his brother, who was driving down with his wife to stay for a few days. A little later that evening Anatole telephoned him to say they were staying at the very comfortable parador at Santo Domingo de la Calzada where they had met up with their mutual friends as arranged and expected to arrive from there late next afternoon.

Back in England, Peter Varlov the same evening was preparing a small dinner party to celebrate the good news he had received a few days before. He would always remember the phone call. Jonathan Hamilton-Gray, after saying hello, had gently asked him to sit down before giving him the wonderful news that the auctioneer's insurance claim had been settled for the full estimated value by Lloyd's and that his bank would be receiving some twenty million pounds for his account very soon.

"There's just one point we should clear up though," Hamilton-Gray had added, wanting to benefit from the goodwill engendered by this news, "The action for negligence your solicitors have begun against us and the other parties involved won't be....." Peter Varlov stopped him,

"You have my assurance that all will be withdrawn - nothing will be pursued or left on the record. You have my word for that, Mr. Hamilton-Gray, I'm not at all vindictive - please don't think I behave like Lloyd's seem to do." They both laughed, although the auctioneer could hear from the tone of Varlov's voice that he wasn't completely joking.

"Thank you, Sir, I can't say how much my colleagues and I appreciate the way you have reacted to all this unfortunate business and I am very happy for you at the way things have turned out." Peter Varlov thought that perhaps the auctioneer would be even happier for him had he known that his dinner guest was Suki Bullioni. His smile faded as he remembered he had one more phone call to make before he could relax and wait happily for her to arrive. Sir George Matthews answered after the fourth ring.

"My dear Peter, let me be the first to congratulate you - I've just heard the wonderful news from my assistant." gushed Sir George, "I'm so pleased I, of course I mean the bank, was able to arrange such a good settlement for you. You know even I wasn't sure myself whether I could pull it off with Lloyd's, but I used all the influence I could and fortunately that finally swung the balance your way." Peter bit his tongue as he thought how Anatole had desperately telephoned him three days before pleading with him to do everything he could to stop Matthews from interfering – the underwriters had made it very clear that his increasingly frantic meddling in things he plainly did not understand was dangerously jeopardising the whole settlement.

"I will always remember what you did for me," Peter replied tactfully, "but I'm afraid there is another reason why I am calling you. I had a letter this morning from the Club secretary about your membership application."

"Oh, good, Lady Matthews will be pleased," interrupted Sir George, "she's planning a small cocktail party there for....."

"Well I'm sorry, George, but she won't be able to, I'm afraid there's been a confidential objection to your candidature and its been suggested you withdraw it to save any further embarrassment to any of us - I'm so very sorry."

Stanislas heard the car draw up and went out to greet his brother and sister-in-law. Natasha quickly followed him and together they helped bring their cases into the house. After they had had some tea all together in the kitchen, the two wives went upstairs to chat while they unpacked. Stanislas ushered his younger brother into his study where his offer of an early drink was gratefully accepted.

"It's a long haul down from Santo Domingo - further than I thought, but all went well there," Anatole opened his brief case and handed a small package to his brother.

"Here it is - it was exactly where Igor said, in the corner of the roof of that little chapel by the bridge," Stanislas gave his brother his drink, "yes, I'm told that Father Fernando was very trusting - he's probably still waiting for the full survey and report on the state of the Church roof which our visiting architect promised him ! I don't know who our friend sent, but finally the plan has worked out all right despite the meddlesome stork! The most extraordinary luck was that the Swiss and Spanish police did not suspect how easy it had been for them to arrest our two Russian friends. I'm meeting them next Wednesday by the way when I go to St. Petersburg."

Unknown to Anatole, Wilhelm had also been in Santo Domingo – this time travelling normally and not as a pilgrim. He was sitting outside a bar in the September sunshine enjoying a beer with Maria. They had read the news of the escape in Switzerland in El Païs the day before, but were more bound up with their own news and had the stork still been sitting on its high perch, and had looked down, it would have seen the sun's rays reflecting this time from the smaller diamond on Maria's finger.

"I'm so pleased you have asked François to be your best man, darling," she said as she kissed her fiancé.

It had been a very happy long weekend and Stanislas and Natasha had enjoyed the visit of Anatole and his wife. They both thought the time had gone quickly when they waved their guests goodbye to continue their journey south to friends in the Algarve. After his brother had left, Stanislas packed for his trip to Russia – he had tried to persuade Natasha to go with him, but she had some old friends staying in Lisbon and finally had decided to remain at home.

Stanislas arrived at St. Petersburg at four o'clock local time and was met by Igor, who whisked him straight through all the entry formalities and after a swift drive he was quickly installed in a very comfortable hotel suite not far from the Hermitage museum. At eight that evening Igor fetched him from his room and together they went to the private dining room where he was introduced to the ten other people already present – including the City's mayor and a very glamorous looking Liza with Eric standing beside her. At the end of the dinner Stanislas got up and formally thanked his host for his welcome, he mentioned that despite some slight hiccups his whole scheme had finally gone well, but in particular he had to thank Igor Yarkov, Aleksei Nicolaevich and Larisa Borisovna – 'who I will always think of as just Eric and Liza' and he apologised to them for making them swallow their pride by ordering them to 'surrender' to the Swiss authorities. The result he said had however fully justified the means, and now this priceless diamond would for ever be back where it truly belonged – in the old Imperial capital of Russia. He ended by saying he was always proud to be a Russian and thankful that his long service with the overseas section of the KGB had ended in such a memorable and worthwhile manner.

"It just remains, Mr. Mayor, for me to hand you this precious jewel, which will henceforth be the property of the Hermitage museum as another reminder of Russia's great history." The host stood to say a few words, "Mr. Stanislas Kortaski, I have been directed by the President of Russia to thank you formally on his behalf, and that of the whole country, for your planning and execution of the successful recuperation of the Tsarina's lost diamond - he wishes to receive you personally in Moscow to decorate you himself."

THE CO-AUTHORS OF FORGOTTEN DIAMOND

Charles Ranald

He retired early from a successful City career to pursue his interests in aviation. In 2001 he undertook a 1000 mile pilgrimage on foot from Le Puy en Velay in France to Santiago de Compostela in Spain. He lives in Hampshire with his wife and two Dachshunds.

John Sorrell

Having formerly been a member of the London Stock Exchange he is now retired from a senior position within a major French finance house. He has lived in France for the past 25 years.

Printed in the United Kingdom
by Lightning Source UK Ltd.
117141UKS00001BA/195